Time
for a
Viscount

MARY ELLEN BOYD

CHAPTER 1

SUMMER, MINNEAPOLIS, MINNESOTA

Olivia's casual gaze, passing over yet another table of so many at the flea market, abruptly caught. The day wasn't a waste at all. She reached out eagerly.

"You are *not* thinking of buying that, are you?"

Olivia felt her jaw tighten at the disgust in her sister's voice, and her hand stopped, suspended over the antique iron sitting amid a pile of what, in all honesty, could only be called junk. The air above the table shimmered in the sun, all that metal soaking up the heat and reflecting it back. "And so what if I am?"

"And you call yourself a decorator!" Renee Underwood's superior, mocking laugh grated on Olivia's already strained nerves. "Fine! I don't know who you think will want that in their design."

"I'm staging right now, not really decorating." The call for her talents was growing, too. It was still a small part of her business, but she liked it.

"Stage, decorate, call it whatever you want. You put that

in a house and no one will buy the place, but it's your money and if you want to throw it away on a piece of worthless scrap metal, go ahead. This is why I own my own condo and you're still renting." She turned and stalked away, her long golden hair twitching with her arrogant stride. Olivia let her go. Renee in one of her moods was not a force to tangle with.

Still, the dig about her little rental made her hesitate, and Olivia hated that her sister had gotten to her again. She hesitated, drawing her hand back with all kinds of second thoughts.

The brutal July sun beat down on her uncovered head, and a drop of sweat crawled down between her breasts. Men in denim shorts and women in halter tops and flip-flops shuffled around them. The heat was as much a smell as a feeling, sticky skin and coconut sunscreen, grease, hot dirt and exhaust-laden dust.

The occasional whiff of broiling polish sausage from the refreshment building, which Olivia had discovered was as hot inside as the air was outside, drifted over the rest of the smells. Conversation was desultory, one-word questions, "This?" "Sure?" "No? Which one, then?" "Oh, okay." "Cash?" Everyone was too hot to talk much.

Vintage chairs sat in clusters at a number of stands, some in mint condition, as if some worker from another time had just set down his tack hammer, and turned the chair around for approval across the centuries. Well-restored chairs had that look, new and fresh, but with an intangible uniqueness that gave their age away.

Other chairs looked their age, and Olivia itched to buy them all. She knew someone who could—for a price, to be sure—give them new springs and new fabric, re-glue dowels, reattach legs, and refinish the sad frames into bright, new life.

Sometimes she used them in her staging and sold them with the house, getting enough back to recoup her costs. It always satisfied her that the old things had found someone else to love them. Once in a while, though, she found a piece just for herself.

She looked around the nearby stalls to distract herself from buying the iron. Maybe Renee was right. It didn't really fit into the design she had planned for her current contract. Something else, perhaps?

Floor lamps from a more modern era, after electricity had been invented and people discovered what this new-fangled lighting could do for a room, poked their naked, bulb-less, shade-less necks toward the clear sky. Cast iron was everywhere, in yard-wide floor registers ripped from some crumbled building, ornate fencing, teakettles, and muffin pans that still held a film of old seasoning—lard or shortening, whatever would keep the rust away. Sadly, the rust had found them eventually.

She shoved a wine-red curl that had escaped the braid out of her eyes. She was the only one in the family that had inherited that color, deeper than auburn, too dark for red, too red for brown.

Renee stood a few tables away. Olivia could see the twist of her mouth even at this distance.

It was becoming increasingly clear that Renee had offi-cially decided she hated flea markets. One more annoyance to her fastidious nature. Flea markets, antiques, and espe-cially the heat had all come under her withering scorn during this jaunt, which was odd, because she spent most of her summers at the fashionable beaches around the lakes that gave Minneapolis its reputation, and should have been immune to summer.

All in all, this sisterly excursion was *not* working out well.

Except for the wonderful slug iron. Olivia looked back down at the table, and knew with absolute certainty if she didn't snap it up, someone else was going to see it and buy it. Antique irons were highly collectable. In this crowd, there had to be at least one or two devoted collectors just looking for a find like it.

She'd never seen one like that outside of reference books, a carved wooden handle, and a door at the back for the chunk of iron that was heated and slid inside. It had to be at least a century and a half old. Olivia was wearing her favorite piece of jewelry, a jade-and-gold link antique bracelet she bought at an auction whose lone drawback was catching on anything that stuck out and giving her wrist a nasty wrench, so she was careful as she reached across the wobbly table set out on the dry grass and grabbed the iron.

Static electricity raced up her arm in a flash of white. The sounds of the flea market vanished. The metal on the table was gone, too, replaced by fabric, piles of it, all the same. A worn gray gown stopped right in front of Olivia, on the opposite side of the table. A young woman, dark hair covered in a limp, almost-white mobcap, leaned over the table, smoothing a bit of the fabric, then reached across toward the iron. The woman was so close Olivia could have touched her.

Olivia jerked her hand away in instinctive reaction, her heart pounding in fright, an odd chill racing through her body. The iron dropped onto the table with a clang of metal on metal, and the woman disappeared.

It had to be the humidity. Heat, humidity, dehydration, and all that metal, of course she'd get a jolt of static electricity. She'd never heard of it causing that kind of reaction, though, not visual, not a scene so real she felt like she was there.

"That's a nice old piece," a male voice said nearby, and Olivia's head snapped up. It was a relief to see a stall holder in modern clothes standing on the opposite side of the table, and get back to reality. A middle-aged man, gray-haired, worn jeans and a dusty t-shirt. Ordinary, reassuring. His blue eyes held hers, darkening into sapphire from the concern in their depths. "You okay?"

"How much?" Olivia asked, knowing no matter what he charged, she was going to pay it. She picked the iron back up off the table, relieved that the electrical charge had dissipated.

Forty-five dollars didn't even seem like a lot. There must have been a residue of electricity left from that jolt because shivers still ran up her arm, but Olivia ignored it and tightened her grip on the iron.

Man, it was heavy! But the wooden handle fit her hand like it belonged there. At least that strange hallucination didn't come back. She held the iron tightly while the man took her money.

"Want to put that in a bag?"

Olivia looked down at the iron. She didn't want to put it in a bag, she wanted to hold it, but there was that slug, and the back opening that might come loose and drop it out. "Yes, please." With reluctance, she handed the piece back, watching like a possessive mother as it was slipped into a used department store bag, clearly the seller's form of economy.

She was limp with relief when the sale was done, and the iron was safely back in her hands.

Such a strange purchase to matter so much.

A residual tingle still ran up her arm as she walked away.

CHAPTER 2

SUMMER, 1811 ENGLAND

Miles Cedric Stewart, Viscount Langley, slid from the saddle in front of his father's country house, in anyone's parlance a mansion, three floors with imposing wings spreading out on either side of the main house, additions built by generations of Stewarts, massive stone, oversized paned windows, and dark wood trimming, wide stone steps leading to an equally imposing front door of the same dark wood, behind which Farley no doubt waited for the exact moment to swing them open. No curtains moved in any of the windows. No one bypassed the faithful butler and rushed out to greet him.

This latest invitation was nothing if not a direct command. He thought back over the last three months, wondering what had annoyed his father.

He'd spent lavishly on the last gift for his latest mistress, but it wasn't as if that amount of money was going to bankrupt him. Father had been prudent in his investments, and the entire family was reaping the rewards. Miles had tried his own hand in the markets, applying what Father had taught him, and flattered himself he had done rather well. If he wanted to be generous, it was, after all, his own business. Besides, he knew his father had taken his own series of mistresses during the dark years after his mother had died and before Father remarried a much younger woman, the daughter of another member of the Landed Gentry.

They seemed content together even now, after eighteen years. The sizeable difference in their ages hardly mattered. That their only child together had been a girl was perhaps a minor disappointment. He knew Father had dreamed of a family of sons. But Cecelia was a charming sister, and Miles had always enjoyed her, despite the thirteen-year difference in their ages. Abby had been young enough to bear more children, but there had only been Cecelia.

He had recently received a letter from his half-sister, still enjoying her new marriage. Seventeen was terribly young to be wed—in Miles's opinion, his sister was much too immature to be a wife—but she had been such a success in her very first season. And after all, wasn't marriage what a Season was for? At least her marriage had taken the attention off himself, and left him to enjoy life on his own terms.

Those terms might account for why Father had summoned him, but the most recent escapades had been minor larks, really.

Although Father might not see them that way. And he could not tell Father the real reason for his reputation. Not that he would be believed if he did tell.

It is better this way, he told himself, and wished that was not so.

A footman he did not recognize opened the door.

Miles met his supercilious gaze. "Lord Langley. I wish to see my father. He is expecting me."

Farley, the aging butler who had served in this same capacity as long as Miles could remember, opened the door and said in his ponderous way, "Welcome home, Lord Langley."

"Thank you, Farley," Miles returned. Never mind that he had his own houses, one in London and the other a few miles down the road. In Farley's mind, this would always be his home.

"The earl is waiting for you in the library. If you will follow me, sir." Farley turned and walked with stately steps down the long hallway that led to, among other rooms, the dark library where Father had always taken him on the occasions when his transgressions had necessitated more severe punishment.

He hardly needed to be shown the way, but Farley would not let anything interfere with his duties.

Miles walked behind, his feet growing heavier with every step. The same dread he had known as a child curled through his stomach, even though he was much too old and experienced for that. He shook off the feeling and straightened his shoulders.

The hallway seemed darker than he remembered, the morbid paintings more oppressive. Miles had never understood the appeal of paintings of hounds baying at a cornered fox, or women weeping over a casket. Life was grim enough without painting the grimmest parts. And if the paintings weren't of death, they were on a similar theme but of a more feminine mien, wilting flowers dropping petals on tables, Abby's own particular attempt to bring some lightness to the house.

The library door loomed ahead. "How is my stepmother?"

He saw Farley's cheeks crease into a smile. "Her ladyship is doing much better, now that the first sickness has passed."

First sickness? Miles suddenly understood what Farley meant. "Abby is with child? After all these years? Are you certain?"

"Yes, sir. I thought you knew."

No, you didn't, Miles thought. *You knew full well I hadn't heard from them in several months, not since Cecelia was married.* He walked the rest of the way in silence.

Farley knocked respectfully on the library door. "Master Miles," he announced formally, and opened the door at some sound from within, then bowed slightly as Miles walked past him. Miles waited until the door was securely shut and Farley was—presumably—out of earshot, not that he would do anything as gauche as listen at keyholes. Farley learned the family's secrets by some magic of his own.

"Good day, Father."

His father raised his head from some papers he was studying and rewarded Miles with a curt nod, then turned his attention back to what he was studying. Miles recognized the ploy, his father's way of making him nervous. It had worked when he was a child, and unfortunately he felt those nerves rising again.

No. He was a man now; he would not let himself be cowed into submission.

The dark blue draperies were partway open, and the sunlight caught his father's white hair, still as thick and wavy as Miles remembered as a child. Only the color had changed. Faint threads of original black added a distinguished contrast. They looked so alike, he and his father. Miles hoped he aged as well as Father had. Even at sixty-one, Adrian Stewart, earl Stafford, rode horses around his lands and even took them over the occasional stile—when he was certain no one was watching who would carry the tale to Abby. His posture was straight and tall, most especially when standing.

He was not standing now.

Miles stiffened his spine, and his courage. "Farley tells me congratulations are in order. Abby is with child."

Father grunted. "You could have learned that a month or more ago if you had bothered to visit. You have land here. You should check on it."

Miles refused to let himself be baited. "Perhaps this will be a son. That should make you happy."

"I just want a healthy mother and a healthy child."

Again that prickle of worry. "Farley told me she is doing well."

Father did not raise his head from the papers. "I did not send for you to discuss the health of your stepmother."

So it was going to go that way again. He had done what he could, had extended the olive branch, and Father had snapped it off. Miles strolled over to a large leather chair set at a relaxed angle from his father's imposing desk, wide and dark, deeply carved to match the bookshelves lining the wall, and big enough to frighten a small boy brought in for discipline, and sat down without waiting for an invitation. He slid down, folded his arms over his chest, stretched out his legs, crossed the ankles, perhaps a tad too defiant, and got to the point. "You ordered me here, I came. Farley, no doubt on your orders, even walked me down the hallway. What is this all about, anyway?"

His father's mouth tightened. "I taught you better manners than that. While you are in my house, I expect you to treat both your stepmother and myself with respect. I will not take cheek from you." His voice was cold with disapproval.

Miles sat up straight, both feet on the floor. "I do beg

your pardon. It will not happen again." Whatever his offense, in The Most Honorable earl Stafford's eyes, it must have been a grave one.

"You wonder why I summoned you home? I have received, from a number of different parties, comment on your behavior in London."

He hadn't heard everything, had he? Miles fought the desire to squirm. He was thirty, after all, far too old for such a childish reaction. "And who are these 'parties' who saw fit to carry tales?"

"That is not important."

"It is to me!" Miles stared at his father while his brain churned. Then he leaned back with a laugh. "Victor, my ever loving cousin, wasn't it? Why do you persist in believing him?"

His father ignored the question.

"He is of no more consequence than a gnat, Father. And that mother of his. The less said about her the better."

"It is not he of whom I am concerned, but you. And you have a title to uphold. I expected far better from my heir than gambling and wenching. Someday, all I have worked for will be yours, and the very thought frightens me. I have worked far too hard to let the fruits of my efforts fall into dissolute, reckless hands, particularly not now, before we are even finished with Napoleon."

"I am neither dissolute nor reckless!" Miles leapt to his feet in outrage and pain at his father's harsh judgment. "If not Victor, I have a right to know who carries such tales!"

Father raised one eyebrow, the way he always had when he was absolutely certain of his facts. "I find your reaction slightly extreme for an innocent man."

"Very well." Miles forced himself back into the chair. "Tell me what reports you have heard."

"Explain the race down the Strand. Just a lark? A diversion?" It sounded as if Father's collar was too tight. His voice was strained and higher pitched than usual, his face was flushed and a vein throbbed on his forehead. Miles had never seen that particular vein before.

"I was chasing a petty thief who had stolen a lady's reticule."

"A *lady*? That is not the version I heard."

Miles felt a growl of rage start low in his throat and swallowed it down. He took several breaths before he answered. "Very well, so she was not exactly a lady. But you always told me we never leave females at the mercy of those bigger and stronger than they. I do not think her profession changes that rule, do you?"

Father scowled at him. "I will ask the questions here. It is bad enough you have so carefully cultivated the reputation of being a neck-or-nothing daredevil who will take on any challenge, no matter how ridiculous."

Miles felt his jaw tighten. This was his *father* at whom all this anger was directed, his father who had to be kept in the dark. He looked away, out the window at the narrow view the heavy curtains left visible, the winding drive with the early flowers in bloom along the sandy path.

Father must have taken that as capitulation. "Very well. We have established that this rumor was true in all the important details. Although you neglected to add that you took this . . . lady as a paramour. I have no doubt she accepted your offer in a rush of gratitude. Did you not suspect it was all a ruse to get you to notice her?"

Miles managed not to blink. She had been a most satisfying mistress for a time, but until his father mentioned it, he had not in fact wondered about the manner of their meeting. It hardly mattered. Women resorted to all manner of tricks and subterfuge to find a new protector. He had no complaints about the affair. "How else was she to meet me? We both got what we wanted out of the assignation."

Father glared. "And you never even bothered to find out her background. A man of your station should be more discreet about his liaisons." A heavy sigh. "Let us go on to the next rumor. Did you or did you not wager my last gift to you, the finest stallion in our stables, on the outcome of a card game?"

Miles clenched his jaw. Again, his father had the basic story, but he did not know the background. "No. I did not wager my stallion. If I know the game you are referring to, I was setting a trap to catch a cheat! A cheat, moreover, who had stolen the entire estate from a young buck who did not have the experience to know he was being fleeced." He was surprised his father let him get that much of the story out.

"I see." There was a chilling softness in Father's voice. "And where did you get the skill to be able to out-cheat a cardsharp? I assume that is what you did? Are you telling me my son is better at cheating than a professional thief?"

"No. But I knew this man, whom you know as well. If you want the name, I will give it to you. I knew he would be so flushed with his victory, and so drunk, that he would not pay attention to the cards. It was a carefully laid out ploy." Miles ignored the part of the question on where he learned his skills. There were things he did not want to admit.

He rose and stalked to the bookshelves, bracing his arms stiffly on the upright dark wood, feeling the deep carvings press into his palms. When he was certain he could speak calmly, he turned around. "You did not deny that someone of our own class could do such a thing, set up a young man, flushed with his new title and lands, his new status in the *ton*, so eager to see what was out there that he could not sense his destruction coming."

His father slumped back in the massive leather chair. The vein under the skin was quiet now, to Miles's relief, but he did not relax his guard. "No, of course I do not deny such predators exist." He steepled his fingers, and tapped them on his chin thoughtfully. "So tell me, son, if it was not in fact the stallion, what *did* you wager on this bet you won?"

Father already suspected. Miles could see it in his eyes. Still, he stood straight and tall, and answered honestly. "My own lands against the return of the youngster's."

"*Your* own lands! You only have those lands because of me! I thought you might like to have something from your mother's dowry. Had I known you would treat them so cavalierly, I would not have made that gesture." Angry red rushed up Father's face, and he clenched his hands on the arms of the chair. His knuckles were totally white, and the muscles in his wrists stood out like ropes. His eyes went blank for a single breath, and then he took a rush of air that whistled in his throat. He said nothing, but Miles felt the struggle even across the room. For a fearsome moment, he feared his father would have an attack of apoplexy, the vein pulsed so hard.

Air rushed out of Father's lungs again with an audible *whoosh*. The red in his face faded, leaving only traces on his cheekbones and around his forehead. In a choked voice, that dangerous softness back, he said, "And tell me about the diamond buttons on your vest that I have heard so much about. Real diamonds, I understand, big enough for a queen's crown."

Miles knew Father had dropped the subject of their lands only to keep control. He was relieved. There had been a few bad moments that night, moments he did not want to relive.

He still felt shaken when he thought of what a near miss it had been. This one thing, at least, his father could have no complaint on. "Those diamonds are not mine. They belong to the young man whose lands I saved. He has his widowed mother and three younger sisters depending on him. The next morning, while he was still suffering pangs of remorse, I forced him to his safe and had him withdraw half the family's gems. I took them and had them securely set into the buttons, so every time he saw me at a party or soiree or musicale, he would remember how close he came to disaster."

"I suppose this remorseful young man gladly gave the gems to you? Did it never occur to you that he could turn around and charge you with theft?" Those red splotches still stood out on Father's face.

Miles slapped one hand against the wood pillar of the bookshelf with a sharp crack, so fiercely his palm stung. "Of course, I thought of that! Do you take me for a total fool? I made him sign a confession to the night of drink and gambling, which I have in my possession for safekeeping. What is more, I have several friends who watched him gamble his lands away, and they will be only too willing to testify to my part in saving them."

He wanted to rub his burning palm, but it would appear as weakness. "It seems to be working. I have not seen him creep into the card rooms since that night. If he ever slips, I promised him I would go to his mother and give her the choice of turning the gems into funds for their future, or keeping them for her daughters."

The color on Father's face flushed again, not so bright as before. "I will not mention what might still happen should you lose so much as a single button. I am glad to hear this story at least reflects better on you than all the other reports

I have heard. However, I find those other stories bad enough, and know full well there are more." He sighed deeply. "At least the tale of the diamond buttons was exaggerated. That relieves me, but only slightly." The earl was speaking now, not Father.

"This wild behavior of yours has to stop, Miles." Stafford folded his hands neatly on the blotter. "I would never dream of doing this unless it was necessary, but . . ." His voice trailed off. He sighed, slumped back in his chair, and waved Miles to his seat. He looked . . . old.

Miles walked back and sat. He had never seen his father look other than vigorous. Was he holding something back? Was there something wrong with Abby's pregnancy? Or with Father's own health? The thought was appalling.

"I do not like being the heavy-handed lord of the manor with you, Miles," the earl went on, "but you simply must get down to business. You have been spending far too much time in your clubs and far too little overseeing your estates. None at all, from what I can see."

"My estates are doing well enough." Miles leaned forward, willing his father to believe him. What could be wrong with enjoying his life? Surely he could not find fault with rescuing younger men from their own folly? "I receive regular letters from my man of affairs. I have not left them unattended."

"No?" Father shook his head. "I wish I could believe you." He sighed deeply again. Miles had the strange suspicion Father was doing it for effect, but shoved the disloyal thought aside, still shaken by the worry that Father might be ill. "Hiring a man of affairs is well and good, but one cannot trust them too far." His intensity was a physical force. "This is not how I taught you. I spent hours, *years*, going over the books with you. You watched me working with my tenants;

you learned all the skills I had learned over a lifetime. I know it is the popular thing today not to even know how much land one owns, or how much rent it brings in, but I have seen men who were my equals lose everything, simply by neglect." Father looked down at the desk. "Perhaps if I had kept a better watch on you these past years . . ." Then he looked back up, directly at his son. "Still, it is not too late. I intend to fix matters. I believe I gave you a solid enough foundation."

Father looked at him, and Miles could see the cold purpose in his eyes. "I am involved in a mission for England that requires the utmost discretion. Men in the government must know that I am above reproach." His eyes grew, if possible, even colder. "And that includes my family. I am going to London to meet with my committee on the issue. I probably should not give you even this much, but no, it is not Napoleon. We have another foe brewing, and that is as much as I can say."

Miles interrupted. "America. If you think this a secret, you are much mistaken, Father. I hear rumors and reports, possibly even before you do. If you want information, you should have a man in the gambling rooms of every ball. The information I hear across the betting table would astound you."

Miles could hear his father's teeth grinding together. His voice went to a deep rumble. "I shudder to think what any such information will do in the hands of such a feckless, foolish group of young men such as the ones you have just been describing to me. Racing down the Strand, gambling away entire estates. Careless talk can undermine whole countries." His eyes were iron as he continued, "I will not have my own son bringing disgrace on my name."

There was a strange satisfaction on his face. Miles braced himself.

"I need a son who commands respect, whose life is above reproach and who can be trusted to take my place when I am gone. I need a son who is a married man with a family. And so, you must find yourself a wife before the end of this coming Season. Go back to London and make preparations for a wedding." He stood, the movement slow and imposing, his voice growing louder. "Because if you do not find a woman for yourself, I will find one for you, and see to it that you go down the aisle with her!" For the second time, his father pounded a fist on the desk. The sound echoed off the walls.

Miles stared at his father for a long moment before his senses came back. "Father, you do not mean that. You cannot mean that! How will you force me? I am far too old to be dragged into the nearest church. Are you threatening to cut me off? Think of the scandal *that* would cause, all to no avail. And what good would it do? I still do have my mother's income."

"Which you nearly lost by gambling." His father looked back at him with a steady gaze. "I would hardly need to drag you. All I need to do is place a notice in the papers and let the *ton* do the rest. You would marry the woman I chose for you or lose your status in society. How long will they tolerate you when you throw a woman over after putting a notice in the papers?"

Miles took a long breath and held it until he could speak without rage. "You would not dare."

"Try me." His father's crystal gray eyes, a match for his own, were cold with resolve.

"Don't dare me, Father." Miles rose and went to the door, and pulled it open. "I will not be forced." He strode down the dark hallway and out into the sun.

His father was right about one thing. It was time to pay

attention to his own inheritance. He did not put it past his father to follow through on his threats, and his mother's land might be all he had left.

It was a short ride. Their lands adjoined, a double-edged blessing. He could flaunt his success.

But his father could watch—closely.

CHAPTER 3

STATIC SPARKED OFF THE METAL AND ARCED AROUND HER, worse than the event at the flea market this afternoon. Flashes burned the air and seared her hand. Olivia dropped the heavy antique iron and jerked backward. Her eyes wouldn't focus, her hands tingled, and a loud clanging noise echoed in her ears.

She'd only been trying to use it for fun, just to see what it had been like for women all those years ago. She shook her arm, shocked at the force of the jolt. There wasn't any other metal around to amplify the static charge, and she wasn't even out in the sun.

"Who the devil are you, and what are you doing in my room?" The question thundered over the sound in her head, the voice deep and male.

Olivia whirled around in alarm. "*Your* room?" Her voice sounded scratchy and hoarse. "How did you get in *here?*"

The sudden movement made the room spin. The man was only a hulking shape in the darkness left by that awesome flash, standing by a doorway, but not the doorway to her kitchen, it was totally the wrong color and in the wrong place, and what did he mean by *his room?* The noise in her head grew louder, the room circled faster. She barely had time to think, *I'm going to faint. How stupid,* before the room went sideways, and then there was nothing.

Voices whispered in the grayness that smothered her. *I must have been sleeping with the television on,* Olivia thought as awareness slipped in. Napping in the middle of the day made her grumpy. It took such a long time to wake up and get moving. She always felt waking up was bad enough in the morning, let alone twice a day.

But it had been such a hot summer, and Renee had been such a pest at the flea market, being sarcastic to all the vendors, making an issue of Olivia's buying the antique iron. No wonder she fell asleep—

Memories returned in a flood. The man in her house, the sparks around the iron she held, and his stupid accusation of *her* being in *his* room—she had not fallen asleep at all. She had fainted.

Something had been wrong even before that, something strange about the room, something odd about the flash that burned her hand.

The voices faded. She heard a door click shut. Just in case the man stayed behind and the silence was a ploy and he was waiting there for her to give herself away before he did . . . whatever he was going to do, Olivia lay perfectly still and took stock of all the sounds.

The clanging in her head had vanished. The room was

mercifully silent, the only one breathing was herself. She was lying down, she didn't hurt anywhere, he hadn't done anything except put her into bed and cover her to her chin.

Which was rather strange for a burglar.

She took the risk and slowly opened her eyes, then blinked several times before things eased into focus.

Olivia blinked again in shock.

She had been in her own kitchen in her own small rented house, standing next to the ironing board with the hot iron in her hand. The air conditioner had been on, the what-not shelf stood in the corner of the living room, right in her line of sight, the Victorian chair sitting beside it.

She wasn't in her kitchen anymore. In fact, she wasn't even in her house. She was in a massive bed, in an equally massive bedroom, with heavy burgundy curtains hanging over windows that seemed two stories high. The biggest dark wood cabinet she had ever seen took up nearly one entire wall, with a simple but solid carved chair at its side. The chair was the hard kind, where someone had forgotten to give the seat any kind of shape at all and they needed good, thick cushions to make them halfway decent to sit on. If the cabinet was an armoire, as she suspected, the chair was merely used as a brief way-station while dressing. A brick fireplace took up most of another wall.

A room divider with the same burgundy fabric as the curtains stood in the far corner, a robe tossed over the top. No doubt that was where he—that man she had seen at first —dressed behind it.

Her entire house would fit in this one room.

This room was a bit elaborate for a kidnapping. It certainly couldn't belong to a thief, at least not an ordinary one. Why anyone would bring her here, she had no idea. She wasn't anyone important, just a self-employed house stager-cum-decorator with a love of antiques. She lived the most ordinary of lives. Who would want to kidnap her, and why bring her here, to this palatial bedroom?

Unless they had an urgent need to stage a house for sale. Which was patently absurd.

Everything was so dim. The only light came around the edges of the curtain.

Olivia eased herself upright. Weakness lingered. She clung to the blankets while the room settled again, then swung her legs over the edge of the bed. Something jabbed her side. "Ouch!"

Her voice sounded loud in the silent room.

She pressed a hand against the poke, and looked down in amazement at the strange fabric beneath her fingers. "What on earth?"

Fragile fabric fell all the way to her feet, gathers and gathers of pale pink with some kind of delicate raised white flower embroidered on a high-waisted, square-bodiced gown. The sleeves sagged off her shoulders and drooped in front, with what seemed like acres of breast on display. She never knew she had that much bosom.

She figured out what poked her, and it only deepened the mystery. Someone put her in a corset. She felt the boning now, running down her sides and front. That partially explained the cleavage showing. A corset!

A tight corset, and a loosened bodice. Had someone been inter-rupted while dressing her?

For a moment Olivia could only stare down at the unfamiliar garments. In a daze, she picked up a fold of the skirt, and held it out, taking a better look. All those delicate flowers must have taken days to hand-stitch, and she knew they didn't come from any machine. The slight imperfections and unevenness marked the design as hand-made.

The fabric of the gown itself was very lightweight, and unless she missed her guess, was silk. She had owned a silk blouse once, and recognized the texture. That blouse had been pricey. This much silk must have cost a fortune.

Olivia pressed a hand to the loose bodice to hold it in place, and leaned forward a bit to see the rest of the gown where it draped over the bed, ignoring another wave of dizziness. A wide ruffle edged the hem all the way around, and lace, of all things, trimmed the bottom. It must be the very devil to keep clean.

Something hugged her legs. She pulled the skirt up to see what it was. Some kind of finely woven stockings went to just above her knees, and tied with a ribbon.

Like *that* would keep them up! Olivia wondered how far she could walk before the stockings slid down to her ankles.

On the floor by the bed sat a pair of slippers, beaded and embroidered, with a thin sole and no heel. They looked like they were the right size.

"Good lord," she blurted. "What happened to me?" She clapped her hand over her mouth, and held her breath, afraid the voices would come back, and the door would open.

But it was still quiet outside the room.

How long had she been out? She looked again at the strange dress. It couldn't have been a drug, she hadn't eaten anything before she fainted, and she didn't think it was possible to force liquids down an unconscious person. The man she remembered could have injected her with something, but Olivia was pretty sure she would feel the soreness from the needle, and there was nothing. No pokes anywhere that she could feel, nothing stabbing except for the corset's boning.

This was rather elaborate for an abduction, she thought. Someone had gone to an awful lot of trouble just for an ordinary house stager on a lazy weekend, indulging her passion for antiques at a flea market.

Ah, yes. The flea-market today—if it still was today—and the iron with the hinged door at the back for the heavy slug. She had been standing by the ironing board holding it when the sparks hit; she remembered dropping it just before she fainted. Thinking about it now, Olivia marveled it hadn't landed on her foot. Those antique irons weighed a ton. It could have done some real damage.

She looked around the bed, but nothing. Only blankets. Of course, she had fallen . . . Olivia leaned off the bed to check the floor, clinging to the bedspread to anchor herself from the wave of lightheadedness that showed no signs of lessening.

There it was, right beside the bed, as if it landed that way, the wooden handle still intact even after its nasty fall. Olivia slid off the mattress, and wobbled as her unsteady legs struggled for balance. A small stepstool sat a few feet away. Nice to know she wasn't the only one who thought the bed a touch too high.

All she wanted right now was to find out where she was, and who brought her here. And why.

She looked again at the strange gown she wore, threatening to slip off her shoulders, and remembered the flash up her arm, the event that seemed to trigger all this mess. Olivia held up her hand and looked at it. There were no burns at all.

Olivia stretched her arms out next, and checked them over. Her hands were familiar, the antique jade-and-gold bracelet she always wore, her gift to herself as a splurge for starting her own decorating business, bought broken at auction and repaired, was still there, as well as the scar on her elbow from when she was ten and fell off a bike.

She reached up to her hair, to find it very different from

how she fixed it for the Minnesota heat. No longer a French braid running down the back of her head in a neat tail, keeping the bulk of her hair off her neck. Now braids circled the top of her head until the plaits ended and the curly mass was pulled into a bun. Hairpins poked out here and there, threatening to fall out as they always did when one had been laying down.

The corset was bad enough—just thinking that someone had dressed her in this strange garb while she was unconscious gave her a chill—but to even fix her hair? And the time it would take to do all of this. Just how long had she been unconscious? The possibilities scared her. Was she even in Minneapolis?

Panic prickled along her skin, clenched like a vise around her chest, smothered her breathing. Her heart pounded in her ears.

Think, Olivia, think! She forced herself to breathe, slow, deep breaths. After a few moments—time seemed to have lost meaning—she began to think, take stock of the situation.

She was not hurt. No one had restrained her, and as prisons went, this was way beyond luxurious.

Why they—whoever they were—had taken her here, it didn't appear they intended to hurt her.

Her gaze shifted over to the window, where the daylight beckoned through a crack in the curtains. A weak smile pulled at her mouth. There was another way to find out at least something about this place with much less risk.

Olivia crept across the room toward that glow, battling dizziness with every step. She passed a shoulder-high, many-branched candlestand of heavy bronze that stood handily in her way and was solid enough to hang onto for a second when her balance slipped. The candles had burned down to nubs at some time recently, the wicks charred black, the wax congealed in the process of dripping off the holders, leaving shiny cold blobs on the polished wooden floor.

A faint draft up her skirt warned her of something vital missing. Apparently whoever brought her here decided she didn't rate panties. Cold fear trickled down her spine, and left dread in her stomach. Olivia froze in place while she took a more thorough stock of her body.

There was no sense of anything wrong, no feeling of violation, just the lingering vertigo. Maybe she awakened too quickly for them.

Air drifted beneath her skirts again. She would have to fix the underwear problem as soon as possible. She was *not* going to sit here with her nether regions unprotected! Surely there had to be underwear of some description in the room. Or, better yet, a nice sturdy pair of blue jeans, something durable enough to escape in.

First things first. She had to know where she was, and if there was any possible way out, even if it meant climbing out the window.

Olivia took a grip on the curtain, only to stop and marvel at its softness. Velvet curtains, finer than anything she'd ever seen or worked on before, and she'd used a lot of excellent materials in her staging. What would someone who could afford velvet curtains on a window a good twelve feet high want with *her*? She was good at her job, but not worth this.

Besides, whoever staged the room had an excellent eye for accuracy.

She pulled the curtain away from the corner of the window only enough to be able to see around it, hoping no one was watching from outside waiting for her to give herself away. It couldn't be helped; she had to know, and it was at least less dangerous than opening the door and being within arm's reach of a guard.

The glass was odd, uneven and spotted with bubbles. Here and there, she saw pits in the surface, as if sand hadn't fully liquefied and had to be brushed free, leaving a dimpled memory behind. It looked cheap, strangely at odds with the luxurious curtains. Surely someone who could afford yards and yards of silk velvet curtains could afford glass without imperfections.

The sectioned window had hinges on the far sides. Right in the center, fastened to the metal divider, an ornate two-sided catch, with levered handles. The window simply shoved open, swinging on the hinges on either side like wings. One of the windows was firmly latched. The left-hand side of the double window was ajar a crack.

A simple shove and it would swing open. As dizzy as she was, she might go right out with it.

Standing out of view of whatever might be outside, Olivia eased as close to the window as she dared and stole a peek. She was on the second floor of the building, which rather effectively ruled the window out as an escape route. There was nothing much in back, just small roofs peeking from behind a small stand of trees, and plenty of bushes.

That left the door. She'd seen adventure movies; she knew someone could be waiting for her outside the room, expecting her to do that very thing. The thought of what might happen if she opened the door and found them there raised the hair on her neck, but there was no other exit.

She wobbled her way back across the room, grabbing at everything that would support her: the candle stand, the armoire, the bedpost.

Goodness, the room was big!

And finally the door. Olivia leaned against it, pressing her ear to the crack between the door and jamb. No sound. One deep breath, and she reached for the doorknob. She stopped when she realized what she saw: a very old knob, oval and worn, with a keyhole complete with an elegant raised cover that perfectly matched the hole in shape. She touched that little cover, and it moved easily. Olivia crouched down and peeked through the keyhole.

CHAPTER 4

A LONG HALLWAY STRETCHED OUT BEFORE HER, WITH WINDOWS spaced down its length, and enough light to illuminate the whole area. Not lamplight, but sunlight.

Sunlight meant windows, and windows might mean another way out.

Another breath, and she twisted that old knob, then pulled the door open. It swung inward without a sound. Someone kept it well-oiled, and Olivia was grateful.

The hall was much wider than it appeared through the keyhole, the windows on her left bigger than she would have thought. Four doors on the right, spaced far enough apart to guess how big the rooms must be. No, she realized, there were five doors, one to the immediate right of the room where she had been.

There would be time to peek inside each of them later.

Perhaps.

At the moment, she needed to see what lurked outside this place. She eased across the hallway to the nearest window, keeping herself in line with the plastered wall and out of view until she could peek out.

Beneath her, two men stood on a wide gravel driveway of some kind, one of them leaning against—she stared in amazement—a carriage! A horse stood in its traces, nodding its head as if eager to move, and snuffled against its restraint. The men were in quaint, costume-like clothes. The sandy-haired man leaning on the carriage was all in black, in an odd formal suit with high, wide lapels, the front of the suit ending at the waist, the back dropping into a square tail. His shirt was white and ruffled, the necktie strange, wrapped around and tied in a bow. He had long sideburns that nearly reached his jaw, and held an actual doctor's bag in one hand, and a top hat, of all things, in the other.

The second man had his back to the window, but he was clearly taller and broader across the shoulders, and his garb was different.

She leaned closer to the window for a better look and discovered it was slightly ajar. Had someone forgotten to check that it was properly latched? Or was it left open on purpose?

The cool air that drifted in was nothing like Minnesota's sticky, hot summer weather.

So where was she?

She needed to find out, and the person who must have the answers was certainly one of the men right beneath her. Tempting as it was to push the window wider so she could hear everything, the chance it might squeak held her back. Instead, she stared at the second man, almost directly beneath the window where she stood.

He wore light-colored, tight-fitting pants, from the bottom of which peeked shining boot toes, so highly polished the sun sparkled off them. On top, where the first man had that strange cropped suitcoat, he merely wore a vest, with the sleeves of his own white shirt billowing out from the shoulders and falling across his hands in tiers of lace.

Oddly, it didn't look effeminate in the least. In fact, an air of power, or menace, surrounded him, emanating from his proud stance, those broad shoulders, the lift of his head, his leashed power reaching out to her even though all she saw was his back. His dark hair curled over the top of the high collar, and Olivia wished he'd turn around so she could see his face.

She didn't remember much about the man who had frightened her so badly in her kitchen, but she'd bet the man standing down there and that intruder were one and the same. And she knew which of those two men down in the driveway would stay behind to guard her, and which was going to leave.

In the carriage.

A voice drifted up from the men below. She pressed her ear against the small opening and held her breath.

"You have no idea the shock she gave me," the dark-haired man with his back to her said in a fabulous rich, deep voice. He had a clipped, upper-class English accent, unusual for the Midwest. "What if she'd been a few minutes earlier? She would have caught me in my bath. How could she have gotten through the house without being seen? And who told her where my bedroom was?"

Olivia jerked at the words, more puzzled than ever. What on earth did he mean, she would have caught him in his bath? And how she got here without being seen, as if her presence was as much a mystery to him as it was to her. He sounded all innocence, so convincing, with his

story down pat and perfect, but there was just one problem. She'd first seen him in her kitchen—but the memory
was off and she couldn't figure out what was wrong
about it.

She pressed her ear back against the slender gap. The
other man's voice was quieter, harder to hear. "... clearly has
been sick. She may have been wandering." Some indistin-
guishable mumbling, then, "You cannot move her. She must
stay in bed until . . ." He, too, had a strong English accent.
Two of them? She didn't even know anyone from England!

"I do not need this right now!" The dark man burst out.
"My father is . . . " there was a sudden pause, "expecting more
war, and he wants . . ." His voice faded, and Olivia fretted at
the missing words. War? What war?

The men's voices stayed too low to make out. Olivia's
gaze wandered from the two men in that odd tableau
straight out of time to the landscape, trying desperately to
explain away what she saw. A long, neatly manicured hedge
edged the outside of the gravel drive, going past the front of
the house, ending somewhere out of view to her right, but
there were no tire tracks. In fact, as far into the distance as
she could see from her window, beyond the hedge, past the
clumps of trees to the left, across the manicured stretch of
green grass in front and to her right, there were no cars, no
trucks, no phone poles or wires of any kind coming to the
house. No satellite dish, no smell of exhaust, no sound of
airplanes or helicopters.

Come to think of it, she hadn't even heard a telephone.
She looked at the wall. No light switch. Her gaze moved
down the hallway. No outlets. Nowhere to plug in a vacuum.
Or a lamp.

Olivia remembered the tall candle stand she had braced
herself on in the bedroom with its well-burned candles, and

its purpose in the room struck her like a blow. There was no lamp. The only lighting in that room was from candles.

She drew back from the window and leaned against the wall. It couldn't be.

Don't panic, she told herself, and concentrated on taking slow, deep breaths. Trembling ran from her shoulders to her toes, and not all of it was from the lingering dizziness.

There had to be an explanation, a logical reason why she was here, in a house with no electricity—at least in part of it —dressed in a rich silk gown, looking down at a carriage and two men with British accents. It wasn't a movie set; where were the cameras?

When the dark-haired man came back—and he would, she knew it—she wanted some answers.

"There's something very strange about her speech, from what few words she said." Miles leaned an elbow against the carriage. "I am familiar with most of the accents of Europe from my travels, and her speech does not match any country I have ever been to."

"Having not heard her speak, I cannot help you there." Edward appeared to be enjoying the predicament far too much, but at least he was trying to be helpful. He had come at a moment's notice when Miles sent a servant for him. "Any number of countries speak English well enough to get by. We have exiles here who fled from France in particular, after first the Terror, and now this endless war. I was young during the Terror, but I remember the trauma in the faces of the refugees from France. Trauma can wipe out memories until the mind is ready to accept what happened."

Miles shook his head. "I think not from Europe, and certainly not France. I would guess . . . America."

Edward raised an eyebrow. "If you are right, she is a long way from home."

"Yes," Miles agreed slowly. "I think many Americans do not want to be forced to take a side in the feud. If this becomes what we fear—what my father wants—they will fight their own neighbors. We certainly hear about those who believe America should never have fought us in the first place. I understand we have some Loyalists from the past war here. If their ship was stopped and boarded, and they went with their heart . . ." He let the sentence trail off.

"I leave the politics to your class, my friend," Edward said with a smile. "I am only concerned with her health. This is not like anything I have ever dealt with. Unconscious as she is, I would expect her to have a fever, but I did not feel any. Nor did I see or feel any wounds on her head. Or anywhere else, for that matter. She is not in any immediate danger that I can see." He stroked a hand through his light brown hair. "Her clothes are quite fine. I saw the bracelet on her arm. Gold and real jade, I believe, very expensive. One does not come by such things without the status that comes from wealth."

"I saw it as well," Miles returned. "I called you here for some answers, Edward, and you have given me none so far. You are the doctor. I can hardly leave her in my bed." Miles glared at his friend. How could the man be so dense? "She is unchaperoned, and she does not wear the clothing of a housemaid."

Edward weighed him with a long, steady look, and a slow grin spread across his face. "I did indeed notice she is a fetching little thing, even with her eyes shut."

"You are not funny." Miles propped his hands on his hips.

"If you think she is in no danger, I shall simply move her to another room, or better yet, send her up to the servants' quarters."

"You have not been paying attention, Miles. I already told you not to move her. This is something I am not familiar with, and her condition could be much worse than I imagine."

"Then you should stay here." Miles managed a smile. "I am hardly qualified for such a case."

"You forget, I have a babe waiting to be born nearby. Birthing is a dangerous process. At the very least, your guest is not in danger of dying that I can see. Take care of her and send for me if you feel she is getting worse. No exertion, under no circumstances wake her until she wakes on her own, do not alarm her, and keep her under close watch. She may be hungry when she wakes. Give her only a light meal." Edward tossed his bag carefully onto the carriage seat, climbed in, and picked up the reins. "You are a clever man, Miles. You can surely handle one sick woman."

She had to figure this out; she had to find out what happened. Renee might be her only sister and the bane of her existence, but she had the right not to worry. Self-centered though she was, Renee would certainly spend at least a little time wondering what happened to her little sister before raiding Grandma's jewelry chest of its heirlooms. Olivia winced at the thought of what might disappear this time—assuming she got back home from wherever this was.

She felt guilty, worrying about what her sister would take when she didn't even know if she'd ever see Renee again.

Surely she could think of other, more favorable things about her sister other than what she might steal.

But nothing came to mind just then.

Carriage wheels crunched on the gravel outside, and from the depths of the house, Olivia felt as much as heard a heavy door slam.

He was coming.

CHAPTER 5

Miles lifted a hand to the departing Edward and turned toward the house. He glanced up at his bedroom window and wondered if the woman in his bed had awakened yet.

She was going to be a problem. Every servant in the house knew he had been bathing before she arrived. It took four footmen just to carry up the water for his oversized copper tub. She certainly had not been there then. At least, not out in the open where he or any of the servants could see her, and definitely not in his own bed!

But she was certainly there now. He knew his staff accepted that there were women in his life, but a man of his stamp kept his mistress in London or, at the very least, away from the family home.

It was bad enough his father thought so little of him, but to come home and find a strange woman in his bedroom, not recognize her, not even be able to explain how she made it through his entire house undetected?

Edward was dependable enough. As a doctor, he was used

to keeping secrets, but how to muzzle dozens of servants? It was an impossible task. News spread among the servant class like lightning across the sky, everywhere at once and leaving no sign of its passage until it hit its target.

Which was himself.

He ran over Edward's parting advice as he made his way back up the stairs. No exertion, under no circumstances wake her until she was ready to wake herself. Do not alarm her, feed her with caution, and keep her under close watch. Miles added his own codicil: *just in case she came for some nefarious purpose.*

Although that seemed unlikely for a woman so ill that she hadn't regained consciousness for several hours. She had not been pretending, either. She hadn't even moved when he loosened the top couple hooks of her gown.

He was very familiar with removing a woman's garments, but this time had been different. She had not known what he was doing. He had never done that before. A woman had to be willing. Only the knowledge that she would breathe easier without the tightness of the bodice had let him undo those few hooks.

Despite his best intentions, no power could have prevented him from looking at the small bits of body he uncovered, slender and yet strong, her arms taut with supple feminine firmness. This was no lazy woman, but rather one who liked to be out and about.

Even in England, a woman could ride her own horse, and walk the lanes. Who knew what freedoms America gave their women?

She had on the gown of a lady, fine silk and stylish, high-waisted, and elegant. Her rich red hair—*beautiful hair*—was styled in intricate braids that only a maid could manage. Then there was the bracelet, pure spring-green jade chunks set in gold. What led her to his house? If she had arrived in poor clothes, he would suspect her of being a servant who stole the bracelet and ran here to hide. Gowns given to maids were usually worn, not crisp, fresh, and of the latest design. And she wore it openly, as one used to fine gems.

He shook his head. How to explain the accent in those few words she had spoken? One generally ran *to* America if one were a criminal, not *from* it.

Assuming that was her country.

She did not have the face of a thief.

Denton, his butler cum confidante and utterly discreet, passed him on the stairs. "Has she awakened yet?"

"There have been no sounds from inside the room." Denton pulled his shoulders back and cleared his throat. "As you asked, I have allowed no one else near. I am keeping them busy in other parts of the house. Your father being who he is, I thought it best to be cautious." He met Miles's eyes with no hint of subservience in his own.

One phrase caught Miles's attention. "My father being who he is?" Miles leaned against the banister and waited for Denton to continue.

"Well, sir," Denton cleared his throat again, "if I may say so, one of the footmen has a brother who works in your father's house, and he said—meaning no offense—there is talk the Earl's entire family is coming under much scrutiny."

Miles shook his head, partly at what was being said about him, partly at the efficiency of the servant's grapevine. "To be blunt, the members of Parliament say that I am a liability, that Father's judgment cannot be trusted because his family life is a disaster. If he cannot get his own son to listen to his advice, he cannot give advice for the country."

Denton nodded. "Your staff, as much as I can tell, is loyal to you, but since there could be political . . . repercussions to this unknown woman's presence, at this delicate time . . . well, we do not know why she picked your house, and as you say, there are those who are looking for something against you." And then he put Miles's worries into words. "She could be a smuggler from France, even a spy."

"True." There was nothing else to say. Miles had put her in his own bed, not the most prudent of moves in hindsight. She had collapsed in his bedroom. What else should he have done, carried her through the house looking for someplace safe to store her, under the eager eyes of every servant? Lock her in the cellar, where someone looking for her could creep around at night and make contact? Secrete her in the carriage house? The stables, where the very same thing could happen?

It was bad enough when the only enemy was France. Adding America to the list only increased the strain on England. "Thank you, Denton." Miles began climbing again, saying over his shoulder, "I shall check on her myself."

"Very good, sir," Denton said, and continued down to the main floor.

Miles pushed open the door at the top of the stairs and headed down the hallway toward his own room. He remembered clearly the body he uncovered while loosing her stays. She had strength in her limbs. Riding horses could give her a strong, fit body; so could long walks on a country lane.

Or hard work, his suspicious mind whispered.

She also had skin as soft as silk, as pale as cream, and unmarked with freckles despite that red hair. Her hair was thick and so dark a red that it seemed almost black until the light reflected off it.

Her face was beautiful, the features were regular and pleasing, the nose pert, her chin firm, almost stubborn. In repose, he could not tell if she smiled often, or was more reserved. He did not know the color of her eyes, he had not seen them in that first moment, but the lashes were thick and surprisingly dark for a redhead. Red hair was not the fashion, but he had never allowed fashion to dictate the women he chose.

And she was not a child. At a guess, he would put her age at five and twenty. She wore no ring, only the bracelet.

As he neared his room, he ran over his suspicions. She had been in his bedroom. There were a limited number of reasons for a woman to be in a man's bedroom. Theft, for one. Spying for another, something he would have to consider carefully. He turned his mind to the last reason on his short list: looking for a new protector.

Edward had not thought her to be that kind of woman, but then, Edward saw the world as more good than evil, saw people as uniformly worthy, and saw all women as chaste. Miles knew his friend had never indulged in the custom of taking a mistress. Perhaps being a doctor, Edward thought it unseemly, but Miles had never had to worry about appearances.

Until now.

Still, a woman was a woman, if she was available and looking for a new man to satisfy her needs, and—it went without mentioning—if she was not here to harm his country. That would change everything.

Father might not think his emotions went deep, but Miles loved his England. He admired its history, was proud of the valiant reputation it had in war, and knew the men of repute that made England what it was, scientists and writers and politicians and kings. He got a thrill when he saw the ships of England on their way out of port, flags straight out in the sea winds as the sails filled.

He relished the chance to thwart a spy. For one, it would

improve his father's opinions of him. If the spy looked like she did, his task would be pleasant, even enjoyable, finding out who she was. Perhaps she had good reason to be here, in his house, unannounced and unrecognized, with no letters of introduction.

Unchaperoned.

In his bedroom.

Good reason? The very idea was laughable.

He stopped outside his own doorway and raised his hand to knock. How very odd, knocking on his own room.

If she was still unconscious, or if she had slipped into a natural sleep as Edward had hoped, knocking might wake her. If she was awake, knocking would warn her. Miles lowered his hand, and listened intently.

There was no sound, as Denton had said, but something was different. He grabbed the knob and pushed.

CHAPTER 6

FOOTSTEPS DRIFTED ON THE AIR, MEASURED BUT QUIET, AS IF not wanting to be heard, the soft sound coming closer and closer. Olivia's heart picked up speed. The air around her tingled; she wasn't sure whether it was her own nerves or that strange aura of power she sensed coming from him as she watched from the window.

She faced the door and held her breath. She'd taken the fireplace poker for a weapon, just in case, relieved that the dizziness was easing its ferocious grip a bit, enough perhaps to fool him.

The door opened abruptly.

It was the man from the driveway, the dark-haired one in the vest and sleeves, the same one who had been in her kitchen—if it had been her kitchen at all. Olivia shoved the thought aside, and hefted the poker over her shoulder. He had looked plenty big from a second story window, and he was even bigger up close, tall, easily over six feet with broad shoulders and long, solid arms roped with muscles not even the flowing shirt he wore could disguise. Even so, a poker could do enough damage to give her a head start. To where, she had no idea, but she wasn't going to stand idly by and do nothing.

It was unfair that he was so stunning.

He had left the door open. The hallway stretched out behind him, the perfect escape if she could make it that far, and get around him.

Which was an impossibility, but seeing that open door gave an odd sense of reassurance.

He looked at that poker, and his eyebrows lifted over gorgeous eyes, a strikingly light gray against his tanned skin and black hair. A smile tugged at one corner of his mouth. Olivia felt her temper rise. This might be funny to him, but it was deadly serious to her, and the poker was getting heavier by the second. Clearly, she wasn't as recovered as she needed to be.

But she didn't want him to know that. She couldn't afford to show weakness. "Who are you?"

He ignored her question and looked pointedly at the poker in her hands. "I see you are awake," he merely said in that rich, dark voice she remembered. Definitely a British accent. She was certain she heard a smile in those words.

Olivia clamped her jaw shut. If he wouldn't answer her first question, she doubted he'd answer any of the others. What she was doing here, for starters. What they wanted with her, why he told that other man he didn't know how she got here.

And most particularly, why there had been a carriage in his front yard, no telephone, or electric lights, and why he and his friend were dressed in costume. There was an obvious, ugly answer, tales of women who woke up with no memory of how they got there or what had happened.

Olivia stared at him. Not stared, exactly, but she fixed her gaze on him and let her thoughts tumble around like ping-pong balls. She shook her head against the frightening thought, and the room lurched.

The man made a move toward her, but she took a better grip on the poker, and he subsided. He looked her over, taking his sweet time while she simmered. "You should not be out of bed." He pointed at it.

She had no intention of climbing meekly back in but she wasn't sure how long she could stand. Her arms trembled; she knew he saw it because the smile crept out of his voice and onto his face. Olivia couldn't look away.

It was almost as if someone had reached into her secret wishes and brought them to life, those fanciful, un-liberated dreams of Tall, Dark and Handsome, who would come and rescue her from her single state, and free her from endless dates with boring men. He didn't look like he would bore her on his worst day.

His dark hair curled along that ridiculous collar on his shirt. A finely sculptured nose, straight and narrow, neat eyebrows, not too thin or too thick, ears that lay close to his head, fabulous cheekbones, and a jaw just exactly strong enough. And those eyes, piercing light eyes, almost a match for her own, more a glittering silver than her own pale green.

They twinkled at her, as if the two of them shared a joke. She wished she could trust the humor in his eyes and his voice, but she knew the smile was at her expense as she stood there, half his size, in a loosened gown she had no idea how to fasten by herself, holding an iron poker on him in what appeared to be his own house.

It was not the beautiful eyes and perfectly sculptured face, tempting as they were, that made her wish she could trust him. It was the air of confidence, of capability, a man secure in himself, a man who knew exactly who he was and where he belonged.

Olivia hardened her resolve. "How did I get here?"

Those eyebrows went up again, and the smile widened. "I think that should be my question, don't you? Only my valet is allowed in here when I'm dressing unless I have invited them beforehand. You made no attempt to knock first. Had you done so, I would have heard you."

Valet?

The smile slipped, and curiosity took its place. "I even brought my butler in to see if he recognized you and knew who you were, and what you were doing in my room during my bath. Delightful surprise though you are, I would have liked a warning. You caught me rather off-guard. I prefer to be appropriately dressed when meeting new . . . guests."

Bath. She'd heard that from him twice now. If she had been in *his* bath, he could hardly have been in *her* kitchen. Someone had abducted her from her house, but she hadn't drunk or eaten anything that could have been tainted, and until he appeared, no one had been with her.

She decided to work that out later, and snapped her attention back to his words.

"I am seldom here, and at first glance thought it possible that you might be a new maid, unacquainted with the rules of the house. I see now that cannot be. You are hardly dressed like a maid." Something flickered in his eyes, but the smile came back. "I assure you, my servants would have seen that you had all the tea and cakes you required while you waited had you merely used the knocker. A woman dressed like you would have been admitted immediately." His gaze slipped down her body, then snapped back up to her face.

"Servants?" Olivia asked faintly. "You have servants, too?" Not just a valet and butler, odd as that was. No one had a valet any more, at least not that she'd heard. And who still had butlers? Certainly no one she knew, not even anyone she worked for.

He drew back. In surprise or offense, Olivia could not tell. "Of course. It is impossible to run an estate of this size without them."

"Your *estate?* Where am I?" Knowing there were servants around might be good if one of them would help her get away, or bad if they were all loyal to him. Which they probably were.

And who did he think she was here to meet?

The man leaned casually against the doorjamb, and folded his arms over his broad chest. "Now I must wonder if I am being insulted. A lovely thing like you, and you might not be in the right house. Where do you think you should be?"

"I don't know." It came out like a wail. "You brought me here. Why me? I can't be of any use to you."

He smiled again, and this time there was no mistaking the wolfish character there. "I can think of any number of reasons you can be of use to me." Then he sobered. "While it pains me to say this, I did not bring you here."

The poker was so heavy, Olivia wasn't sure how much longer she'd be able to hold it. Her legs were shaking, but under the dress she wore, she doubted he'd be able to tell.

She was naturally pale, with the fair coloring that went along with her red hair, but from the way his gaze suddenly sharpened, Olivia suspected she'd gone a whole new shade of ashen.

Her muscles abruptly gave up the struggle. The poker dropped, its point hitting the beautiful wooden floor with a frightening scrape, and she braced herself against the handle like a cane, hoping it hadn't done too much damage to the wood, hoping the thing would hold her up long enough for the man to leave the room. The dizziness that had plagued her since she woke up attacked with a vengeance, and she felt her balance go.

Strong arms caught her, lifted her. "No more arguments. This is my bed, and I shall have to find another place to sleep for the night, but I can hardly let an ill woman sleep on the floor."

Now that she was no longer standing, Olivia's head cleared slightly. Whatever had happened to her wasn't out of her system yet, but she could tell that with a little more rest, she'd be herself. "What did you give me?" she asked desperately as the man laid her on the bed with more care than she expected.

"Nothing at all. Why? Are you hungry? Thirsty?" His face was close to hers as he pulled his arm from under her shoulders. His eyes suddenly grew dark as his pupils widened, leaving that strange silvery ring around the edge of the darkness.

A darkness that threatened to draw her in, warm and close, very close. She felt his breath on her skin.

"*Are* you hungry?" he asked again, those eyes with that odd silver rim of iris fixed on hers, still so close that it was becoming hard to breathe.

Olivia forced her mind back to the subject at hand. Food.

Feeding her might be an excuse to get a drug down her again, but for some strange reason, she doubted he meant any harm. He'd had all kinds of chances to hurt her, even frighten her, and he'd done nothing except put her to bed, and catch her when she started to fall.

Of course, there was still that unlaced corset, and the gown. She hadn't been wearing *them* in her kitchen.

"I won't eat," she warned him. *Something* had made her

weak and woozy, with no memories between her kitchen and this room. He didn't act like any kidnapper she'd ever heard about, but something was very strange here.

"If you won't eat, a cup of tea, then." He straightened at last, his arms sliding away from beneath her, leaving a trail of warmth.

Olivia grabbed at his sleeve before he turned to walk away. She had to try, one more time. "Please. Tell me where I am?"

A frown of genuine worry creased his forehead. "Do you honestly not know?"

She shook her head, something she quickly reminded herself not to do for a while as the room moved again. "No."

He stared down at her. "If you don't know where you are, do you remember how you got here? By stage? Walking? Did you get a ride on some farmer's cart?"

"No." As he had listed off the choices, Olivia felt panic stir. "This isn't some reality show, is it? You aren't doing this to stay in character?"

"Some *what*? Stay in character? What is this you are asking?" He backed up a step, and Olivia lost her grip on his sleeve.

"Can you answer one question for me?" She heard the rising desperation in her voice, so he must have heard it, too.

"What?" The man sounded wary. He folded his arms, probably to keep her from reaching for him again.

"If you won't tell me where I am, can you at least tell me" —it was so hard to ask, but she had to, all the signs pointed to it, no matter how impossible it was—"*when* I am?"

He looked aghast. "You are more ill than any of us realized. I will have someone bring tea for you soon. Drink it or not, as you wish."

Despite her fear, Olivia felt a laugh threaten. Tea, of all things!

"*Please,*" it sounded strange to have him use the word, "stay in bed."

And then he slipped out the door, leaving Olivia more unsettled than ever. Nothing here made sense. He was so decidedly English, his speech oddly stilted and formal.

The wild idea rose up again, leaving Olivia nauseous with dread.

It was ridiculous. Absurd.

Insane.

Maybe she had lost her mind.

But she didn't think so.

CHAPTER 7

NOTHING OF THE TWENTY-FIRST CENTURY EXISTED. DESPITE the dizziness that kept coming in unexpected waves, Olivia clung to the window and scoured the landscape in both directions. She should at least hear something, some engine, the hum of distant traffic, the vibration of an air conditioner.

Nothing.

The room faced the back of the house. She wished she paid more attention to the drive when she peeked outside earlier, checked for what kind of tracks showed in the pebbles, looked for any churning modern tires would leave, but she had been so distracted by the carriage and the men that she had forgotten to look.

No garage sat behind the house. No asphalt driveway, not even the pebbled type that ran along the front. Instead, a rough brick pathway hugged the house so closely she could only see a portion of it. More paths led away from the house, and she could see buildings through the boughs, but nothing from the shape of them gave away their purpose.

She caught a distinct whiff of manure.

Everything hinted at some rural setting, from the extra buildings tucked away from any arriving guests to the trees to the smell of animal.

Which, if someone wanted to kidnap a person, made sense.

But what anyone with a house this size needed with her, a self-employed house stager—despite how good at her job she was—Olivia could not imagine. If they wanted her services, all they had to do was hire her.

No television noises drifted from another room or another floor, no vacuum, no scent of a clothes dryer. She heard wet clothes flapping in the breeze on a line somewhere very close, but she couldn't see them. She'd already discovered there was no light switch anywhere, no overhead lamp in the center of the room, and no outlets, either.

If there were any, she would have discovered them. She had prowled the room, checked behind the door in the wall that did not lead to the hallway, even looked under the bed.

When she peeked out the hallway window and saw her host standing by the carriage, she had been surprised to discover that grooved lead held the panes of glass in place, not dried putty. She'd seen similar windows in older houses when she went in to stage for sale, but these were far more intricate. It was almost as if every single item had to be both beautiful and functional.

Olivia took stock of what she knew so far.

Someone had dressed her in a silk gown, complete with a corset and stockings, but either it was supposed to slide off the shoulders—which she doubted—or they had left something unfastened.

As far as this room, her elegant prison, it was as elegant as her gown. The beautiful bedposts with carved vines winding up to blossoms at the top were done by hand. She had traced her fingers along the grooves, down the leaves and stems, and recognized the skill of a master. While staging houses, she had worked with enough modern, machine-made furniture to find the faint imperfections that only happened in hand-carving.

The same burgundy velvet as the curtains had been draped into a canopy over those magnificent posts to protect the occupant from any dust drifting from above. In a nod to the masculine resident, the canopy had no frills, just a long stretch across the top that dropped into a plain fall over at the foot.

She looked back to the door in one side wall and shivered, remembering her first look inside.

The copper tub had been a surprise. Like everything else, it was elegant, four heavy clawed feet, but the real surprise had been the lack of pipes. No drain in the bottom, and not a faucet in sight. It was not there for decoration, though, because a faint dusting of soap scum lay in the bottom.

Someone used this tub. But how? It would have to be filled by hand, and emptied the same way.

That same room also held a wooden-framed screen with more of the burgundy fabric from the bedroom, only thickly gathered. She had peeked around it. Even now, as she stood by the window, she remembered the shock of seeing a genuine commode in place of a modern toilet.

It was time to think, coldly and rationally. Olivia held tightly to the window frame and went over everything she remembered, step by step, until she woke here.

She knew absolutely and positively she had gone with Renee to the flea market. She knew absolutely she had bought that iron, the very one lying on the foot of the bed. And she knew positively she had been ironing in her own kitchen.

Everything after that went a bit strange.

Can you at least tell me when I am? She heard herself ask it, and saw again the appalled look on his face.

Could she believe what all the evidence was saying?

Olivia closed her eyes. She remembered it all, her kitchen, the ironing board, the air conditioner's hum, and the iron, surprisingly hot, heavy in her hand.

Then the next image, the man in the doorway, just a quick flash before she fainted, but suddenly Olivia realized what had been tantalizing her all this time.

The doorway had been in the wrong place. She heard his words now, as clearly as when he first spoke. *"Who the devil are you, and what are you doing in my room?"*

She hadn't seen the man in *her* house at all. She had been in *his*.

Olivia trembled as the first part of the answer settled into place. One second she had been ironing in her own kitchen. The next instant she had been here, in this room. And the man had been in the doorway of that odd bathroom. He probably told the truth to his friend when he said she had nearly caught him in his bath.

No one had drugged her. No one had kidnapped her. He was innocent.

That was the good news.

The bad news was so unbelievable she was not sure she even dared ask the question of herself.

Where was she—when was she—and how had it happened?

Could she believe what she saw? What she wore?

Her gaze fell on the iron, sitting undiscovered on the floor. Aside from her bracelet, it was the only familiar thing around her. Olivia looked down at the bracelet. It, too, was an antique, but she had worn it for several years without a flicker of anything odd. Surely if it had been the catalyst, something would have happened long ago.

Not so the iron. She remembered the hallucination from that first touch in the flea market, when she saw the woman in the strange mobcap and the pile of fabric and blamed the vision on static electricity.

Only it hadn't been an illusion at all, had it? It had been the iron getting ready, warming up, so to speak. Olivia grimaced at the macabre pun. She gave the iron a narrow-eyed glare, but there was no warning shimmer like in the flea market. In fact, it looked frighteningly at home.

"What are you?" she asked it, half expecting it to answer.

Although, now that she thought about it, something about it was different. It looked so much . . . newer. The wood of the handle was cleaner, the iron absolutely devoid of rust, the metal unpitted.

"You did this to me, didn't you?" Good thing she was alone. If anyone saw her talking to an inanimate object, they would think she had gone around the bend.

But they weren't the ones who had just been whisked through time. And left here without instructions, without friends. Without even knowing exactly where she was.

Still, she was on to that innocent-looking iron now. All she had to do was figure out how to make it work again. Surely that couldn't be too hard. She'd done it once without even trying. Surely she could reproduce the events that started this, at least close enough to send it into reverse. Back home.

If she was right, she had to find a stove.

But where to find one, in a place this huge?

M iles paced the study. He had heard of people forgetting their past, but that belonged to the elderly, not the young. And not this severe.

Can you at least tell me when I am?

When. What an odd question. How much time did she think she had lost?

He had been right from the first. There was something odd about his uninvited guest's speech. It was even more pronounced than he at first suspected, an accent he had never heard before, that unusual cadence and the way she elongated her words. After hearing her say entire sentences, it was clear she wasn't from England, nor anyplace else with which he was familiar.

His thoughts returned to his first suspicion. America.

Everyone knew there were Americans in England, displaced from their home when the war for independence made their British leanings unwelcome. No doubt they sounded just like her. He wished now that he had met them. Perhaps it would help identify her accent.

He had heard enough political rumblings to be aware that America was still torn between political leanings, and debates for and against war raged in the papers that made it across the Atlantic to England. Whispers had reached even his ears that in some states, Federalists had mentioned secession from America in order to keep their cherished link to England open, although thus far that movement had gone nowhere.

Adding to that was the ongoing threat of Napoleon. The Americans longed to trust Boney, despite the growing list of broken promises. His surprise guest might have come to England for safety now that Americans were rattling their sabres again, only this time the upstart country included

Canada in their targets. America hoped to split England's attention with two wars to fight simultaneously.

Of course, there was always the possibility that she was no friend of England and instead had come under false colors. She showed up, not in the home of a companion or confidante, but in his house, the only son of a member of Parliament.

She was newly come to England's shores. He was certain of that. Now to find out what cause brought her here. There should have been someone waiting for her at the docks to take her into the bosom of friends, family—or conspirator.

What did she hope to accomplish for whoever had sent her?

If that was the case, the confederates had a problem. Their agent seemed to have lost her memory.

Miles slipped his coat on. Until he knew more, he had to present at least the *appearance* of abiding by the proprieties, and going before a woman once in his shirtsleeves was once too much.

Edward Reed, who had come so readily when summoned, was a doctor, but not a specialist in anything this extreme. And Edward was always busy, delivering babes, treating axe wounds, gorings, and all the other accidents that happened in the rural communities. He did not work with illnesses of the brain.

Assuming this was a true illness and not a ploy on the part of his uninvited guest to fool him.

It was time to find out.

Olivia looked around the room. There had to be a place to hide the iron before someone found it, decided it had been misplaced, and took it off to wherever the ironing was done.

Where it might well turn on.

If anyone was going to be wafted to another time, it had better be herself! She could only hope the thing had a homing device in it.

Where to put it? Someplace no one would think to dust, so under the bed was out. The room had no chest of drawers, just the armoire. Her gaze traced the massive piece. Two doors that opened in the middle—although she refused to look inside, that was a bridge too far even for this situation—antique hardware on the sides, dark metal handles, and carvings up the sides to the scalloped top. The iron only had to hide for a little while, until she could find a better spot.

And find out how to make it send her back home again.

Olivia climbed onto the chair, and clenched one hand onto the carvings for support. She raised the iron above her head. The armoire top was so tauntingly close. She held the iron a little higher, risked going up on tiptoe on the chair. Just a little higher, one more inch—and the room lurched, the floor rushing back toward her, coming fast.

An ominous thump came from inside the room, loud enough to be a person hitting the floor from a height. Miles ran down the hall, bursting in through the door.

His guest was sprawled on the floor in a tangle of skirts and slender legs, her hand clenched around an iron from his servants' quarters, his chair on its side next to her. She had clearly fallen.

Holding an iron?

He reached her side and scooped her up, ignoring her startled gasp. She still held the iron, clutched tightly in her hands.

"Did you think to drop that on my head?" he snapped at her. "And what were you doing out of bed at all?" He laid her down on the bed with a thump.

Miles braced his hands on either side of her, glaring down at her from too close a distance. Her eyes were wide, the pale green of her iris nearly swallowed by the black centers. He grabbed the iron with one hand, wrenched it out of her surprisingly determined grip, then thrust it toward the foot of the bed and turned back to her, keeping her trapped between his arms.

He refused to give in to the panic in her eyes. "What did I do to deserve you dropping an iron on me? Do you know what kind of damage that iron could do? Of course you do," he corrected the ridiculous question without letting her answer. "Why would you want me dead?"

"I wasn't trying to kill you! That iron's mine!" she gasped. "I need it. I was just trying to find a safe place to keep it." She reached around his arms, a foolish thing because the bed was large, and so was he, and the iron was too far away.

"On top of my armoire? Where it might fall down on the nearest head? Why do you need to hide an iron? Would it not be better to leave it nearby for use?" He pretended to look around. "Odd, since I see no travel trunks, nor anything that might have been in one. And why would you press it your-self? An iron is a servant's tool, and no servant would wear jewelry like this." His gaze fell on that gold and jade bracelet. The piece was too expensive for any servant to afford. He let his sleeve brush against the fancy thing.

"Please," she begged, and kept her arm out, as if that would induce him to hand it over. "It's mine, give it back!"

Give it back? "Who are you, that you think you can give orders?"

"It's mine!" Her eyes grew wider, and she struggled to sit up. Her bracelet made a faint sound, the links sliding down her wrist as she pushed against the mattress, but he did not give her room.

Which, he realized as her gown slid off one shoulder, was a good thing. Too much movement and it might drop below decency, although he had not unfastened *that* many hooks and eyes.

Miles kept eyes on her face and his hands braced on either side of her, holding her in place. "Stay where you are. Do you want to fall over again?" An iron was a servant's utensil, and she wanted it back too badly.

He turned his head toward it, sitting on the edge of the bed where he had shoved it, and froze. The back of the iron was open. He had never looked at an iron before, never knew that they had a door. A rather large door for such a small tool, taking up the entire back of the tool.

What a handy place to hide a missive. Who would think to look in such an unlikely object?

He looked back down at the woman, and straightened. She immediately sat up, just as he expected, and one hand clapped the gown he had unfastened to her bosom, holding it just inside the bounds of modesty.

"If you are well enough to go climbing on chairs and dropping irons on my head, you are well enough to get out of my room." He caught her upper arms, and picked her off the bed, setting her firmly on her feet, and grasped her free wrist like a manacle. "Come with me."

She tugged against his grip, twisting, tugging toward the

foot of the bed where the iron rested, her hand grasping at nothing. The gown slipped over a shoulder again, but she did not notice, just kept pulling against his grip. "I need my iron!"

He kept moving. Her stockings had no resistance on the floor, and she slid away from the bed, nearly bent double in her attempt to get at the thing.

Miles stopped pulling long enough to scowl down at her. "You are going to hurt yourself if you do not stop this. I am not giving you that iron. You have nearly dropped it on my head once already, and that is plenty. I will give you your own room, and you will stay there until I figure out what to do with you."

If she struggled any harder, she was going to get slivers in her feet. "My shoes, then!"

He glanced down at her feet, but they were mostly hidden under her skirts. "I will go back for them once I get you settled."

They were out in the hallway. Olivia switched from the useless effort at grabbing for the iron to trying to pry his fingers off her wrist.

He slammed to a stop, and she stumbled the last step. "Stop it! You are wasting your strength, and I do not appreciate getting scratched."

He wrenched the knob of the door in front of him, shoved it open, and pulled her forward, letting go of her wrist only long enough to give her a gentle push into the room.

He stopped in the doorway. "Here. This will be your room. You will stay here until I can decide what to do with you."

But she wasn't listening. Olivia just stared at the room before her, open-mouthed.

CHAPTER 8

THE ROOM WAS DONE IN SOFT YELLOW, THE COLOR OF daffodils in the spring. Yellow wallpaper accented with—she squinted to identify the design that overlaid up the color, yes, silver *fleur-de-lis*—covered the walls from floor to ceiling, and was duplicated in the curtains at the wide window on the far wall. The pattern would have been overwhelming if not so subtle.

From the *de rigueur* armoire to a pair of slipper chairs by the window, upholstered in the same shade of yellow, to a dressing table complete with a mirror and matching chair, everything was original, and in pristine shape.

Even the mantel for the fireplace on the other side of the armoire had been painted yellow. It would have blended into the room if not for the brick interior she could barely see from where she stood.

Happily, someone had wisely left the all the lovely carved wood unpainted. It gave warmth to the room and added a needed contrast to all the bright tones.

Olivia's professional eye admired the skill of whoever did

the decorating. She wanted every piece here. What she could do with them! Minneapolis had enough old houses that this furniture would be perfect for those who liked things unspoiled and authentic.

There was a bed, too, and what a bed! A full tester complete with massive posts and an arched canopy over-head, not the flat one of her host's room. Someone had decided the room was yellow enough because the fabric hangings were the exact silver of the design.

His rich voice broke her thoughts, and she whirled around.

The door was still open behind him. The iron was only steps away. But she couldn't let him guess where her thoughts went, so kept her gaze on his face. It was easy enough to do, with those grey eyes so riveting against his richly tanned face, and the dark hair that tumbled over his forehead. "There is a bell pull by the bed, so you can ring for assistance." His voice went gruff, and he stepped back.

"It's a beautiful room." She looked up at him, and found a smile. "Thank you." The smile faded as reality intruded. "What do you intend to do with me?"

"That all depends on why you are here. Surely you heard the rumors of war before you left. I am not sure whether it was brave or foolhardy to take such a trip at this time." He braced his hands on either side of the door, and leaned in, something warm in his eyes. "Although I confess I am delighted you arrived safely."

"War? What war?" He had not answered before, but Olivia tried again, more desperately. "You can't mean . . . What year is it?"

His face went blank except for a slight crease between his eyebrows. "That is the second time you have asked that, only before you wanted the day. Am I to believe you truly do not know the year? Is that sort of forgetfulness not something reserved for the old?"

Olivia looked at him, her brain whirling. If she was right, if the unimaginable had occurred and she had left her own time behind, how much damage could she do by telling him what she thought, feared? Every time-travel movie and tv show she'd ever watched zipped through her memory. What would she change in the future?

What was that place where they threw the insane in this time period? Bedlam? She would never get her iron and go return home! Her scalp tingled with the prickle of fear. "I tell you, I do not know how I got here. I do not know how much time I lost. Please. What is the year?"

That worried crease stayed between his eyes, but he did give one nod. "Very well. It is 1811. July, should you need the month. Do you wish the date as well?"

Her mouth went dry, his shape blurred, her ears rang, and she grabbed at the bedpost for support. 1811. For a moment, she thought she might faint. She had lost over two hundred years.

The man shifted, and her attention snapped away from her shock and into the present. The ringing in her ears subsided as his form became solid again, but her fingers could not unclasp from the bedpost. It took her a moment to remember his last question.

The date. Did a date matter when two centuries were gone?

But having gotten that much, getting the rest couldn't hurt. It probably wouldn't help—1811!—but she needed all the information she could get. "Yes, please. What is the date?"

"It is the twenty-fifth. Before you ask, it is a Thursday."

July twenty-fifth. The same date she had gone to the flea market with Renee, except two hundred years earlier.

A single brow rose on his face. "You seem surprised. Did more time pass than you thought?"

A laugh burst out, sharp with a tinge of stifled hysteria. "Yes. Oh, yes."

He straightened, his arms dropping from their braced position on the jambs. "How much time have you lost? What is the last date you remember?"

Olivia's brain couldn't come up with a believable lie. "It was summer."

His brows rose, his eyes went wide. "Summer? But it is still summer."

Keep it simple, she told herself. "I remember it was July."

He gave a single shake of the head, almost as if struggling to comprehend what he heard. "That is not good. It takes months to cross the ocean. You have lost more than one year. Do you not recall getting on the ship? Or with whom you traveled?"

Denial seemed to be her only friend right now. "No. Neither."

His brows came down, any mirth gone. "You must have been quite ill. I am surprised whoever left you here did not stay to see to your health." That dark gaze drifted past her, toward the window with its yellow curtains. "Perhaps they have not gone far. I should send the servants out to see if someone is wandering the countryside looking for you. I will send someone off to Posset and check the docks, see if you have been reported missing."

"No!" His eyebrows rose, Olivia caught herself, and floundered for an explanation he might believe. "They would have come knocking, wouldn't they?"

He shook his head. "For now, you are here and . . . safe." That mischievous twinkle started in his eyes. "And recovering. I can alert the village to watch for someone asking for a woman of your appearance."

What would he do when no one ever appeared, when all his searching was in vain? It would be, of course. She had to get out of here. She had to go back. She had to get that iron and *make* it work.

It was all she could do to keep her gaze on his, and not let it drift past him and toward his room.

As soon as he left, she was going to zip down the hall and grab her iron.

For now, she had to keep him distracted. It was easy enough to frown. "I wish you would answer my questions. You still haven't told me where I am."

CHAPTER 9

MILES FOUND THIS WOMAN CONFOUNDING. SHE SEEMED SO lost, and oddly sad.

His nature was to protect women, natural for a man with a younger sister, but he had never been in a predicament like this.

How could he discover what she was hiding when she did not even remember what year it was? He could not threaten her, not just because he would never do such a thing, but also because that was not the way to win her confidence.

And he needed to win it if he was going to learn her secrets.

He had distrusted the faint when he walked in on her after his bath. It was far too convenient, with him standing wet and barely covered, staring at a woman where she had no business being, but his suspicions had been unwarranted; she had truly been unconscious.

She was not a diamond of the first water, not with that red hair. Oh, she was pretty enough, with those delicate features, slender eyebrows, and pale skin, and certainly had allure. Goodness knows, she had drawn him like a magnet since he first walked into his room and found her there.

Her face had character and her spring-green eyes showed her intelligence—and her thoughts—like a beacon. Not the kind of woman to be an effective spy. And then there was the red hair. One could hardly escape notice with a feature that distinctive, and weren't spies supposed to be unobtrusive?

She had held him at bay with fireplace tools and tried to assault him with the iron, hardly the action of someone being secretive.

He admired her audacity, and the very believability of her performance, whatever her purpose here.

She frowned now. "I wish you would answer my questions." Irritation suffused her voice. "You still haven't told me where I am."

If she was pretending, she already knew the answer to that. If this loss of memory was real, finding out where she was might be enough to jog her memory. "You are in England," he said, and watched her closely.

She gave one nod. "I suspected I was in England, but where?"

"Between Bristol and Posset." He waited for her reaction.

A light flickered in her gaze. "Bristol. I know that name. Never heard of the other, but thank you."

"Perhaps you know it better as Portishead?"

She frowned. "No. You made that up, didn't you?"

"Made it up? No. I assure you, that is its real name." He felt his lips twitch as a smile threatened, but firmed his mouth and his willpower. "I asked you earlier how you got here. Have you remembered anything yet?"

She looked away instantly, and Miles felt his suspicions sharpen. Disappointment flooded him. How he had wanted her to be innocent! Of spying, at least. But then she raised her eyes and met his gaze straight on. "I was at home, in my own kitchen, and then I was here."

"Kitchen, eh?" He scarcely knew what his own looked like, and was positive neither Abby nor Cecelia had ever been in one. Her own kitchen? In those clothes? He remembered the strength in her arms, and his thought that she was familiar with work, but a kitchen maid? With her educated style of speech, and her clothes? It hardly made sense. "Nothing in between?"

"No."

That felt like the truth. But her gaze drifted away. She was holding back something. "Do you remember your name?"

"Olivia Underwood."

Miles smiled in satisfaction. That came so quickly it had to be her real name, although he did not know how that information helped. Yet. "Hello, Miss Underwood. I am Miles Stewart." He gave a quick bow and waited to see if there was any sign of recognition. Nothing. Not a blink, not a flicker in her eyes, but then he had left off his title deliberately. If he gave it, she should recognize it. Even if she did not, merely hearing it might make her stop talking. Titles had that effect. "Welcome to my house."

"I know my presence here is . . . unexpected." At that last, the faint smile grew, and genuine amusement lit her face. She held him with her eyes and he was reluctant to look away.

H is amazing eyes drew her in, the surprising crystal color holding mysteries. Their initial effect hadn't faded in the least. Eyes were supposed to be mirrors of the soul, but his reflected her thoughts back while hiding his own. She saw her face in the darkness of his pupils, and felt herself blush.

She forced herself to look away. *Watch yourself, girl,* she thought. *This man is dangerous. And very attractive, a perilous combination.*

And she had to figure out how to out-think him and get the iron back?

The sound of his voice startled her, shattering the silence that had begun to stretch. "From where do you come? What country?"

She met his gaze again. The heat in his eyes was gone, as if it had never been there at all. "America," she said, and waited for his reaction.

His gaze didn't so much as flicker, but Olivia knew she felt a strange satisfaction coming from him, as if she'd confirmed something he had expected.

Miles's gaze did not flicker, but she could feel his mind drift away. His fingers tapped a rhythm on the jamb, no doubt in sync with his thoughts, and then his eyes sharpened again. He gave the wood a slap. "I shall have to find you a maid."

"Why? I've never needed a maid."

"Indeed?" One eyebrow rose. "Never?"

"No. No one I know has maids. We're perfectly capable of taking care of ourselves."

He stepped inside, and pushed the door partially closed. "Our conversation is not for all and sundry." Then he fixed those crystal-grey eyes on her. "We? How many of you are there?"

Stick as close to the truth as possible, she told herself. "Just two, myself and my sister."

"Older? Younger?" The questions came quickly, one after another.

She would have to be cautious. "Older."

"Did she try to talk you out of coming? Is she married? Did her husband not convince you to stay safely in America?"

Another memory came from Jane Austin: if she told this man that her sister was older and still unmarried and happy to be that way and still living in America, it would lead to all sorts of questions and—from the look in his eyes—suspicions. She pressed her lips together, and looked away.

"Or did your sister accompany you on the trip? Did something happen to her?" His voice went soft and warm with concern. "Is that what you've forgotten? Forgive me the questions, but I must know something before I begin the search. I only want to help."

She couldn't stop the wince. However incompatible she and Renee were, they were still sisters, and Olivia realized with a sting of pain how very far away she was.

He tilted his head as if weighing his thoughts. "I find myself in a quandary. I have in my house an American woman alone and missing an entire year of your life. You claim never to have had a maid, and will not admit to having your sister with you. The ports are filled with French ships stopping any vessels that get close, yet you got in." A faint edge colored the last sentence. He took a breath, and in that gentle voice of a moment ago went on, "I cannot explain your presence, nor can I turn you loose in the English countryside without a protector."

The room was quiet. He drummed his fingers against the doorjamb, and she could feel the thoughts churning in his head. "As you certainly must know, our two countries are on the verge of war, as if Napoleon were not bad enough for England to endure."

His shrewd eyes sharpened; his whole body was far too

still, except for those fingers tapping on the jamb. "So now I must ask if you are in sympathy with the War Hawks who are so busily beating their war drums."

"War Hawks?" What tidbit of history was going to trip her up now? Honestly, who ever thought her safety, her survival, would depend on knowing what happened between England and America in 1811? "I don't like war. I try not to listen to the news much."

"It appears the officials of your America aren't listening." That gaze stayed fixed on her face.

CHAPTER 10

"Since neither of us wishes to discuss the potential war, we must decide what to do with you. Surely you know you are making my search for your companion very difficult?"

"I'm sorry. I can't tell you what I don't know." Nor could she tell him what she did know. Olivia fought the shudder that wanted to run through her body.

He didn't seem to notice, just gave a single nod. "As I mentioned, we find ourselves in a difficult situation. You, an unwed woman, should not be in my house unattended." His brow furrowed. "I wish whoever brought you here had stayed. 'Tis beyond strange that they did not."

Keeping secrets, some secrets, was only going to make things worse. "I will answer what I can." That sounded amnesiac enough. "I live in the middle of the country, in"—she thought fast and tried desperately to remember her Minneapolis history. What was it called in this time?—"St. Anthony Falls, in the"—she hoped she had her dates and locations right—"Louisiana Territories. We don't get the news like so many other places do." *Please let that be accurate.*

TIME FOR A VISCOUNT

"Ah. So you are in War Hawks territory? Or are you too far west even for that?"

She was going to have to figure out this War Hawks fixation he seemed to have. "I don't know anything about that," she said quickly. "I'm not very political."

"No? So you live safely in a city?" The eyebrows went back up in apparently genuine curiosity, but she was certain she felt a strange tension in him.

She had been dropped on him without warning or reason. And there was so much she could not share. Anyone would be suspicious.

What was his question, again? Oh, yes. Did she live safely in a city. The answer should be innocuous enough. "If cities can be considered safe."

"True, unfortunately," he returned, and she could have sworn he was fighting a smile. Again.

For an unwitting host, he was being surprisingly genial about this whole thing.

Still standing straight, the Colossus of Rhodes blocking the barely-open doorway, he said with that surprising calm, "Whoever you were to meet here in England, they will be most concerned. I will alert my staff that if anyone asks for you, they are to be admitted immediately. For now, you need rest. It was not that long ago that you were insensible. Until we know more, you will stay here as my guest. I will tell the servants . . . I'll think of something. You will be cared for and treated as a lady unless I find out otherwise. I will send someone up to see to your needs."

He bowed, and turned around, leaving the door fully open.

Olivia held her breath, wondering which way he would turn. One side went back to his room, the other toward whatever lay down the rest of the hallway.

His bedroom was to the right.

He stopped in the hallway and turned back to look at her. Something in her face must have given her away. "Ah, yes," he said softly. "Your iron. Thank you for reminding me." He turned right, toward his own room.

She stuck her tongue out at his back, a useless, childish gesture. He reappeared quickly, her shoes in one hand, the iron in the other. "We must not forget your shoes." He set them down on the dark wood floor just inside the room, two bright spots against a somber background, and gave her a mocking wink as he lifted the iron. "You will not be needing a weapon." His footsteps moved down the hallway with a steady pace.

He whistled.

Miles Stewart clearly loved to gloat.

The whistling faded, the footsteps paused for an instant as she heard him open one of the doors she had seen in her peek into the hall. It snicked shut behind him.

Olivia unclenched hands she hadn't realized had gone tight, and strode over to the door to collect the one thing he allowed her. The shoes fit, of course, just as the gown did—or would once it was fastened back up.

Although how she was going to do that, Olivia did not know.

She went back to staring at the shoes. The soles were a thin skin of leather, virtually soundless on the floor, and certainly not designed for any long walks. She turned around and flopped down on one of the yellow chairs.

Now what to do? No books to read, no one to talk to, not even a phone to call for help. She could hardly walk around his house uninvited. Besides, although she felt better, she was not up to a stroll, particularly in a place this large.

Somewhere nearby, clear in the quiet of the house, a door

opened with a creak. No murmur of voices, just the barest scraping of footsteps, someone trying not to be heard, and the sensation of air shifting with the movement.

If anyone asks for you, they are to be admitted immediately.

The footsteps came closer. For some reason, an instinct she didn't understand, Olivia knew she had to be absolutely quiet.

She stared at the open door. It was too late to close it. She was grateful that the chair was off to one side, so no one could see her without stepping into the room.

Mr. Stewart had said he was sending a maid, but these were not the steps of a maid. First of all, they weren't light. Quiet, but definitely a man's footfalls. More soft sounds, faint scrapings of soles on the floor.

An echo, like noise through a tunnel, more vibration than sound, crept along her skin. Voices. Men, at least two, rumbled, and the air around her suddenly went cold.

CHAPTER 11

FOR THE SPACE OF A SINGLE BREATH OLIVIA SHIVERED, AND then she realized the chill came from just outside the room, from the men somewhere in the hallway. The very furtiveness of the voices screamed danger. She scarcely dared to breathe as she listened, afraid even her heartbeat was too loud.

"How long has Stewart been here?" The speaker's voice was dark, menacing, and crisp with authority. "I hoped to get what I need without him looming over me, and I get here to find out he is in residence. My creditors are traipsing about England to find me. I have no desire to run into a Bow Street Runner, and I would not put it past them to hire one. I have no intention of staying here any longer than necessary, but I cannot go back without funds."

Stewart. The name her host gave her. They had to be talking about Mr. Miles Stewart. Olivia stayed still and kept her breathing quiet and slow.

"He got here yesterday." The second man's voice lacked the threat of the first, and was softer, more subservient. "I do not know how long he intends to be here before he heads back. Why are you trying to get something from him?" The man seemed to stiffen his spine. Likely not employer and employee, or he would not answer back. "His father is the family head, not Mr. Stewart. If you think you were slighted, why not go to the earl and ask for an advance on your allowance?"

Family head? Allowance? This man was related to her host? She couldn't decide whether that was better or worse.

"That, my good man, is none of your business."

"You gambled it away, am I not right? How many clubs have you been tossed out of? Will any let you back?"

Olivia felt her heart skip at the taunting tone. She wouldn't dare to take the scary man on.

The cold voice growled back, "Best you not ask too many questions. Miles is always plump enough in the pocket. I need some of that. You were to find something useful, not get curious. Wouldn't you like some of his dosh? Do not tell me he pays you enough that you can buy whatever you want. I see the age of your suits, and the wear on your boots. Furthermore, I happen to know you do not own that gelding you ride. It comes from *his* stables."

Someone shifted, feet scraping slightly on the polished wood floor, and Olivia realized with horror that she could see a bit of a sleeve. If the owner turned just right, would he see her, too? "Find me something I can use," that disturbing voice went on, "and I will make it worth your while. Get some boots you won't be ashamed to be seen in." Ugly humor laced the words.

"You know there is always staff here. How am I supposed to find anything with servants crawling all over this place?" The second man's voice managed to be both ingratiating and insistent. "I can hardly go rummaging through his room. His valet watches over his possessions as if they were the Crown Jewels."

"There has to be a safe somewhere." The scary man's voice took on a tinge of panic. Just how much money did he need? "You are with him enough; you must see where he puts things."

"He has his office. I believe he keeps some things of importance there, register payments from the villagers, rent records, crop reports."

"I don't want paper, man! I want a cravat pin, or jeweled cufflinks. Maybe one of his rings."

A gasp came from the hall, pale enough to belong to the weaker man. "I cannot do that! I have never even been in his bedroom, and I have no desire to confront Thomas."

"Everyone knows he wears diamonds on his vests." A special hiss accented the last word. "Surely he can stand the loss of a single diamond. Buttons fall off—"

"No!" the weak man interrupted. "I have not seen the vest. He might have left it in London. He is not a fool to travel with it." The response was quick, the voice surprisingly firm. Maybe the second man wasn't as weak as she thought. "I will find something. Just give me a little time."

"You do that. He is a valuable prize with or without the diamonds. London is a long way away. He might be robbed on the return trip. In fact, I am surprised he made it here without incident. It would not surprise me to hear that he was murdered by a highwayman on the return trip."

If she had been cold a moment ago, it was nothing compared to the ice that crept in from that hallway. She must have watched too many crime dramas, because Olivia knew she had just heard a murder plot. That was much too casual a statement. How could the second man not notice?

But the villain changed the subject. "Keep looking. You

know well enough that I am staying nearby. I will come tonight when the servants are asleep. Have something for me."

"I cannot find what you want in that amount of time!" The quieter man's voice carried the tinge of panic.

"Then we will look together. Meantime, find his safe. He might surprise both of us by keeping something useful there. Let me slip away before the servants stroll past. Oh, and keep your mouth shut. I do not want word to get back to London about where I am until I have something in hand. I cannot have word drift back on a loose tongue."

"I will let you out the back way." A shoe scuffed; the men must be leaving.

The last sentence came from a distance, but still clear enough to overhear. "Not past the kitchens. They have seen me before; some of them know who I am."

Any other response was lost. Olivia held her breath, listening for a sound that indicated they were still nearby. The hallway was so quiet the men had to be gone.

Miles Stewart would never believe her if she told him what she'd overheard.

Maybe that's why she was here. Perhaps she was *supposed* to intervene.

CHAPTER 12

AN AMERICAN.

A pretty woman with appealing manners—just the thing, many would say, to wear down his own reputed meagre patriotic defenses.

Just how wily was this woman, that she could play ignorant and lost so convincingly? She was hiding something, and it was not related to her memory loss.

No one in her country could be so unaware of the building swell to war. He had never heard of St. Anthony Falls, but that meant nothing. He had not heard of most of the cities in America.

And how did she get here? Here in his house, and here in his country? Father was the more likely target, and his own house a mistake.

Miles stopped in the middle of the entrance hall, forcing himself to look at the matter coldly and analytically. How many knew of the rift between his father and himself? As an only son, perhaps someone thought he knew more than he did. It was expected for an earl to ensure his heir was well-trained for the role he would someday have to assume.

If America was searching for information behind the scenes and wanted details on England's next step, they might have their own spies lurking about the country, searching for any scrap of particulars that fell from unruly lips.

Father being who he was, they perhaps fixed their attention on the son. Himself. Was his father right about his reputation? If someone was looking for loose lips, his daredevil reputation could make someone think him a big enough fool to fall for a pretty woman, and careless enough to indulge in reckless bedroom talk.

His enemies did not know the real Miles Stewart or they would know he never discussed important matters of this sort with anyone, least of all a mistress.

He needed to look over the iron that meant so much to his strange guest, and carefully. At the moment, it was safely hidden. He doubted even any of his servants would find it.

The woman's escorts had chosen his house for a reason, or so he had to believe until he proved otherwise.

Two footmen came through the doorway of the stairs that led down to the kitchen, carrying elegant china vases of flowers, translucent white with a design of intricate gold and purple lines. He could not see the pattern from where he stood but knew it by heart. Clearly the good china had been brought out for use now that the master was back. Miles stood quiet and unnoticed as he watched them walk with unfaltering stride. The men scarcely paused long enough for the dining room door to be opened from inside by some unseen servant.

Dinner would be perfumed as much by his garden as the scent of well-cooked food. They were going through a lot of effort for his meal.

Unless they knew about the woman in his bedroom. Perhaps they expected her to join him for dinner.

That explained the flowers.

The footmen were all tall and handsome, as protocol dictated, but despite their admirable physique, still nameless and faceless cogs in the working of the estate, standing unnoticed behind guests at dinner parties, merely arms appearing from behind guests with wine, soup or fresh foods. Their other tasks brought them into most rooms of the house, carrying water, delivering polished boots, and freshly ironed clothing.

The dining room door clicked shut behind the men and their burdens. Not a single petal had dropped. Men who moved like that could slip in and out of rooms easily and unnoticed, and were strong enough to carry a woman, particularly one as slender as his surprise guest. Had one of them smuggled her into his bedroom? Was one of them Miss Underwood's contact?

"My lord?" Denton appeared, as was his way, seemingly out of nowhere. "Do you need something?"

Miles looked at him. His thoughts must have shown, going by the worried expression on Denton's face.

"My lord? Is something wrong?"

The traitor she came to meet could not be Denton. Not Denton, his loyal butler-cum-manservant who had kept his secrets for many years. The man would never betray Miles, nor would he betray England for America. "No, Denton. I was just thinking, that is all. Pay me no heed."

He waved Denton away and went into his study, where he could be certain of privacy, or at least a knock in warning. He walked to the window and stared at the garden outside. It was in full bloom, the rosebushes preparing for their second set of buds, the yellow flowers planted between each bush bobbing on their stems in the summer breeze. Ivy clung to the wall, a few sprigs dancing against the window. He was going to have to remind the gardener to prune them back before they covered his view.

Footmen, gardeners, groomsmen, and farriers, even the cooks in the kitchen. His house was full of workers, any one of whom might have reason to undermine England. Miles looked at his reflection in the window, his image translucent, alone, and thought about his guest and the problems she had brought with her, the iron and its mysteries.

I will send someone up to tend to your needs. He turned away from the window and abruptly tugged the bellpull, then sat down behind his desk to wait.

Denton arrived within the minute, although Miles had not been watching the clock. "Yes, my lord?"

"I need to speak with Mrs. Flaherty."

"Yes, my lord. I will have her here momentarily." Denton gave his quick bow and exited.

Leaving Miles to his thoughts again. He tapped his fingers on the desk, a rhythm to the ruminations in his head. Edward had said the woman was not to be moved, but despite what he told Miss Underwood, she simply could not stay here. If his suspicions were right and she was sent here to find out information that could undermine England's policies toward the upstart country, bringing her to Father's house would put her directly in contact with someone in Parliament.

But then, she did not remember her assignment.

Would it all come back after she heard his father's name?

He and his father might have their difficulties, but he knew no secrets would ever escape Father's lips. Besides, with Abby there to help watch Miss Underwood, they could interrupt any plans that might be brewing.

The thought pricked him. He did not like the idea of spying on his guest even though she might be doing the same to them. Or at least, had been sent for that purpose.

And as he had realized earlier, if she was sent on a mission, it was no longer in her memory.

A tap came on the door. "Enter!"

Denton opened the door and stepped aside as Mrs. Flaherty walked in, a worried look on her face. "Yes, my lord? You were wantin' me? I assure you, supper is well underway."

"I have every confidence in you, Mrs. Flaherty. That is not why I wanted to see you. I need a female servant."

She pulled herself up to her full height, and puffed out her chest in affronted dignity. "All my girls are good girls," she said stiffly.

His reputation had certainly reached to the bowels of the manor house. He decided to put the woman straight immediately, before his name got any blacker than it already was. "One good enough to serve as a lady's maid and chaperone to a guest?"

Mrs. Flaherty's mouth formed a silent O. "A maid, you'd be wantin', it is? A lady's maid, you said?"

"One and the same," Miles said, and smiled in an attempt to look trustworthy. "I need someone willing to report to me and only to me, and whose loyalty is above reproach." He wondered if Miss Olivia would like whoever Mrs. Flaherty assigned. And then he wondered why he even cared.

He had no choice, either way. Olivia needed a maid to protect her name—and his—until he got the answers he sought, and serve as loyal observer.

Mrs. Flaherty looked off into space for a moment, then her gaze came back to him. "I might have just the one."

"Send her to me, if you will. I will give her instructions."

CHAPTER 13

OLIVIA HEARD FAINT FOOTSTEPS IN THE HALLWAY AS SHE stared out the window at the trees and the shed roofs, wondering what each building held, and stiffened. Her first thought was that one of the conspirators from the hall had learned of her presence and come to eliminate her. She looked frantically around for a place to hide.

Until the knock came at the door. They would hardly knock, would they? And that didn't sound like a man's hand. "Come?"

A woman with hair so dark a brown it appeared nearly black and eyes to match stepped inside, leaving the door open. Olivia guessed her age at mid-twenties, from the smooth skin of her face, the absence of lines, and the slenderness of her figure, but her eyes looked older, and her mouth wanted to turn down.

Being a maid in this time probably aged women faster than usual.

She wore a dress, high-waisted like Olivia's, but there the resemblance stopped. Olivia's gown had embroidered flowers and lace; this one had a narrower skirt with no decorations of any kind, the color a nondescript washed-out blue. Altogether more functional.

"Hello." The woman paused, then curtseyed, hesitant and awkward.

"Hello." They looked at each other for a moment. Olivia decided someone had to break the silence. "Who are you?"

"My name is Clara. I'm supposed to be your maid. His Lordship said there was a woman here, but I didn't know how that could be because no carriage had arrived." Clara clapped a hand over her mouth. "Oh, I'm sorry. I shouldn't have said that. Pardon me." Her face turned red.

"*His Lordship?* Who is that?"

"He owns this house."

"Then who is Miles Stewart?"

Clara chuckled. "He's the same man. He has his family name, and his title."

Olivia stumbled over and sat down hard on the bed. "The man I've been talking to is a lord? I knew it was a big house, I could tell just from the size of the hallway, but he's a *lord?*"

"Well, a viscount, actually."

Like that made it better? "How many people in the house now know about me?"

"Oh, most of them, now."

Olivia fell back onto the bed with a groan. "Wonderful. Just wonderful."

"That's why I'm here. He wants to save your reputation. If you have a maid, it will blunt the gossip."

"Gossip. Great. Just great." She knew just enough about Regency England to know that reputation was everything for a woman. Olivia sat up again. "What are they saying about how I got here? Because he didn't bring me. How I got here is all a blur."

"Forgive me if I spoke out of turn." The maid bobbed again, as if she didn't know the protocol and decided to err on the side of caution. "Lord Langley told me you had lost your memory. I'm not supposed to get you upset." Her brows came together, and her hands clasped tight, as if needed something for support. "I don't want to lose this position. I'm lucky to get it."

"I remember some things, but I don't know where I am, and I don't know anyone." Olivia kept the rest to herself.

The maid opened her mouth and hesitated for a brief pause. In a cautious voice, she said, "You sound just like me and I am originally from America. Does that help your memory?"

Another American. Olivia should have noticed it, but she had so much on her mind that the similarity had slipped past. How interesting that the accents had not changed in all this time.

Still in that hesitant voice, as if afraid she was breaking some rule, the maid went on, "Don't be surprised if you run into more of us. Many Americans didn't want any part in the Revolution, and came back to England. They consider it their rightful home."

As long as the woman was willing to share, Olivia decided to find out as much as she could. "And that's what happened to you?"

There was a pause. "Of a sort, I guess."

Of a sort? That was an odd answer. Still . . . another American, whatever the difference in time, was comforting. "Did you come with your family?"

The woman winced. "No. I came alone. But enough of me. I shouldn't be too familiar, anyway."

Too familiar? Talking to the person to whom you were assigned was getting too familiar? Perhaps it was time to stop asking questions. She needed the company of this woman, and if a maid could admit to being from America, why would it matter if she admitted it herself? Maybe the maid already knew. If Lord Langley told her that Olivia had lost her memory, what else had he told her? Sooner or later, everyone would probably find out. There was no point in hiding it. "We do sound alike, don't we? And I *am* American."

The maid did a strange thing. She stepped over, pushed the door shut, and walked in a few feet closer than she had been before. Her mouth opened, then closed. Her lips pressed closely together, and her gaze drifted past Olivia and onto something far away.

"Is something wrong?" Olivia wanted to tell this pretty woman that it was fine, she could talk freely, but she herself didn't know the rules of this house. Besides, her own situation was unclear. Perhaps it was best to keep her distance.

The maid's gaze came back, and she gave a sharp shake of the head. "No. No, it's nothing."

It was rude to press in any era. Probably more so here. Time to change the subject. "So you are supposed to be my maid? What does that entail?" Olivia needed someone to teach her how to survive until she could figure out how to get back, someone who could explain how to take a bath without running water, and what to do for a toothbrush or toothpaste. And where to find a comb, and how to style her hair, because this current hairstyle was well beyond her own skills.

"Well, now, I'm not quite sure. I've never been a lady's maid before." The woman's hands worried each other again.

Her host chose an inexperienced maid? As Olivia thought about it, the situation made sense. He was presumably a bachelor. Why would there be a lady's maid in the house?

This could be a good thing all around. There had to be a

way to swing the woman over to her side. She held out a hand. "I'm Olivia Underwood."

The maid looked surprised, but she came the rest of the way over and held out her own hand. "I'm Clara."

The second introduction wasn't necessary, but Olivia let it go. "Nice to meet you, Clara." Miles Stewart might not want to tell her anything, but maybe this maid would. "Can you tell me where in England this is? Miles—Mr. Stewart—said we aren't near the seacoast."

Clara hesitated, but then said, "I think that would be allowed. The closest big city is Bristol, but we are in the country."

Bristol? "I don't know where that is. Is this the north, south, east, or west of the country?"

"Oh!" Clara blinked, and a frown furrowed her brow. "I guess . . . the west?" She made it a question.

She didn't know? Olivia suddenly realized in this time the servants probably did not get an education, or learn geography. She changed the subject again. This was getting awkward, not knowing what she could safely talk about without embarrassing or even jeopardizing the poor woman. "I had an iron when I came. If Mr. Stewart—I mean, Lord Langley—took it, where would he put it?"

Clara made an odd sound. "You had an *iron?* And His Lordship took it? A pressing clothes-type iron?"

Olivia nodded.

Clara's brows went up. "I can't believe Langley would take such a thing. What would he need with it? What would"—she cut herself off but Olivia could guess what the rest of the sentence would have been: *what would you need with the thing?*

She could hardly give the real answer: *He thought I was trying to drop it on his head.* Olivia kept that to herself and hedged her words. "He didn't think it belonged to me." She tried again. "Where would he put it?"

Clara shook her head, but the movement was jerky. "Most likely, he just sent it down to the laundry maids."

"Oh no!" Olivia almost shrieked the words. "You can't let anyone else use it!"

Clara blinked at Olivia's vehemence. Her hands worried themselves again. "I have no say in this place. I do what I'm told, and for that I have a roof over my head, and food to eat."

Olivia's skin prickled with the imminence of the danger, but poor Clara's words forced her to drop the subject, despite the danger. *I have no say in this place.* Clara had her own loyalties. How dire would the poor woman's situation be without this position, however lowly? Olivia knew she shouldn't be selfish, but with Clara gone, she would lose her only connection to her own land, however tenuous and distant.

Of course, she would feel worse if the iron whisked the wrong person back to her own time. Assuming, she reminded herself, that the iron traveled both ways.

Her stomach growled, and she suddenly realized how long it had been since she ate. "Can you bring me something to eat and drink?"

Clara nodded. "That's what I'm here for. What would you like? Tea? You don't want to eat a lot, because the cook is almost finished with supper, and you don't want to miss that. He's been working hard on it."

A sandwich, Olivia thought, but didn't know when the word came into common use. "Tea would be lovely." She had refused food from mere Mr. Stewart, but things had changed. A twenty-first century man might be suspected of a nefarious deed like kidnapping, but not in this world, not with a *His Lordship*, and not with a whole household of servants watching and gossiping. She should be able to eat and drink without fear.

Especially at supper. After all, wouldn't they be eating the same thing?

Clara shifted her feet, as if eager to go do something. "It might just be bread, or a cake with your tea. Would that be enough?"

"Anything you get me is fine. Thank you."

Clara turned to go, but stopped abruptly, turned back just long enough to bob a curtsey, then slipped out the door.

Now all I have to do, Olivia thought, *is find the iron and figure out how to make it work again.*

And then—if all went well—she could go back home.

CHAPTER 14

CLARA CAME BACK A FEW MINUTES LATER WITH A SMALL TRAY complete with a teapot, a small pitcher that likely held milk, a cup and saucer, and plate of bread with an orange-y jam. The way she balanced everything as she eased herself through the door made Olivia suspect she had done quite a bit of kitchen detail.

The tray was set on the dressing table without spilling a drop, or even having anything slide around. Clara stepped back. "Would you like your tea with milk?"

She had heard of milk with tea, but . . . "No, thank you."

Clara poured the tea neatly in the cup, and handed it over. "There is a bit of bread and gooseberry jam, if you want."

Olivia's stomach rumbled at the scent of the fresh bread. "Yes, please." The tea was surprisingly good. No wonder the English had such an affinity for the stuff, she thought as she took another sip. Then she moved on to the single slice of bread, and orange-colored jam. The bread was smaller than the kind she was used to and home-made.

Olivia had never seen jam that color before. It was delicious, sweet but with a sharp zing. There wasn't much, no doubt Clara had to grab what she could, and it was gone in just a few bites.

Clara watched her eat. After her last swallow, Olivia looked down at the plate, crumbs and a smudge of the jam, then back up at the maid. She couldn't make out the expression there, but Clara was watching the plate fixedly. "Are you hungry?"

The shake of the head came a little too quickly. "No, I get enough to eat. If anything is left from dinner, we can have it, but there is always something made for us. We get stews and fish, and sometimes mutton. The chef here is really excellent, and our housekeeper—although it's not really her job—bakes an excellent bread." A smile tugged at Clara's mouth. "When Henri lets her. He views it as infringing on his place."

She leaned closer. "But he wants to bake only French stuff, croissants and brioche and baguettes. They're all delicious, but sometimes I just want plain bread."

With Clara being so open, it might be the best time for her to find out all the things she needed to know. "What do you use to brush your teeth?"

Clara winced. "We do have a couple brushes but the servants share them. I use frayed sticks instead. Then there is tooth powder, but I can never get to the market, so I mainly use a mixture of salt and baking soda. And there are always comfits to freshen your breath, but they're almost completely made of sugar."

Olivia shuddered. No toothpaste? A stick for a toothbrush? Sugared breath mints wasn't so shocking. She suspected the ones she occasionally used in her own time were the same. But she needed something for tonight, so she better plan on getting supplies. "Can you get me one of those sticks, and some salt and baking soda? And what about soap?"

Clara looked over at the pitcher and bowl right next to Olivia. "Isn't there soap over there?"

"I didn't look." And why would she, Olivia thought to herself. She had not wanted to think that she would be here long enough that a bath would be necessary, but as the day grew longer and no way home appeared, it was time to make longer-term plans.

And hope they weren't necessary.

So she shoved her plate and cup aside, and stood to look down inside the pitcher. Sure enough, a cloth lay tumbled in the bottom.

Did that mean someone had already used it? A bracing breath, and Olivia reached down inside and caught the cloth. As she pulled it up, something inside fell out into the pitcher bottom with a soft *thump.*

She looked down. It was brownish and semi-clear, but she knew what it was. "Oh, lovely! Soap!"

Clara came over and peered down as Olivia tilted the pitcher. She breathed, "Bar soap. Real bar soap. And Pears, as I live and breathe. I heard of it, but I have never seen it."

Olivia glanced over at her maid. "You don't have soap?"

Clara straightened. "Oh, no, I have soap, but it's soft and I just pour a bit out on a cloth. The housekeeper buys it by the barrel, and we use it for everything. For washing the floors, and the dishes, and the laundry, and the servants. It works, we get clean, but it's very drying." She stared back down at the soap.

Impulsively, Olivia said, "You can use this if you want. Just bring it back."

"Oh, no!" Wide-eyed, Clara held out a blocking hand. "I can't do that." Then her eyes narrowed. "Although I might be taken from the servants' quarters and given a room nearby. No one has said anything official yet, but there is a lady's maid room next door."

She took a few steps back, moving closer to the bed as if being too close to the soap was too much temptation. "If they do move me there, I would be happy to borrow your soap, but I wouldn't use it often because it must be expensive. Maybe just once. Right now, I need to get you all laced back up because he almost certainly will invite you down to dinner, and you simply cannot go down with your gown falling open."

Olivia turned around. Clara tugged something, and the gown pulled up and up as it tightened, the neck finally settling in place. A few more tugs, some brushing and movement behind her, and Clara sighed. "There! All presentable."

A tap on the wooden jamb startled Olivia. She turned to the doorway. An unfamiliar man with dark hair pulled back into some kind of ponytail stood there, straight and tall, wearing what was obviously a uniform. A dark blue coat with brass buttons, a white shirt with stiff collar points standing up, and a cravat tied in a neat bow and tucked into a gold-colored vest that matched the buttons.

He wore breeches that buttoned under the knee, white socks that the buttoned cuff of the breeches probably helped hold in place, and pumps. Nothing feminine about those pumps, though. They had a solid sole and the heels, which she barely glimpsed, were wide and solid.

His deep, gravelly voice pulled her attention away from his clothes. "Excuse me, my lady, but 'is Lordship would like you to join him for supper. If you will follow me?"

The bread and jam had taken the edge off her hunger, but it wasn't going to last until tomorrow, and in this strange uncertain world, she might not get another meal. "Thank you."

The footman noticed the plate and cup on the dressing table, and his lip curled. "Clara, bring that down to the kitchen and give it to the scullery maid. We do not want to attract vermin by leaving food about."

Clara gave her a satisfied nod, stacked the dishes with professional skill, and followed them out. The footman turned right toward the long hallway; Clara turned left, where a door sat at an angle. Olivia knew a round tower stood roughly in that space; she had seen it from the corner of her eye the first day. No doubt it held a stairway.

Balancing the dishes against her hip, Clara pulled the door open and Olivia caught a glimpse of a railing.

So, yes, that door led to a curving stairway, which explained the round wall outside. Olivia tucked the knowledge in her mind. One never knew when one might need a quick escape.

As they walked down the hallway, she looked out the line of windows. She knew the pebbled drive would not hold a carriage now, since the doctor was gone, but she could see the rolling hills in the distance. Keeping the footman in the edge of her vision, she glanced out the windows as they appeared between the brick wall that divided them.

A long fence that she had not noticed at first cut the hillside, and on the right, trees made a border closer to the house. She thought she saw a dirt path between the trees, and wondered where it led.

Not that it would get her out of here, but it was something to know . . . just in case.

The footman opened one of the doors she had counted. It was not a room, though, and the flutter of panic that he might have led her here to get her alone subsided. Instead, it hid a wide stairway of polished white stone that despite the shine showed a faint wear in the center.

This was an old house, as old as she first suspected, she realized as she trailed her hand along the carved wooden railing on the inside. She stopped briefly, letting her silent guide keep going, and leaned over to look down.

The stairway ended one floor below. Olivia glanced upward, but there were no treads above her. From what she could tell, these white stairs connected her level to the next one down, which she knew had to be the ground floor.

So this was the main stairway. She thought back to that narrow staircase that Clara had gone down. Poor Clara, going down the dark tower while she got the white stairs.

But her escort—who she suspected was a footman, although she had never seen one before—was already on the second half of the stairs. Olivia caught her skirt to keep it out of the way, and followed.

As he neared the door, she decided to pry a little. "Are there other guests here?"

The footman looked up at her from a few steps below. "No, me lady. You are the only . . . *guest* . . . here." His voice was polite, but the pause spoke volumes. He continued down the stairs.

No one believed she was here innocently.

She let the pause and its inference go. He might deny anyone else being here, might not even know, but *someone* had been in the house. Someone who knew their boss and hated him, someone who expected the staff to recognize him. Someone hiding from pursuers, likely debt collectors.

The villain had found a way inside. Had his co-conspirator smuggled him in? Or had the villain hidden his horse somewhere close, slipping in to catch his fellow off guard?

Watching the man in front of her, thinking over his

words and behavior, Olivia decided a footman wouldn't have the control over his own schedule long enough to slip away and meet someone, not knowing how long the conversation would last. No doubt someone below stairs was counting the time with every errand, and expecting this man to return for the next chore on the list.

The man reached the bottom, pulled the door open and held it, waving her through, then stepped around her, and began to walk back the way they came, passing a closed door hiding mysteries. From what she'd seen so far, the house was a long rectangle with a hallway in front and all the rooms on a single side.

She had been lucky to work once with another crew to stage a mansion for sale, but it hadn't been anything like this. That one had been ultra modern, almost without personality, not like this place, which breathed history.

"'Is Lordship is waitin' inside." The footman paused outside the last door, open and inviting.

Light streamed out and gave a single stripe of brightness across the wooden floor. She didn't know what to expect, but she was still hungry, and furthermore, her host held the secret to her way home. So Olivia stepped into the room, and stopped, amazed by the beauty of it, the walls a soft cream with three-pronged candle sconces mounted a few feet apart. Every other sconce had been lit, with the bulk of the light coming from the lowering sun.

A long wooden table and matching chairs filled most of the room, with a sideboard on her left.

But not even the elegance of the room could offset her host, standing like a statue in the center of the room, his dark clothes stark against the soft ivory walls and the pale green curtains. The entire room shimmered in the sunset, with him as the focus.

She barely registered the long dining table, white cloth covering it and already laid out with two place settings on the far end. Instead, Miles Stewart Langley captured the room, standing silhouetted against those glowing windows, the sun limning him in gold, and throwing his face into shadow.

He bowed from the waist, a quick gesture. "Good evening. Are you ready to eat?" He didn't move after that, just stood there in front of the tall windows that arched over him and the sun glowing a frame around his tall body, touching the harsh black garment with an outline of gold.

She knew he could see every expression on her face, standing as she was in direct sunlight. Did she look as nervous as she felt? "Yes, thank you."

His head dipped, and the faint candlelight caught his face with that gesture, giving her a quick peek at the wariness there before the shadows hid him again. A footman she hadn't seen before appeared at his side, and stopped next to the chair that had been already been pulled out, waiting for the lord to be seated. Miles—or should she call him Your Lordship like the rest of his staff?—waved toward her side of the table. "Sit."

A man materialized at her side, startling her. She glanced up at him, recognizing her guide, but his face was expressionless. Irritation prickled her skin. She didn't belong with the lord. She was one of the servants, and belonged wherever they congregated, talking and grousing, laughing and sympathizing.

But she couldn't make the footman talk to her if he didn't want to, and especially not under the watchful eye of his employer. The servant merely walked to the chair just around the table's corner from her host, pulled it out, and stood there waiting. Olivia forced herself to walk along the table, getting nearer to her host, whose face somehow remained shadowed. She stepped in front of the chair, and in a move so smooth that she couldn't have done better seating herself, he eased it in as she sat.

Her host politely waited to take his own chair until she was seated. Now that he was sitting, the candles did a better job of showing his face. Either that or the sun had gone down just enough to reduce the glow from behind.

"I know you believed that you had been poisoned, but I hope you have decided you can trust me. We will both be served from the same dishes, so you need not worry."

"I was confused." She remembered those first few moments, and the sensation that something had gone very wrong.

"Now that I know how ill you must have been, that is most understandable." He leaned back in his chair, and his face fell into shadow again. Olivia wondered if he knew exactly how the setting sun would illuminate the room so he could keep the rays at his back. "You certainly have made a miraculous recovery. While I am pleased, it leaves me with a quandary. I might be forgiven for giving shelter to a woman who was too ill to move, but now that you can walk about, your reputation is in danger. I can only hope that your maid will provide the protection you . . . need."

That was an odd pause. Almost as if he wasn't certain she deserved protection? She wished she could challenge him on the hesitation, find out what he implied, but the silent footman who had shifted to the wall suddenly moved, startling her. He had been so still, she had forgotten him. Now he picked up a decanter and filled her host's crystal wineglass.

She would have loved a glass of cool water, but wasn't water contaminated in this time? Olivia watched as the footman stepped around to her and filled her own glass. A fruity aroma tickled her nose.

Was she allowed to take a sip before her host? And where was the tea? She would be drunk if she only had wine with her food!

The footman set the decanter down and stepped to one side. Olivia folded her hands in her lap, grateful for the bread and jam so her stomach didn't rumble, and waited for Miles-His-Lordship to give her a clue what to do next.

A door she hadn't noticed opened, and a man came in carrying a tureen, which he set down in front of her host, and left.

"Ah. Chestnut soup." He looked at her, the candlelight catching his eyes again.

"*Chestnut* soup? How lovely!" She waited while the footman behind her host scooped out a ladle of soup and poured it into his bowl without a single drip. It was golden-brown, almost the color of squash. She could smell it, vaguely nutty with the rich aroma of cream mixed in.

Chestnuts were almost a thing of the past in the America of her time, Olivia knew, due to some blight that killed them off. She loved nuts of all kinds, but chestnuts were so rare that she had never eaten one.

"I'm glad you like it."

"Oh, I don't know if I like it yet. I've never tasted it before."

CHAPTER 15

SHE FELT HIS GAZE ON HER, EVEN THOUGH HIS FACE WAS STILL in shadow. "Why did you call it lovely, then?"

"Because now I get to taste it." Surely that was obvious.

The footman stepped away from Stewart-Langley and turned toward her. The movement broke the pull of her host's presence, and she looked down at her dish with a sense of relief.

Something about him was the magnet, and she was the poor filings, dragged into his pull.

She looked down at the design on her dish. White with rows of pink and purple around the edges. A *lot* of pink and purple for a man. The inside base was decorated with a yellow flower in the center that vaguely resembled a dandelion, complete with roots. Her finger gently traced the gold around the brim.

Who would paint dandelions on china plates? She folded her hands as the footman filled her bowl with great ceremony, covering the picture. "Lovely china," she said and hoped Langley would say something that answered her unasked question.

"Thank you. It was my mother's." But he gave no more information. China makers were obviously not of interest to him, but it did explain the pink and purple edging.

One word of his reply stuck in her ear like a burr. "Was?" A clutch of sympathy caught her heart. She knew what it was like to lose a mother.

"Yes. She died when I was quite young."

"I'm sorry. I lost my own mother last year." She suddenly realized what she had said.

And sure enough, her host caught it. "Was that the year you are missing? Or was it the year before? Has she been gone one year or two?"

There was a limit to how many lies and evasions she could keep straight. "One."

He lifted a finger, as if in remonstration. "Ah, but you cannot know that."

She took a deep breath and let her frustration out with the exhale. "To me, it *is* a year. And we aren't talking about me, anyway. We are talking about you." She wanted to ask how young he was when his mother died, but that was too personal. "I don't think anyone is ever old enough to lose a mother, but it's especially sad when it's a child. I know how much I miss my mother, and I was an adult. She was done raising me."

"What about your father? Did you not have him to step in and ease the grief, or was he mourning too much to take note of his daughters?"

So he had not forgotten that she had a sister. She suspected he hadn't forgotten anything she told him. "My father died when I was in my teens. My mother was a widow. So both of my parents were gone."

He was silent, his spoon hovering above his bowl as still as a statue. Clearly, he didn't suffer from nerves. "Perhaps the grief was too much for you?"

"No. I don't think so." Her father's death was filled with unresolved complexity: love and anger, loss and resentment, unresolved after all these years. Renee had been his favorite, and Olivia often wondered if he had something against her own red hair.

Mom's death was harder to deal with, because she had loved her mother unreservedly, and admired her for picking up and carrying on after losing her husband. Their marriage hadn't been the stuff of legend, but after he died, raising two squabbling daughters on her own could not have been easy. The life insurance hadn't paid off the house, her mother had to work harder than ever, leaving Renee and herself to argue whenever she wasn't there to mediate.

Thank goodness Mom had left a will, or Renee would have walked off with everything of value. Not that there was much of that, anyway.

She drew her spoon through the soup, unable to take a swallow. Just a few breaths to let her throat loosen.

"My apologies for asking such an impertinent question." He swallowed that spoonful, and gestured toward her bowl. "You have not tasted the soup. Why does an American from a country full of chestnut trees not know how it tastes? Surely you have had any number of chances."

She scooped up a spoonful and stared down at the thick soup. How could she answer without revealing where she was really from? *There are almost no chestnut trees left in my country now?* That was too easy to check, even though the question had to go across the Atlantic by ship, and the answer return the same way.

When in doubt, she decided, *stick as close to the truth as possible.* "They don't grow well where I live."

W *here I live.* She had just handed him the opening he needed. "So where in America do you live, that chestnuts won't grow?"

She hesitated. He forced himself to remain relaxed, although his mind immediately went on alert. That pause had to mean something, so Miles sat and waited, and watched. The sun had gone down enough that he feared the candlelight now matched its illumination, which meant that she could see his face almost as well as he saw hers.

And he saw her very well, had all along. Someone had chosen her well, picking a woman with intelligence, determination—and beauty. The sun turned her red hair into burnished fire, and her eyes were like the first leaves of spring. He remembered thinking her lashes were dark for a redhead, and even in the setting sun, they made a perfect frame for those big eyes. The golden glow gave rich color to her flawless skin, and his fingers itched to stroke it, see if it was as smooth as it looked.

Only the gown spoiled the view. She wore the same one she had been in all day. It showed the wrinkles of the day's events. He had the sudden urge to deck her in new gowns: golds and greens, ivories and purples. The thought jolted him.

It was time to get her under someone else's care.

She sighed, snapping his attention back to their conversation. That stubborn chin lifted, along with the spoon holding that untasted soup. "I'm from Minnesota, and it's very cold there in the winter. A lot of plants that grow well in other places can't survive."

"Minne-what? I have never heard of it." Had she concocted the word? If she made it up, he could not think of anything in the room that might trigger such an odd combination of letters. "Where is this place?"

Her eyes flickered away, and back, and she sipped the soup off the spoon before lowering it back into the bowl. He watched her swallow, and knew every move to be a deliberate ploy to give herself time to think.

"Oh! This is good!" She took another swallow and savored the mouthful while he waited for his answer. When she met his eyes again, her gaze was straightforward, no sign of artifice despite her obvious delay. "You would call it the frontier, I believe. It's in the middle of the country." Her eyes widened, and he saw them brighten with an idea.

If she was a spy, she was either the most skilled or the most inept one he had ever heard of. He was almost ready to exonerate her of any such accusation.

She cocked her head, and kept her gaze on his. "I did mention that I live in the part of the country that came from the Louisiana Purchase."

Miles had ignored that it the first time she mentioned it, but could not ignore it now. He looked at her gown. "The wilderness Jefferson acquired must be far more inhabited than we have heard, for you to come wearing silk and lace. I thought your country to be still in the process of clearing the land. Your attire speaks of a city and civilization."

"You'd be surprised how civilized it is," she said in response, and her mouth curved up in secret humor.

"Undoubtedly I would, since I have never been there." He waited until she had swallowed another spoonful of soup with obvious delight before he asked the next question. "So, in which part of that vast land do you come?" When her brows rose at his question, he added, "Come, come, now. Surely you realize we have heard about the size of the land deal. You could be from anywhere in that area."

"Yes," she said slowly, and looked down at her soup. He watched her spoon drag through the thick liquid. "Well, Minnesota is in the northern part."

"Northern? That takes you from the middle of the country, and puts you in the land of the voyageurs."

She blinked, and he watched her head lift. "Yes, I suppose it does."

"But you do not see them, either, I suppose, being from the city?"

A smile tugged at her mouth. "No, I don't."

The door opened again, interrupting his questioning. The main courses had arrived. He breathed in the rich scent of venison, and caught the second, somewhat stronger aroma of fish. Sole, no doubt.

Henri had indeed come through. The venison looked tender enough to fall apart, and the crust on the sole was browned to perfection. The herb pie smelled delicious, the wonderful greens blending into their own delicious fragrance.

She ate with clear enjoyment. "What kind of meat is this?"

"Venison. Have you never had it before?"

"As a child, but it never tasted like this. I didn't like it then." She smiled at him, a guileless smile. "Maybe I was too young to appreciate it, or maybe it wasn't prepared right."

"I am indeed fortunate with my chef." How he wished he could believe her! He waited until she swallowed her mouthful. She had given him the perfect opening. "Surely there are enough deer in America that anyone would know how to prepare it properly."

She smiled. "Not when you have beef to eat."

"So you are from a land of farming? How does that fit into the country of the voyageurs? They are hunters and trappers and live around the forests. Not good farming land." He raised a brow, and waited for her answer.

"But my state is on the edge of the prairie. The northern part is more forests, but the southern part is rich farmland."

He lowered his fork and looked at her. So America got farmland in the deal. *Rich* farmland, she said. Was that one of the reasons Jefferson was so eager for the purchase?

It was best to leave this subject. They ate in silence for several minutes before he realized she had finished her venison, the herb pie, and was picking at the fish that had just been put on her plate. "What do you think of the sole?"

Miss Underwood wrinkled her perfect nose. "I'm not a fan of fish."

"Henri is as good with fish as he is with venison. You should give it a try."

She forked off the smallest bite, and hesitated before putting it in her mouth. A tentative chew, and he had to bite his cheek to keep from smiling as she swallowed.

"Better than you thought?" He took a healthy bite himself.

"It's not as fishy as I expected." But she did not take a second bite. Maybe she was getting full; maybe she really did not like fish.

Every subject that occurred to him was a potential argument. He preferred to eat his meal and continue the inquisition later. She might not want to eat her sole, but it was one of his favorites, and he did not want it spoiled with anger or suspicion.

He was having enough of a struggle with attraction.

And then the salmagundi was set in front of him. Ah ha! So

that was how Henri stretched the meal! The salad was a virtual tower of food, fish and chunks of some kind of roasted bird meat—he would know once he tasted it—chunks of cucumber and apple, chopped eggs, red cabbage, and beans, and other bits, all stacked to a point, with grapes around the edge.

Miles held up a hand to stop the footman from filling his plate. "I will serve myself." He took a good helping. Henri's salmagundi was always worth a generous serving.

After each food was on his plate, the footmen turned to serve the dishes and platters to his guest. She smiled easily at the men, and Miles was pleased to notice she did not turn her nose up at this latest course, but dug in easily. She had been as courteous, if not as enthusiastic, with the sole. Although she did not like fish, she had given it a try. Clearly, she had been raised with manners, unexpected from someone out of the wilderness. Assuming she was telling the truth.

The dessert came, plum cake with rum sauce. Her eyes lit up.

Ah, so the lady loved sweets. Although he suspected she was full since her last courses had become smaller and smaller—not counting the sole, which she barely touched— she had room for the cake, and even allowed the footman to give her an extra spoon of the sauce.

Miles waited until her mouth was empty before asking the rest of his questions. He had enjoyed enough of the meal. And nothing could spoil plum cake with that run sauce. It might even have enough alcohol left to mellow his temper, should she spark it. "Tell me about this city you come from. What is it like to live in the new territory? How big is it for being set in the wilderness?"

She cleared her throat. "Big. It's quite a big city."

"As big as London? Or Bath? Or is it more the size of Bristol?"

An impish smile that caused his breath to catch tilted her mouth, and Miles could swear he saw the twinkle in her eyes. "Since I haven't been to any of those cities, I have no way to compare."

"You may have been, but simply don't remember."

Her smile faded, and he wished he could take the words back. He wanted to see that smile again. But even as he fought the prick of regret, something cynical inside him wished there was a way to check her answers. Unfortunately, he knew no one to send across the sea to find out if her tale was true.

"Tell me about this city you are from again."

She took another bite of dessert, and dabbed at her chin with her napkin to catch a dribble of the sauce.

Miles had the sudden desire to lick away that sauce, so close to her mouth, and he quickly took a sip of his wine.

"Minneapolis?" Red rushed up her porcelain skin. "I mean, Saint Anthony." Her gaze flicked up to him, stayed for only the length of a blink, then dropped back to her plate.

"Two names? And so different?" He could hardly challenge her too much on it, living as he did not far from a village with the same double name.

Miss Underwood raised her chin, despite the flush on her face, and held his eyes with her own. "I don't know where Saint Anthony comes from, but both Minneapolis and Minnesota are from the native language. I think they both mean something about water, and we are known as the land of 10,000 lakes. And Minneapolis means City of Lakes."

He took another sip of wine. The native language bit had to be true. The names of both territory and city did have a foreign ring to them. Surely, if she was making them up, she would stumble as she tried to recall the lie, but they flowed from her tongue easily. "Would you like a tour of the house?" He could tell a lot about her reaction. For instance, whether any of the rooms looked familiar. And if one interested her more than the others.

Who had brought her here?

CHAPTER 16

"I THINK I'M DONE." SHE SMILED AGAIN, SO GUILELESS. "MY compliments to your chef."

"I will pass your regards on." The footman appeared behind her, and Miles rose as the man moved her chair out of the way. He held out his elbow. "Shall we walk?"

Miss Underwood slipped her hand into the crook, and looked up at him. "I have heard your servants call you Lordship. Are you really a lord?"

He paused in the doorway. Someone had spoken out of turn. He had deliberately withheld his title when they first met. Oh, well, too late to change things now. "Why do you want to know?"

"I need to know what to call you. In my . . . city, we are casual, and usually use first names, but I suspect here you are more formal. Do I call you Miles, or Mr. Stewart, or Your Lordship?"

His Christian name slipped so easily off her tongue. He rather liked the sound of it, better than the title. It could not have been kept secret much longer anyway, but the anonymity had been delightful, despite his suspicions about her. Still, until he knew more about her and why she was here, the formality was necessary. "Your Lordship or Lord Langley, even *my lord*, will do until we know each other better."

He watched her expression, but there was no surprise or disappointment; she just mouthed the words as if committing them to memory.

They walked out into the hallway, and he looked down the long stretch with familiar pride. The servants had lit the sconces, and the light fought back the growing dimness that dusk pressed against the glass. Portraits lined the walls between the doors on the one side and the windows on the other. He periodically had them switched just to ensure they did not fade.

"Who are they?" Miss Underwood waved her hand toward the images on the walls. "Ancestors?"

"Most of them. And not all of them were nice." He glanced down at her. "Most families have the usual number of rogues and villains, if they care to look."

Olivia managed a smile, the pang of the distance between herself and Renee sharp again. "I suspect you are right. I was never that interested in my ancestors. My own family is enough for me to handle."

"Ah, yes. You and your sister." The flicker of pain that slipped across her face told him to leave the subject alone. For now. He pointed at the nearest painting, a dour-looking man in an Elizabethan ruff and a stiff-looking doublet. "My several-times-great grandfather. Known to be a rogue and a scoundrel. He fought many a duel over accusations of cheating at cards, and with other men's wives. I understand his own wife had a difficult time."

Lord Langley—*she had to remember that name*—waved a hand down toward the far end of the corridor. "Her portrait is down there. Perhaps I will show you later, when the sun is high." The smile that warmed her each time it appeared creased his face, and his eyes sparkled with humor. "I decided she had endured enough from the man in life; there was no reason to punish her after death."

Olivia chuckled. "Very kind of you."

They walked a few steps further, and stopped next to a closed door. "This is the parlor, should you ever need to know. It was my grandmother's favorite room."

An old line popped into her head. *Step into my parlor, said the spider to the fly.* "May I see it? I've never seen a real parlor."

His brows raised. "Is that so? Perhaps it is called something else in your country." He turned the handle and pushed the door open. "I hope you like it."

Olivia let go of his arm and walked inside. The room was large, and her footfalls whispered an echo in the space. *It is straight out of a Jane Austen movie*, she thought, and wished she could share the thought with him.

But he would not understand, so she kept the delight to herself, and swiveled slowly around to absorb as much as she could in the fading light.

The room was large, at least twenty feet square, maybe larger. The walls were done with whitewashed wainscoting on the bottom, and rich gold wallpaper above, giving the room a feminine flair. Several seating areas sat in groups, straight-backed chairs with Queen Anne legs next to small round tables at the right height for teacups and plates.

Two wooden settees with straight backs and square legs

faced each other on either side of the white fireplace. On the room's far side, the curtains had been drawn for the night, but she knew they faced the sunset because her room—all the rooms—were on the same side. In the evening, those windows should glow with golden color. Indeed, they no doubt had been illuminated by the sun's dying glow while they ate.

A small whitewashed desk that had to be a woman's, and probably belonged to his grandmother—*Good grief! How old would that make it?*—narrow and delicate, with a low top and tiny drawers underneath, sat tucked in one corner of the window wall, close enough that someone could read, or write, and watch the birds at the same time, although the nearest trees she had seen from her window were set back from the house.

What books did they have to read? She knew of a scant few authors from this time, but were any of Jane Austen's books even in existence yet?

Olivia dragged her attention back to the room, and chills ran over her skin. *She was really here.* Everything was in perfect shape, and screamed of a time where she did not belong. She had seen original pieces on rare occasions when staging large houses, but most of the time she handled repro-ductions, and simple modern furniture.

She took a deep breath to calm her heart, and looked over her shoulder at Langley. "May I touch them?"

His brows rose. "Touch what?"

"The furniture. Everything is so . . . perfect."

"Certainly. Furniture is meant to be used. Even sat upon." One side of his mouth quirked up. "I presume you sit on your furniture? Or do you need to keep it perfect?"

Olivia felt the blush heat her cheeks. "Of course not. I mean, yes we use our furniture, but by the time I see anything this original, it's too delicate to do more than look at."

Langley's brows went down this time, and a furrow formed between them. "Perhaps the journey and the sea air are hard on them."

And the centuries, she thought, but her brain caught her mouth before the words came out. "I have heard that."

Olivia walked around the room, running her fingers over each piece, the chairs, the desk, the curtains, with the barest of whisper-touches. Even the sturdy settees with their thick arms and solid legs intrigued her.

Did any of this make it through to her time? Was this house still lived in, or had it been turned into a museum? She couldn't bear the thought that it might have been torn down to make room for apartment buildings or—worst of all— factories.

Thank goodness England was a country that valued its past.

Finally, she turned back to her host, to see him watching her with a strange look on his face.

Had she given something away?

At some point while she was browsing, he had relaxed against the door frame, and stood there now, arms folded across his chest, letting the jamb hold him up while he watched her.

He straightened when their gazes met, and the expression vanished, leaving him the courteous host again. "So you like the room?"

"It's beautiful." She rested a hand on the settee back, and reminded herself that it was still new, and should survive her perusal. She gestured toward the desk, and couldn't hold back the smile. "I don't think you could even fit under that desk."

To her surprise, a chuckle warmed the room. "You are quite right." He walked slowly in, as if giving her time to scoot away. But she felt no urge to move, just stood there as he came near. He didn't stop, though, and walked past her to that small desk.

With his back to her, she couldn't see the expression on his face, but there was a vulnerability to his stance. His hand reached out, stopped short of touching the small piece, then pulled those fingers back, to curl them into a fist.

Olivia felt her heart clench. It was obvious he had loved his grandmother very much. Or had that desk been passed down to his mother, and was he mourning her?

No wonder the room still looked like a woman's room. Undoubtedly, when he had guests, they were men and would convene in his office, to talk and drink liquor and pretend this feminine room did not exist.

Lord Langley's spine straightened, and he turned around, again the lord of the manor, and held out his arm. Olivia slipped her hand into the crook, surprised at how easy it was becoming.

"Shall we move on to the library?"

When she looked up, he was watching her, his eyes shrewd. This was all a ploy to find out if she was a spy!

Regardless, she wanted to see everything about this house. There was no telling how long she would stay. If she suddenly got pulled back, she didn't want to leave anything unexplored. "Yes, please, I very much want to see your library."

They moved down to the next door. Langley opened the door and waved her in with a flourish. "My library, and my favorite room of the house."

The sconces had been lit here, too, she noticed. Either he

kept the house well-lit, or the servants expected him to show her around, and wanted her to get a good impression.

It worked. Olivia stared at the room, the gold paint on the walls, the arched windows that looked out over the dark shadows of the trees but in the daylight would have filled the room with vivid color.

But what really caught her attention was the books. Rows and rows of books in recessed shelves of dark wood that reached most of the way to the ceiling, where the gold paint picked out the grain. The faint scent of leather teased her nose.

She stared at the room, traced the tall shelves with her gaze. Seeing this many books was not uncommon in her world, but she knew from the tickle of leather perfume that most, possibly all, of these books were bound in leather.

Were they chained to the wall now like they would be in her time?

A chuckle behind her made her spin around. "What?"

He tapped her under her chin. "Your mouth was hanging open. You look like you have never seen books before."

A reluctant smile tugged her lips. "I suppose I did, but no. I have seen lots and lots of books. The thing is, I smell leather, and any old leather-bound books are chained wh-"— she caught herself—"where I come from."

He looked around the room with pride. "I will not say the idea has not occurred to me, but I read them too often to want to unlock a book every time I wish to enjoy it." He strolled over to the wall, the candle sconces casting odd shadows as he moved. "I have little to worry about, as most of my servants do not read. The odds of any wanting to steal my books are negligible."

"How sad. That is not fair! Everyone should be able to read."

He turned around, and his face fell into shadow. Olivia was quite sure he knew exactly how to position himself with each candle, each sconce, even the sunlight, to reveal or conceal what he wished. "They do not need it for their work."

"But they should have some time off, and be able to read when they're resting. Reading is a wonderful escape."

He folded his arms. "So you are one of those."

Those arms looked ominous. "One of what?"

"A radical." His voice had lost all warmth. "Were you sent to England to bring your American ideas? Perhaps I was wrong about why you came here."

She knew only one servant, and that was her bare-acquaintance of a maid, but she highly doubted time sent her back here to teach every servant to read. Not when she had overheard the plot against him. And preventing his murder that was why she came here, she had to keep on his good side or he might send her away. "I am not a radical, but I wish everyone could read." She sighed. "Just knowing how doesn't make them do it, though. I know plenty of people who can read perfectly well but don't."

His arms loosened, although they stayed folded against his sizable chest. "I know the same." Then his arms relaxed by his side. "Since you clearly read, I invite you to peruse my library. Perhaps you will find something you like."

Ancient English authors were not her strong suit, and she suspected there wouldn't be any Jane Austens in his collection, but she was perfectly willing to search. Since most of the books looked similar, with no colored covers to give her a clue to the contents, she walked over to the closest bookshelf, and squinted at the spine.

A nice LED lamp would come in handy right now, she thought. Or even a flashlight. Her eyes adjusted, and some author names came into view. Isaac Newton, Thomas Young, John Dalton, Adam Smith. Titles such as *Opticks, Experiments and Calculations Relative to Physical Optics, A New System of Chemical Philosophy, An Inquiry into the Nature and Causes of the Wealth of Nations.*

Good grief! Had Langley actually read these books? If so, he was more educated than she even suspected. She wondered how many of the subjects here led to the discoveries of her time.

On a hunch, she pulled out his *Wealth of Nations* book, and looked at the page edges. They were worn, a few corners actually frayed. Olivia turned to her host. "You actually read these books, don't you?"

One brow went up. "Of course. Why own books you do not want to read?"

She pushed the book back onto the shelf, and brushed the fine layer of dust off her hands before facing him again. "Do you have any light reading?"

One side of his mouth lifted. "You are not interested in economic theory?"

Olivia grinned. "Not particularly. I would much rather read a good mystery, or a romance. Do you have anything like that?"

Langley smiled. "My mother might have something that would fit your requirements. I think I saw it here when I was looking for something else." With surprisingly gentle hands on her shoulders, he moved her aside, and walked past her down the long shelves. "Let me see, it was right . . ." His finger ran along the spines, and he leaned back at one point to scan the shelves above. "No, not here. Was it . . ." His voice trailed off as he cocked his head. Olivia could see his eyes tracking along the books.

Then Langley leaned down. "Ah yes." And he pulled a

book off the shelf. "I knew I had seen it." He held out a reddish-brown book with a red banner on the spine. "This is Volume 1, but you can see the other two volumes are there as well."

Olivia took the book. "The Mysteries of Udolpho," she read aloud. "I heard about this book, but I've never read it." She also recalled it was a bit of a tragedy and she had enough disasters on her hands right now, but maybe reading about someone else's problems would be welcome. "Thank you."

He leaned against the shelves and crossed one foot over the other. He would have looked relaxed except for his watchful eyes, glittering in the candlelight. "I must tell you, I have given this much thought, and tomorrow I will contact my father. You cannot stay here. A bachelor and an unmarried woman with only servants for chaperones? I must protect your reputation. As you have been ill, Edward can vouch for you. But the sooner we get you to my father's house, the better."

How far away would that put her? "I need my iron!"

Those eyes got more alert. "I think not. I assure you, I will take good care of it, and if it puts you in danger, I will step in, but until I find out why such a mundane thing means so much to you, it remains under my control."

Her hands tightened on the book. "How far away is your father?"

He smiled. "I suppose if I told you he lived on the other side of the country, you would find a way to walk back just to keep an eye on it." Olivia did not answer. He sighed. "As it is, my father's lands adjoin with my property. That is how Father met my mother. So you see, you will not be far away from your iron."

His eyes narrowed then. "Whoever brought you here will have to deal with me. And if that iron hides some secret

code, some message in the metal, I will find out what it is and
see that they are turned over to the authorities. My country
has enough on its hands with Napoleon. We do not need
your nation complicating matters any more than they
already are."

It felt like another protest was required, and she didn't
want to disappoint him. "If I tell you again that I am not a
spy, I suppose I'll just be wasting my breath."

"Yes." His eyes softened. "I do not believe you are the
mastermind, but since you cannot remember, that puts you
in danger. My father will keep you safe, and between the two
of us, we will intercept them before they can get to you."

Olivia wanted to argue, but she hadn't gotten far before,
and pushing would only annoy him further. At least she
knew the iron was still here, and that she would not be too
far away.

The sun must have slipped below the horizon, because
the only light in the library now came from the sconces.
Langley must have noticed, because he took the few steps up
to her and held out his arm. "Since it is getting dark, I will
take you to your room. No doubt your maid is eager to get
you to bed."

They walked out into the gloomy hall. Olivia glanced
back at the candles burning in the sconces, and at the fortune
in first editions on the shelves. "Are we going to leave the
candles burning? Aren't you worried they might start a fire?"

He gave a single chuckle. "That is why I have servants."

That reminded her of something. "Clara doesn't have
more work to do, does she? I mean, she won't have to go to
the kitchen now and help clean, or mop the floors or dust?"

Langley sighed, she could feel the movement of his chest
against the back of her hand as it brushed his elegant coat. "I
pulled her from there to wait on you. I prefer her to stick to

her new duties. She will go with you to my father's house, but once we solve the mystery and it is safe for you to return to your home, she will return to her position. For now, it is best she stay close and watch over you."

Safe to return to your home. When would that happen? Was she here to stay? Olivia felt her fingers tighten, and forced them to relax. If he noticed—and he was very observant—she did not want to have to explain.

CHAPTER 17

CLARA WAS SITTING ON THE BED FACING THE WINDOW, waiting, when Olivia opened the door. She rose, and slipped around the bed.

Strangely, although Olivia hadn't been tired when walking down the hall, as soon as she saw the bed, a yawn threatened to crack her jaw. If she was tired, she could only imagine how tired Clara was. At least she didn't have to do more work once she was done here. "I'm sorry we kept you so late."

"This isn't late. I have been up much later than this." Clara pulled out the dressing table chair. "Let's take this hair down. You can't sleep with your hair like that. Those pins will stab you all night." She patted the chair's curved back. "Sit." Then she blushed. "Sorry. I mean, sit, please."

Olivia sat down in the chair and turned to her reflection.

She looked as tired as she felt. Had she looked this tired during dinner?

Clara began pulling out pins and lining them up on the dressing table. The braids came loose, releasing some of the pressure from Olivia's scalp. She watched idly in the mirror as her maid worked her way through the red curls, looking for more hairpins to add to the growing pile. Some pins were straight, a single spine with jewels at the top, no doubt for sticking between braids where their only purpose was to be decorative.

Others were similar to some she had occasionally seen, a U-curve at the top, and two tines. Those weren't nearly as efficient as bobby pins, but clearly did their job well enough, since her hair had stayed in place all day.

Her head felt more like itself once freed from the other-worldly style. Olivia reached up and started running her fingers through the tangled mass, scratching places the hair-pins had been poking her all day. She sighed in relief.

"No, no, that is my job. Let me." From somewhere, Clara produced a comb and started to work out the tangles. Olivia watched as she became herself again, her hair falling around her shoulders and down her back like normal, the natural waves springing back from their artificial curves.

But while the face was familiar, the setting and the pink gown with the embroidery belonged firmly in the past. She was still in a world that could not exist, but did. The canopy bed glowed in the growing twilight. Clara slid the comb through her hair, something no one did outside of a hair salon. The faint comb-scratches against her scalp lulled her into a dreamlike state.

A maid. A canopy bed in a room with a fireplace and armoire. And the gown, all embroidery and lace. Oh—reality intruded—and she couldn't forget the commode behind the screen.

Clara set the comb aside and cleared her throat. "You will never get out of that gown by yourself. What's more, your corset undoubtedly fastens in the back. It is my job to get you ready for bed, so if you could turn around, I will start undressing you."

The maid was right about the corset, Olivia had already discovered that, so she turned her back and let Clara begin the unhooking and unlacing.

It was a weird feeling to have someone undress her. And Clara was as uncertain, because her fingers hesitated first before she began the unhooking, and a slightly longer time before they slid into the corset lacing.

The gown slid down her arms, and the corset followed. "Step out, if you will," Clara said, and Olivia let the clothes slide off, leaving her in a little slip-like dress.

"I think you should take the chemise off as well." Clara lifted a pile of fabric off the bed. Chemise. So that's what it was called. Olivia turned her attention to the fabric she hadn't noticed before. "I found a nightgown in one of the armoire drawers, as well as some kerchiefs, a few stockings, and some straw bonnets."

Lifting off that last layer was embarrassing, but Clara held the nightgown high enough that it formed a kind of shield.

It was nice of the maid to protect her modesty, Olivia thought as she let Clara tuck her into a long-sleeved, white floor-length nightgown with lace-edged ruffles on the neck, sleeves, and bottom. *It had better be cool tonight*, she thought, as the garment was slipped over her head.

Clara hung Olivia's only gown on a hook in the empty armoire, with the corset and the slip on the neighboring ones. "It should be fit for tomorrow, once it hangs out overnight." She straightened the gown's short sleeves and brushed down the skirt with her hands, tugging here and there to even out the layers.

Fit for tomorrow. Olivia suppressed her shudder. No

shower, no deodorant, yet she would be back in the same gown. The nightgown was thick enough for daytime, and had the advantage of smelling of fresh air and sunshine.

She highly doubted wandering around in a nightgown, however modest and frilly, was allowed.

How did one go about getting more clothes in this time? She didn't dare ask Clara to get her something from the other women in the house because, based on what she saw of the maid's gown, the odds of any of them having one to spare were slim.

She had to find that iron. If only she wasn't so tired! Now she had to search the house when all she wanted to do was sleep. Exhaustion would make her careless, or cause her to miss a clue. Maybe just a short nap would help.

"Is there anything else I can get you?"

Olivia shook her head. "No, you go to bed."

Clara nodded. "They gave me the room next door, so if you need anything, just yell." She slipped out, shutting the door softly behind her.

Sleep pulled at Olivia, and she let her eyes close. . .

S he woke with a jerk. What time was it? Popping upright with a brief bout of dizziness before her head caught up with her body, she found herself staring into almost stygian darkness. It took her a moment to catch her breath, remember her mission, and let her eyes adjust to the variations of blackness. Gradually the furniture took shape.

The house was utterly still.

In such quiet, even the softest of footfalls—sounds out of the ordinary—might be enough to trigger an alert. With exquisite slowness, she moved the covers back, listened for a

moment, and swung her feet off the bed. The mattress gave
the softest of rustles; whatever was inside sounded dry and
crispy, but at least it wasn't the squeak of metal springs.

The air was surprisingly cool for a summer night, but she
reminded herself England was surrounded by ocean, which
would keep the temperature down. She didn't have a robe,
but Olivia looked down at the nightgown. Hopefully she
wouldn't run into anyone else wandering the house, but if
she did, she would be modest—and hopefully warm—
enough.

She tiptoed to the door, holding her breath against any
creaks of the floorboards, but the house had been built
sturdy and even with the passage of centuries, the wood held
tight. One door creaked; she remembered the sound just
before the appearance of the co-conspirators.

She couldn't remember if this particular one did any
creaking. Olivia turned the knob slowly, and pulled the door
with the same caution. It wasn't the expected noises that
woke her, it was the unexpected sounds, like the swish of
leather soles, or a whisper louder than a shout.

A tiny groan from the hinges almost stopped her heart,
but it was so quiet she hardly thought anyone would have
heard it. She kept easing the door wider, but thankfully, that
lone protest was the only sound it made.

Nowhere to go now but forward. Amazing the difference
city lights made! She had never seen a night this dark.

The walls took shape in the small bit of moonlight that
seeped through the windows. Almost in slow motion, she
eased down the hallway. Langley's room was right next door,
and she paused outside, listening for any hint of movement,
but all she heard was the softest, most tactful of snores.

Once past what she knew to be his room, she made it to
the servants' stairway door, which was closer than the white

stairway and had the added advantage of being tucked in the tower, and eased it open with the same care. Another gentle groan from the hinges, barely a breath on the air, and she was inside, to pull the door shut with the same caution she had opened it.

Only to be plunged again into blackness. Olivia froze, unable to see where the stairs began. Gradually her eyes adjusted once more to what little light the moon and stars shared through the small windows spaced along the length. She grabbed the railing, but still had to feel her way down.

She hesitated at the door at the bottom of the stairs, and eased it open. The doors to the rooms had been shut, no doubt to keep whatever warmth remained inside. Poor servants, to wake to a cold house, and need to warm themselves by their own hard work.

She knew where the parlor was, but that wasn't where she would hide something she didn't want found. No, if she was going to hide something, she would keep it in a private place.

Like a bedroom. But it wasn't there. He had made quite a point of removing it. The other likely place was an office, and in all the historical movies she had watched, the man of the manor had his own private sanctum. She had decorated enough houses to know most studies or offices were tucked away from the everyday bustle of family life.

And if she was going to guess . . . Olivia turned right, toward the last door in the hall. A place where someone could work in peace, away from the bustle of the rest of the house.

It was also the closest room to the stairs, in case she needed to make a quick escape back to her room.

Olivia felt for the knob, and to her relief it turned. One quick look over her shoulder, and she slipped inside, closing it behind her. The room was dark, but she was growing used to the darkness. A bare slit between the curtains showed the faintest glow of moonlight. She felt her way over, step by careful step, barely enough moonlight to notice shapes. His massive desk faced the room. A chair of equal size sat behind it, with a smaller chair in front—for guests, no doubt. She passed a footstool, and then a globe on a stand. He seemed to like his room simple and uncluttered, a good thing for her feet and shins.

She reached the curtains without injury and felt around until she found a rod tucked in the fabric, right in the center where the moonlight peeked through. With a careful pull, one side opened enough, and Olivia turned to examine the room better. The moonlight must have come out from behind an invisible cloud, because it obligingly cast a silver glow into the room. Bookshelves lined entire the wall behind the desk, reaching from floor to ceiling. He had a wonderful sliding ladder to get to the top ones.

But she needed to find a hiding place, and there wasn't time for more than this quick look. The iron would never fit behind the neat lines of books, so that was out. Olivia tiptoed over to the back side of the desk, and looked at the drawers. There were nine of them, four on each side and one in the center, much like modern desks, but apparently no one had invented hanging folders yet because none of them was that deep. However, the drawers could hold the iron if it was placed on its side.

The house was still silent, and she knew alarms wouldn't be invented for a hundred years or more, so she tugged on the first drawer.

Locked.

As were each of the others on that side. It might be a futile effort, but she moved to the opposite side and tried again, with the same results. Olivia stood back and glared at the desk.

Now what? Her iron had to be in this room. She was certain of it, more now than before. He had certainly taken care to keep it from her, and unfortunately, he had succeeded.

Olivia's shoulders slumped, and she dropped back into the chair behind her. The sudden comfort jerked her out of her funk. She stroked her hands over the leather wrapping on the arms. Foam hadn't been invented yet, she knew that. This chair must have been the work of a gifted craftsman who created luxury from careful carving of the wood, because the leather tacked to the seat, arms, and back was only there for design and yet the chair molded to her.

Someone who knew his stuff made this chair, and Langley apparently wanted comfort when he worked. He seemed to be the type that would demand nothing less.

A creak broke the silence, and Olivia froze. She couldn't breathe. The thunder of her heart was so loud if anyone walked in, surely they would hear it. She slipped off the chair, and crouched behind the desk, waiting for the sound to happen again.

It did, and a third came after that. Someone was walking through the house.

CHAPTER 18

THE FOOTSTEPS CAME CLOSER, AND ON THE SAME FLOOR, NOT from overhead. Olivia shivered, but this cold wasn't from the night air. Nearly silent, the steps were stealthy and slow, the movements of a burglar, not an owner.

Unless the owner had discovered she was missing and was hunting her.

If he had heard her slipping down the hall and found her bed empty, he would roust the servants and send them through the house, and even out onto the road, looking for her.

But someone in the house wanted him dead. Or at least didn't care if he died.

The faint creaks got closer. Olivia looked around frantically, but there was only one place to hide. She scooted under the desk, pulled the chair as close as she could—praying no one would notice it was still out about a body's width—and tucked her nightgown as close as possible without banging her elbows against the wood. As she scooped another swath of fabric, her fingers found the gap beneath the bottom of the desk front and the floor.

If whoever was coming brought a candle, would he see the white of her nightgown in that crack? She pulled the ruffles closer, pushing the folds into her bent knees and pressing her already bent head tighter against her thighs.

Now if she could just get out when she had to . . .

The footsteps stopped outside the room. Olivia curled tighter in her little cubby and held her breath. The knob whispered, and then a faint snick as the latch slipped free of the plate. Something in the air changed, a coolness drifted in, and with it, the sound of breathing.

Olivia caught her breath. If she could hear him, he could hear her.

And it was a man. The weight of the footsteps, the depth of the breathing, told her that. He must be one of the co-conspirators. And he was here, in the room.

She didn't see the flicker of candlelight, or smell anything that hinted at a candle. He had no better vision than herself, only moonlight and his own eyesight.

The shoes came closer; the man stopped beside the desk. "Where would he hide things?"

She didn't think it was possible to go any colder, but she was wrong. Who was he talking to? Himself? She had only heard one set of footsteps.

He didn't see her, did he?

"Hmmm." The voice was still hushed, as if he was as afraid of being overheard as she was. He moved a step away, and Olivia let out her breath so quietly she couldn't hear it herself.

Something scraped, once and then a second time. He was looking behind the pictures. Hunting for some hidden safe?

"Are you done?" A different voice this time, but equally quiet.

There were two now!

"I thought you said he had a safe." The scraping came, either another painting being pulled away from the wall, or one being set back.

"He does, but I don't know where it is." The second man stepped inside; Olivia could tell from the vibration through the floor. "You gave me too little time to look. Besides, I assumed you would know what to look for."

"Don't taunt me." That warning note she had heard from the hallway was back. Even though they both spoke in whispers, this was certainly the same two men. But what were they looking for?

She longed to close her eyes, like a child who couldn't be seen if they couldn't see, but she had to be ready. What if one of them decided to go through the desk? They wouldn't miss her then!

Neither man seemed interested in the desk, though. Which made sense, since they were looking for a hidden safe. The desk was big, but not big enough to hide a safe.

A scraping sound came from the other side of the desk, followed by a strange hum. "I have seen globes like this before," the ominous voice went on, followed by a stillness and a rustle. Olivia could almost see him leaning back and looking at the globe. "Ah, yes. There it is."

He made a disgusted noise in his throat. "Too obvious. I should think he could find something less predictable." A click, and a thump, probably the globe top flipping open and settling back on its hinges. "What have we here?"

More sounds, the rustling of paper. "This is useless, nothing more than his mother's diary. She was the most inoffensive of women. I know. My own mother told me about her. She never put a foot wrong, but if she hadn't died in childbirth, Stafford would likely have smothered her in her sleep just to be rid of the boredom."

The faint thump—a sole on the floor?—from above them sent an electric shock through the room. The ominous man inhaled sharply. "I thought you told me we had enough time."

"If that is the servants, they are rising early." The second man moved away; Olivia followed his steps by the sound and the vibrations through her feet. "I thought we would find the safe in time."

More footsteps from inside the room, also moving away, but one last comment reached her. "Find that safe, if you do nothing else. And see if his mother left any jewelry here. Maybe check her rooms. I care not whether I pawn men's baubles or women's."

Relief left Olivia limp. Wait, she told herself, fighting the urge to scramble out from beneath the desk and run for the door, and then the stairs. She stayed put, growing colder by the minute, and listened as hard as she could. No door opened, nor any closed. Some instinct told her the men were far enough away to make her escape.

Inch by inch, she worked herself out from under the desk, crouching behind it once she cleared the walls of the cubbyhole. She didn't dare peek over the top, just listened for any sound that carried a threat.

But nothing came. Olivia held her breath and peeked over the top of the desk. Shapes in the darkness reminded her of where the globe was, and the other chair. The door was open. One quick breath, and she bolted to her feet, and was around the desk.

She paused before slipping into the hallway, but no sounds greeted her. A look to the right, where the hallway stretched out past the dining room and the parlor and went on. No shadows moved, no whispers came. The door to the curving stairs was only a few feet away. One glance down at her white nightgown, a quick prayer for safety, and she was out of his office and through that barrier.

It opened easily enough, but Olivia forced herself to catch it before it could slam, easing it that last inch until it clicked with no more sound than a mouse's feet. The stairs curved above her. Grabbing the overlarge skirt of that overlarge nightgown, she held it as high as she could and raced up those stairs.

Then she was at the top, just one more door to slip through before she reached the safety of her room.

And all for nothing, she thought as she eased the stairway door open. The iron was still as lost to her as it was before she ventured out.

The hallway was quiet. Olivia eased through, closed the door behind her with exquisite care, and crept down the hall, struggling to listen over the pounding of her heart.

Running up stairs was not the way to keep both breathing and heartbeat calm.

Something creaked as she passed Miles' room, and she gasped. Her hand clamped over her mouth, muffling the rest of the sound. Another creak, and Olivia catapulted into movement. Thank goodness she had left her room door ajar. Down those last few yards she flew, slipped through the opening, then whirled and caught the door and her common sense at the same time. With shaking hands, she eased it shut, grateful that it didn't rattle when the latch caught.

Then her legs gave way, and she slid down the wall, landing with a puff of white cotton on the floor.

A third creak, directly overhead, and she finally realized what those sounds had been. The servants were rising for the day as the man had guessed, poor creatures, and it wasn't even sunrise yet.

Or was it? She could see shapes here, not just varying shades of grey. The sun might not be over the horizon, but the first harbingers of the new day were here. Olivia pulled herself to her feet and crept over to her bed on legs that shook as badly as her hands had. She sat down, brushed off the dust from her feet, and tucked herself under the covers.

Sleep was last thing in her mind, though. She had a decision to make, and her thoughts tumbled around, scrambling for guidance. What was she going to do about what she had heard?

Olivia sat up, wrapped her arms around her legs, and rested her chin on the covers over her knees. She replayed the conversation. *I thought you said he had a safe. I care not whether I pawn men's baubles or women's.*

She knew little else. His enemy was bold enough to stroll in and not just meet a cohort but actually search the house. This time the cold-voiced villain hadn't brought up any threat against anyone's life, but that didn't mean the threat was gone.

So now what? If she told Langley about the threat, would he think she was involved?

But could she say nothing? He was sending her to live with his father. She might help him if she stayed here, but what could she do from miles away?

Give me some answers, she thought desperately, and wished she had the iron in front of her. Yelling at it would do nothing, but the thought broke through the tension and made her chuckle.

Olivia flopped back down and pulled the covers up. If she was lucky, she could get a few more hours of sleep. And as worn out as she was, despite the lingering pounding of her heart and her jangled nerves, she thought she might. She pulled the covers over her head, closed her eyes, and concentrated on slowing her breathing. In, out, in, out, she let the pattern lull her brain.

Maybe, just maybe, when she opened her eyes again, she would find herself back in her Minneapolis bedroom, listening to her clock radio blare music.

In, out, in, out, she felt her heartbeat slow, and a yawn cracked her jaw. In, out, in . . .

CHAPTER 19

SUNLIGHT FLASHED A RUDE BAR ACROSS MILES'S FACE, AND HE groaned, dragging his arm from under the covers to shield his eyes. "I did not ask you to pull the curtains open." His morning growl lacked the authority it normally had.

Thomas merely cleared his throat. "The sun is up, my lord, and so should you be. There was quite a to-do downstairs this morning."

Miles didn't move his arm from his eyes, merely sighed. "A to-do? What happened? Did the cat catch a mouse and leave it in the middle of the room? Did Henri throw another fit in the kitchen?"

"No, my lord." Thomas moved across the room from the window to the armoire. Miles could hear his footsteps.

"So why am I up so early?"

The thing with having a valet who had known one since leading strings was that if he didn't feel like answering, he didn't. Instead, the armoire doors opened. Miles heard him pull out a shirt from the drawer, and felt it land on the foot of the bed. Then came the trousers and the coat. He gave up. Thomas was determined he rise.

He suddenly remembered his uninvited guest, and sat upright, the covers falling to his waist. "Miss Underwood! Is she still here?"

"Yes, my lord. She is." Thomas did that throat-clearing thing again. Despite the grey hair and the creases that lined his face, Miles knew those throat sounds were done for effect, and had nothing to do with his valet's age. "In fact, you might wish to talk to her about what went on in your office last night."

That got him out of bed. Thomas had seen him without clothes often enough not to even blink, merely handed him his dressing robe. Miles slipped his arms into the sleeves and wrapped the robe tight, then tied the belt. If he had to run down to his office, he preferred to do it with at least *something* on. "What do you mean about my office? What happened?"

"Your water is warm. I recommend you make your ablutions quickly."

"My office, man! What happened in my office?" Miles propped his hands on his hips and glared at his valet, but he knew from long experience that Thomas was not overly impressed by titles, or by his young master. Still, Miles would not think of replacing him with a younger man.

Thomas stepped around him and pulled the covers back into place on the bed, smoothing them into pristine order. "Your door was left open, and the curtain had not been shut. I know for a fact that both were closed last night, as they are every night. All the staff were brought in and examined. Denton had their beds searched to make certain nothing was taken. All denied being in the room other than the maid who closed it up for the night, but since she was the one who noticed it, he went easy on her."

"You are certain someone was in there? It was not just an oversight?" Miles tightened the belt of his robe.

"The maid was positive. She has never failed to properly close it for the night. She would certainly know how she left it. The only explanation is that someone paid your office a visit in the night."

"And you suspect Miss Underwood?" He hardly needed to ask the question. He suspected her as well, and chuckled. As long as he kept his desk locked, he need not fear losing anything from there, and the odds of her finding his hiding place for the iron were slim at best. God knew why she wanted the thing so badly. He'd find out why, but still . . . "Was anything else disturbed?"

"No, sir. At least, not that anyone could tell. But I do not like it, anyway. No one should have been in your office after it was closed for the night."

Miles remembered the diary hidden in the globe. It was precious to him, but worthless to anyone seeking to sell it for money. There was nothing in it even worth blackmailing. Still, it had been his mother's, and he didn't like the thought of anyone finding it. He headed for his dressing room and blessed the ancestor who put a door into the hallway so the servants could fill his bath without waking him. "I will be out in a moment."

He shut the door behind himself, dropped his dressing gown, and climbed into the tub. Not many of his acquaintance believed in regular bathing, but he liked the feel and smell of clean skin. Today, however, he made quick work of his bath, and took care of his own shaving. Thomas despaired of not doing it himself, so on important occasions

Miles gave in, but he liked knowing exactly where the razor was.

Besides, there was something satisfying about using his skills to care for himself.

He came out to see Thomas standing by the bed, the shirt ready, and the boots, trousers, coat, and vest set out. "Let me take your robe, my lord, and let's get you dressed."

This was the one battle he had never won with his valet. Miles pulled on the trousers and boots and, in short order, Thomas had his shirt on, the vest buttoned, and his coat on, and the cravat crisply tied.

"Now you look fit, my lord." Thomas stepped back and nodded in approval. "Wherever your guest came from, she can have no complaint against her English host."

Miles stopped at his bedroom door and looked back. "Check in the village and see if there is a dressmaker there, will you? My guest is still awaiting her trunks, and despite what propriety says about purchasing clothing for a woman not of one's family, she can hardly go around in the same gown day after day, however elegant."

Something nibbled at his brain. "Thomas, did my sister leave any gowns here? Our guest might be about the same size." If Cecelia had left some gowns for the occasional visits to their grandparents, it would be a quick solution until the dressmaker arrived. "Tell her maid to check the rooms. If she finds any gowns, shoes, or any other thing a female would need under the circumstances, tell her to bring them to my guest's room and have the lady try them on for size. That will spare her embarrassment until either the dressmaker or her own trunks arrive."

"I will have it done, my lord. I will also send someone to Bristol. 'Tis further away, more anonymous. The city abounds with dressmakers, and surely we can have one come to us. 'Tis scarcely a ten-mile trip. Even if she is busy, she can pack her supplies and be here within a day."

"See to it." Miles headed for the main staircase, and took the steps at a quick clip.

Two footmen stood outside the office door. "Standing guard?" he asked when he stopped in front of them.

"Yes, m'lord," one of them answered as he stepped aside. "Denton told us no one goes in or out until you get here."

"Good men." Miles looked at the room. The curtain had been opened only on one side, but nothing else looked disturbed. He turned to the footmen. "You may go. Thank you." And he shut the door.

He pulled the curtain tight first. Not that the prowler would be watching from outside, but he took no chances. If his trusted servants believed someone had been in the room, the most likely culprit was his lovely guest. Someone had left her here; that was not in question. Whoever it was, they would certainly keep an eye on her.

It was disappointing to think that she might be a common thief. There was that elegant bracelet on her wrist, but she wasn't protective of it. Instead, she wore it as easily as if she forgot it was there.

Instead of guarding her single bit of jewelry, she wanted that iron.

It raised the annoying question of why. Why would any lady want an everyday implement used by servants? It made no sense. But he loved a good mystery, and this one he would solve. With or without his visitor.

The thought made him smile a bit. A delightful prospect indeed. Unless she was a spy, of course. Then he would do what was necessary, however unpleasant.

All the desk drawers were locked. He found the tiny secret door so well concealed in the wooden corner of the desk that no one could find it unless they knew where it was. The key was still in its place, and Miles felt his shoulders relax.

Drawer after drawer was opened and checked, but nothing was missing, nothing even out of order. Everything was exactly as he had left it. Miles tucked the key back into its spot, and turned to the shelves behind his desk. He pushed down firmly on a piece of one of the shelves, and a portion of the bookshelf clicked free. A pull, and the hinges hissed open, revealing a gap in the wall.

The iron was still safely there. She hadn't found it, although he suspected she had looked hard. He opened the iron's back door, and the slug was still there, too.

What secret did it hold?

He slid the iron back into the gap, clicked the shelf back into place, made sure the books looked undisturbed, and turned to the globe. The lid had been opened—*clever girl*—and hadn't fully latched when she was done. The diary had been removed, at least for a look, but at least it was still there. He always took care to fit it exactly in the small notch at the bottom, designed at some time in the past to hold something rectangular. It was a nearly perfect fit.

Now the diary was not in its place. It was close, but his searcher hadn't been quite careful enough.

Miles set the little book neatly back in the notch, and closed the globe, making certain to hear that solid click.

Someone had indeed searched his office.

He leaned back against his desk and stared down at the globe. This didn't have the feel of his guest, with her open face and obvious confusion, but what did he know of female spies? Female thieves were more common for anyone who walked the streets of London, but she didn't behave like one of them, either. He had encountered his fair share in his life.

He checked to make certain everything was back to normal before opening the curtain exactly as it had been. Then he tugged the cord to summon his butler, took his chair, folded his hands on the desk, and waited for Denton to appear.

The man arrived in less than a minute, looking impeccable as usual. "Yes, my lord?"

"Shut the door, if you would." Miles waited until the door snicked shut, and Denton was in his usual place in front of the desk. "Tell me again exactly how the office was found this morning."

Denton stood at attention, and cleared his throat. "One of the maids noticed it. She particularly remarked on it because closing up the room is always the last thing she does before retiring. And this morning the door was open and the curtains ajar." Denton waved to the window. "Exactly as you see them."

"And she touched nothing?"

Denton shook his head. "No, my lord. She is too experienced for that."

Miles gave a nod. "As I expected." He tapped his fingers together. "Did you check with Clara?"

"Clara?"

"The maid assigned to our unexpected guest."

"No, sir." Denton straightened.

"Bring the maid and the lady both to me."

CHAPTER 20

OLIVIA WOKE, A SINGLE LINE OF THE SUN DANCING AGAINST her eyelids from a crack in the curtains. She should have pulled the shade . . . She shaded her face with one hand and cracked an eye open.

But nothing was familiar.

Oh! She clapped that hand over her eyes and groaned. She was still here.

"Morning, Miss Olivia. Did I wake you?" Clara. A now-familiar voice.

"No, but the sun did." Olivia struggled to sit upright. It couldn't be morning already. She had barely slept. "What time is it?" A yawn nearly cut off the last word.

"I don't know. I filled your water jug so you can wash up."

Wash up. Water jug. No shower. Olivia dragged herself over to the dressing table with the bowl and pitcher still dripping water, and sagged down on the chair. She longed to just rest her head on the dressing table and sleep, but a tray of food and a teapot sat right where her head would land.

She had no choice but to wake up now.

"Here, let me get you something to eat before we take that nightgown off you. I brought you some tea and a scone with jam."

Clara turned the cup upright and poured the tea in. "That might have steeped too much. I hope it's not too strong." She stepped back and started gnawing her bottom lip again. *How hard it must be to be a servant.* "Don't worry. Today, the stronger the better." Olivia took a sip, and forced herself not to wince. It *was* strong and bitter, but she could feel the caffeine start to work.

The scone was delicious, only a faint hint of warmth from fresh baking but still soft, the jam the same tangy gooseberry that Clara had fed her yesterday.

The tea and scone helped wake her, but another day in this strange world stretched out ahead, along with the new secrets and threats she had to find some way to unravel.

And share?

Who would believe her?

"Let's get you dressed now." Clara's voice pulled Olivia away from her thoughts. "The water is fresh. Arms up, and I'll take your nightgown off."

"Oh, no, really. I don't need any help."

Clara pulled back and fear slipped into her eyes. "But this is my assignment." Her shoulders straightened, and Olivia saw an idea spark in her face. "Besides, you need help getting into your corset."

Guilt pricked Olivia. My assignment. The poor maid had come from the kitchen, she knew, and if she wasn't needed would have to go back. She couldn't let that happen. A bit of embarrassment wasn't that much to endure if it saved Clara from drudgery.

If she had any doubts about being here in real time, the new morning routine was a forceful reminder. Clara's idea of 'warm' water and her own were entirely different! Doing her bathing in a simple bowl of *cold* water—which cleared the last cobwebs out of her head in a hurry—having a maid there to comb her hair, being strapped into a corset.

Worst of all, having to put on the same gown. It had the faintest smell of wear. She could only hope her deodorant lasted.

Olivia turned back to the mirror when Clara was done. She was again the woman from yesterday, her reflection stuck in a different time.

Olivia looked down at the gown. It had been amazing when she first found herself in it, but right now she would love something else. If she had anything else to wear.

A solid rap came at the door, and Clara hurried over to open it. A male servant stood there, one of the footmen from last night's supper, Olivia realized.

"What are you doing here?" Her maid was certainly taking her protective duties seriously.

"'Is Lordship wants to see both of you down in 'is office." The man looked down his nose at Clara. "If you will follow me."

Olivia looked at Clara, and Clara looked back. There was nothing to do but follow the footman.

Something must have shown on her face as they walked in a group down the fancy white staircase, because Clara leaned over as they neared the bottom, and whispered, "Don't worry. He's a fair man. I've only heard word of him throwing one servant out in the months I've been here, and that was for stealing. I know you didn't steal anything, and I'm going to tell him so."

The footman glared over his shoulder and took the last steps, then opened the hallway door. "'Is Lordship is waitin' in the office." He stepped aside, and as they passed him,

Olivia heard the suspicion in his voice as he added, "I presume you know where it is."

Even if she hadn't, Langley stood in the opening of the room in which she had spent long, frightening minutes last night. "Miss Underwood, if you will come inside."

"What about my maid? Shouldn't she be in, too?" Resentment and guilt roiled inside and the snide comment popped out. "After all, I wouldn't want to compromise you."

No smile tugged at his mouth, and his brows came together. "No. I think it best that I talk to you separately." He turned to the footmen. "Watch the door, and keep the maid there with you."

A chill slithered down her spine. He was truly angry. The amiable, charming host had vanished. In its place was an imposing English gentleman ready to defend his country against all intruders.

The chill spread from her spine through the rest of her, running down to her feet, and out to her fingers.

The door shut behind her with a solid thunk. Olivia stopped a few feet in, placing herself in the daylight to her movements of the night. Window, globe, chairs, and the desk that had shielded her. Two walls held bookshelves, the books a study in monochromatic color, leather bindings in shades of brown.

He motioned her further into the room. "If you would sit, Miss Underwood, we have much to discuss." He walked around her to the opposite side of the desk.

There was nothing to do but take the chair in front of that imposing piece of furniture that had yielded nothing to her search last night. She tried not to look at it, sure her guilt would show if she did. Instead, she looked down at her hands, folded them neatly in her lap, the fingers cold against each other, and lifted her head, meeting his fierce gaze.

"Someone was in my office last night." He had waited to sit until she was down, and now his hands were folded on the desk, his posture ramrod straight in the chair, but even in his stillness, he exuded power. "I do not suppose you know anything about it."

There was no question at the end. She knew it meant the exact opposite. *You know everything about it*, that voice, those words, said.

How to tell him what she knew? Maybe the two men had pocketed a piece or two. They didn't sound like they found what they had been looking for, but she had only heard words; she hadn't seen anything from her hiding place. "Is something missing?"

"That is not the point." His fingers tightened. "This place is my private sanctum, off limits without an invitation. I think you knew that. I made no move to show it to you last night, did I? So why did you come in and search it?"

"What makes you think it was me?" It was a stupid question, but she needed another moment to think.

A growling sound came from his throat. "Come, come, Miss Underwood. Who else could it be? My servants are all well trained, and know it would be worth their position if they were to take so much as a single fork. And I have something you want badly. Of course it was you. I just wonder how far into this plot you have involved the innocent maid I assigned you."

That was too much. Olivia bounced out of the chair. "She had nothing to do with it!" She saw come alert, his eyes keen on hers as he suddenly seemed closer, and she sank down again.

"Ahh." His hands relaxed, and he leaned back in that great big chair. It didn't dwarf him as it had done her. "So it was you. How did you figure out the latch to the globe?" He took a deep breath, and she felt him struggle for control. "Are you a thief, or are you a spy? I want to know what hides in the back of that iron. Did it hold papers and have you already managed to turn them over? Or were you searching for something to hide in there and bring back to your country? Is there a message etched in the metal slab I saw inside your so-precious iron?"

Olivia's heart pounded in her chest, squeezing her lungs. "None of that. I never touched your globe." Aside from bumping into it, but that wasn't what he meant. She hurried on, "And I most definitely am not a thief!"

"Explain your bracelet, then." One hand moved in a gesture around his own wrist, as if she didn't know what he was referring to.

Olivia looked down at her bracelet. She was so used to wearing it that she seldom gave it a thought. At least now she had a guess of its age. Nothing else had come through the iron's gate. It had to belong to this time. She cupped her hand over it. "It was a gift to myself. I was able to afford it because it was broken. I brought it to a jeweler, who fixed it for me. It doesn't look exactly the same, but pretty close."

"You bought a broken bracelet? And a servant's iron?" His brows had gone up on his forehead, and his eyes were wide. They narrowed again, and he gave a brief shake of the head. "I find myself struggling to believe what you say."

"I don't know what to tell you. I don't know why I'm here, either."

"I would find it easier to trust you," he spoke softly and slowly, "if you did not have the gaps in your memory. I find myself wondering if they are as real as you say."

She couldn't tell him everything, but he only needed to know that he was in danger. "Okay, fine. Yes, I did come in to search for the iron, but I didn't find it. I had very little time

to look and I didn't open anything. Your desk was locked."
His brows came down, but she hurried on. "I wouldn't have
taken anything but my iron. You know I want it back. What
is more, I had no idea the globe was a safe. It was the other
two men who found that out."

She felt the anger around him like a cold chill. He sat up,
and his fingers clenched so hard on the edge of the desk she
expected the wood to dent. "So you have already met your
co-conspirators?"

"No! I have no conspirators!" She leaned forward and
pressed her hands onto the desk, half-rising from her chair.
"I first heard them outside the yellow room when you left me
there. Remember when you walked off with my iron? I heard
a door creak, and footsteps. I thought at first it was you
coming back, but they were too stealthy. There were two of
them, two men, and they talked about you, and something
about diamond buttons."

Some of the words from the first time she heard them
talking came back. Olivia made herself sit back, and kept her
voice calm, rational. "One of the men talked about a family
head and some money, and said the other man should go to
an earl if he needed funds, and then there was talk about
stealing those buttons. They were both in here last night. I
recognized the voices."

His eyes were slits. "A pretty story. Two men in my house
twice, plotting a robbery, and you tell me nothing until now?
And the three of you were in my office, yet you claim they
are not conspirators of yours. Am I supposed to believe
you?"

Olivia jumped to her feet. "Yes, you are! I hid under your
desk when I heard them come in; they didn't see me. Why
would I tell you a story that ridiculous? How else would I
know about diamond buttons? You never showed them to

me. How would I know about them? But those men knew, and one of them wants whatever he can get out of your house. If he can find the diamond buttons, all the better. You are in danger, and I'm trying to save your life!"

He scowled. "How did we get from robbery to murder? I presume that is what you are talking about? Someone was plotting my murder?"

She sank back into the chair. "Well, that's what it sounded like to me. The first time I heard them, one of the men said it was a wonder you hadn't been waylaid on the way here, and that everyone knows about the diamond buttons."

"And from that you deduced that this mythical man wanted to kill me."

She glared at him. "It wasn't a mythical man, and I thought it a logical deduction."

M iles looked at his guest. Somehow she found out about the buttons, but if she wanted to steal them, she was going about it all wrong. To warn him first?

Go to the earl for money. Which earl? His father? There were plenty of other earls about England.

Although—he did know one man about whom this description fit.

Assuming she had heard what she thought she had heard.

Granted, by the time he brought her to the yellow room, she was walking on her own and well enough to climb on a chair with that heavy iron—although not stable enough to hold it—and talking lucidly. She claimed never to have been in London.

Still, the mails were most efficient. Someone might well

have mentioned them in a letter. It was not beyond the realm of possibility.

"A pity for these men, assuming they exist, that the buttons are still in London." Locked in his safe, where they stayed when he wasn't wearing the vest.

She leaned so far forward he thought she might fall out of the chair. "But they didn't know that. And if you have anything else of value, I'd lock that up, too, because whoever wants to get your buttons won't stop there. The one man told the other man to find something else to steal, something that wouldn't be missed for a while."

So, she was not a thief. No self-respecting thief would tell her victim to lock up all his valuables. That left the other possibility, the one he had suspected all along.

Spy.

And that without a memory. But why here? And why him? He remembered thinking she had been dropped off at the wrong house. Even if his house was the deliberate target, what made them think he knew anything that would help them? Did they think his relationship with his father was so poor that he would betray the man that way?

Or did they think the two were so close and trusting that his father would confide government business to him?

There was one other person to question, although the possibility of finding something out from her was slim at best.

He rose. "You may leave. Send your maid in, if you will."

CHAPTER 21

MILES DID NOT MISS THE QUICK SQUEEZE OLIVIA GAVE Clara's hand on the way out. She also made no effort to lower her voice when she said, "Just tell the truth."

"Good advice," he drawled to her back, and switched his gaze to the maid, who hesitated in the door. "Come in."

The maid walked in a few steps, stopping at the typical servant's distance, and gave a start as the door was pulled shut behind her with a solid *snap*.

"You wanted to speak to me?"

Miles raised his eyebrows. Impertinent chit. She should know she was not to speak first. He sat. "Yes, I did. And before you answer that, remember you are in my employ. I pay your wages, not Miss Olivia."

The maid met his gaze without flinching. "I am well aware of that, my lord."

Something about her speech and behavior caught his ear. He had not noticed it before, but then, he had hardly spoken to her. This maid spoke like someone who had always been free to speak. Was she the daughter of a gentleman who had fallen on hard times?

Perhaps her freeness would serve him now. "Then answer me honestly. Has she sent or received any messages?"

The maid shook her head. "No. None."

"Has she told you where she is from?"

"She told me the same thing I believe she told you. She is from America."

He steepled his fingers and tapped them against his chin. "And what did she tell you she remembers about her journey here?"

"She said it was a blur." The maid's brows came together, and she opened her mouth, but then closed it again.

"Say what you were about to. Remember, your first loyalty is to me."

The maid—Clara, was it?—took a deep breath, and let it out in a rush. "She never had a maid. She doesn't know where she is, and said she doesn't know anyone here. She doesn't even know what a maid is supposed to do. I know, because she asked me what my duties were."

Miles nodded. "She said the same to me." Clara's hands clenched and released; he did not know if she even realized she was doing it. "Is there more?"

"She doesn't know where she is. Truly." Clara leaned forward earnestly, blinked as she seemed to realize what she had done, and straightened again. "She asked me where in the country this house was."

Her head lifted in a movement of confidence, and he thought again of a gentleman's family. "She would not ask where she was unless she honestly didn't know. If she was here to cause problems for England, wouldn't she have to know the countryside, at the very least? What good is a spy who knows nothing about the country she's supposed to be spying in?"

Before he could ask the next question, she added, "And she really wants to know where her iron is."

How convenient an opening. "She admitted she was in this office last night."

Clara started. "She did? I can't believe she left her bed all night. I heard nothing."

Miles jumped on that admittance. If Miss Underwood went to the main staircase, she would have passed right by the maid's tiny room. "So she could have slipped out and you would not have noticed?"

Her brows came together. "Was I supposed to stay awake?"

He had some idea how hard his servants worked. "No, you are entitled to your rest." It just would have been helpful if she had awakened at the faintest sound. Miss Underwood must have been careful moving about. But then, if she had used the servants' staircase in the round tower, she would have had to pass his room, and he heard nothing, either.

Clara leaned forward again. "She was in her bed this morning when I woke, and I got up early. But I do not believe she would have taken anything, or done whatever you think she did. If she admits she was in here, it was just because you took her iron and won't give it back."

"You are right on that last point. I will not give it back." Miles leaned back and thought. Clara's hands did that clenching and unclenching thing again. "How well do you know the rest of the household staff?"

She drew back, even took a step away. "Hardly at all, my lord. I haven't been here long."

"All the better. You should not feel the need to protect any of them, then." He resisted the urge to lean forward, press his hands on the desk, and bark the question, but kept his voice low and calm. "Have you ever heard talk in the servant's area about America? Does anyone ever pay too much interest in the subject? You are aware that war is on the horizon?" He honestly did not know how much his servants heard, but since men of all classes were going to be pulled into the fighting and some of their women intended to follow them, he suspected they knew as much as anyone.

He was sure a smile tugged at her mouth, but she didn't let it loose. "I don't think any of them care much about America. They are more worried about Napoleon."

As was most of England. This was going nowhere. "Thank you, Clara. You may leave, but find your mistress a bonnet and shawl. I have a desire to take her out and see if the view brings back her memory."

She bobbed a quick curtsey, turned, and slipped out of the room.

Olivia looked at that closed office door and wished she could go in and give moral support to her maid. She could barely hear a murmur, let alone words. But she wasn't doing anyone any good standing outside, not even herself. She could hardly stand in the corridor and wait for someone to guide her.

She turned her back on the office and looked at the hallway, where the sun through the spaced windows provided illumination. There were all those family portraits to look at. Olivia strolled down to the nearest portrait, a man from a long-ago century, painted with unsmiling face and an Elizabethan ruff.

Was the man in the portrait really that grim in life, or did the painter just not know how to capture a smile?

Her skirt swished as she moved to the next portrait, thrusting her predicament firmly back to her mind. She shivered, but it wasn't a shiver that a shawl could warm.

The door to Langley's office remained firmly shut, so she moved down the corridor, looking at men in clothes old even in this time, women wearing square-necked gowns that showed off heavy jewelry. Most had been painted in strange hats, some peaked with veils hanging from the top, others fitting tight to the head, sparing the artist from having to paint hair. Here and there, she saw more Elizabethan ruffs, both on men and women. A few paintings looked so lifelike she almost expected the figures to step out of the canvas and join her.

And why not? After all, if she could travel through time, why not them?

As the paintings grew more ancient, the faces became more stilted. Many had to predate the flowering of the Renaissance, when artists learned how to bring realism into their work.

Olivia shivered again, and this time she realized that despite the flat wall of windows on her left, the house was actually cold. No Minnesota summer, here.

The office door opened, Clara stepped out, and that door snicked shut again. Olivia wanted to call to her, but one of the footmen said something she couldn't hear, and gestured toward the door of the tower with the curving stairs. Her maid slipped through.

Olivia knew she could rush back down the hall and try to catch up with Clara, but the footmen remained in their place, and they would almost certainly carry tales to their boss.

So she opened the nearest door, and stepped inside. The

sunshine that had passed the hallway windows on its journey poked its first rays through this room's open curtains, adding a tinge of gold to the room. Olivia stopped in one of the sunny stripes, and let the warmth sink in while she stared at the display before her. *I'm here*, she thought, *I'm really here.*

The room wasn't large, maybe thirty feet square. The upper walls had been done in the same pale yellow as her own, a wash above the chair rail, as if the designer was inspired by the morning sun that would shine in.

The lower part was wainscoting, dark wood set in elegant panels. Chairs of the same dark wood sat around the outside edges, and the walls were decorated with more paintings, landscapes this time instead of people. The oddest piano with a vague resemblance to a grand but with a keyboard about half the size, a more flat box, and strange spindly legs, the cover closed as if waiting, sat in a corner, with an ordinary chair in front of it. No bench, no piano stool, just a chair.

Olivia glanced over her shoulder, where she had left the door partially open, but no one looked back, so she walked over to the piano. She didn't know how to play, but couldn't resist pressing a few keys. The odd little piano gave a clear tinkle that drifted in the room.

If only she had learned. She sighed, and let her fingers trail over the keys without pressing.

It was lonely here. At home, she had coworkers to chat with as they arranged furniture, brought in knick-knacks, or ate lunch together. There was the cellphone with messages waiting for response—often too many messages—and television to keep up on what was happening around the world. She was never alone unless she chose to be.

Right now, the outside was quiet. The only sounds

drifting in came from the back of the house where there must be stables, because she heard the whinny of a horse.

She left the strange piano and turned to examine the room in front of her. She could see it now, a small family gathering where fathers danced with their daughters, and brothers with their sisters. They would bring the chairs back from the walls to sit close and listen as someone played the piano and sang.

Such a simple life. Were teenagers easier to raise in this time? Or did they get bored and find trouble here, too? She looked at the openness of the room again, and imagined swirling around on a man's arm while someone played the piano.

A melody slipped in from somewhere in her memories, and she started humming. Olivia tried a few steps. What would it be like, swirling around this magnificent room with a gorgeous man's arms around her? She closed her eyes and dreamed as she swayed to the notes in her head. The man had Miles's face, so clear behind her closed eyes Olivia could almost smell the scent she remembered from yesterday, spicy and masculine.

She collided abruptly with a large and muscled male body. Firm hands closed on her arms and caught her before she fell. Big, warm, strong hands that held her easily.

CHAPTER 22

HER EYES POPPED OPEN. DIRECTLY IN HER LINE OF SIGHT, A blue vest with gold buttons appeared, and a white shirt. Her gaze went upward, over a lopsided white cravat, a chiseled chin shaved clean, firm lips, a sculpted nose, and those crystal-green eyes under that tumble of dark hair that looked as if he had run his fingers through it.

Had he been afraid for her? Or perhaps afraid of her? That could account for the difference between his rumpled appearance now and the tidy man she had left earlier.

Olivia braced herself for a scolding, especially since his fingers were still wrapped around her arms.

That supportive grip loosened, but he left his fingers there, almost as if he had forgotten what he was doing. His thumb moved on her arm, a barely-there stroke.

Maybe he wasn't thinking of scolding after all. She snapped her attention back to his gaze, staring into those pale eyes for guidance.

Langley suddenly released her and took a step back.

Olivia managed a breath, not realizing until then that she had barely breathed from the moment he had caught her. Wishing his hands were still on her arms. Strange, for a man she barely knew. Heat ran up her face, the bane of redheads.

His long fingers ran through the rumpled hair, combing it into order. A bit of color stained his cheeks, too, but that could be the odd lighting. "I am done questioning your maid. You will be pleased to know that she defended you valiantly. When I told her you admitted to being in the office, she said you were in here simply to find the iron, and would not have taken anything else."

"She did? How nice. Besides, she's right."

"We are not going to resolve that until I find out why someone like you wants it so badly. Right now, I wish to know more about you if I'm to decide whether I can trust you."

"Ask away." She caught herself and added, "I'll tell you what I can." He would hardly ask what year she was born, would he? She did quick math counting back from 1811, landed at 1783, and waited for the first question.

He seemed to think they were still too close together, because he strolled over to the strange piano, then looked over his shoulder at her. "Do you play?"

Olivia laughed. That was easy enough to answer. "Not hardly."

"No?" His eyebrows rose. "Did no one think to teach you? Most young women learn."

"Well, I did not. Not that I didn't want to. It just wasn't that important."

"Important. That is a good word." He stepped away from the piano. "I confess, I do not understand why it is considered of such *importance* for young women, and yet it seems the indicator of a proper education. One might think they should learn instead how to run a household, give orders to servants, tell if a child is ill, or what to do for fever."

Run a household? Olivia's spine stiffened. "Yes, I think medicine is a good field for women, too. We seem to have the compassion necessary to make good doctors."

His brows came down in a frown. "I said nothing about medicine. I merely meant that it is good for a woman to be able to care for children, to know when something is wrong and it is time to send for a doctor. Those things are essential for mothers."

"Imagine how much better for a mother to be a doctor herself."

"So you are one of those radical females who believe in educating women along with men." He shook his head. "It will never happen. Women are not made for that kind of learning. They do better in the more refined arts. Music and painting, languages, and needlework."

Her jaw tightened. "I'll have you know women can learn just as easily as men! Easier, in many cases. I received an"— her brain finally caught up with her mouth. "An excellent education myself. I might not know how to play the piano, but I know mathematics, finance, and some of the sciences."

Although, now that she thought about it, her own career fell under what he might consider a womanly skill. Staging was an art, but it still was done in a house. He wouldn't care that she had studied business, architectural styles, the history of furniture, color schemes, and even some psychology, essential to understanding how to appeal to both buyers and sellers. She wasn't even sure he knew what psychology was.

He seemed to realize he had insulted her because he gave a graceful bow. "I am hardly surprised to hear that. You struck me from the very beginning as an intelligent woman.

Besides, we do know that women in America have very strong wills."

This time it was her turn to frown. "I suspect if you took the time to really *look* at your British women, you would find them to have equally strong wills." Before he could say anything, she added, "And equal intelligence."

His head was shaking in negation before she even finished. "A man does not want a woman who is in competition. A woman is a helpmeet of a man, a support. Is that not what God said at Eve's creation? A man wants someone who will support his decisions, not go about making her own."

Her fingers tingled with the building irritation, and it took effort not to slam her fists onto her hips. "So are you looking for someone without a brain? Or without a will of her own?"

Langley chuckled. "Neither. I just do not want a woman who will challenge me at every turn. What kind of household would that make? Mother and father at each other's throats? Imagine what that would do to the children." He shook his head. "No, much better to look for a woman with a gentle, meek spirit, one who will stand beside me, and present a united front for the children."

Olivia flexed her fingers in hopes of making the tingling ease. She might be stuck here, with these antiquated ideas! How would she survive? "You don't want a companion. You want a servant. I wish you luck in your search." She turned around and started for the door.

Right now, she wanted out of the house, some place to run off her irritation. Her skirt started to wrap around her legs, and she was forced to slow, which only exacerbated her temper. At the pace her gown required to keep from tangling in fabric around her ankles, it would take her hours to cool down enough to put on a pleasant, unruffled face for her host.

Only he had other ideas. She was barely at the door when a hand caught her arm, the gentle restraint preventing her from stomping out of the room.

"Where did you think you were going? You hardly know my house. I hate to think you would get lost, and I shall have to send the servants out to find you."

He drew her hand through the crook of his elbow, and held it there, gently but implacably. "I seem to have offended you yet again. Forgive me. I do not want a servant, if by that you mean not a literal servant but a weak, cowering woman who will jump at my every command. As far as the other, I could not marry a servant with my position. It simply is not done."

"You understood me perfectly. That is exactly what I meant." She took a deep breath to calm her temper and settle her racing heart. "You see, my lord, in America—at least where I live—women have so much more freedom. And men as well. If a man wants to marry a woman of lesser status, he can. *If* she is willing. We believe in marrying for love, not for convenience."

He began strolling down the hallway, a pace that easily accommodated her long skirts. "Today is not a day for arguments, but for getting to know each other better. After all, I accused you of theft and spying. You denied both. I must determine whether to believe you."

He paused at the big doors set in the middle of the wide hallway. Through the wavy glass, she could see the brown of the pebbled drive, and the green beyond.

One of the footmen stood by the door, and at some signal she didn't see, pulled it open. Langley paused. "When the lady's maid comes down, have her meet us by the maze."

"Yes, my lord." The man dipped his head.

Olivia ran the brief sound of the footman's voice through her memory, but it did not match either of the two men who held such threat. Whoever was plotting against the man at her side, it was likely not this footman.

Langley could not know what she was thinking. In a calm gesture, he waved her on ahead. "If you can walk around my small garden, then I might be convinced you have recovered." His eyes twinkled. "You must promise not to tell Dr. Reed I let you do this." Then he sobered. "Tell me the moment you feel the least faint. Your maid will be with us momentarily. There is no one about to see you without a bonnet, so we shall walk slowly and let her catch up."

They began a sedate stroll along the front of the house. Olivia looked at the red brick walls soaring up three stories, and the stark white stone edging around the windows. "What a strange layout your house has. I have never been in a house where a hallway ran down the front and all the rooms branched off it on one side. Where I am from, the hallways usually run down the center, and rooms branch off on both sides." She thought of her little rented house, and a pang jabbed her. Would she ever see it again?

Lord Langley shifted at her side. Olivia glanced up to see him looking down at her. He never broke his step, just continued along the pebbled drive. "I inherited this house from my mother's family. I had no say on how it was built." It was his turn to glance around, and his face softened, his lips curved up, and she felt his deep, satisfied breath.

"You love this place, don't you?"

His gaze returned to her, and she saw that calm reflected in his pale eyes. "Yes. I do." Then his jaw firmed, and the peace left his face and body. His eyes moved from hers back to the tall wall on her right. The arm beneath her hand tightened. "It is mine, and I will not let anyone take it from me."

His gaze moved down to her. "Not even whatever you are involved in. I know not what it is, but I will not let you destroy my family's reputation by dragging us into some traitorous conspiracy. I let your claim of my impending murder wipe the questions I should have asked out of my mind." He stopped just inside the outer door. "Convince me you are not a spy."

Olivia felt her shoulders slump. "I have always heard it's difficult to disprove a negative. I say I'm not a spy, you don't believe me, but I have no proof of my innocence."

"Let us not forget that you also have no proof of your missing memory, either."

She pulled her hand out of his arm. "Just as you have no proof that I'm lying about that."

"True." He took her hand again and looped it through the crook of his elbow. "So where does that leave us?"

"You said you wanted to get to know me better. If you do, you will see that I am no spy." As long as she could keep from letting the real truth slip out. She would go from a spy to a lunatic. "I've already told you a bit about my family, and where I'm from. What more do you need to know?"

His brows puckered, then smoothed, he rubbed his free hand over the back of his neck. "I am not certain. Something will come, though, I am confident."

Footsteps scuffed behind them, and they both turned around. Clara slowed to a stop, a straw bonnet—no doubt one of the ones from the armoire—dangling from her hand, and a shawl draped over her arm. "The footman told me you had gone this way."

She handed over the bonnet, and Olivia took it. Langley waited for her to put it on, and the shawl.

She hadn't thought she would need it, but there was a definite freshness, almost a chill, in the summer air here. A bird chirped nearby. She couldn't see it, but just hearing birdsong was like a piece of home.

He tucked her hand back into the crook of his arm as they rounded the corner of the house. Langley looked down again. "This is not too much for you, is it? If you are becoming tired, we can turn back."

Olivia met his worried gaze, and smothered a frustrated sigh. Was that why he had slid her arm through his? Not as an excuse to be close to her, but to monitor her strength? "No. I feel perfectly fine." Besides, she needed this break from the house that had become a beautiful prison.

His silvery eyes searched her face. "You are pale, but perhaps that is normal for you. Most redheads have that coloring." One side of his mouth tilted up. "Perhaps it is nature's way of compensating for the richness of your hair."

He gestured at a wall of greenery in front of them. "Would you like to take a stroll in my maze? It is not large, we are not far from the house, and if you get tired, I can get you back inside quickly." His pale eyes twinkled again. "I assure you, I know the best way out of this from any place we may be."

As they drew near the hedge, she saw that the living walls were higher than the average man, even than Miles, and he was quite tall.

No one would be able to cheat by looking over those sides for the exit, she thought with a smile. A gap appeared, obviously the entrance. Two metal benches sat on either side, perhaps for those who had gotten lost inside to rest once they found their way out.

"I would like that." That opening with those tall green

sides drew her. The lure of a maze: *come in and see if you can get out.*

CHAPTER 23

SHE GLANCED BEHIND THEM AT HER MAID. *POOR CLARA*, OLIVIA thought as the maid stood pretending not to watch. It wasn't enough that she had work to do, but now she had to set everything aside for a stroll through a maze.

But maybe an hour or two in the sunshine would be welcome. "Can Clara have time off to come with us?"

Langley gave a start. "Of course. While we are visible from the windows, and that is powerful restraint from damaging gossip, I would not think of taking you into a maze without her. I assure you, with her along, your name is safe, and no one can fault either of us."

Even for a walk in the bright sunshine? Olivia shrugged, smiled at Clara, and turned back to the entrance.

Lord Langley held out an elbow. Olivia slid her hand through the crook, and looked up at him. "I presume you know your way around? We won't get lost, will we?"

He didn't smile, but a twinkle grew in his eyes. "I have been through it any number of times. I know my way around." He looked at the opening. "I find it an excellent place to walk and think."

Olivia smiled, both at the coming adventure and at the scene, him in his suit and vest, and her in a long gown with a bonnet and shawl. "I don't know whether that reassures me, or disappoints me. I rather liked the idea of getting lost in the maze, especially since I know all I have to do is yell and someone will come and lead me out."

He dipped his head, and peered under her bonnet's brim. "I shall let you lead. As soon as you are ready to give up, let me know and I will lead us safely out."

"Oh, ye of little faith," Olivia laughed, the words slipping out easily. She turned around to Clara. "Stay close. I'm going to try not to get us lost, but no guarantees."

"I won't get lost," Clara said, something certain in her voice.

With the reassurances from both companions, Olivia turned around and headed for the opening.

The sun tipped the green leaves, and she saw the cut edges where some gardener had gone through, keeping the maze neatly trimmed. A bird twitted somewhere nearby, but she couldn't see it, couldn't tell if it was inside, clinging to some small branch, or outside. The hedge made a sound barrier, but she realized with a new jolt that there would not be any familiarity noises, no lawn mower, no car, or motorcycle, no radio.

Olivia dragged herself back to this new and strange present, looked down the long walls on either side, and began walking. She took the first left turn, inexplicably relieved at the firmness of Langley's arm beneath her hand. They reached the curve of that wall in silence, just their feet crunching on the pebbled path, Clara's heavy work shoes thumping behind them, and birds chirping a distance away.

If he was thinking of some question to trap her, it was hard to tell, but he remained silent and walked alongside her, making no attempt to steer.

A path split off, going to the right, and she followed its leading, only to come to a dead end. She glanced up at Langley, but his face was carefully blank. The sun glowed on his hair, turning the tips white and casting his eyes into shadow, but the silver orbs glinted at her, and she thought she saw a smile there.

He was doing a lot of smiling with his eyes. She would have to watch them, which was no hardship at all.

"I took a wrong turn." Color warmed her cheeks, from both embarrassment and her wayward thoughts, and she knew he saw it. Hopefully, he thought it from her mistake, and did not guess what else put it there.

One side of his mouth twitched. "So I see."

They backtracked to the original path and continued on. Another path split off to the right again, and she glanced up at him. He raised one brow. "Wherever you wish."

"Okay." Olivia took this second turning, and tried to guess from his arm beneath her hand and the rhythm of his breathing if she had made another mistake. But he didn't tense, his breaths stayed regular. The path turned again, and she followed its lead. Another turn, and she suddenly felt lost. How many turns had it been? Greenery surrounded her, and the walls that had been tall from the outside now began to close in.

But the sunshine reached down through the open sky above, and she took a deep breath to quell the flutter of nerves.

"Tell me about America." His voice pierced the quiet.

Aha! Here came the questions. Either that, or he was deliberately interrupting her concentration. All the movies about one wrong word changing the outcome of history pricked at her. What was happening even now in the world she left behind? "What do you want to know?"

"Tell me about this place where you live. Where voyageurs roam yet you have never seen one, and chestnut trees do not grow."

That should be safe enough. "As cities go, it's a very pretty city. Lots of trees and green. There are rivers and streams running through it, and walking paths around them. There is a park with a rose garden by a lake, and it is very popular. People drive from all over to see it."

"And what did you say the name was, again?"

She decided to stick with what she knew of the city's history. "Saint Anthony."

A sharp intake of breath came from behind them, and Olivia turned around. "Clara? Are you hurt?"

Clara shook her head quickly, her mobcap bobbing and threatening to fall off. She reached up and pulled it down tighter over her dark hair. "No. I thought I saw a bee, that's all."

"You aren't allergic, are you?"

"No."

Two voices spoke at the same time. "What is that?" from Langley, and her own "Good."

But he had asked a question, and she had to come up with an answer. "Allergy means that you get sick from something. Like a food that makes you break out in a rash." Another bit of history that she didn't know: when were allergies first recognized? There was no internet to do quick research.

"I have a friend who cannot eat strawberries. His nose itches every time he tries."

"Yes, well, it's more than food. Do you sneeze in the spring?"

He smiled. "Not I, but some of the servants do."

It was time to end the subject. "In America, we call those allergies."

Olivia looked at Clara again, but the maid was still struggling with the mobcap and her stubborn hair, and didn't meet her eyes.

Clara's face looked pale. Was she too hot in her heavy maid's clothes?

Hopefully they—*she*—would find the way out of the maze before Clara fainted.

A small shiver ran across her skin. A tremor in the fabric of time? Or Langley's movement beneath her hand? Clara's cap was securely on her head again, and she was staring at the top of the hedge wall.

Neither seemed to notice anything different.

Olivia was struck by her maid's stillness, though. Poor gal, who interrupted their conversation a moment ago with the bee. Was she afraid she'd done something wrong? Thinking of all the work she still had to do? Or was she just enjoying the sunshine and wishing she could stay out longer?

Olivia knew servants weren't supposed to mingle, and she didn't want to get her maid in trouble, so she bit back the questions and began walking again. A right turn, a left turn, another dead end.

She glanced at the roofline and the windows, not sure how they would help her, but perhaps if she kept working her way in that direction . . . Back to the junction, and this time she turned the other way.

"Do you want help?" His voice held no teasing, just a bit of surprise.

"No." A smile tugged at her mouth, and she looked up at him from under her bonnet brim. "This is fun!"

Langley's brows rose a fraction. "You like a challenge?"

"Yes." She thought about what she had done with her life, about starting her own business, and ignored the pang of loss. That other world would have to take care of itself until she got back. Instead, she turned her attention back to the maze, and measured where she was in the windows looking down at her.

Another turn, another guess, and another lift of the brows in the man walking quietly beside her. Olivia knew she was on the right track. It took longer than she wanted, and a few more wrong turns and backtracking, but finally light came not just from overhead, but brightness from ahead lit the walls as well.

"Very good." Langley patted her hand, still tucked in his elbow. "You impress me."

The compliment warmed her and sent a flutter along her skin, lifting her spirits, wiping away the worries of earlier. "Thank you. I would love to do it again, until I get it memorized myself."

He stopped within sight of the exit, and turned to face her fully. Her hand fell away from its temporary home on his arm. "I think we can do that. If you wander through it again, I will stay with you until I am certain you will come to no harm in it."

"I can always yell. Someone will hear me and come."

His forehead furrowed with a sudden frown. "They will do you no good if they cannot find you. No, I think it best that I continue to accompany you until I am confident you will be safe."

Olivia didn't argue. The thought of him with her was actually exciting. Intriguing.

"Do you want to go back inside? Or would you dare to risk the doctor's scolding and walk around the house?"

"I would love to walk further. The maze was fun, but you have to admit, it isn't the same as real exercise."

They walked out of the maze; Langley kept his pace slow, to accommodate her supposedly healing body, she was certain. "Odd that you speak of exercise. Women usually do not, at least not as men do. We fence and study pugilism, ride and jump fences, and all manner of sport. Most women find dancing exercise enough."

She could hardly challenge him on that. America was renowned for its overweight population. In this time, she wondered what women were even permitted to do.

Most of the women she knew back home—*home, that thought again*—loved exercise and enjoyed a daily jog, One couldn't live in Minnesota, surrounded by lakes, creeks and rivers, not to mention hundreds of miles of bike and walking trails, and not enjoy some kind of exercise. Even the winter didn't stop people from getting out, and she had her own favorite winter activities.

Would she be back in time to ski?

"You must let me know if you feel weak." He paused as they neared the corner of the house, the pebbled drive poking through her soft shoes. "Dr. Reed will undoubtedly scold me soundly for this."

Olivia looked up at him. His gaze was steady, but his brows puckered, no doubt in second thoughts. "I'm fine. Truly. I really want to walk. The fresh air feels wonderful. You have no idea how good it smells." She took a deep breath. No exhaust, no scent of hot road with the lingering bitterness of rubber tires worn into it. As she lifted her gaze to the blueness overhead, she knew no jet contrails had left their own pollution there yet, and felt a pang of sadness for the destruction yet to come.

"If you are certain."

She felt his gaze on her, and hoped her bonnet brim hid her expression. He must not have seen anything that worried him because his pace never faltered.

Miles wondered if he was making a mistake. Take a potential spy for a stroll about the countryside? Let her get the lay of the land?

But he would not take the offer back, and this might be for the best. Her face, her very manner, was so open that if anything triggered a memory, he would see it. Feel it in her hand on his arm, see it in her bright eyes and pink cheeks, at the moment flushed with her victory.

A pretty face framed by her borrowed bonnet, wisps of her vibrant hair escaping the sides. Very attractive, indeed, the perfect lure for someone trying to find a British traitor.

So he stayed where he stood and looked down at her head, waiting for her reaction.

"The land is flatter than I thought it would be." Miss Underwood sounded disappointed as she slid her hand away from his elbow. It felt like a rejection, but he had no control over the land he inherited. She looked up at him, a faint furrow between her eyes. "I always thought of England as rolling green hills."

Miles pulled his gaze away from hers, looked over the fence that barely reached his waist. "I assure you, there are hills aplenty." He pointed at the distant trees on the opposite side of the road. "Beyond the windbreak over there, the land begins to roll. My ancestors claimed this bit because it was flat and would be easy to put a house this size on it. Or so the family legend goes."

"Oh." She reached out and ran a finger along the tips of the fence. "Why do you have the fence so close to the house? Wouldn't it make more sense to put it on the other side of your yard? You know, as a barrier? To say, this is my property, keep off?"

He chuckled. "Rumor has it that at some time in the past, a carriage and four broke loose when dropping off guests at the door and raced across the lawn, tearing up all the grass. No one remembers what spooked them, but once the damage to the ground was fixed, the fence went up to keep it from happening again." He motioned to where the drive and its white barrier took a bend. "When we reach the gate, we can walk across the lawn, if you wish."

She looked down at her shoes, and then back up. "I don't know if my shoes are up to it."

He knew he should not look at her feet, but his eyes refused to obey. Her delicate footwear peeked out from her hem. "Perhaps you had trunks in the ship, and your missing gowns and shoes are there. Did you bring half-boots?"

She gave him a blank look. "Half boots?"

"Perhaps they are called something else in your country." And perhaps she could not remember what she packed. At some point she would slip, and he would learn what he needed. "Once we reach the gate, the grass should cause less damage than the stones."

"Then by all means, let's walk across the grass." The words were light with a smile.

He pulled his gaze from the tips of her feet back to her face, where the color looked good, her cheeks tinted pink to match the gown he was becoming heartily tired of, her lips were equally rosy, soft and curved, inviting . . . He pulled his mind from that alluring mouth, and forced himself to concentrate on her health.

No trace of the pallor lingered. Her eyes sparkled with delight.

Who would have thought a walk across his lawn held such appeal?

Beware, he told himself. *Spy or not, this woman is dangerous.*

CHAPTER 24

Olivia turned around to check on Clara. She caught the maid at the very moment of blowing a breath upward to cool her forehead. One hand pulled her bodice away from her waist. The fabric had already begun to darken with sweat.

Poor gal. Such a pretty young woman to be stuck in an ugly gown of heavy fabric, and clunky shoes on her feet. Did she want to wander the countryside? Servant or not, she had the right to her own wishes. "Clara, do you want to go inside?"

Clara immediately let go of her bodice and shook her head. "No, I like the fresh air. I'd rather go with you."

Her host looked down in surprise. "Even if we are in sight of the house, it is still best that you have your maid. We have enough worries about explaining your presence here without throwing the conventions of proper behavior aside."

He continued his steady pace down the gravel drive, and Olivia immediately envied her maid those ugly shoes. Her own were no more durable than a pair of slippers, and the pebbles beneath her feet left their imprint with every step. Langley might well have to replace them. Still, she refused to miss this opportunity.

So she stepped with care, watched the stony path beneath her feet, and hoped they would reach the gate soon.

Thin furrows marked the drive, not much wider than a bicycle tire but with edges sharp enough to scrape the rocks.

Carriage wheels, she knew, and had to resist the urge to kneel down and run her fingers along the tracks.

More marks scarred the gravel, faint large ovals that had to be horse hooves. They must have been left by the doctor's carriage, since that was the only vehicle of any kind she had seen since arriving.

And just like that, her mind was back to the men in the office. If they had come on horses, they certainly would not have ridden boldly in front of the house. The horses must have been left a distance away. She thought of the road just the other side of the swath of green. Would they have dared tie horses to the trees that dotted it? Or would they have come the other way, sneaking up from behind the house, creeping around those little buildings with the roofs she had seen?

She was glad she had warned Langley, even though he plainly did not believe her. She would keep her eyes and ears open. One of the men belonged to the house in some way. If she heard his voice, she would report him.

Which would be easier said than done, she knew. But she had to be here for a reason, and that was the only thing that presented itself.

"You are quiet."

His voice startled her, and Olivia knew he felt the flinch. "My feet hurt. I don't think these shoes are going to last. I might have to walk around in stocking feet."

"We are here." Langley stopped, lifted her hand from his arm, and unlatched the gate, then waved her through. "Grass, my lady." As she passed him, he said, "As far as getting you shoes, when you remember how you got here and the name of the ship, we can send for your luggage. No doubt any unclaimed trunks will only be kept for a short time. After that, we must expect the captain will sell them, but we will deal with that when the time comes."

Olivia ignored his subtle prying and stepped onto the grass with relief. "Oh, this is much better." She looked up at him and smiled. "I don't normally wear shoes like these. They are about as useless as shoes come."

He made no move to walk, just stood there in the grassy softness as if to let her feet rest and recover from the rocky drive. "Has your memory returned at all? Do you remember coming to my house, now that you have seen it from the outside?"

She scowled at him. "No, so if that is the only reason you brought me here, it is doomed to fail. I recognize nothing."

He gave slow shake of the head. "I had hoped something would be familiar. That is all." His eyes softened. "Would you not feel better if you remembered? Surely this must be frustrating for you as well, not knowing why you came, or even how you got here."

Olivia couldn't hold his gaze, just looked off into space. The lie sat heavily on her conscience, but she had no choice except to let it stand. "I can't deny that, but I have to accept that the memories likely won't come back. I could let myself stay frustrated, or I can enjoy my time here."

Enjoy my time here. Where did that thought come from? But she had to admit, in an odd sort of way, she was beginning to have fun.

"I should send for Dr. Reed, but I know not when he can

come. I am hardly qualified to determine if you are as recovered as you seem. I can guess what he will say when he finds out I have let you wander about my property so soon after being ill."

She looked at him, and saw the concern in his eyes. "Blame it all on me. You gave me the choice, and I wanted to walk. I feel fine, I promise you."

"Well, I will see that we walk with care and I will not let you overdo." His gaze trapped her own and Olivia could only stare and wonder what he was thinking. He held out his arm, and she slipped her hand through the elbow's crook easily. "You will let me know if the ground causes more pain, will you not?"

"Of course, but you don't have to worry." Olivia looked down at the rich green lawn beneath her. "You don't cut the grass short. It makes an excellent carpet."

He looked over the grassy expanse with obvious pride. "I have servants who take care of it, but it is a time-consuming chore and they have plenty of other work to keep them busy." She felt him shift and knew he was looking down. "Let us walk."

He started across the green swath, keeping his steps short to accommodate her own. "We have something to discuss." His voice was flat.

A chill settled on her, at odds with the sun.

"You know you cannot stay in my house any longer."

She had known it was going to be bad, and stopped, pulling her arm away from his and whirling on him. "I have nowhere else to go! You aren't going to throw me out into the street, are you?" Her hands closed into fists, catching her gown and giving her something to hold on to.

He pulled himself as upright as a soldier, and glared down at her. "What kind of man do you think I am? I would never throw a woman into the street." A stillness came over him, and his eyes went dark. He opened his mouth, just to shut it again, before clearing his throat. "I hesitate to ask, but I must know. Is that why you left? Did some man abuse you?"

Olivia's mouth fell open. "No!" Then she took a breath to settle her voice. "No."

His face relaxed, his shoulders eased their stiffness. "Well then, if you were not running away, did you leave a man behind? Was someone courting you? Did the grief of leaving him cause the illness?"

It was a good thing they weren't walking, or she might have tripped. A laugh bubbled up, and burst out, "Heavens, no!"

"You answered that far too quickly."

Olivia blinked, and thought fast. "I remember everything before my journey."

"So you say. How can you be so certain? You admit your memory is faulty." He sighed. "We will have to hope nothing more is missing. I must ask, though, based on what you think you recall, whether a man has claim on your affections? I feel I must prepare for some man to track you here to England, anxious to bring you back home."

Olivia shook her head. "I guarantee that won't happen." The memory of her latest boyfriend slid in. They had been almost-dating, and she soon realized she liked it better when he didn't call. The dates—boring dinners listening to him talk about cars and his job at a computer programming firm making video games or some such thing—got further and further apart, much to her relief. She hadn't heard from him in weeks.

"And you are certain you are not wed."

"Positive."

"Why not? Most women of your class here are married in

their first season. Are there no men in your city you wish to marry?" His eyes still held hers. She couldn't read the expression there.

"Not so far. I decided I was better off alone than with the men I've met."

He chuckled. "A rather harsh condemnation of men."

She glanced away from that steady gaze. "Not *all* men, just the ones I knew." If she had met *this* man there . . .

"What about this sister of which you spoke? Did she find a man she could wed?"

Olivia looked up. "My sister is not married."

"Ah. So you cannot find a husband until she does." He held out his arm again, and looped her hand through, holding it in place, turned and started walking.

"No, it doesn't work that way in America. I don't have to wait for her. I just haven't found a man I could tolerate being married to. In my opinion, the good ones are already taken."

"Taken where?"

A snicker came from behind them, and Olivia smiled. "It means they are already married."

"Are you sure your sister would not mind if you marry before her?"

"Positive."

"You mentioned your parents are no longer living."

"Yes. Both are gone." Was he checking to see if her stories matched? Her father's death was still filled with complexity, love and anger, loss and resentment, unresolved after all these years. Renee had been his favorite, and Olivia often wondered if he had something against her red hair.

Mom's death was harder to deal with, because she had loved her mother unreservedly, and admired her for picking up and carrying on after losing her husband. Their marriage hadn't been the stuff of legend, but raising two squabbling daughters on her own couldn't have been easy. The life insurance hadn't paid off the house, and she'd gone to work, leaving Renee and herself to argue whenever she wasn't there to mediate.

He stopped, and turned to face her. "Miss Underwood? Did I say something wrong?"

She jolted back to the present. "Oh, no. Not at all."

He leaned closer, peering under the edge of her bonnet. "I did say the wrong thing. My apologies. I know what it is like to lose a parent. I should have suspected you would not be here unless you had nothing to keep you in America." He straightened, releasing her from the strength of his gaze.

"Thank you." She wasn't sure why she was thanking him, so added, "For being so understanding."

"Have you remembered whether your sister came as well?"

She was still jangled from the sudden reminder of grief and couldn't summon even a pretense of anger, couldn't prevaricate. "No. She did not come."

"Ah." His satisfaction landed like a punch to the gut. "I thought the memories would return."

CHAPTER 25

I THOUGHT THE MEMORIES WOULD RETURN. HE HAD DENIED plotting this walk as a way of prodding her supposedly forgotten memory. Well, he had not hidden his suspicions, and she could hardly blame him for them.

"That wasn't a real memory, not like those of my family. Those are part of myself. I couldn't forget them if I wanted to."

His gait faltered. "I lost my mother when I was five."

Olivia looked at him. When had her hand slipped from his elbow? They were facing each other, but his gaze was fixed on something far off in the distance. "I'm sorry. I was an adult when I lost my mother, and I miss her terribly, but at least I had her all those years when I was growing up. It must be very difficult to lose a mother so young."

He didn't take his gaze from the distance. "I had my father."

But something was off in his voice. Perhaps it was the sunshine, perhaps it was the fresh air. Perhaps it was because she was centuries away and nothing she said could hurt anyone now. Something pulled the story out. "I still haven't figured out how I feel about mine."

His gaze snapped back to her. "About him? Or about his death?"

"Both." She sighed. "My sister was his favorite. I always knew that, and she played on it constantly. Renee wanted a new"—she caught herself, and stopped in alarm. She had been about to say *bicycle*. Olivia thought fast—"gown, and she got it. I got her hand-me-downs. Always."

A smile tugged at his mouth. "She was the oldest. I understand that is one of the risks of being a younger child. I am the oldest, and was the only child for a good long time, so I never had that problem, but I heard it from my friends at Cambridge."

She stepped on his last words, knowing it was rude but unable to stop. "But it was worse than that. She was spoiled. Rotten." Olivia paused, but she had wanted to talk to someone, confide in someone, for so long. Mother had listened, but she could hardly take sides between her two daughters.

Langley tilted his head, the very posture of inviting her to continue. "Is that not the very feeling of every younger child? I have a younger sister, and she always thought *I* was the favored one." Again, that off note. "I was not, but I could never convince her. No doubt your own sister tried to reassure you that you were both loved the same."

A bitter laugh burst from Olivia's throat. "Not hardly! She wasn't even nice to me about it. She loved that Dad had a favorite and it was her, rubbed it in my face all the time. I wasn't as pretty as her, I wasn't as popular as her, she had better friends, and Dad always took her side. Even after he died, she still found ways to hurt me. In fact, the last day I was there, she was still poking fun at me, at my taste in furniture." Her brain finally stopped her mouth.

"Your American informality is slipping through. I call my own parent *Father*." But he did not smile, instead his gaze darkened and his eyes flicked away before coming back, the shadow gone. "Your sister said you were not as pretty as she? I have not met her but I already do not like her. Perhaps that is unfair of me, but she sounds like she was the jealous one. To be more beautiful than you, she must be a diamond of the first water."

"Oh!" Olivia didn't know what to say. *To be more beautiful than you.* He thought her beautiful? No one had ever said that to her. She felt her cheeks heat, the flush running down her neck and below her neckline.

Her face must match her hair now.

If he noticed, he said nothing, merely tucked her hand back into his elbow, and started them walking again. The grass was soft and springy beneath the thin soles, and her feet were grateful for the softness. Even the cool seeped through. No trees were nearby to give shade, and she understood his insisting on the bonnet. His own hat shaded his eyes and blocked their expression, but his brows were furrowed and frowning.

"My sister is thirteen years younger than myself. We get along quite well." He gave a hollow chuckle. "She recently married. At seventeen. I think her too young, but it is a good match, and she is happy not to be on the shelf. Her husband is older than her by ten years, so he can temper her youthful exuberance without crushing her spirit."

Olivia found her voice. "*On the shelf?* Seventeen is on the shelf?"

He shifted beneath her hand, and she felt him looking at her. "No, but in another year, she would be in her second season, and young girls feel that failing to secure a match in the first season is certain social failure. I realize that sounds awful to your independent American sensibilities, but that is the way of things here."

"So I am firmly on the shelf, then?"

He stopped, and turned to face her. Once again, her hand slipped from its home on his arm. "It is beyond the pale for a man to ask a woman her age. I would not insult you that way."

A strangled laugh came out. "A few minutes ago, I wouldn't have felt insulted to offer it. Now, when a seventeen-year-old considers eighteen on the shelf, I'm not sure I want to share it."

He smiled. "And I, as I said, will certainly not ask."

Olivia turned and studied the house in search of a new topic of conversation. The house was old; that was as apparent from the outside as from the inside. It was almost flat in front, brick with the same white stone edging the windows outside that she had noticed inside. A decorative cornice ran under the roof's slight overhang, and where the second and third floors started, a decorative banding of some kind ran along the house, but nothing projected out, no columns, no parapets, no balconies.

A shallow pediment added elegance to the double doorway, but there was no portico to offer protection from rain or sun. She counted the windows, six evenly spaced, providing light for the hallway and likely saving on candles for the sconces between the rooms.

And on the far right side as she faced it, there was the round tower that hid the servant's stairway. "I wondered what it looked like from the front. Now I know." She looked up at him. "It's a beautiful house. America has nothing this old. Modern houses lack the character of these old buildings. They don't put the time and effort into it. It's more, how fast can it go up."

Langley glanced at the house himself, and then gazed down at her. "America is a young country, and impatient. We are older, and have learned the value of taking our time."

A smile lifted one side of his mouth. "Besides, when this house was built, they had no choice. It was built about three hundred years ago by serfs and vassals; this was the only work they had, and they were happy to take their time and do it right. The longer it took, the more work they had." He pointed at the white blocks that marked the corners and edged the windows and the door. "The white edging is Bath limestone." He looked down at her. "You have heard of Bath, have you not?"

"Of course," she said. "I have never been there, but it has hot springs, doesn't it?"

He shook his head slowly. "You confuse me. You appear out of nowhere, you claim not to know where you are, and yet you have heard of Bath, and even know of the hot springs."

Olivia folded her arms. "America is not the moon, and we hear of all manner of cities from countries all over the place. I have heard of Berlin, and Paris, even St. Petersburg, Russia."

"I can tell that you are very well educated. I meant no disrespect." He looked over her head, and she could see his brain churning. Then his gaze came back to hers. "I find myself in a quandary. I am an unmarried man with no wife to give this situation respectability. My father's property adjoins mine, and he does have a wife but his lady is . . . indisposed right now."

Olivia wondered at that odd pause. What did he mean by indisposed? Was she sick? Did he mean she had something awful like cancer?

He faced her and took both of her hands. "I have given this much thought. For whatever reason you were left at my house, it is not advisable for you to remain here. If we get you to Father's house, and you take along your maid, perhaps we can salvage your reputation. Lady Stafford will be an excellent protection, and I believe you would be good for her."

He meant what he said before. He was sending her away. Olivia stared up at him. She had felt oddly safe. Plus, the iron was somewhere in this house. The thought of leaving the last place she had seen it, not to mention leaving her gracious, aggravating, appealing host, left a pit in her stomach.

For a moment, she didn't know what to say, just stared into those crystal eyes. "You are sending me away?"

"I must." His hands tightened on hers, and then he let them go. Olivia could hardly grab his hands again for support; instead, she clenched her fingers in her skirt as he continued. "You cannot stay here. I have jeopardized your reputation enough. Only the fact of your illness will protect you, but you are well enough now that we can no longer hide behind that. You simply must be someplace where you will have more than a maid to protect your name."

Protect her name. Nice of him to ignore the supposed spying, she thought with a flash of pain. "Ah, yes. The concept of chaperones."

"Is that not done in America?"

She shook her head. "No. Not where I live." But as his brow furrowed and his jaw tightened, Olivia hurried on, "You got me Clara. Surely that's what she's for."

The worry on his face didn't fade. His hands clenched and unclenched, as if grasping for something. "We already have pushed the bounds of propriety. My servants know of your presence, and reports of a woman in my house will spread. My father knows I am here. He will hear about you soon enough."

Langley stroked his jaw, then gave a strange shrug. "I gave orders to have your maid look about the house to see if my sister left any gowns. We often visited my grandparents when this was their house, and it is like her to leave something behind. I make no promises, she might have taken them away before she married, but it hurts nothing to look."

He turned to Clara. "Have you done that yet?"

Clara looked down. "No, my lord. I was about to when I was asked to bring the bonnet and shawl. I will check in the other rooms as soon as I get back in."

"You do that. I shall expect a report."

"Yes, my lord."

Olivia barely listened to the conversation, her mind stuck on where these potential gowns were coming from. His sister's clothes? That was awfully presumptuous. "Will she mind having a stranger wear her gowns?"

"I hardly think so. She got a whole trousseau upon her marriage. I hardly think she will even remember them." Another pause. "If they exist. If we cannot find anything here, I am certain there will be leftover gowns at my father's house. Surely Lady Stafford will have no objections to allowing you to borrow them until we find out what happened to your trunks."

Langley ran a hand through his hair. "This might all come to naught, but I have also sent for a dressmaker from Bristol." He paused. "Perhaps, in hindsight, that was not the best move. I should have sent for someone further away, but you cannot go about in only one gown. Either there will be some forgotten gowns here, or you will find some in my father's house. I will send the dressmaker there when she comes. I expect her soon."

He turned toward the house, extending his arm for her, and Olivia slipped her hand through it. They started back across the green lawn. How many times would she be able to do this?

He continued his conversation, and she was glad he didn't require a response. "I must see what I can find out about the ships that arrived in the last couple days."

He shifted, Olivia knew he was looking down at her, and she was grateful for the protection of the bonnet's brim. "It is best that it appears Lady Stafford is paying for your gowns. Your trunks might already have been sold." Then his voice took on a teasing smile. "Even if they are found safe, I have learned that a woman can never have too many gowns."

Olivia suddenly stepped out of one of her delicate shoes. "Hold up!"

He stopped while she worked it back on, grateful for the support of his arm. The smile remained in his voice. "I will also suggest Father send for the local cobbler. Cecelia's shoes might not fit. I also cannot be sure if she left behind anything sturdier than dancing slippers, but you surely need something to walk in."

Then they were through the gate. Langley latched it behind Clara, and they crunched back along the pebbled drive. When they reached the front door, he stopped and turned around. The sun was still high, and his hat brim cast a shadow over his eyes, but she thought she saw worry in them. "I asked earlier if you left a man behind, someone who wants to find you."

"Yes, you did, and I said no."

He took a deep breath. "I have been assuming you came here for a nefarious reason, to spy on my country. I should have worried equally if you came to save yourself from harm. You said you were not running from abuse, but was there something else? If I begin asking questions about the shipyards in Bristol, will I put you in any jeopardy?"

She reached out and touched his arm in a fleeting gesture. "No. I assure you, no one is chasing me. But . . ." How to tell him this? "Don't waste too much time on it. I don't think you'll find any ship."

The furrowed brow turned into a frown. "You have not been here long enough for it to go out to sea again. There has not been time to unload the cargo, let alone refill the ship for the return voyage." His spine stiffened, and she saw his shoulders tense again. "Did you come on a smuggler's boat, or were you rowed across from France? Perhaps taken ashore in a skiff?"

"No." *She wasn't supposed to remember!* Olivia hurried back into speech. "I don't know how I could have been."

"No ship, no rowboat, no skiff. How do you think you got here? There is no other way."

Olivia refused to blink, and forced herself to hold his harsh gaze. "I feel like I thought myself here. I remember my home in Minnesota, and the next thing I knew, I was in your room not even knowing where I was."

He gave a visible start. "*Thought* yourself here? Are you ill again? I must send for Edward right away." He looked over her shoulder and addressed Clara. "Take your mistress up to her room. Watch over her. Make certain she is not running a fever."

"I am feeling fine, honestly." Olivia swiveled from him to Clara. If he had looked shocked, Clara looked even more alarmed, all wide eyes and slack jaw. Even her skin had gone pale. "Clara? I really feel fine."

A sudden rush of red brought the color back to her maid's face. "I'll take her up."

Maid on one side, Langley on the other, Olivia felt like she was being marched like a prisoner up the few steps, through a door that had opened as if by magic until she saw the footman waiting beside it, into a short hallway, and from there into the long corridor.

"Get her into her bed," Langley ordered Clara, and waited as they started down the hall toward the turret with the stairs.

CHAPTER 26

CLARA CLOSED THE BEDROOM DOOR BEHIND THEM, AND JUST stood there, looking at it. Olivia didn't know what to say. Was her maid frightened? In this time, anyone would be scared to wait on a woman who claimed she could move across an ocean by thought alone.

She had been keeping this secret so tightly, and it had finally popped out. For herself, she was amazed she hadn't blurted out everything before. Keeping so much back was a testament to self-control. Or fear.

More fear than self-control.

She stood in silence, looking at the tense back of her maid, the tightness of Clara's shoulders, the bent head, and wondered which was the more scared.

A person out of time. Or a maid responsible for the care of a woman who claimed to cross an ocean by merely thinking it.

"Clara? I'm still me." She decided to use the tale they had spun. "I've been sick. I had no concept of time."

Clara turned around, and gave her a strange look. "Time.

How odd you should use that word. I've been wondering, and listening, and now I have to know." Her hands clenched at her sides, and Olivia watched her force them to relax.

"Ask me anything. I'll answer whatever I can."

Clara glanced around, and lurched for the dressing table, pulling out the small chair and flopping down on it as if her legs had suddenly lost the ability to stand. She looked up at Olivia, her dark eyes almost burning with some strange fear. "You told me you were from America. And so am I, just as I said." A strange strangled laugh burst out, one single gust. "I can't believe I'm going to ask this, but I have to know."

The room went quiet, except for the pulse Olivia could feel surging through her veins, pounding in her ears. What was going on with Clara? Was she the spy Langley was looking for? *Not Clara! Please, not Clara!*

She heard the maid take a deep breath, and Olivia made herself meet Clara's firm gaze. "This is going to sound ridiculous, I don't know how to ask, but . . . America *when?*"

"What?"

"What *year*, Miss Olivia? What *year* was it when you came?" Clara leaned forward, her eyes wide, her hands shaking, and high color on her oddly pale cheeks.

Olivia felt her own legs give way, and she sank onto the edge of the bed. "It was the future." She took her own breath. There was a limit to what she could say, even if what she thought might be happening was really true. "I'm from the future."

The tension washed out of Clara with such force that Olivia watched her shoulders relax, the stiffness leave her spine, the high color of her cheeks fade to normal, even saw her hands ease. "I thought so. I wondered if I was losing my mind. I kept hearing you say things that would make sense in my own time, but felt out of place here, even if you were from the America of this day."

Then Clara laughed, round and bubbling. She stumbled over to grab Olivia's hands, and dropped to her knees, almost in supplication. "So, future when? The world of speakeasies, the Depression and Prohibition, the world of black and white television, or the world of the Internet and cell phones?"

Olivia took a chance. "I'm from 2023."

"Oh, thank God." Clara laughed again. "Me, too. I'm from Minnesota. Where are you from?" She let go of Olivia's hands and clasped her own against her heart as if holding the excitement in.

Olivia realized she had done the same thing. Her heart thrummed against her palms. "Me, too! Oh, my goodness. Can this really be true?" She stared at Clara. "You are really from the future? I'm not alone?"

Clara's hands were still clasped against her chest. "I can't believe it! I have been all alone." Her voice broke, and she took a breath so shuddering that Olivia could hear it. "You have no idea how good it is to have you here!"

Then a thought came. "How long has it been for you?"

The smile faded from Clara's face. "Three months. Three very long months."

It was a good thing Olivia was sitting. The words came out in a whisper, *"Three months?"*

"Yeah."

Her voice came back, loud with dismay. "In the kitchen? Working as a maid?"

Clara nodded, and her hands dropped onto her knees as if too heavy to hold up any longer. "It hasn't been fun, let me tell you."

An ominous thought pricked Olivia with sharp edges. "How did you get here? What did you use?"

This time Clara actually laughed. "An antique iron. Can you believe it? I thought it was interesting, and my grandfather had an antique iron collection. He gave it to me when he died, and I thought the iron would make a nice addition. So I heated it up, and was using it, just for fun." She spread her hands to encompass the room. "I have all the antique irons I could imagine now, but I never thought I'd actually have to *use* them for real."

The ominous fear grew. "What did your iron look like?"

Clara smiled. "It was a nice old slug iron with a kind of swooping wooden handle, and this clever door on the back. I don't know how old it was—is—but I liked it. Until I was having fun with it and the next thing I knew, I was stuck here. I no sooner got here than that iron disappeared. I bet if it could have laughed all the way back to my real time, it would have."

Her throat went tight. "Do you think it only goes one way? That it dropped us here, and each time, it went back? That we're stuck here forever?"

Clara looked down at her hands as if remembering how hard they had worked, then back at Olivia. "I wondered."

"Because that sounds exactly like the iron that brought me here."

Clara nodded. "You kept asking for an iron, but I didn't want to believe that it could be the same one. Because if it did to you what it did to me, it's long gone. And we are both stuck here."

The image of Langley walking back from his room with her shoes and the iron that first day came back as clear as a photograph. "It didn't disappear right away for me. He had it

for a while after I got here. I know. I saw it. He said he was
going to hide it until he figured out if it's concealing some
spy information against England."

The distance between lady and maid was gone; they were
simply two women lost in time who needed each other.
Clara rubbed her forehead. "How long did you see it?"

"I don't know. A while at least. Fifteen minutes? Maybe
half an hour?"

Clara chewed her lip. "I never saw it after I arrived.
Where did he take it?"

"I suspect it's in his office. That's why I was in there.
Maybe it was just desperation on my part, but I was sure I
would be able to sense it if it was nearby. Unfortunately, I
didn't notice a thing. I'm still pretty sure that's where he put
it, but it's hidden somewhere. Maybe in his desk. All the
drawers are locked." She gave a weak smile. "I know. I tried
every single one."

"There are rumors of a secret safe in this place, but no
one knows where it is." Still on her knees, as if the strength
had not come back, Clara looked around the room. "This
house is centuries old. It was probably built in the Middle
Ages, and must have been in his family for all that time. Who
knows how old any safe would be, or even if it still works."

Olivia thought of that elegant office and his beautiful
desk, even the comfortable chair. Granted, furniture wasn't a
house, but if the house was built with the same care, she was
certain the safe—wherever it was—still worked as well.

She looked at Clara with new eyes. A fellow time-trav-
eler! It still didn't feel real. How many had the iron brought
over? "Do you think there are any others like us here?"

Clara shrugged. "If there are, I sure haven't met them yet.
But why here, and why now, and why the both of us?"

Olivia slipped off the bed, and sat on the floor in a puff of pink. "Does it mean anything? That's what I want to know. I wondered if I was supposed to change something that is about to happen." She leaned forward, and kept her voice low. "I overheard a plot that sounded like Langley's life is in danger. Is that why I was sent here?"

Clara sighed. "How would I fit in? Why me a maid, and you a lady?" She rolled off her knees and shifted on her bottom until she was sitting next to Olivia, turning her head to meet Olivia's gaze. "I'm just beyond happy to finally have someone that I can talk to about this and everything. I seriously thought I was going crazy."

"Me, too." As if pulled together by a magnet, the two women embraced each other. Olivia felt the shudders running through Clara's arms as they clung together. Was her own body shaking, too?

They let go, exhales coming from each pair of lungs in harmony. Olivia leaned against the bed frame, Clara slumping against it, too.

The room was quiet for a minute. Clara broke the silence first. "I can't worry about that now. We have to find the iron; that's all I can think. And hope against hope that if it didn't go back right away, it might still be here." She gave Olivia a long look. "Don't be surprised if it has already vanished, though. Maybe it went back without me because it misfired. Maybe I was supposed to go back with it, but something went wrong. It might have gone back again."

The thought that she would be stuck here had occurred to Olivia. Clara's theory that the iron might be broken was not what she wanted to hear. "What are we going to do?"

Clara rose. "For now, I guess we just play out the roles we were assigned. I stay your maid, and you find a way to break through his resistance and get him to *tell you where that iron is!*" She added the last bit with such emphasis that Olivia could almost see the exclamation point hovering in the air.

Another thought occurred to her. "As a maid, you can probably go in and out of rooms without needing permission. Do you think you can do some snooping, see if you can find it?"

Clara shook her head. "Being a maid isn't that simple. I only go where I'm assigned, and since becoming your maid, I'm expected to stay up here most of the time, going between your room and mine. I can head down and do some pressing, but as we both know, I have to use the irons I'm given, and none of them are the one we want."

"Well, how about offering to help any maid that's assigned to clean his office? I'm positive he put it there because it's the most private room and I know he took it downstairs, but those are my only clues."

Clara thought for a moment, then nodded. "I'll try. For now, I expect his Lordship will ask if you had a chance to rest."

"I'm too wired to sleep."

"Of course you are." Clara grinned. "Going to bed is the solution for everything here. I'm supposed to see if there are any left-over gowns from his sister. If you want to peek around, all the bedrooms are on this floor so if we hear him coming, you can scurry back to your room and sit on the bed."

"That sounds like fun." Olivia scrunched up her gown to roll onto her knees, braced herself on the bed, and pulled herself up. Nothing tore, she didn't hear any stitches pop. One less worry.

Clara got herself up with much less effort, a testament

both to the durability of her clothes and how long she'd been here. A strange look passed over her face. Sadness, maybe?

"Is something wrong, Clara?"

"No. Just . . . I know we're both in a pickle, but I'm sure glad you're here."

Olivia smiled. "So am I."

CHAPTER 27

THEY PEEKED OUT THE DOOR INTO THE HALLWAY, BRIGHT FROM the daylight through the windows that lined it. Clara slipped out and beckoned Olivia to follow. She whispered, "Wait for a moment. I'm going to open the servants' door, so if any of them show up, we'll have warning. They'll tell Langley, so be prepared to move fast."

They hurried past the first door—"That's my room. It's really small, but it's convenient."—and Clara opened the second one, which Olivia knew held the white stone stairs, and left it barely ajar. "If Langley comes up, this is the way he'll take. I've never seen him go up the servants' tower. If we leave it ajar, we'll hear him coming. Unfortunately, the rest of the bedrooms are on the other side of these stairs, so if we have to hurry back, we're taking a risk, but I don't expect he'll come up. He's sure you'll be sleeping, so he won't want to wake you."

Olivia sighed with relief. "I hadn't thought of that." Then she smiled. "This is my first chance to explore where I can actually see what I'm looking at. Last night doesn't count. I was so scared I could hardly think, and it was really dark." But even with Clara as a guide, she couldn't bring herself to reach for the door handle. It just felt too . . . intrusive. She stopped a few feet away, feeling very much the interloper.

But Clara had been a maid, and she opened the door like someone who had been in and out dozens of times. Perhaps she had.

She strode in and looked back at Olivia. "Come on. We don't have all day."

Olivia peeked in. This room was smaller than the one she had been given, but not by much. Where hers was yellow, this one was done in an elegant blue-and-white rose pattern. Very like Wedgewood in color, she thought. She didn't know much about Wedgewood, but she did know it was old, and maybe the same age as this room's design.

A big bed with a canopy just like hers sat in the middle of the left side, the blue comforter woven with the same design as the wall. On the wall, facing them, near the window, a washstand stood, the bowl inset in a hole cut for that purpose instead of sitting on top. And, on the right, the ubiquitous armoire.

In the far corner, a three-panel room divider sporting the same fabric as the rest of the room was clearly meant to hide the commode.

Olivia didn't have to look because she had the same setup in her room.

The wood was whitewashed, no doubt to keep everything matching. *Go figure*, she thought with sudden humor, *interior decorating was going strong even in this time.*

Maybe if she couldn't get back, she could find work in her own field. After all, house staging was interior decorating, just with a different end goal.

But the thought wiped away the humor. She dragged her attention away from the furniture and back to Clara.

Hands on hips, Clara stared fixedly at the armoire. "We clean these rooms occasionally, but I have never looked in that thing." She looked over at Olivia. "Here goes nothing."

Marching over, she pulled open the doors, and gasped. "Oh my goodness! Will you look at that?" She whirled around. "Olivia, come look!"

But Olivia could see right from where she stood. "Gowns!" She met Clara's wide eyes. "How many do you think there are?"

Clara reached in and did a quick count. "Four. Only four, but with your own gown, that gives you five." Her hand ran lightly across the fabrics and delicately touched the embroidery. "Aren't they gorgeous?" A faint smile twitched her lips. "Look at all the pastels. And white lace on everything."

Olivia looked from the gowns to Clara, a new worry tormenting her. They were all so light-colored, soft blue, a barely-there pink, and two mostly white ones. Even in her own time, keeping those colors clean would frighten her. "What if I spill something on them? His sister will hate me!"

But Clara only chuckled. "He wouldn't have offered them to you if he worried about them being damaged. Besides, he did say she got a whole new wardrobe when she got married, and probably doesn't remember them." Her smile faded. "They have some interesting ways of removing stains in this time. No bleach, but what they use works surprisingly well. It burns the skin, but it cleans the clothes."

She plucked the first gown off the hook, and Olivia stepped over to start at the other side. Two gowns apiece.

They were lighter than they looked, and she was positive she felt the slide of silk from at least one of them. "We better get back to my room. We might hear him coming, but then again—"

"We might not." Clara finished her sentence. "Let's get back."

When they passed the door to the white staircase, Clara nudged it shut with her foot. "No sense giving him any clues. I'll have to close the servants' door, too, but then we'll have a clothes party."

Clara dashed out to take care of the tower door, and was back in less than a minute. "There! Everything is shipshape again." She looked down at the pile of gowns on the bed and pointed at the top one, small embroidered yellow flowers on a white background. "We need to see if they fit. They won't do you any good if they're too small. Turn around, and I'll get you out of this one."

Olivia turned her back, and felt Clara unbutton as efficiently as she had buttoned it this morning. The gown loosened, slid off the shoulders, and with a shrug and a tug from Clara, landed on the floor.

"This is too gorgeous to leave it lying about." Clara picked it up and spread it out on the bed, then lifted the embroidered confection. She slid her arm inside with care, separating the layers inch by inch, treating it as if it might break.

It felt strange to be waited on, but Olivia had to admit that these clothes weren't made for women who dressed themselves. She looked at Clara's gown, "And to think your clothes are sewn specifically for women without maids."

"I've heard of maids getting their mistresses' cast off gowns," Clara said as she lifted the fabric mass over Olivia's head and guided her arms into the tiny sleeve openings, "but I have no idea how they manage."

With a rustle, the embroidered gown slid over her head, falling down to settle in a float of silk. A tug here, a fluff there, and it was ready to be laced. Clara's fingers were busy again in the back, and Olivia felt the gown tightening.

Clara kept a running monologue as she tugged and pulled. "It's lovely. And in such good shape. Just imagine it in a museum. I hope it survives. Maybe if we get back, I'll check if I can find it somewhere." She adjusted the shoulders again. "I think it's a perfect fit. You and his sister must be about the same size."

Olivia watched the bodice tighten across her breasts. A teenage girl was generally not fully developed, unlike herself, and the cleavage got deeper and deeper as the gown molded itself to her. "Oh, boy. Just what I need. A gown from a flat-chested girl."

Clara stepped around in front and tilted her head from one side to the other, giving it a thorough once-over. "It's not as revealing as you think. Even the housekeeper has a low neckline, but she's forever tucking fichus in it." She looked up. "I'll go back in a bit and see if there are any hiding in the drawers we didn't check. There might be more shoes, too."

In addition to the chill drifting over her chest, her ankles felt the cold, too. Clara noticed. "It's a bit short, though. Not too much, but a bit." She met Olivia's gaze, and there was a wistfulness in her eyes. "It would be the perfect length for me. I'm not as tall as you."

"You're smaller on top, too." Olivia looked at the pile on the bed. "I wish I could loan you a couple. It's so unfair."

"Agreed." Clara looked down at her faded blue dress, and the stained apron over it, then back at Olivia. "But we're stuck with the roles we have to play."

Play. "I know!" Olivia stepped back to the bed, looked over the colors, and plucked the pink one out. "You'll look fabulous in this, with your dark hair and pale skin. If we're having a dress-up party, by all means, let's have fun."

Clara's gaze went from Olivia to the bed's bounty, and back. A brief hesitation, probably from the three months of subservience, and then her twenty-first century self came back. "Okay. I think I will!"

W ithout a clock, they had no idea how much time had passed, but Clara was on the last gown when a solid rap came on the door. They stared at each other, and Olivia suspected her own eyes were as wide as Clara's. "I'll get it. You hide behind the door."

With Clara hidden—and hopefully not visible in the seam between the door and the jamb—Olivia pulled the door open. A footman stood there, not Lord Langley, and the tension slipped away. "Yes?"

"The physician has arrived. You are supposed to come down."

The doctor! She had completely forgotten that Langley thought she was suffering from some desperate brain fever. Olivia glanced down at the yellow-embroidered silk gown, the only one she had tried on, and refused to peek at Clara, lest she give the maid's presence away. "Tell him I will be down in a moment."

"I am supposed to take you."

"One moment." Olivia shut the door and whirled to Clara, wearing the last of the borrowed gowns. In a rushed whisper, she said, "Let's get you out of this. You're sure you can get into your own clothes?"

"Yes." Clara's eyes were wide as she whirled around. "Get it off me! I need to get your hair done before you leave. We're both a mess, but I can get away with it. You can't."

Olivia glanced over at the small mirror, and her eyes

went as wide as Clara's. "How long do you think he will give me?" Her fingers flew down the buttons, and the gown slipped off her friend's shoulders.

Clara stood in her chemise, looking very like a modern woman wearing an oversized t-shirt. "Sit." She pointed at the chair. As soon as Olivia was seated, Clara reached around her, and picked up the brush. "Now for your hair, and then down to the doctor."

CHAPTER 28

OLIVIA SAW THE FOOTMAN WAITING BY THE OFFICE AS SHE
stepped out of the stairway. He gave a nod and tapped at the
office door.

"Come in," that familiar deep voice called.

The footman opened the door, and she stepped inside.
The door clicked shut behind her. Langley was there, of
course, standing behind the desk, but he wasn't alone. A
vaguely familiar man leaned against it with the air of
someone welcome in the house. He took one look at her and
straightened.

She was the focus of two interested pairs of eyes. And
then the recognition gelled. The visitor was the man beside
the carriage when she first looked out the window right after
she regained consciousness.

He seemed smaller to her now, standing close to Langley,
and yet she could see he wasn't a small man by any means,
probably six feet. His clothes were more simple than Langley's, a white cravat in a simple bow, black trousers, a plain

black coat, and—in what looked like his lone bit of elegance —black riding boots that went up to his knees.

He was also more pale, less substantial, slender where Langley was built, with fair hair and friendly hazel eyes compared to Langley's vivid black hair and striking gray eyes that turned silver in a certain light. Eyes that seemed to read Olivia's thoughts, eyes that penetrated her secrets . . .

Eyes that noticed the new gown, and the ample cleavage on display, and glittered with approval. "My friend, Dr. Edward Reed," her host said, his voice giving away nothing of what his eyes said. "The nosiest, most interfering doctor in England."

The doctor merely grinned. "You should be grateful that I am."

"I didn't do so badly in doctoring her myself. As you see, she is well enough to stroll about my house." Langley came around the desk and stopped next to Dr. Reed.

The doctor laughed outright. "Fine. Take the credit. I will check her and make sure she is as well as she looks."

Dr. Reed fixed his gaze on her, the expression there only professional, thank goodness. One man admiring her breasts was all she could take right now. "Well, he is right about one thing. You look much better. After only a day. Remarkable. But he also tells me you remember nothing of the journey?"

Olivia answered honestly. "No. Nothing." There hadn't been a journey, just a flash.

"Interesting." He looked over at Langley. "I have heard of amnesia, even talked to a doctor who thought he had a case. She does not fit the true definition of the word. 'Tis a new concept, scarcely recognized for fifty years. 'Tis common enough for people to lose track of the days when they are that ill, but that is not the same thing at all." He turned back to Olivia. "I can only assume you were most ill on the journey. You were still insensible when I first saw you, so I can at least diagnose that part of it."

He came forward, crossing the room slowly. "I, however, will not go on appearances alone." He stopped beside her and turned to give Langley a pointed look. "We cannot have you lapsing back into unconsciousness."

The two men were obviously good friends, because Langley merely grinned at him. "I told you, she appears to be in fine fettle."

"It's a good thing I am the doctor here, and not you." Dr. Reed scowled at his friend, but it held no anger. "'Tis too early to make that determination. Now I must ask you to leave. Send in her maid, if you will."

Langley strolled to the door. "Her maid will not be hard to find."

With the master of the house gone, the doctor turned his shrewd gaze on Olivia. She met his look with her own and tried not to quail. *Dare she trust him with the truth?*

"I know not what kind of illness could make one sick for the entire course of a sea voyage, most people recover after a time, but we are constantly learning new things. Is there anything you want to tell me, anything you dared not say with him around?"

I'm from the future, I don't belong here, and I need to go home. He would clap her into an asylum. At the very least, jerk her out of his friend's house and lock her into a shed somewhere. Still, his gaze was warm and exuded caring, and she suddenly realized he might be the answer to one of her quandaries. "There is something."

"I assure you, whatever you tell me will remain in confidence. I do not spread reports about my patients around the countryside."

Olivia started shaking her head before he was halfway

through. "No, it's not about me. It's about Langley." She leaned forward. "The first day I was here, I overheard two men outside my room. They didn't know I was there, so they talked freely."

She glanced over her shoulder at the door, then lowered her voice. "I think somebody is planning to kill Langley, and one of his servants is in on it. Is there anyone who would inherit this place if he dies?"

Dr. Reed gave her a strange look, part amusement, part disbelief, very much the man indulging the silly woman's delirium. "What exactly did you hear? Are you sure it was real? After being so ill, your mind might be playing tricks on you."

"Trust me, it was real." He didn't need to know about the men in the office. Besides, she'd already confessed that part, and revived her host's suspicions. Still, he had been kind enough to send for the doctor, who had access to the homes in the area and might hear confidences from both servants and the upper class.

Olivia took a breath. "Someone with some connection to someone in this house is in need of money, and wanted the servant to find something he could sell. But the truly frightening thing was that apparently Langley has diamond buttons, and the man who needs money said it was a wonder he made it here without being killed for them."

The amusement vanished. "The buttons. Those—" He took a sharp breath. "You must tell Langley. He needs to know."

Before she had the chance to tell him she already had and that he didn't believe her, a tap on the door made both of them jump and turn. Reed smiled at her. "Your maid, of course." With a raise of the voice, he called, "Yes, come in."

Clara stepped in, back in the faded blue gown and stained apron. "His lordship said I was wanted in here."

"Yes, thank you. You may stand there." Reed pointed to a spot near the closest shelves, and turned back to Olivia. "Shall we begin? I must get on with the rest of my calls, delightful as our conversation has been."

He pulled over Langley's great chair without any seeming effort, and seated himself very close. Olivia noticed his black bag and wondered what 1811 medical horror might be hiding in it. She had to force herself not to glance over at Clara.

With narrowed eyes, he gave her face the most severe scrutiny she had ever had. "Your color is good. You were pale before. Your pupils are the same size, so I doubt you suffered a blow to the head. Have you had any headaches?"

"No." She didn't want to mention the early dizziness, since she was now convinced it was a side effect of time travel. She should have asked Clara if she went through the same thing when she first arrived. But Dr. Reed was still asking questions, and she had to pull her attention back.

"Any nausea? How are you eating? Does it stay down? Sore throat?" It went on like that, the questions so ordinary she didn't know what he expected to discern from them, but then, this was long before anything remotely resembling modern medicine. He wouldn't be pulling a medical flashlight out of his bag to check her eyes or throat, and she highly doubted he'd test her reflexes with rubber hammers.

But then he slid closer and put his head on her chest. Olivia braced her hands against his shoulders and gave a solid push. "Excuse me! What are you doing?"

Dr. Reed plucked her hands from his shoulders and pressed them together between his own. At least he straightened in his chair, giving her back her own personal space, not that he'd know what that was. "I need to listen to your lungs and check your heart. Surely you have had a doctor's exam before?"

"Well, yes, but not like this."

"Perhaps you do not remember." She watched the excitement surface in his eyes, a medical mystery in his care. "Perhaps you might be missing more of your memory than you realized. This may be true amnesia. We know so little about it. I shall have to make a note. Someone might have heard of a case like this."

"I assure you, I do remember going to the doctor. They used a"—she caught herself—"something to listen to my lungs and heart."

His brows furrowed. "I wish I could see your American doctors' tools." He set her hands back down on her knees. "Now that you know what I am doing, might I continue?"

Olivia nodded. Even knowing, it still felt strange, like an invasion, to feel his hair against her skin. She reminded herself that Reed, with his head resting so snugly on her chest, was a doctor, but she felt a blush heat her face, anyway. With a sudden start, she realized he could see right down her bodice! She peeked down at him, wondering if he had his eyes open, but all she saw was his sandy hair.

Her heart must have done something, because he pressed his ear harder against her. Olivia looked away, only to find herself gazing into the laughing eyes of Clara.

Dr. Reed finally leaned back, patted her shoulder, and stood. "Your lungs are clear. You have no fever, and you certainly appear to have your strength back. 'Tis nice to see you so recovered." He glanced over at Clara, and looked back down at Olivia. "I believe your hearing is also perfect. The only lingering concern is the inconvenience of your loss of memory, but that does not seem to have affected your health in any way."

"It's not that big an inconvenience," she blurted.

"No, I see you are functioning well enough here." He picked up his medical bag, which he had not opened, so the medical horrors remained a mystery. "I will give Langley the good news. He must be about to come bursting in. If you feel any strange symptoms, tell him, and insist he send for me right away." He gave her an elegant bow, nodded at Clara, and headed for the door.

As soon as it shut behind him, Clara burst into giggles. "Olivia, if you could have seen your face! You looked like you thought he was going to . . . to . . . well, I don't know, but if your eyes could have fallen out, they would have."

She was off again. The blush that had faded with the doctor's matter-of-fact manner came back, warming her face, but there was no malice in her new friend's laughter, and the giggles were so infectious that Olivia started laughing with her.

"So what is your verdict?" Miles straightened from the wall, and started Edward toward the outer door. He knew how busy his friend was, but they had much to discuss. He trusted Edward as a doctor, but he was also a man, and Cecelia's gowns fit his guest entirely too well, and showed far too much.

Edward did not seem in a hurry, if his leisurely pace was any indication. "Rather a miraculous recovery, I must say. I do think that her memory loss is real. She acted as if she had never been treated by a doctor before, yet she assured me she has been. She insists American doctors have tools for listening to hearts and lungs." Edward's brows furrowed, and he glanced around the empty hall, then leaned closer. "Her reaction when I pressed my ear to her chest was so startling, I am convinced no one had ever done that before."

The sudden jealousy that spiked through Miles caught him off guard. Edward would have to lean against Miss Underwood to hear. More than lean against her. He would have put his head on her chest. In Cecelia's gowns—Miles recognized the one she had on, so clearly the maid had found something—there was nothing of her beauty, or her bosom, to hide.

Perhaps loaning her his sister's gowns had not been the best idea. But what else could he do?

Edward had done that very examination yesterday when he checked Miss Olivia, and Miles recalled watching without a flicker of emotion. But then, yesterday he had not talked to Miss Underwood, had not eaten with her, had not walked through the maze with her.

The man is a doctor, Miles reminded himself now, but the irritation still lingered.

He forced his mind back to the subject of Olivia's memory, or lack of it, and willed his fists to relax. "Interesting. I noticed that what she remembers is very clear, and what she has forgotten seems related to the journey."

Edward's hand clamped on his arm, and he dragged Miles to a stop. "I think we are far enough away to speak freely. There is something you should know. Miss Underwood says that on her first day here, she overheard some men in the hallway outside her room, and she is convinced they were discussing your murder, and that you are in danger. Even worse, she knows about the diamond buttons."

Miles frowned. "I already knew. She did tell me. As far as those buttons, you know of their existence because I told you. Have you heard word about them from anyone else? Has the tale reached this area?"

"No, but you give me far more credit than I deserve. I hear a great many things, but people have secrets even from me."

Miles shook his head. "If you hear so much as a whisper, you must tell me."

"Agreed. So what do you say about this tale of the men in the hallway, and the threat against your life?"

Miles sighed. "I cannot decide what to make of it. I do not like to speak ill of a woman, but there can be nefarious reasons why she knows about the buttons. I find the tale of two men very suspicious, even more than her knowing about those blasted buttons."

He lowered his voice. "What do you think, now that you have spoken to her? Is she a thief? A spy? Delusional? Or a combination of the three?"

"She did not mention them in the context of theft. Rather, she was frightened that they might get you killed. And that by the unknown man who mentioned them. I believe she knew nothing about them until she heard the conversation."

"You are too trusting, Edward."

"And you, my friend, were not there. Miss Underwood is frightened for you. You are too quick to brush aside this threat to yourself."

Miles smiled. "We both know that she was not fully herself. Still might not be herself." To be sure, she had come after him with a poker and the iron when he came into that room unexpectedly, but he doubted he was in any danger from her. More likely, she just wanted to protect herself.

Whatever she thought she had overheard, she probably

misunderstood, and assigned some nefarious meaning to it. "So what do you want me to do?"

"I can hardly give you advice in matters of intrigue. I am merely a doctor. I deal with illness of the body. I do not look concern myself with plots and conspiracies. I can tell you that regardless of what caused her illness, she is recovered, but to what extent I cannot say. What you do with her from here on in, I only request that you not stress her too much. I do not want to deal with a relapse after she has come this far. Can you agree with that?"

"Certainly, but this has left me with a decision to make. She cannot stay here. She has been here too long already, but with your reputation as a physician, and requiring that she rest, plus with her now having her own maid, I believe we can cover over the past day." Miles folded his arms. "However, now that she is well, she simply cannot stay here. I plan to bring her to my father's house, and I have told her as much."

Edward nodded. "I have been thinking the same. Not that she go to your father's house, but that for her own sake, she cannot stay here." A smile lifted one side of his mouth. "If you will forgive me, if word gets out that she spent even one day here unchaperoned, she will be ruined."

Miles raised an eyebrow. "Even with all the mitigating circumstances? Would people find it more acceptable if I threw an ill woman out onto the road?"

"Having a maid will help. Thank goodness you assigned one quickly." Edward's smile was gone. "Even so, maid or not, I recommend you get her to your father's house as soon as possible."

"I will do that tomorrow. I want her to have another day to recover. I can hardly bring a woman who might suffer a relapse to my father." He took a deep breath. "There is another issue at stake here. If she was sent to get information for her country, bringing her to Father's house will put her in the very spot they wished to have her." A prickle of dread slithered down his spine. "And Lady Stafford is with child." Miles raised an eyebrow. "I would not share something so personal, but I assume you already know."

Edward did smile. "Of course I know."

"I would not risk Lady Stafford's health, nor that of the child." That dread grew tighter, and moved to his chest. "I could not live with myself if that happened."

"Your father is experienced, and has a staff much larger than you have here. He can alert them to be on the watch, and even assign a guard to your mother." Edward did a rare thing; he clapped a hand on Miles's shoulder. "I worry more about you. Remember, Miss Underwood was left at your house, not at the earl's."

Miles felt his brow furrow as he thought it over. His friend was right. Miss Underwood had been left here. Whoever did it had to know the connection between him and his father, maybe even knew the committees on which Father sat.

He thought out loud. "She does not remember her assignment, but they cannot know that. I have wondered if she might be in as much danger as she fears for me. And you are right, Father has a large and devoted staff."

The dread in his stomach eased. He looked at Edward. "Everyone might well be better off if she is there. Whoever brought her here will come here, and I will be waiting."

I t wasn't until Edward was on his way to his next patient that Miles realized he had forgotten to say anything about the iron with the clever door that could hide all manner of papers, and the iron chunk inside that might have something hidden on it. He would find some way to examine it, scrub it clean, or heat it up, something.

If there was a message etched in its surface, he would find it.

CHAPTER 29

THE FOOTMAN—SHE DIDN'T KNOW WHICH ONE, BUT AT LEAST she and Clara got to leave the office—ushered them out. "Ye're ta leave now. 'Is Lordship will be needin' th' room."

She and Clara stood there after the footman closed the door behind them with a sharp *snick*, and Olivia wondered if Clara had the same urge to wander around as she did. Wandering might be harder than she thought, because Langley and the doctor stood halfway down the hall and right by the outside door, talking in low tones. The doctor didn't say she had to go back to her bed, but Langley might disagree.

She looked at Clara. "I refuse to hide in my room. Can I walk around the house? I'm to go to his father's house, but I don't know exactly when. What would happen if I popped into the kitchen? I want to see as much of the house as I can." Not that she knew what she would do with the knowledge, but maybe, just maybe, she would go home. It would be one piece of knowledge to use in her work.

"Oh, you don't want to go down there." Clara wrinkled

her nose. "Actually, *I* don't want to go there. I have spent more than enough time in that room."

"I'm sorry. I should have thought of that." Olivia glanced back down the hall at the two men, and wished she could eavesdrop. As long as the men were in conference, though, she and Clara had time to get better acquainted. "What about going back outside? Is there some way to sneak out without having to push those guys aside?"

Clara nodded. "There's a door between the dining room and the kitchen that leads outside."

They strolled the few feet down the hall with casual movements that shouldn't attract attention, then ducked into a narrow hallway with a single door on either side halfway down, and one at the end. A fanlight above an elegantly narrow door of carved dark wood showed the sunlight. The dark wood matched the wood in the rest of the house.

Did a whole forest give its life for this house?

Olivia smelled the fragrance of cooking food, meat and something lighter, potato-like, as they moved toward the outer door. They slipped past the kitchen without being noticed, and made it outside with no one calling them back. Olivia took another breath of the wonderful, clean air. "I have to say, Minneapolis never smelled this good."

Clara sighed. "True, but there are a lot of things I miss from the future. Electricity, running water, television, and the time to sit and watch it."

Olivia thought about her gown. "Permanent press. Dry cleaning."

"Gas stoves. Dishwashers." Clara's thoughts seemed stuck on her last few months, and the work she had done.

Olivia tried to lighten things. "Computers. Cars. Cell phones."

"Vacuum cleaners. Washers and dryers." Then, as if she

thought back to their earlier discussion, Clara added with vigor, "Flush toilets."

Olivia looked at Clara with renewed sympathy. "It really has been hard for you here, hasn't it?"

Clara lifted her hands. The nicks and redness hadn't faded in the short day she had been a lady's maid. "It has. I was a waitress in our own time, so it's not like I didn't know about hard work, but nothing like this. And my hands"—she held them up—"they are so chapped from the harsh soap and being in water that they burn most of the time. I wish I had the lotions I used to use. I thought my hands got chapped in the winter. That was nothing compared to now!"

Olivia looked at Clara's hands. "There must be some lotion around. I didn't look in my room. I haven't needed it" —yet, she added silently—"but if I find any, you can have it." She had another thought. "Did you check in the room where we found the gowns? I bet Langley's sister had all kinds of stuff to make her beautiful."

"No doubt," Clara said dryly. "But if it was that good, wouldn't she have taken it with her when she got married? Besides, this was the grandparents' house. She didn't live here, as I understand. She just visited."

"It's still worth a check." Olivia decided she would search her room, and if anything remotely looked like it might help, she would give it to Clara. "Let's get out of sight of the house. I want to find out everything you know since you got here, and all about your previous life, and tell you about mine. Maybe the clue to why we're here is in there."

Clara's brows raised as she thought over the idea. "You know, you might be right. I want to get back so bad!" Her voice broke, and the very air went still, as if in sympathy. "I had a boyfriend, and I am so afraid of what he's going through." A sniff, and she wiped her nose on her sleeve, then gave a wet chuckle. "One more thing I miss. I miss tissues."

Olivia tried to smile, but her lips didn't curve. A smile would lighten the mood, but Clara was right. What would a boyfriend think if his girlfriend suddenly disappeared? And was gone this long?

Might he even be arrested and charged with her murder? Fear clamped around her own heart. She had been gone less than two days. No one would worry yet.

Soon. But not yet. It was still the weekend. It would take a lot longer than that for Renee to call.

Unless she wanted to taunt Olivia about buying the iron.

That stupid iron! Everything came back to it.

"We need to plan." She gave Clara's sleeve a tug, not knowing where they would go, but just needing to get out of sight and sound of the windows. "Do you think Langley will change his mind about taking me to his father? What will I do if he was serious? He said their lands adjoin but from the size of the property, that could mean anything. I might be stranded miles away!"

"I don't know how far apart the houses are, but I'd be surprised if it's too far to walk."

"Still, walking is a slow way to get from one place to another."

Clara's mouth curved. "You could always try running. Did you ever do jogging?"

Olivia gave Clara what she hoped was a mock glare. "No. First things first, we have to find the iron, and if I am even a little bit away"—the very thought frightened Olivia. Not be in the same house?—"If you have to stay behind, can you keep an eye out for it? Do you ever get close enough to hear him talk to his valet, or his butler? Surely one of them knows where it is. I don't know how you will get word to me, but surely it's possible."

"Shhh!" Clara's head whipped toward the windows they were passing. "It's open."

They hurried past, and Olivia kept an eye on it until they reached the edge of the house. No figures passed it, no voices rumbled through the air, but that didn't mean no one was there.

Clara stopped at the corner of the house. "I know where we can skulk. Let's go around the maze and talk on the far side." Her pace picked up. Olivia clutched her skirt and tried to keep up.

The maze was large from the inside but it felt even larger from the outside, and with her corset digging in, Olivia soon was out of breath, but she kept going. When they slipped around the far corner, she felt about to collapse. She made it, then bent over and wrapped her arms around her waist to ease the stitch in her side as she fought for air.

Clara put a hand on her shoulder. "I'm sorry, I forgot about your corset. I can do anything I need to in mine."

After a moment, her lungs no longer felt like they were going to seize up, and Olivia managed to get a full breath. "It's not the corset. Exactly." She thought while she took another, easier breath. "Well, maybe it is. It's different from a bra, that's for sure." She looked down at her gown. "It's the clothes, too, and having to hold up the gown when I run."

Clara chuckled. "At least we landed in this time. I recall that corsets get worse in the future." She sobered. "To get back to what we were talking about, maids can slip in and out of rooms, but we're supposed to be as efficient and silent as possible. I'd never get away with stretching out a task just to eavesdrop."

They looked at each other, and Olivia saw the same frus-

tration in Clara's eyes that churned in herself. She leaned
carefully against the hedge, and stared out past the short
lawn to the trees that bordered it. Her heart burned with
unease. "Why are we here?" She turned her head to look at
Clara. "Don't you think there's supposed to be some purpose
to Time sending us back? I suspect I came to stop Langley's
murder, but how can I do that if I'm not even here? And the
guy who threatened him isn't going to do anything until
Langley heads back to London. He will not take me with
him, and it probably wouldn't matter if he did. I don't know
who the killer is!"

An appalling thought occurred to her. "Am I supposed to
die here, in the past?"

Clara gasped. "Don't say that! There has to be a way to get
back!" She whirled in front of Olivia, her hands in fists at her
side. "I want to go back! I *need* to go back! I want to marry
my boyfriend!"

Olivia didn't dare bring up the thought that he might
already be under arrest, and the police be searching for her
body. "I just have my sister. I suppose she might worry." That
was unfair. "No, she *will* worry, but we don't keep in touch
like sisters should, and we always fight. Both of my parents
are dead, so at least I don't have to worry about them
worrying about me."

"I was a server, and can't figure out what good that does
to Time." She gave a little hiccup that could have been a
stifled sob. Olivia waited, and Clara finally continued in a
wavering voice, "I have my parents and my brothers, and my
sister-in-law is expecting a baby. I haven't let myself think
about them. It would have driven me crazy."

"I have my own business, but it's just a small one. I stage
houses for sale, and I have contracts with a few realtors. I
hire people to help me; it's too much for me to do alone, but

if I don't go back, the other stagers will gladly snap up my accounts."

They looked at each other. Clara was the one to put it in words. "So why are we here?"

Neither had an answer. The silence stretched long. Birds chirped nearby, no doubt relaxed by their quiet.

Clara stared into the nearby woods and heaved a wet sigh. "You might have some kind of answer because of what you overheard, but I have nothing. No higher purpose. I wish I'd never come, and I want to go back."

For some odd reason, Olivia couldn't make her mouth echo the same words.

CHAPTER 30

MILES LOOKED AT THE METAL CHUNK HE HAD SLID FROM THE iron's back. It did not look like much, but that might be its very purpose. It was surprisingly heavy, about the size of a small woman's hand, and tapered to match the iron's outer shell since it had to fit inside.

It did not look like it held secrets, but the surface was rough enough that it could hide letters. He walked over to the window and tilted it, side to side, up and down, but nothing jumped out at him.

If there was something etched on the surface, it was well disguised.

He looked down at his desk. Dark flecks liberally covered it. Ashes. What a perfect way to disguise an imprint.

He pulled the bell, and within a minute, Denton appeared. "Yes, my lord?"

"Give this to a maid and have her wash it clean." He held it out, and Denton's eyes went wide.

"That? You want that cleaned?" His gaze went from the

iron chunk to Miles and back. He did not ask the question, but it was there in his eyes: *why wash a dirty piece of metal?*

Miles handed it over, wincing as he saw the soot rub off on Denton's white gloves. No doubt this was the last time his butler would wear that particular pair. They would likely wind up in the fireplace.

Before Denton got to the doorway, he turned around. "I forgot to mention. Your man of affairs is coming up the drive."

Miles looked at the calendar and blinked. He had totally lost track of the days. It was a good thing Crofts was precise. "Very well. Send him in when he arrives."

Denton gave a quick bow and walked out, leaving the door open. Miles smiled. That oversight might be because his gloves were too dirty now, or perhaps he thought since Crofts was nearly here, the door would no sooner be closed than have to be opened again.

Miles would bet on the dirty gloves.

In the meantime, he had his own hands to wash. If he hurried, he could make it to his bedroom, use the washbasin, and make it back before Crofts was ushered in.

H e stepped out of the stairway door just as the footman announced his man of affairs.

They walked to the office together; Miles opened the door, and walked in. Crofts closed it behind them, and remained by it. "What is this I overheard about footmen guarding your office? Or did I mis-hear?" He took a quick breath. "I assure you, I do not listen at keyholes. The footmen were talking right in front of me as I was let in. Perhaps they thought I should know?"

"It is just as well that you do. We had at least one intruder in this office a night ago." Miles left the iron's shell sitting on his desk, and took his seat. His man of affairs was trustworthy, but Miles did not want anyone knowing about the safe behind the books. His grandfather had kept it a secret, and he felt honor-bound to do the same. Let the man wonder why he had an iron on his desk. "Sit down, man. No need to stand on ceremony."

Crofts hesitated a moment, then walked in and sat in the guest chair, his normal place when not standing beside the desk as they went over figures together, and set the pouch on the floor. "So, was anything missing?"

"No. Nothing."

"Who do you think the intruder was? One of the servants?"

Miles looked at the iron, and leaned back in his chair. "I believe in my staff, but if it was any of them, I will find out and he will immediately be dismissed."

"You believe the intruder to be a man?"

"I make no predictions either way." He ruled out Miss Underwood as being the one who opened his globe, despite —or perhaps because—of her admitting being here.

He sighed. Crofts was likely to find out anyway. The whole staff knew. Why not him? "You might as well hear the rest. Someone left a young woman in my house. She had been ill. No one saw her come, no one will admit to seeing whoever smuggled her in, but somehow she is here. I am surprised you have not heard the tale yet."

"I do not live in the house, and the servants do not consider me one of them. They might talk around me, but they do not confide in me. But, if you forgive my forwardness, having a woman in your house is not a surprise."

Miles gave him a mock scowl. "My reputation precedes me, I see."

His man of affairs chuckled. "You would be surprised how effectively the servants carry stories. So," his brows rose, "what does this woman look like? A diamond of the first water? Or is she an antidote?"

"Not a diamond, but definitely someone worth a second look." He felt his mouth curve, and stiffened it. "She has red hair. Hardly someone who could pass unnoticed in a crowd."

"Red hair?" Crofts smiled. "This hardly surprises me. I have not known you to discriminate." His eyes widened. "Are you saying she is the one who was in this office? Why not throw her out, or turn her over to the magistrate? She could have slipped in herself, and the tale about her being ill might be fustian. Perhaps she is trying to force you into marriage? I pay your bills; I know you are worth the attempt."

The scowl became real. "I have assigned her a maid. I took care of that immediately, so there is no question of compromise."

"A man can as easily be hanged for a sheep as for a lamb, you know."

"I am not easy to trap."

"That is so." Crofts motioned to the iron, and his mouth twitched in another smile. "A rather odd decoration for your desk, is it not? What are you doing with an iron? Are the servants not pressing your clothes properly and you wish a go at it yourself?"

Miles shook his head. "It is a strange decoration, but it is not mine. It belongs to this woman. She tried to drop it on my head the first day, so I have removed it from her possession. She insists she was not trying to kill me, but better to be safe. I know she was in this office the night of the intruders, searching for it."

He touched the smooth wooden handle. "As you can see, she did not find it. I thought it might hold secrets, but so far have found nothing. Why it means so much to her, I do not know."

Crofts had gone pale, or maybe it was the daylight through the window. "So you have solved the problem of who was in your office. If you know this woman was in here, you have the answer to your intruder."

"No, I think not. She said there were others in here, but she hid."

"Others? We are back to your servants, then." His eyes flicked around the room. "So where is this woman now? And why have you allowed her to stay?"

"I put her in the room next to mine. There is no connecting door, and her maid has the next room, close enough to hear anything going on." Miles sighed. "As for why I have allowed her to stay, you are aware that America is rattling their swords and begging for a war. She is American, my father is in the House of Lords, and I am his son. I find the sudden appearance of an American in my house to be suspicious. And now this iron," he tapped it with a finger, "has a perfect hiding place. I think this uninvited woman was left here by mistake."

Crofts's hands were tight on the chair. "So you think you have a spy in your house?"

"Yes, and no. You see, she cannot remember the journey, and claims—most believably—not to know why she is here. Edward suspects she lost part of her memory from the fever. As she recovers, I expect it to return. And then there is her red hair. Someone could assume that it is so distinctive no one would suspect her. After all, are not spies supposed to blend in?"

"And you have her in the room next door? If she got into

your office, why did you not hear her moving about? One might think you should have heard something and caught her in the act."

Miles nodded. "Interesting, is it not, that she could slip about the house without a soul being aware? She might remember her training without realizing she remembers, and being able to slip in and out without being caught must be one of the first things spies are taught."

Crofts still looked pale. "And you are certain she was the one in your office?"

"She is working hard to get the iron from me. She brings it up at every opportunity. Yes, she was in my office."

Crofts's hands unclenched from the chair's arms, and he reached down for the pouch. "I have been collecting rents, and paid a few of the bills. Would you like to go over them?"

Miles nodded. "By all means. I need something to distract me."

Miles watched Crofts ride away. The accounts were all in order, and instructions had been given regarding some of the tenants' repairs.

But he may have made a mistake in telling his servant about Miss Underwood. Not that a simple man of affairs was a threat, but it would not do to have the word spread about.

Still, if one could not confide in one's trusted advisor, what was the point of employing him?

For now, he had to find the maid that was scrubbing the iron's chunk and give it a good examination. A pity he did not use a quizzing glass. That would give him a better look, but he had good vision so no doubt he saw well enough to find letters.

He pulled the bell and waited until Denton appeared. "Has the maid finished cleaning that iron piece?"

"I believe it is as clean as it will get, my lord."

"Bring it here, then." Before Denton could leave, he added, "Make sure it is thoroughly dried."

"Indeed." Denton disappeared, his boots clicking on the wooden floor.

Miles tapped his fingers together while he waited, a subtle releasing of the tension. Within a few minutes, he would either find out what had brought Miss Underwood here, what the purpose of her mission was . . .

. . . **O**r he would not. Miles glared at the dull grey slug, as Denton informed him the maid had called it. No letters. No markings, nothing that could pass as a code at all.

Just rough, pitted metal.

It had no message printed into its surface. It was nothing more than a slug of iron.

So what made it so important to her? Why did Miss Underwood want it so badly?

He opened the little door at the back of iron, slid the now-clean slug inside, and closed it. It would go back into the hidden safe, and she would go to his father's house.

He would warn Father to keep an eye on her. Miles could not shake the feeling that it held the clue to her mysterious and forgotten journey here. If she came to get it, he would not give up until he had the answers he sought.

CHAPTER 31

CROFTS DROPPED THE KNOCKER AGAINST THE PLATE WITH more force than necessary and waited for the response. What the man would do with this information, he did not know, but their plans were in jeopardy.

When they talked in the hall for their initial meeting, she must have been in a nearby room. And the night they slipped into the office? *She said there were others in here, but she hid,* Langley had said. Where? How much did the woman hear?

They needed to learn more about her. He gave the bell another turn.

The door opened so quickly he didn't have time to let go and nearly fell as his arm was grabbed and he was pulled inside. The door slammed shut behind them.

Stewart let go and stood there, fury in every line, his hands on his hips. "I told you not to contact me, that I would contact you. This had better be important. What brings you here?"

"We have been overheard." Crofts had a gratifying surge of power that mingled with the dread in his stomach after hearing where this woman had been while they talked. The combination left him somewhat nauseous.

"What nonsense is this?" Stewart folded his arms and leaned against the wall by the door. The hallway was dim; the glass in the door had not been cleaned in some time. The man always seemed to have darkness around him, with his thick brown hair and his swarthy skin, but in the dim hallway, even the air felt heavy. "You are not becoming a hysterical woman on me, are you?"

"Never." Crofts tried to stand taller. A pity the other man had inherited the Stewart height. "I was in the office with the reports, and Langley told me there is a woman in the house. He does not know where she came from, but he suspects someone left her there instead of at his father's house."

"Tell me how this matters to us." Stewart shoved the half-open door at his left wide and strode in, then turned around in front of the cold fireplace on the wall directly opposite, his arms folded again, his legs braced apart, his very stance a threat. "Well?"

Crofts followed him in. This room was as dimly lit as the hallway, but he realized only one candle was burning in a sconce on the wall. The room was sparsely furnished, merely two chairs and a settee, with a low table in the centre. While the furniture was of good quality, it had seen better days, as had the rug on the floor. The edges were fraying, and Crofts feared he might catch his boots on the loose strands and make a fool of himself.

Stewart must be low on funds, if this is all he could afford.

"What makes this woman important? Langley has women all the time, although it is not like him to flaunt one so close to his father's land."

Crofts jerked his attention back to the matter. "The

woman was put in the room next to his own." If the situation were not so dire, he would have smiled. "And you do recall where we had our first discussion?"

"There was no one around at our first meeting. You chose that spot yourself."

The urge to smile faded. Typical of Stewart to remember that, and turn the blame around. "We share the responsibility. You never looked in any of the rooms, either. And you are the one who selected the meeting place. If you recall, I seldom go farther than the office. So why did you not think to check and make sure the rooms were empty?"

Stewart leaned forward, enough that the spittle from his mouth landed on Crofts's hands. "I am not even supposed to be in the area, I told you that, if you recall. Why would I go announcing my presence?"

Crofts brushed his hands on his breeches, but he could still feel the spatter there. "It is much worse. She was in the office while we were there!"

That caught Stewart's attention. "That is impossible!"

Crofts shifted his feet, and felt the heat crawl up his face. "It must be true. Langley said the woman told him there were others."

Stewart remained still; Crofts could almost feel him thinking. "I heard and saw no one. Where did she hide? Behind the curtains? Under the desk?"

"I don't know, but how else could she have known we were there?"

Stewart's gaze went some place in the distance, and he was quiet for a moment. A carriage rattled past, and boys shouted something in the street. Then those cold eyes came back to Crofts. "She must have been gone before we got there, but this changes things. If she was hiding in another room, waiting to slip away or even to come in, she already knows too much. You have to find out who she is. We need to get her out of the way."

"We will know her by her hair. It is red, and Langley used the word distinctive.".

"Red hair." Stewart drummed his fingers on the wall beside him. "Can you go back with some tenant complaint? Does anyone have a hole in the roof that you forgot to mention? If you arrive unexpectedly, you might catch a glimpse of the woman."

Crofts shook his head. "We covered all that. He would begin to doubt my memory." He bit back the smug smile, knowing how this was going to irritate the other man. "Come out of hiding and pay your cousin a visit. He would hardly suspect you if you are out and about publicly, making no move to hide your presence. You have friends all over England. Surely one of them lives near enough to make a handy excuse for being in the area. He will invite you in, and you can see her."

Stewart's brows came down and his mouth opened, only to shut again. His forehead smoothed. "I wonder if the woman is beautiful despite the hair, since he wants to keep her close."

"I would not know. I have not seen her." Crofts watched the man closely. "We left something undone, some clue, or he never would have believed her word."

Stewart took a step closer, and it was all Crofts could do not to back up. "You are supposed to know how things are done in that house. What did you forget?"

"Nothing! I even closed the globe!" Hope flickered, and Crofts wondered if maybe, just maybe, Stewart would call this off.

Although he would miss the money. Stewart's taunts about his worn clothes and tattered boots still rankled. There was always the risk when dealing with thieves that bargains would be broken, forgotten, or ignored.

His own family had a name once. He could have had stature and a place in the *ton* if his father hadn't—he shoved the old pain aside. It was too late for that. What his father did was done, but it had been a long, hard life making his own way.

Now, as he watched the other man clench and unclench his hands, and purse his lips while his brow furrowed and his breathing came harsh, Crofts knew he had his own choices to face. Either stay with Stewart, regain something of his family's wealth and run to America or even New South Wales, live as the gentleman he could have been, or have Stewart give up the plan altogether and continue working as he had been, watching someone else get richer and richer while he did the bowing and scraping.

He could not even skim anything off the top of the rents with Langley as he had done before with earlier employers. The man was too smart. And unlike most lords, he paid attention to his finances and what went on in his estate. Crofts believed Langley was honestly interested in the people in the village. He was also quick with mathematics and had a mind like a steel trap.

The first time he had made a deliberate mistake to see how far he could go, Langley had noticed immediately, and he had been forced to pass it off as a mistake. He had been doubly careful after that, knowing that his position could hang by a single error.

If his other employers had been as careful, he might have found himself in Newgate.

Or in the Australian penal colony.

And to think, he might wind up there, anyway. It was all

in the circumstances: go of his own free will, or go on a convict ship.

The room was quiet. Stewart walked over to the closed curtains and touched the seam between the two panels. He looked at the dark green fabric and, with a vicious jerk, yanked them apart. Dust puffed out, catching the glow as the sun poured in, bright and jarring. "Very well. I will stop in, tell him I left London to escape the clutches of a woman. That he would believe. I will find a way to meet this red-haired ladybird of his. I know how to read females. If she recognizes me, I will know it."

"And then what? You can hardly pull out a pistol and do away with her on the spot." Crofts surprised himself with his temerity.

Stewart turned to Crofts. "I can do better than that. Let Miles think this woman in his house is a thief. If he put her in the room next to his, there must be something between them. I can easily find an excuse to get away from his company while I am there. He has cufflinks and cravat pins, all kinds of things that I can take. I will get back in the amount of time he would expect me to use the necessary and have no problem conversing for the next hour."

He paused. A smile creased his mouth, and chilled Crofts, as if ice slid down his spine. Stewart's teeth glinted in the candlelight. "No, not an hour. I hardly think either of us could tolerate the other's presence for that long. I rather enjoy the thought of talking to him while my pockets are full of his trinkets. As soon as I see her and know who to watch for, it should be easy enough to do away with her. Women like to stroll about the gardens, and there are enough trees about the place that I can easily hide until I find my opportunity."

He actually rubbed his hands together. The man was

enjoying this! In an even, unruffled voice, Stewart continued with his plan. "After she is out of the way, I will stay in the vicinity long enough to enjoy watching him agonize about a faithless woman who stole his worldly goods and fled. Once I have amused myself sufficiently, I will pack up my ill-gotten gains and leave, supposedly back to London, and wait for him on the road. If I hurry back to London once the deed is done, I can join the mourners as they grieve over the death of such a promising and wealthy man. Then I will, with great humility, take my position as the next heir."

He stroked his chin. "Even better, I will then own the gems I appropriated. There will be no need to sell them. The theft will have served its purpose admirably."

He smiled at Crofts, something chilling in that curve of the lips. "And of course, you will be well paid for your help."

Crofts's stomach gave another lurch. It was one thing to talk idly about Langley possibly being waylaid by a highwayman for his own foolishness. It was quite another to listen to someone plot Langley's death, and that of the poor unknown woman, and detail the schemes so blithely.

But he was in too deep now.

CHAPTER 32

Olivia strolled down the hallway, looking at the portraits Langley had not managed to show her on their first jaunt. Clara was in the bedroom, doing some stitching on the gowns where the seams were coming loose.

No doubt one of the reasons why Cecelia had left them in her grandparents' house.

She had been in this world for parts of three days, and the other world, her real world, didn't intrude as often as it should have.

But then, how could it, when she was living in a world she had only seen in movies?

Olivia gave herself a mental shake and moved on to the next portrait. She had recognized occasional features that—assuming the artist got the proportions right—had passed down to the man she was coming to know.

She ignored the portrait of his many-times-great grand-father with the stern, unyielding face, but she hadn't seen the poor, long-suffering wife. Not that she would know which woman on the wall was her, but Langley did say he kept them far apart.

Just outside the library, a portrait caught her attention, a woman with the same Elizabethan ruff as the man. This must be the wife. Portraits from this time period seemed to have the same shape, the same painting style, as if the same artist had done them, the expressions all looked flat to her inexperienced eye, but despite that, she thought she saw a deep sadness there that had not been in the others.

"So you found the wife."

Olivia jumped and whirled around. Langley stood there in his topcoat over a full suit, with shiny black boots that went up to his knees.

It must be time to leave. Behind him, at the far end of the hallway, she glimpsed the closed office door, but her gaze slid easily back to his face.

Unless she was imaging it, his face held a shadow of the sadness in the portrait next to her.

No, that wasn't likely. It must be the odd lighting in the hallway, with the sconces snuffed for the daytime, and the windows now sliding into shadow as the sun passed midday's peak.

She pretended he wasn't dressed for travel, and pointed at the woman. "So this is the woman with the awful husband?"

He glanced over and back to her. "Yes. That is the one." He took a breath, deeper than seemed necessary. "I told your maid to pack the gowns for both of you, as well as whatever else you found that you can use. It is time to take you to my father's house. He knows you are coming."

His gaze drifted down to her exposed bodice, then snapped back to her face. "My father is quite conservative. Your maid should find you a shawl. I will send some men to Bristol to see if there are any unclaimed trunks by the docks." A faint twinkle lightened his sober face. "Despite what you remember, or rather, what you cannot remember, one does not fly across the sea. There has to be something left, if we can get to it before it is sold."

Olivia caught her hand before it clapped over the cleavage his sister's gown left, and clenched her fingers in the skirt, the embroidered flowers nubby against her palms.

He held out his arm, and Olivia hesitated before she slid her hand into the curve. Was this the last time she did that with him?

Thumps came from the end of the hallway, and the door to the round tower opened. A footman backed out, his hands gripping the handle of a good-sized wooden trunk. A second footman followed, holding the other end. Clara came through behind them, gave a quick curtsey—likely to Langley—and followed them out the door.

Langley looked down at Olivia. She felt the movement, and lifted her head to meet his gaze. "Your gowns. And you should know, I am sending your maid with you." He touched her hand where it rested on his arm, and his fingers seemed to linger a moment longer than necessary. "I thought it would help if she joined you there. You prefer a maid you already know, do you not?"

Relief and fear tangled inside Olivia. Clara being with her, someone she could talk freely to, an actual friend, but that left no one here to find the iron.

She knew better than to bring it up again. Instead, she smiled. "I like that. Thank you."

They started down the hallway, and again, she had the odd feeling that he was reluctant, that they were walking slower than normal.

She was right. He stopped abruptly and sighed. "We must discuss this before we get in the carriage. I do not want this spread about among the servants. They know too much already."

He turned to face her. Olivia's hand slid away, and she clasped her fingers together to give them something to do, since they—silly things—seemed to miss their place on his arm. "I should tell you about my father. The earl. Things are not always . . . comfortable between us. He thinks I am a rakehell, and always puts the worst possible meaning on what I do. I fear this may cause you difficulties, as he will almost certainly assume you are as deficient in character as he believes I am. I will have to tell him the situation. He will no doubt fill you with tales of my escapades, but I promise you, I am not the scoundrel he thinks."

She wanted to touch him, just a simple gesture of reassurance, but put her support in her voice instead. "I know that."

Despite the dimness in the hallway, there was enough daylight for her to see his eyes. An odd vulnerability swirled in the crystal depths. "You do? On such short acquaintance?"

"Of course. A real scoundrel would have taken advantage of my . . . incapacity. You did nothing to hurt me. Instead, you sent for the doctor, and got me Clara." She gestured toward the carriage visible in the window, the carriage he was going to put her in shortly. "And now you're even taking me someplace where my reputation will be pristine. If you feel you must defend yourself, I promise I'll listen and believe your version."

He looked out the window, and back. "Father's biggest annoyance right now is a set of diamond buttons I have. They are not even mine, but belong to a young man who nearly lost his entire family's estate in foolish gambling."

"So how did you get the diamonds? Did he lose them gambling with you?"

He straightened, or else his spine stiffened at an intended

insult, because he seemed to be taller. "No, certainly not! I took his place in another game, and got his lands back, but I forced him to give me something to keep safe for his mother and sisters."

His hand clenched on his thigh, Olivia saw it in her peripheral vision while her eyes stayed on his. "I still fear he will find the gaming hells too much of a draw, and lose everything when I am not around to rescue him a second time. Those diamonds are to guarantee his mother and sisters a future."

Now he had her entire attention. "You are a very nice man."

It might have been a trick of the shadows, but she thought his cheeks got a stain of high color.

Langley could blush?

He cleared his throat. "That is kind of you to say, but I will wait and see if you feel the same way after you have spent some time with my father."

She folded her arms. "If he can't see your good qualities, I don't know if I will like being there. And if he judges me just because I landed here—and not of my own free will—then I'm not sure I want to go."

His brows came down, and he tapped his fingers against his thigh. "You do know that it is impossible to stay at my house any longer? You must see that. Surely your country cannot be so lost to all proprieties."

"I think each country must have their own set of values. What works for one might not work at all for another." *And what was expected in one era was considered old-fashioned in another.* She changed the subject. "So how far away is this place?"

"We will be there in moments. Our lands adjoin." His mouth lifted in a smile. "An easy journey on a horse, and not even a bad one on foot. It's a mere morning's walk." Then he sobered. "You realize I will have to tell him the whole story. That you are from America, that you cannot remember anything after getting on the ship, and that someone might be threatening you."

Threatening you. Not herself, Olivia thought, but him. Two fears now: distance from the iron, and distance from the real threat: the person who wanted *him* dead.

Apparently, her face gave nothing away, because he held out his arm again. "Shall we go?"

There was nothing to do. Somehow, she would have to find a way to save his life. The time tunnel had brought her to his house, and the only conclusion she came to was that she was supposed to overhear the threat. More than overhear, though. She was supposed to do something about it.

Right now, Langley was still safe, and still waiting to take her out to the carriage. Olivia slid her hand back into the crook of his elbow—where she wanted it to be anyway—and they headed for the door and the patient footman waiting there.

They walked outside together, and Olivia thrust down the surge of dismay as the door shut behind them. The other footmen had hefted the trunk onto the back and was done lashing it down.

Clara had a shawl over her arm and that same straw bonnet. As Olivia and Langley drew near, she unfolded the shawl, and held it out one-handed. *My father is quite conservative.* Olivia let go of Langley's arm and let her friend drape it over her shoulders. Then the bonnet was tied.

They were ready to leave.

Perhaps not ready, but the last delay was gone.

A small set of steps had been put in place. Clara glanced at Langley, and he gestured her in. She climbed up, the carriage rocking with each step, and crossed to the far side, bracing herself against the shifting of the box with one hand on the roof before sitting tight against the wall, looking half alarmed and half excited.

For herself, he did no simple gesture toward the fragile-looking vehicle as he had with Clara. Instead, Langley held out a hand, and Olivia put her own in his. He held it steady, a strong hand for a strong man. The carriage did the same rocking thing as she climbed up, her skirt in one hand, clutching his fingers with the other.

As she settled in place next to Clara, the words he had said minutes ago came back. *He will assume you are as deficient in character as he believes I am.* It was bad enough that she was going to be miles away from the iron, but even worse, now she was going to be around someone who thought she was, at a minimum, unacceptable.

Langley settled on the seat opposite, the steps were folded back up, the driver shut the door, and the carriage lurched into motion.

CHAPTER 33

A SOFT BREEZE CAME THROUGH DOOR'S OPEN WINDOW, bringing summer scents, tree, grass, a bit of manure, and tinged with dust.

Olivia suddenly sneezed.

Langley pulled a large handkerchief out of his pocket and handed it over. "Is the road dirt bothering you?"

She nodded. The dust that had tickled her nose made its way down her throat. Olivia covered her mouth to stifle a cough.

"Do you want me to roll the leather down?"

Much as she wanted to see the countryside, she wasn't seeing much with the coughing and sneezing, so she nodded reluctantly. With the smoothness of long practice, he leaned forward, untied the strings, and a supple leather shade flopped down. More strings unrolled from the inside as it opened, and he tied them to clever flat knobs in the wall by the door on either side.

Once both sides were tight, he settled back. "There. That should help."

Two more coughs, and Olivia could catch her breath. The leather hadn't eliminated all the dust, but it blocked enough.

"When the road is wet, we don't have this problem, but the rain brings its own difficulties." He raised an eyebrow. "Surely you have the same problem in your country. England cannot be the only place on earth that gets rain."

She thought back to some camping trips, and the muddy trails they had hiked when they were still a complete family. "Yes, rain can turn a road into slop in a hurry."

Perhaps Clara's presence stifled the conversation. Olivia noticed that he glanced from the maid to herself and back again, and shifted in his seat.

Maybe he wasn't used to riding in a carriage. No doubt he was more comfortable on a horse. Odd, then, that he had chosen to ride with her.

Although . . . every time she looked up, he was watching her. She had smiled, but he did not smile back, so Olivia pulled her gaze away and glanced at Clara.

Who had a slight smile pulling at her mouth. He might not be smiling, but Clara was having a good time watching them without watching.

Since neither companion was any help, Olivia fiddled with her bracelet and wondered if she dared ask him to lift the leather curtain. If she could look outside, it would keep her from wanting to look at him.

Finally, she decided to risk it. "I think I've adjusted to the dust. Can I lift the curtain?"

He raised an eyebrow. "Are you certain the dust will not bother you again?"

"I think I'll be okay."

He shook his head. "You and your American words, but I think I understand this one. Very well." He rolled the leather up with the same skill as he had lowered it, settled back, and folded his arms, looking at her with narrowed eyes. "You realize if you start coughing, I will drop them down again."

But either the road had transitioned to more rock than dirt or she really was growing more used to the particles tossed up, because Olivia found herself absorbed in the scenery, clumps of trees along the road, scattered in the distance, climbing green hills with low bushes for company, and white dots that must be sheep, or maybe rocks. She preferred the idea of sheep. The sky overhead was a perfect blue, the clouds white and looking as soft as cotton balls.

He said the distance between his house and his father's was an easy morning's walk. She wondered how that translated into a horse and carriage trip, because the journey was taking longer than she thought. Maybe it was the silence that made the trip feel long, or Langley's ill-disguised discomfort.

Maybe it was because she still thought in automobile speeds.

The carriage turned down a long drive, and finally a house appeared.

A big house, massive slabs of a glistening white stone running the entire length of the structure, giving the whole building a glow.

Someone wanted to advertise their wealth.

Olivia managed to keep her mouth from dropping open, but it was hard. She had never seen a house like this up close. It wasn't just the stone. Even the windows were oversized and multi-paned, each rectangle of glass no doubt held in place by real lead solder. Dark wood outlined them, making the house a study in black and white.

Wings spread out on either side, set back slightly from

the center building but equally impressive, the same stone, the same dark trim, the same large windows.

The carriage stopped directly in front of wide stone steps. The front entrance matched the house in grandeur, the single door as wide as a double.

It probably did not do to gape. Olivia took one last stare before she swiveled and looked at Langley. "Is this it?"

He smiled down at her. "Yes." He climbed past her and out, and held out his hand. Olivia slid off the seat and accepted Langley's help down the wobbly steps. His hand was solid and firm.

And she wished he wasn't leaving her here with strangers.

He looked down at her, she felt it in the faint shift of his arm under her palm, and Olivia could not stop herself from glancing up. Their gazes met and held. "Courage," he said softly. "All will be well."

The door opened and a tall young man in fancy livery—a footman of the house, she guessed—came out and waited for them to reach him, holding the door wide and undoubtedly letting in all manner of bugs. "Welcome, my lord." He looked at Olivia with undisguised curiosity, but pulled his attention away when Langley spoke.

"Where is my father?" Langley strode up the few steps and through the door. Olivia caught her borrowed gown with her free hand and tried to keep up. They both stopped as the footman closed the door behind them, and Olivia's attention went between the two men. Her heart was beating too fast, and this place was far too big and too elegant.

She wondered when they would let Clara in and how they would meet up because she really needed her friend's company now!

The footman stole another look at her as he answered. "He is in the office with Farley, I believe."

"Tell him I am here. He is expecting me."

The footman nodded, and hurried down the long hall, and around a corner.

"You have to wait for your father to admit you?" Neither she nor Renee ever stood on ceremony with Mom. They both had keys, and walked in and out as if they still lived there. If they had waited for permission, Mom would have wondered if they were ill.

The grief rose again, softer now but still real.

"Of course I wait. It is my father's house." Langley strolled over and stared at a depressing painting on the wall, drooping flowers in a bowl, with dried petals on the table beneath.

Olivia took advantage of his distraction to examine the house, which dwarfed his own. They were in a wide cream-colored hallway that stretched out into the distance, where an elegantly carved stairway of what she guessed to be mahogany filled the entire width, rising on the left, a wide landing in the middle, and finishing its journey to the next floor on the right, a vivid contrast to the pale plaster.

Her entire house could fit in this hallway!

Three sets of double doors in the same wood as that stairway appeared to mark rooms, two on the left side, and one on the right.

Frames filled the spaces between the doors, gloomy pictures like the one Langley still stared at, and a large oval mirror.

"Miles!" A soft feminine voice drifted down the hall.

Langley turned, and smiled, then strode toward her. Olivia didn't know what she was supposed to do, so stayed where she was and watched.

A pretty brunette woman of late thirties or early forties leaned over the landing. She was in a beautiful rose-colored gown, with long sleeves, a lace fichu filling the low neckline. Olivia would have bet every inch of the garment was pure silk.

A faint swelling announced she was pregnant.

"Abby! What are you doing walking about the house? I understood you were to rest."

She laughed. "I am not ill any longer. Besides, I thought I heard your voice, and had to see if it was real, or if my ears were playing tricks on me."

Without a glance her way, Abby went on, "Your father told me you were at your house, and I hoped you would come and grace us with your presence. And here you are."

Langley seemed to realize that Olivia had not followed him, because he turned around and gestured toward her. "Please come meet my stepmother." Then he turned back to his stepmother as she walked down the stairs with the grace of a queen. "Abby, I have a situation, and I need your help. I have someone for you to meet. I hope this will not cause you any difficulty but I did not know what else to do. I brought her maid as well."

There might as well have been a spotlight on her because Olivia felt the center of attention as she walked up to Langley.

She reached him at about the same time as the woman. "This is Miss Olivia Underwood of America, and I believe she is in danger. She has been ill, but Dr. Reed assures me she has recovered." Then, with a respectful bow toward Abby, he added, "Miss Underwood, this is my father's wife, Lady Stafford."

Olivia kept her hands folded rather than assume she could take his arm in front of this elegant woman, and unobtrusively tried to clear her throat. Thankfully, her voice worked. "How do you do?"

Shrewd green eyes looked her over. "There must be a story behind this, as there has been no mention of a woman in Miles's life." Those eyes turned to Langley. "I presume she is of good family."

Movement from the side hallway the footman had gone down caught Olivia's eye, and she turned to see an older man, a veritable duplicate of Langley, striding toward them. The young footman followed like a shadow.

She touched Langley's arm, but before she could say anything, a deep voice boomed toward them.

"Miles!"

Langley flinched; Olivia was positive she felt the wince. "Father."

The man kept coming, his voice leading the way. "You did not give us much notice."

"There has not been time." The strain between the two men was obvious in Langley's stilted voice, Would that strain be turned against her as Langley feared? She noticed that neither the father nor the wife had actually agreed to this yet.

Stafford stopped a few feet away and gave her the same thorough going-over that his wife had. "American, huh? And what brings you to my fair country?"

"I don't know." She had a guess, but still more questions than answers. Through it all, it came back to: why her?

"I must be honest. I do not tolerate deceit. Our countries are in the middle of . . . difficulties, and I find your presence here suspicious. I am not a callow youth to be taken in by a pretty face."

Olivia wanted to give as straightforward a reply as he, but her very presence was thick with secrets she dared not share. So she held his gaze, and said nothing.

Stafford waved down the hallway from which he had just come. "Come, son. We should discuss this in my office." He bowed to Olivia. "Please forgive me, but this is a time for men to talk. I will have you escorted to the parlor, and have tea and cakes delivered." Then his gaze got harder, and his voice, too, turned to iron. "If you cause my wife a single moment of pain, I will see that you regret it."

Without waiting for her to respond, Langley's father turned and strolled down the hallway, clearly expecting his son to catch up.

Langley did the oddest thing. He picked up her hand, pressed a kiss to the back, and gestured to the footman, waiting so silently she had forgotten he was there. "Take good care of my guest."

"Yes, m'lord." The man turned to her. "If you will follow me?"

She took one more look down the hallway where Langley walked beside his father before following the footman and Lady Stafford back down the hall toward the first set of double doors. What would he say when he and his father were alone?

The footman pushed one tall panel open. The door was shut quietly behind the two of them, the footman on the other side, leaving Olivia in a stunningly beautiful room with a woman who held—at least in part—her own security. The wrong thing could get her thrown out onto the dusty road.

She glanced around the room. Where Langley's home bore only signs of previous occupants and little of his own personality aside from his office, this house was replete with a woman's touch.

Lady Stafford strolled over to a little grouping of two chairs and a table. "It might be a moment before the tea and cakes come. You may sit with me and we can get better acquainted." She smiled. "It is always easier to talk over tea, don't you agree?"

"It does break the ice," Olivia smiled back. The lady was remarkably gracious, considering the situation. She tried to absorb the room as she crossed to her hostess, looking out of the corner of her eye in case an obvious stare would be considered rude.

Several small tables like the one Lady Stafford seated herself next to littered the room, each holding a lamp. She supposed even in the daytime, without the advantage of electricity, the room could get dark early, since it faced east just as Langley's did. The candles showed signs of use, melted wax frozen in drips, the wicks burned black, the tips of the glass shades stained with smoke.

Flowers sat in astonishingly large vases, the walls were painted a bright rose-pink, the furniture looked freshly upholstered, curtains of matching fabric were pulled aside to let the sun in. Pictures hung on the walls, scenes instead of portraits, which probably hung in some gallery elsewhere in the house. The family hanging on Langley's walls was from his mother's side. Was his father's side equally ancient?

In contrast to the bright fabrics and walls, the artwork was rather morose, just like the paintings in the entry hall. Lots of still life and scenes of hunting and dead birds dangling from dog's mouths. She shuddered. When she staged houses, she made sure the artwork and knickknacks were always bright and cheerful, designed to put potential buyers in a happy, purchasing mood. Artwork like this would send them screaming out the door.

She did not have that option.

Olivia reached the chair, sat down with an attempt at the elegance of the other woman, and folded her gloved hands.

No sooner was she seated than Lady Stafford asked the first question. "Does your house look anything like this?"

"No, not at all. Mine is quite small." She decided not to share just how small, and added, "Compared to this one."

"Yes, Stafford's family is a very old one, and they have done well for themselves." Lady Stafford's eyes went firm for the first time. "But you must not think our marriage is based on such mercenary considerations."

"I never thought that, not for a second." Goodness, but this woman was frank!

"You heard Miles—Langley—explain he is my stepson."

"Yes."

"It is not easy to become an instant mother." Lady Stafford folded her own hands and pinned Olivia in her gaze. "Miles was old enough to remember his own mother, and it had been just himself and his father for a number of years before I came into his life." She paused, but not to let Olivia speak. "I worked hard to win his trust and affection."

A tap came at the door, and it opened. Olivia swiveled on her chair, grateful for the interruption. A different footman held a tray with a floral china teapot, some matching cups, a plate of some fancy cupcakes, a silver-hued creamer, and a sugar bowl.

Olivia bet nothing on that tray, nor the tray itself, was silverplate.

She looked down at her own embroidered white dress, and wondered when Lady Stafford would comment on it. As a mother who almost certainly picked out the fabric and was there for every fitting, she must have recognized it instantly.

The footman set the tray down without jarring any of the china, turned, and disappeared. The door clicked shut. Langley's stepmother fixed her gaze on Olivia. "Good. As you heard my husband say, this is a bad time for a sea journey. I leave politics to my husband, but even I am aware of the tensions. It must have been frightening." She reached for the teapot, but her gaze kept returning to Olivia as she filled the cup and set the teapot down without filling her own. "At least you had your maid with you."

That stopped Olivia. That she had no maid before Langley gave her Clara was far too easy to prove. The only thing she could do now was stick to as much of the story as he had told. "I remember nothing of the trip."

Lady Stafford handed over the cup and saucer. "I have heard of people who are not good sailors. I never had the chance to find out whether I would sail well, and I now think it is a good thing."

Olivia held the fancy china carefully and looked down at the white gown. She dared not spill. Tea was a known dye, and this gown would certainly absorb it immediately.

Odd that Lady Stafford said nothing about it. If she didn't mention it, Olivia wasn't going to.

Tea was tea, as far as she was concerned, but even so, she could tell this was well made. She had just set the cup and saucer down when the other woman spoke.

"What brought you here? And to my stepson?"

"As I said, I don't know. I remember nothing of the journey."

"Nothing? At all?"

"Nothing."

"You must have been quite se*verely* ill." Despite the sympathetic words, Olivia could see lingering suspicion and doubt. Lady Stafford finally glanced at the gown, and back to Olivia's face. "You hardly look it now. You have recovered quickly."

As long as she was stuck with the lie, she would have to make it good. "Dr. Reed thinks I was on the way to recovery already. He was there the day I was dropped off, or so I understand, so he can tell you the state they found me in."

Lady Stafford seemed to relax. Not much, but some. At least her eyes relaxed. "So you have already seen our local physician. That is good. I am sure you understand, but we must check your story."

"Langley believes there is more to the story, too." She sank back against the chair. "I don't know why I'm here. I don't know what I am supposed to do." Then she straightened. This she could say with complete sincerity. "I am only grateful that he is willing to protect me. Without him, I don't know where I would have ended up, or what I would have been forced to do."

Fixing her gaze on Lady Stafford, Olivia almost snapped out the words. "I am not here to take advantage of him. I am not here to cause him, or you, or your country, problems. And if there had been any other way to handle this, I promise you I would have taken it."

Lady Stafford held her gaze with equal strength, and then with a blink, turned back to the teapot. She picked it up and tilted it over her own cup. "I believe you." Her gaze came back to Olivia, while the teapot hovered, the spout empty and waiting. "Which is a good thing, because I could make your life a misery if you hurt Miles."

Olivia had to smile. "And I believe you, as well."

CHAPTER 34

FATHER'S WALK WAS STIFF AS HE STRODE DOWN THE HALL. Miles reminded himself that he was not the young boy who feared his father's switch, but the memories walked with him.

He thought he heard Olivia's voice, and his spine suddenly became as straight as his father's. She needed help that Father could provide—if he chose.

All he had to do was convince the man the help he needed was as important as his every instinct shouted it was.

Father pushed his office door wider and strode inside, leaving Miles to shut the door behind them just before the footman reached for it. He turned around and faced his father much as he had done mere days ago.

The afternoon sun poured through the open curtains, caught in his father's white hair, and cast his face into shadow, leaving Miles's own facing the brightness.

There would be no hiding of secrets. At least this time, he had no secrets to hide.

He looked at the large leather chair in which he had sat

the last time he was here, still angled for easy conversation in front of his father's desk, and as imposing in the daylight as in the gloom.

He did not turn to the bookshelves, but the memory of those carvings pressing into his palms on that last visit made his hands sting.

When he turned back, Father had not seated himself in that massive chair yet, but was leaning on the desk. Miles noticed his father's hands were clenched, and the knuckles he leaned on were white.

His resolve hardened.

"We are alone. There is no need for false courtesy to protect your . . . guest. I find your tale sketchy, but I hope I am right in believing you would not bring any lightskirt of yours into my house and present her to your stepmother. You had better have a very good reason for foisting that young woman onto your family." Father took a hissing breath, and burst out, *"So what have you gotten yourself into this time?"* Then he sank down into his big chair with a thump.

"We need your help. *Miss Underwood* needs your help."

Father pressed both palms down on his desk, hunching over the desk, threat in his posture. "What are you involved in? How bad is it?"

Miles tamped his old resentment down and rested a hand on the desktop. "She was found in my house, unaccompanied and ill. So ill that it took her several hours to gain any kind of awareness."

Father's brows rose, but he said nothing, although Miles could feel the growing anger thrumming on the air. He braced himself, both on that hand and inside, where years of his father's disapproval still lingered, and continued, "I sent for Edward—Dr. Reed—immediately. You remember him?"

"I do indeed." The words came out through gritted teeth.

"He was most concerned when he first came, and told me I must not move her."

"How very convenient—for *her*."

Miles stiffened, the insult to Miss Underwood pricking him, perhaps more than it should. "Do you want the story, or don't you?"

A sound like a growl came from Father's throat, but he gave a nod.

"We were both quite surprised when she came to herself. She had no trunks, nor did she know where she was or how she got there. The only thing she remembered was her name."

Only the width of the desk kept them from touching. The pale eyes that matched his own had turned to ice. "And you brought this woman into my house?"

"This woman believes she overheard a plot to murder me!"

The words rang in the air. His father slumped into his seat, his face suddenly gone slack.

"Tell me everything."

Miles lowered himself into the visitor chair, took a deep breath, and fought to keep his voice calm. "I must go back to the beginning. At the time I sent for Edward, I knew nothing of her, not her name, nor how she got there. I was more suspicious of her than you even are. But once she began to recover, I did my best to learn what I could about her."

"And what did you find out?"

"Only that she came from America."

Father closed his eyes.

Miles went on, "She remembers nothing of the journey. Edward believes she was desperately ill, and that is why she cannot remember. I suspect she was left at my house by mistake, that she was supposed to be left in your house."

"My house?" Miles saw the instant his father made the connection. *"You brought me a spy?"*

"No, not a spy. Or if she was supposed to be one, she has forgotten all about it. She does not know what she was sent here to do."

Father slowly rose back to his feet, the ominous growl of his words a match for his movements. "You said someone is trying to kill you? Did it not occur to you she might be the one?"

Miles kept his seat, aggravating though it was to have to look up. "Would she warn me if she was sent to kill me? And why would America care what happened to me? Would they not rather get rid of you, with your seat in Parliament and all the committees and secret societies to which you belong?"

He took a breath. Father waited, though he did not sit down. "I do believe she might have been sent on some urgent mission, but her illness wiped that from her mind and left her with the pure essence of herself." He smiled at the memories that rose. "She has taken nothing that did not belong to her, an honesty that is rare."

He did not mention Olivia's nighttime visit to his office. She admitted it herself, and the iron was hers; she made no secret of wanting it back. Someone had riffled through the office, but his suspicions went in a different direction. He continued, "The maidservant I gave her adores her, and I suspect would obey her instead of myself despite being in my employ. She is charming and open and too stubborn to let herself be easily used."

"Appealing though such qualities may be," Father said in a dry tone as he lowered himself and settled in his chair, "they are easy to mimic for a short period. As you say, she has not been in your house long. And pretending to overhear a threat against you is an easy way to win your trust. Which it appears she has already done." He shook his head. "You just said she is more of a threat to me than to you. So why did you bring her here, to the very place you suspect she should have been all along?"

Miles's hands tightened on the arms of the chair, even as he had to admit that he had shared the same suspicions at the start. They grated now, knowing Miss Underwood better. "No one can be this convincing unless it is real. You did not see her fear when she first awoke. Whatever happened to her on the journey to make her that ill wiped out whatever mission she was to perform. Edward knows a little about her condition. He called it amnesia, and says it is a new discovery in injury to the mind."

His father gave a disgusted snort. "So you are not just bringing me an American woman who might well be a spy, but one who could also be a candidate for Bedlam."

Miles had had enough. "You saw her. You talked to her. You know she is no more suited for Bedlam than you or I. She is an intelligent woman who is recovering from a serious illness that has left her with missing parts of her memory, but her mind is fully intact in all other ways."

Father gave him a measuring look, then a single nod. "I will treat her with every courtesy unless and until I find cause to do otherwise." He leaned back into his chair and tapped a finger on the heavy wooden arm. "Now what is this about her hearing a threat against your life?"

"I do not believe she actually heard any such thing. I believe it to have been a fever dream, but she is thoroughly convinced it happened. You know how real fever dreams can be. It is possible the danger she fears for me might well be danger against herself. That is what concerns me. I believe she might have been sent here by force to find something that her country can use. When whoever left her at my house discovers that she has not completed her mission and does not even remember what that mission was, they would have no further use for her."

He leaned forward, willing his father to believe him. "What would you do if you had a spy who could not fulfill his mission?"

Father's gaze drifted past him, and a frown furrowed his brows. "It would depend on the seriousness of his assignment, but you have a point. If the mission was of utmost importance, it might be necessary to do away with him. Perhaps not by killing him, but at least put him someplace where he cannot do any harm to England if the memory comes back in pieces."

"We teeter on the brink of war with America. I worry that someone will come back and try to force her—against her will—to find out information." He met his father's eyes and spoke with total conviction. "Which she will not do. She believes someone will compel her to return to America. I fear for her life as much as she fears for mine."

"Your faith in her is admirable, if misplaced."

Miles forced himself to speak calmly. "She is in enemy country. I believe they will eliminate her once they find out what has happened." He gave a deep sigh. "I would not put Abby in danger, but Edward reminded me that you have a larger staff than I do, and are in a better position to both watch over her safety and watch out for any strangers who might wander near. I will not ask details, but you may have heard about America sending spies to learn something about our plans, assuming they decide to declare war on us."

Father was surprisingly silent. For the first time since entering the room, Miles heard the mantel clock tick. He could feel the struggle inside his father, years of weighing what to reveal and what to keep hidden.

A soft sigh came. "Nothing you have told me connects with what I am working on." Then Father's brows came down. "You might be right. They might have left her at the wrong house. If they wanted to find something out, much better to bring her here. They would hardly know that I keep nothing confidential lying about."

"There is one more thing. If I knew of a better place to put her, I would have done so, but I must warn you. They smuggled her into my house without being spotted. If they could bring her in, they can take her out as easily."

Father's brow furrowed, his gaze became distant again. "I will send for a Bow Street Runner. He will check the ships from America in the harbors nearby, and more thoroughly than your servants. No doubt he can get the passenger list, and then begin tracing them. She would have her traveling companions listed on the ship's manifest."

"He will have quite a job on his hands. She does not remember the ship, nor the harbor. There are any number of places along the coast to check."

"That is their specialty, finding the unfindable." Father pushed himself to his feet. "For now, I should like to speak more with this woman who appeared so mysteriously in your house." He stood, and Miles stood with him. "You, of course, may come, but I do not want you interfering. You give me credit for knowing political wiles and ways. Allow me to use my experience unimpeded."

"Yes. I will." He followed his father out the door and back down the hallway. The parlor doors were shut, but the footman stood just outside, saw them coming, and opened it.

CHAPTER 35

THE TWO WOMEN SAT ON EITHER SIDE OF ONE OF THE TEA tables. They had been sipping tea, because the cups in both hands were nearly empty, and crumbs on the plate were all that was left of whatever food had been brought. He thought he caught the scent of cake, and despite his full stomach, his mouth watered.

"Are there any cakes left for us?" He walked over to Miss Underwood and took the nearest chair. "And have you two had a pleasant time?"

"We've had a lovely talk." But her voice was a bit breathless, and she glanced at the earl with some alarm. "And yes, the footman said there is more cake in the kitchen."

Although he had expected his father to begin an inquisition immediately, the earl directed his first question to Abby. "My darling, how are you feeling?"

"The tea has settled well, and I feel quite fine."

"You know you are not to overdo." Father strode over to collect another chair, and placed it next to his wife. Only then did he turn to Olivia. "So you are from America. The trip did not suit you?"

She glanced over at Miles, and he nodded, not sure what he was nodding to except that her eyes definitely held a question. She turned back to his father. "You would have to ask Langley, because I don't remember anything about arriving at his house."

"So I heard. And you have been there a short time. You recovered quickly."

Miles stepped in. "Dr. Reed believes she was already on the road to recovery. The people who smuggled her into my house must not have known that, but how often would there be a surgeon on the ship to make such a diagnosis?"

There was nothing to do but stick with what Langley had believed all along. "The first thing I remember is finding myself in his . . . house." Best not to tell them she landed in his bedroom and nearly caught him in his bath. Obviously, he hadn't given that detail, so she certainly wasn't going to share it.

"And with whom did you travel?" His eyes reminded her of Langley's: piercing and sharp with intelligence. She remembered his warning: *I do not tolerate deceit.*

"I was alone."

He scowled. "I know you were *found* alone, but women do not travel unaccompanied. If we are to keep you—not to mention my own wife—safe, we need to know everything. How can you guarantee that they will not find you here and threaten my family for the information you were to collect?"

Olivia was sorely tempted to fold her arms and glare back at him. *What about the real threat, the threat to your son?* But she had no proof. So she turned the question around. "What if I was sent here for my own safety? Some in America still consider themselves English." Or so she thought she remembered.

Stafford drew back and rubbed his jaw as he stared into the distance. The room went quiet. Then his gaze returned to her, sharp with intelligence. "If that were the case, why did they leave you in my son's house? Surely, if they thought they were still British and favored the British cause, they would have had family or friends with whom to stay. There was no need to leave you with strangers."

A flicker of admiration at his comeback almost triggered a smile, but the urge faded in the next breath. "I will have to grant you that."

"My dear," Lady Stafford interrupted, "do you recognize her gown? She is wearing one of Cecelia's old dresses. She told me that she has no trunks. Would someone using her as a spy allow all her trunks to be taken? Would they not rather stand guard over them?"

Gratitude washed over Olivia for this bare acquaintance who took her side.

And then Langley opened his mouth. "We do not know that her trunks were stolen, only that when she was left at my house, she had none."

"Regardless, my point still stands." Lady Stafford turned her attention back to her husband. "If someone wanted her to spy for them, they would hardly leave her without supplies. And a woman? They would make sure she had gowns aplenty, because she has to mingle with those who knew the Crown's secrets." She shook her head. "No, my dear. I do not think you are looking in the right direction. She is American, and I have heard their women have far more freedom to come and go." Lady Stafford looked over at

Olivia. "Am I not right, Miss Underwood? You have more freedom there than we have here?"

Olivia struggled against a burst of hysterical laughter and nodded. She swallowed down the bubble and immediately choked.

"Oh, my dear!" Lady Stafford immediately poured some tea, and held it out while Olivia cleared her throat. "Here you are. Drink it slowly now. You might have a crumb caught. I have done that. It is most distressing."

Olivia cleared her throat one last time and reached for the tea. After a couple of sips, she could talk again. "Yes, I had a great deal of freedom." The laughter still threatened, so she closed her mouth and let it go at that.

"There! You see?" Lady Stafford turned to her husband. "We must not assume the worst. No doubt her family wanted her away from any dangers, should this miserable disagreement become war."

Lord Stafford turned to his wife. "What do you know about any threats of war? I do not want you reading anything that might distress you and cause any harm to either you or our child."

The lady gave him a saucy look, a twinkle in her eye. "You cannot keep all communications from me. My friends write and have been most distracting during the time of my illness. I have been grateful for their company, even if only by letter."

Olivia would have bet any amount of money that Lady Stafford had servants bring the newspaper, but she was too protective of her staff to get them in any trouble with the master of the house.

He harrumphed. "I should have made my concerns more clear to one and all."

A stolen glance at Langley told Olivia nothing about whether he agreed with this kind of protectiveness. She bit her tongue hard to keep any protest inside. Their marriage was their own business, but if she couldn't get back home and had to live out her life in this world, she didn't know if she dared to marry.

It was a depressing thought, but she had a pretty good idea of what happened to women who never married. She suspected the term 'poor relation' was coined mainly for them.

Lord Stafford turned his attention back to Olivia. "My wife raises valid points. Perhaps my suspicions are too harsh. I will permit you to stay, and your maid, but do not think I have lowered my guard. I will keep a close eye on both you and on any visitors to my property. There had better not be any unexpected guests asking to talk with you."

That she could guarantee. "I assure you, there will not be any."

His eyes narrowed. "I would not make any promises you cannot keep. I do not forget that your memory is lacking. But for now, as I said, I will allow you to stay. My butler has assigned your maid a room next to the one I will give you, but she will be under as close supervision as yourself."

The last hope that Clara might be able to get back to Langley's house to look for the iron shriveled. The houses were five miles apart. She could walk that distance, maybe run part of the way if she had to. Clara was in better shape after the hard work she'd done these past three months, and she was just as motivated.

But if both of them were being watched, how could they ever make their way back there?

Even more, she still had the worry about the men she had overheard. While the Staffords and Langley were worried about her situation, she knew the real danger was to Langley. And neither of them took her seriously.

Whatever time force dropped her here, if she was to save his life, she had to be near enough to prevent it.

And if she couldn't?

But everyone rose, and Olivia finally heard her name through the tumult in her brain.

Somehow she had to get past Lord Stafford's suspicions, convince him of what she had heard, and have him do . . . what? Set his men about Langley's property, too? She had no idea how many male servants Stafford had, let alone have enough to spare to watch two properties.

But she got to her feet and face her hosts. "Thank you so much for your hospitality. I apologize for the inconvenience this is causing you." She couldn't promise anything in return.

Not even that she would save their son's life.

CHAPTER 36

THE HOUSE FELT ODDLY STILL WHEN MILES WALKED BACK IN. Denton closed the door behind him. "I see the lady is no longer with you."

"Feel free to ask where she is, Denton. You know I have no secrets from you." Or at least none that Denton need know about. He flipped his gloves into the hat he pulled off and handed the lot to his butler. "Yes, my father agreed to watch over Miss Underwood and her maid."

"So life can get back to normal again." Denton stood there holding the hat and gloves, and Miles could have sworn a smile tugged at the man's mouth.

"Yes." He should be glad. Riding the countryside if he wished, reading whatever he wanted in the peace of his library, walking about his own house without worrying that he be caught in his banyan.

The carriage drove off to the carriage house, but not even the scraping of the wheels offset the odd void inside.

"I will be in my office." Where the only thing he possessed

of Miss Underwood's was. "Bring me a banyan, if you will." He intended to go through any mail that may have been delivered—and that he had not even looked at—since his own arrival. And he was going to do it in comfort.

As he walked down the hall toward his office, he realized he would be eating that meal, and all future ones here, alone.

Odd that a woman he had sheltered for scarcely two days could leave such a presence behind.

This is nonsense, he scolded himself. *You will read your mail and answer your letters, and life will go back to normal.*

He shut the office door behind himself and defiantly removed his coat. The day's warmth was fading, and he gave a shiver while he waited for his valet to bring down the comfortable wrap.

He pulled the mail out of his center drawer along with a quill and ink, and settled in to work.

Keeping his back defiantly toward the hidden safe where Miss Underwood's iron hid. No matter how badly he wanted to open the cubby and set the thing on his desk.

The better part of an hour had passed when a tap came on the door. Denton stood there, with Victor right behind, lip curled, expression mocking.

"Your cousin is here, Lord Langley."

Miles stifled a groan. "Let him in." Annoying as it was, Miles made himself stand. Courtesy was, after all, courtesy.

"The viscount will see you." Denton turned to Victor and stepped aside.

He knew his butler deliberately used his title just to annoy the man. The contrast of the looks on the two faces, one smug, the other irritated, was almost worth having to visit with Victor.

Perhaps he would get an answer to the question planted by Miss Underwood.

Denton pulled the door shut firmly behind Victor. Miles waved his cousin to the nearest chair and took his own seat again, folding his hands on the desk. He would never have chosen the man for a relative, but there it was. Relative, yes. Friend, definitely not.

"So what brings you here? When I left, you were still in London. Creditors hot on your trail again?"

Victor smiled the smug smile that always annoyed Miles. After all these years, he should be immune, but each time he saw that expression, the question arose whether Victor actually did harbor some secret knowledge.

His cousin settled himself in the chair on the other side of the desk, and folded his hands across his flat stomach. "As it happens, I have a line on an investment that should pay off nicely." His mouth went tight, and the smile disappeared. "You are hardly in a position to criticize. Your path was laid out at birth. The only son of the heir? What do you know about having to beg for an income?"

Miles scoffed. "You have plenty to live on. Our grandfather provided well enough for both of us. With only two sons, and three grandchildren, there is more than enough to go around. It is hardly anyone's fault but your own that you do not manage it properly."

Victor leapt to his feet and slammed his hands on the desk, propping himself there. He was much too close, but Miles did not let himself move back. "I still must wait every quarter for your father to dole out my funds. And then I must listen to his lecture about how important it is to manage money wisely. Does he not remember what it is to be young? I am certain you never have to listen to his pious lectures."

He straightened, and Miles felt his own shoulders relax.

But Victor was not done. "I intend to free myself from my dear uncle's thumb." He fairly threw himself back down into the chair. "So what is this I hear about you having a woman hidden in your house? And so close to your father, too. Did you haul her here from London, or is she a local lass?"

"I have no woman in my house." Let Victor make of that what he would. Miles leaned back and watched the flicker of confusion cross his cousin's face, to be replaced by shrewd intelligence. No doubt the wheels were spinning madly inside that wily brain.

He would have to warn his father. And Miss Underwood.

One of his past mistresses had gone directly from his own patronage to Victor. That had occasioned comment for a while.

But Miss Underwood was no courtesan. And she had warned him that someone wanted him dead. His suspicion had gone directly to Victor.

And here the man was.

Coincidence? Or was there more to this visit?

"Still holding the lovely Mrs. Tiptin against me," Victor taunted, both in posture and in voice. Miles knew it offended him to have to sit on the opposite side of the desk, but his cousin pretended to be relaxed, one leg over the arm of the chair, his body slouched against the back, his lip curling as he spoke. "You cast her off. Why should I not have taken her? If you want a woman, Miles, you keep her. Once you reject her, she is fair game."

"I will not discuss Mrs. Tiptin with you." Nor this one,

either. He would do his best to keep Miss Underwood out of the conversation, but Victor's curiosity was well and truly aroused. How he found out about Miss Underwood, Miles did not know, but servants talked and he did not keep as close watch on the comings and goings at the servants' door as perhaps he should have.

His hands had clenched against the wooden arms, and Miles forced them to relax. "Tell me why you are really here. I do not control the family finances. That responsibility, as you so loudly said, belongs to my father."

"Can I not drop in for a pleasant chat with my cousin?" Victor still slouched in the chair, but his eyes were sharp.

Miles braced himself for a verbal sparring match. Victor might be odious, but he was hardly stupid. "Certainly you can drop in, but how many times in the course of our lives has the chat ever been pleasant?"

Victor threw back his head and laughed. "Well taken, Miles." Then he untangled his long limbs from the chair, sat up straight, and folded his hands across his stomach. His gaze never left Miles's face. "So who is this woman that you say is not here? Since I know you will hold my stealing a second mistress away, I will merely ask if she has a sister."

It took real effort to keep his hands from clenching on the chair arms again. "Unlike you, I do not discuss women."

Victor's brows rose. "Oho. So she is a woman of means, and you are keeping her reputation from stain." He leaned back in the chair again. "I will have to ask around London when I return, see which lady is missing.."

"Ask away. You will only add to your reputation as a man who cannot find his own women, but must take my left-overs." The dig was beneath him, Miles knew, but he could not resist.

Victor lurched as if to rise, but settled back. "So she is not from London. A local conquest, then, although Bath is not so very far away. Bristol is even closer, and both cities offer plenty of choice."

"Why not go there yourself, then, and find a woman, if you need one?" Miles watched his uninvited guest closely and saw his knee bounce. So Victor's feet were having trouble staying still? Interesting. The man was nervous about something.

Go to the earl for money. Miss Underwood's words from all those weeks ago whispered in his mind, and Miles followed his instincts. "If you need an advance, why have you not been to Father?"

"Did I say I had not been?"

"I know you, remember? You only come to me when you are afraid to go to Father and ask for more. You know full well he will want an accounting, and you are afraid to confess your gambling."

"As if you have never played too deep!" Victor shifted in his chair. "I know you, as well. You enjoy a night in the card room instead of wandering the ballroom floor dodging the voracious mamas and their less-than-appealing daughters."

"Ah, but I know when to stop." With words as well as cards, Miles thought, and wondered if Victor had heard about the card game when he won back the young man's lands and nearly lost his own in the process.

Everyone knows about the diamond buttons.

He decided to play a new card. "So you did not find what you were looking for here in this office last night?"

Victor's knee stopped its jiggling, his spine straightened and his chin came up in affront. "I cannot believe I heard that. You saw me arrive just now. Are you accusing me of breaking into your house like a common thief?"

The first inklings of doubt pricked Miles. Would Victor

bring it up so easily if he was guilty? "Someone did. Someone was in my office last night."

"And here I am today, so of course it would have to be me. It could not be one of your servants, or even, God forbid, the woman you have installed here. Miles, I am ashamed to be related to you at this moment."

"I assure you, I have questioned all of them." Miles could not read the look on Victor's face, which alone was unusual. He knew his cousin too well, and to have his face devoid of any expression was a first. He even could tell when Victor was cheating at cards, and had blocked many an attempt to fleece someone who did not deserve it.

A faint chill ran down his spine. If not Victor, then who was in here? And why?

Victor rose. "I believe we both need time away from each other. I will take my leave, and perhaps by the next time we are together, I will have found it within myself to forgive your accusation."

"I will have Denton give you your hat and gloves." Courtesy demanded Miles rise, so he did, keeping his gaze fixed on Victor.

His cousin gave a far-too-elegant bow of blatant mockery. "I bid you good day, which is more than you deserve."

Miles gave his own bow, but he did not try to match Victor's effusive performance. "I return the wishes in the same spirit." He pulled the cord for Denton, but Victor was already on his way out.

And he shut the office door behind himself with remarkable restraint. Miles would not have been surprised if Victor had slammed it hard enough to break the hinges, but it shut with barely a whisper.

Tempting as it was to peek out the door and make sure his cousin had actually left, Miles remained by his desk, listening to the clock tick. It was about time to wind it again. In fact, it would take the exact amount of time as Victor needed to leave the house. He turned the key, waiting for the sound of hoofbeats to match.

And there they were. He was gone. For now.

CHAPTER 37

WHEN OLIVIA GOT UP TO HER ROOM, CLARA HAD FINISHED unpacking, and the borrowed gowns hung in the armoire.

The room was large, but then, in a house this big, what room wouldn't be? Large orange-canopied bed with matching coverlet and shams, pale orange wallpaper, orange curtains on the window that faced the front of the house. The inevitable armoire, and a commode, if that was what the little curtain in the corner hid.

She'd find out soon enough.

She couldn't help but notice they were right next door to Lady Stafford's room, which also put them one room away from the earl.

The man wanted to keep an eye on them, didn't he? She had expected him to put them at the other end of the long hallway,

Clara walked over and peeked out into the hallway, then closed the door. She dragged Olivia over to the window, which was tightly shut. In a soft voice, Clara hissed, "I heard they are watching us. One of the footmen who brought your trunk told me. Our nifty plan has gone to pieces."

"I'll admit, this is a major complication." She glared at the orange walls while ideas tumbled around her head. "I refuse to let this stop us. I'm going to start wandering around the gardens. There must be a path to keep us out of sight of the road. The properties are linked by marriage. One would think a courting couple would find a place to sneak off and meet. A stream would work nicely, if it links the two properties. It's a better route than out where everyone can see us."

Clara shook her head, not in disagreement, more in disapproval. "First of all, marriage in this time isn't always two giddy people skulking around to see each other. Often it's arranged, they barely know each other, and they are stuck. Secondly. you did hear me say they're going to be watching you. And me."

"Yes, but what else can we do?" Olivia sighed and flopped back onto the bed, her legs dangling off the edge. She stared up at the orange canopy. "Somehow we have to get back there and find that iron."

Clara leaned over. braced both arms on the mattress, and looked down at Olivia. "First of all, we don't know where it is. Second, he'll never tell us. Third, they are going to watch us like hawks."

Olivia sat back up. "Fourth, they have no idea how resourceful modern women are." She paused. "Or will be."

Clara straightened, too, and gave Olivia a long look. "I'm on your side, remember that, but we both have a lot to lose if we get caught. Me more than you, because you have that bracelet. Don't think I haven't noticed it. You could sell that and live for a while on the proceeds. But me? I came as a maid. If I get fired, I'm so out of luck."

"And if we can't get back there and find that iron, we both are going to be stuck here."

They looked at each other for a long moment.

Another concern rose. "We're about what? Two miles away from Langley's? Maybe three?"

Clara shrugged. "I didn't have an odometer, and no one in the kitchen ever mentioned it. Not that I would have remembered if they had."

Olivia tilted her head and looked Clara up and down. "I know you've been here for months, but have you ever jogged? I had a gym membership and ran on the treadmill, but I don't know how well that compares with running on roads like they have here." She leaned over the edge of the bed, lifted her skirt, and looked down at her silly shoes. "And in these?"

"Do you think Langley will still get you clothes? He mentioned half-boots."

Olivia dropped her skirt back into place. "I think it all depends on his father, and right now, I don't think his father wants to give me much of anything."

Clara wiggled her feet in their sturdy boots. "To get back to jogging, I've never done running like marathons, but I was on my feet all day as a waitress. I never got much time to sit down here until you came. If I had to run to Langley's place" —Clara's voice got grim, and her face set in determined lines —"I promise you, I'd make it."

"Good. Because somehow we have to get back there." Olivia sighed. "Something will come up. I have to believe that. We'll start walking around. I'll tell them I need the fresh air. If they get used to seeing us strolling the property, we'll stretch it farther and farther."

Clara frowned. "Assuming they let us out of the house."

Olivia looked at the orange walls again, and an old tidbit

of information slid like a warning into her mind. "One thing to watch out for. I studied wallpaper for my work, and green in this era is so poisonous that you can't even touch it today." She caught herself. "I mean *today* like in our time. It's not every green, I don't think, but some for sure. If they have wallpaper anywhere that's green, try to stay out of that room."

Clara looked at the wallpaper. "That sounds familiar. My room is white, so I'll be okay."

"That's one less worry. Let's see how far we can stroll today." Olivia found a grin. "We might as well get them used to seeing us outside."

O ddly, no one refused permission to going outside, although they had to wait in the grand hallway while Lady Stafford sent her maid. "To escort you about the place," the footman said as they stood by the door.

The woman who came was late thirties or early forties, smiling face, curly dark hair under the requisite mobcap, and wearing a blue muslin gown with embroidered white flowers.

The gown was clearly second-hand. Olivia noticed some of the flowers had been mended, likely by the maid herself, but she had done a nice job. Lady's maids were expected to be quick with a needle. It almost slipped past her attention. No doubt someone not as used to spotting inconsistencies wouldn't even notice.

"Are you the one sent to take us about?" Olivia took a stab that this was Lady Stafford'a maid.

"Call me Maribelle," the woman said, and dipped a quick curtsey. "Yes, I am to show you about the garden, but we must stay close to the house. What do you want to see first?"

Olivia thought. What did she know about flowers? "Are there roses? I love roses!" One of the few flowers she could identify by sight.

"Oh, there are indeed, but they are close to the gazebo." She glanced at the staircase at the hall's end, and Olivia had to force herself not to turn and look. "What is most fun, I have found, is to wander through the flagstone paths and find the flowers the gardener hid among the bushes. We have lavender and foxglove, and sweet peas, and peonies. Oh, and hollyhocks and wisteria and delphinium."

Clearly they weren't going to be able to see the far end of the garden today, so Olivia gave in. For now. "Whatever path has the most hidden flowers. That sounds like a lovely walk."

While Langley had a maze, this house's maze had been ripped out and replaced with trees and bushes and flowers, Maribelle told them as they walked out the door. "And I quite like what he did. The earl hired Capability Brown, you know."

They strolled down the long extravagant front and around the side, where a flagstone walk took them past more windows, some large enough to step through into a room she hadn't seen yet. The curtains were drawn, so she didn't know what was inside.

But it was what stretched out ahead and to the side that captivated her. Olivia swiveled around to see it all. Close to the house, tall bushes had been shaped into large rounded contours, one after another, some larger, some smaller, running along the whole side. A thicket of trees began where the bushes ended, and the flagstone path wandered between the low-hanging branches, keeping it from looking like a forest.

The flagstones between the boughs seemed to beckon them to enter.

"Where does that go?" Olivia pointed down the path into the dark shadows beneath the trees.

"Oh, just down to one end of the long pond. The pond winds around, but if you follow this path"—Maribelle gestured ahead, where the main walkway wandered between the tall bushes—"which goes behind the house, it will lead you through the main garden and past a gazebo. From the gazebo, a short stairway goes down the other end of the pond, and the stream."

A stream. Was it the route they needed?

The maid started down the very direction she had described. Olivia looked at Clara, who shrugged. "I guess we follow her," she whispered.

So they strolled behind, close to the house and past more sculpted bushes.

"You will be glad we came this way." Maribelle smiled back over her shoulder, and stepped around the final bush into the late afternoon sun.

Olivia and Clara followed. Ahead of them spread a vista of green dotted with a rainbow of colors, flowers in clusters with bricked edging, while more bushes curved and split, giving them options of which colors and flowers they wanted to stroll through.

Where the bushes leading around the house were too tall to see over, this area was like strolling through a meadow lush with flowers that beckoned for attention, while paths wove around, in and out of the clusters. More trees in the distance, a green background to this carpet of technicolor, surrounded something that glinted in the sun, likely the gazebo the maid just mentioned.

Olivia couldn't decide which way to look first. "Oh, it's

lovely!" She turned to the maid. "I could spend all day out here."

Clara was more blunt. "Can we stroll out here whenever we wish? It would take weeks, maybe months, to see everything."

Maribelle's smile faded. "I cannot give you permission to wander at will, but I shall ask my lady. Now that she is feeling better, she might wish to join you. There are benches scattered about where she can rest, if she needs." The smile came back. "The benches are always a surprise. Capability Brown arranged each bench with special plants that give you something to enjoy."

Those distant trees reminded Olivia of something else the maid said. "And you said the pond is beyond the gazebo? Can we go down and look at it?"

Maribelle shifted uncomfortably. "I can only ask."

Obviously, that wasn't going to happen today. "Did you say the pond ends in a stream? Or is it fully enclosed?" *Because if understood right and the pond became a stream and if the stream headed toward Langley's house, it was exactly what they hoped for, the perfect escape, more private than running along the road.*

"I think it continues, but I have never gone that far. There is no need, and my lady would never trudge along the riverbank."

That was an obvious verbal hedge. Olivia would have bet money that the woman had been warned not to reveal too much.

No sense pushing her. It was time to talk to Clara in private. She smiled at the maid. "I think I have seen enough for today. We should go back inside. There is so much here, it will take me days to see it all."

The woman relaxed. "It will indeed."

CHAPTER 38

"MISS UNDERWOOD?" THE BUTLER—FARLEY, WAS IT?—STOOD in the parlor door. "Are you receiving guests?"

Olivia put down the book she had chosen from the library—Diderot's *The Nun,* since *The Mysteries of Udolpho* was nowhere to be found in Stafford's library—and nodded. She hadn't gotten far enough in to figure out the story, anyway.

In walked Langley, and her heart gave a happy skip. Not just because he looked gorgeous all dressed up—blue suit jacket, gold waistcoat, crisp white shirt, a cravat tied in an elaborate knot, tight tan knee breeches, shining black boots —but because he was here.

She had been gone for one day. Did he miss her already?

More likely, he had come to see his family and thought it rude not to at least check on her. It was barely afternoon. Not that she knew what time was considered appropriate for visiting, but it just felt a bit soon for him to come back and ask to see her. Not that she was complaining.

Olivia tried to stifle the happy patter inside, and rose. "Hello. How nice of you to come."

He bowed. "Miss Underwood. It is good to see you again. How are you settling in? Are you being well-treated?" He motioned to the book she had set down. "I am interrupting your reading. I apologize."

Olivia laughed. "I've hardly started it, and don't even know what's going on yet. You haven't interrupted a thing." Her mind went blank. Did she ask what brought him here? What he had done with the iron?

He looked around the room as if he didn't know what to say next, himself. "I have always hated the paintings in this room."

Another bubble of laughter broke free. "I'm so glad to hear that. I hate them, too. I wouldn't read here except that Lady Stafford fell asleep in the library, and I wanted to let her doze in private."

His gaze came back to her, his brows furrowed in genuine concern. "How is she?"

The obvious affection in this family toward Lady Stafford was such a contrast between herself and her sister. If only the father and son got along as well.

Last night's supper had been tense, with Stafford needling her about just how long she had known his son, and if she had been to London, and what she thought about England.

Whether Stafford was satisfied with her replies, she didn't know.

But Langley was waiting for an answer. "I think she is fine. She's young enough still so I think she should make it through the"—Olivia caught herself. Did women say 'pregnancy' in this time?

Langley understood what she hadn't said, though. "I

know my father is worried. I confess his concern has rubbed off on me."

"I'm no expert," Olivia said, wishing she could give more reassurance, "but I've known women who have had children at an older age than your stepmother and did fine." Although that was in an era where births were monitored every step of the way, and there were specialists in older mothers to guard against tragedy.

Langley gave a single nod, then motioned to the door. "Would you like to go for a walk in the garden?"

That was easy. She hadn't even had to hint. Maybe he would let her see what Lady Stafford's maid hadn't. "I would love it!" She didn't even realize she was smiling until he smiled back.

"I have never had someone be so happy at a simple walk. Are the walls closing in on you?"

"Now, that would make me sound ungrateful." She wrapped her shawl tighter against the goosebumps. Despite the summer day, the house felt cool most of the time, especially in rooms like this one that faced east and lost the sun early in the day.

Langley walked over and pulled the bell cord. "We will get you outside, and the fresh air and sunshine will wash away any malaise." He held out his arm.

She had missed that courtesy, and it had only been one day. Olivia slid her hand into the crook and he led her to the door.

A footman stood outside. "Yes, my lord?"

"We are going outside." Langley led her past the footman and out into that oversized hallway. "Send for Miss Underwood's maid, and have her bring a bonnet, shawl, and gloves. She will accompany us. And bring me my own hat and gloves, if you will."

"Yes, m'lord." The footman scurried off toward the staircase.

Langley looked down at Olivia. "I have some news. The dressmaker is at my house at this moment. I gave her driver directions here. She should arrive within the half hour."

"Oh!" In some strange trick of time, having five gowns had seemed enough. At least for now. No doubt in another day or two, when she had run through the last of her borrowed clothing, she would have wished for more.

Five gowns. Who would have thought she would be happy with a mere five gowns?

They waited in a strangely peaceful silence until Clara's boots sounded on the floor. She came around the hallway that led to the library and the servants' stairs, Olivia's straw bonnet in one hand, a shawl and a pair of gloves in the other.

Five gowns might be easy enough to adapt to in the first days of this strange new life, but forcing her new friend to avoid the fancy staircase and have come down the narrow, dark servants' stairs? Never!

She was not here to fix the plight of servants, much as she would like to, if only for Clara's sake. For right now, they could enjoy the sunshine.

———

The day was lovely, the sun high and bright, the breeze a bare whisper of air. Enough to stir the leaves, but not enough to chill her through the shawl.

Besides, she was walking close to Langley again, and his body's warmth was enough to offset a deeper chill than this.

The sun sparkled ahead. Langley kept his pace slow. He was in no hurry to reach the sunshine. Her hope that he would take them to the gazebo where they might see the bend of the river, even ask where it went, began to fade.

He didn't need to know she and Clara were planning to hike its distance to get back to his house and search for the iron. "I heard about the gazebo. Can we go find it? I've never been in one, never even seen one in real life." She looked up at him, and hoped her innocent look wasn't overdone.

He stopped walking, forcing her to stop as well, held her gaze for a long moment, and then one side of his mouth curved. "No gazebo? Does no one in America have a garden big enough for one?"

"Does a garden have to be big to have one?"

He dipped his head. "I stand corrected. Undoubtedly, a gazebo would be a lovely addition even to a small garden."

"At least for someplace to hide if it rains." She smiled and looked up from under her brim at the sky.

He tilted his head up as well. "I don't think we need to worry about that today."

"No, it looks lovely out. But then, this is England, and aren't you known for rain?"

The playfulness left his eyes, replaced by the watchfulness she was getting heartily sick of. "You know of our weather?"

Olivia pulled her hand out of his elbow and stopped in place. "*Everyone* knows about England's weather. You'd have to be living in a cave not to know." Then she started walking again, and he moved with her, but they did not touch. "I'm sure there are gardens with gazebos in my country, but I just have never been in one."

"I have offended you again, have I not?" He did not look down; she knew because she looked up at the question and his gaze was on something far away. "I beg your forgiveness."

He looked down at her now as they stood in the path. "I may have to beg your forgiveness for another thing, as well. I have news other than the dressmaker. My cousin came yesterday. I did not even know he was in the neighborhood."

A cousin. In the neighborhood. Nearby.

A cousin would know things, hear things. Like diamond buttons.

A strange expression darkened his face. Sadness maybe, or regret. "I still cannot believe someone wants me dead, It must be a fever dream jumbling together your own danger, added to your being left in my house. However, I admit I found it strange to have him suddenly appear in my house here, and not be in London."

Olivia made herself keep silent.

Langley continued his tale. "I did accuse him of being in my office in the night and he became very angry. He even said he was ashamed to be related to me." He gave a mocking laugh. "Can you imagine? He, the black sheep of the family, had the temerity to turn the blame around to me."

"You know him, and I don't, but what do you think? Did he sound guilty to you?" She wished she could hear the man, listen to him speak, because then she could determine if he was the voice she had heard twice now, and let Langley know if his cousin was the man in both hallway and the office.

Fever dream, indeed!

At least she had him somewhat on the alert. That had to be good.

Langley started walking again, forgetting to hold out his arm. She strolled beside him, her arms at her side feeling useless and awkward without him to hold on to. The sculpted bushes began to thin, the path at her feet brightened as the green branches no longer blocked those golden rays.

"Did Stewart sound guilty?" He repeated her question and shook his head, but it looked more in thought than in answer. "No, but he tried too hard to sound innocent. He never said he was not in the house, and that would be the most logical response."

They passed the last bush, and the garden stretched out again, flagstones winding between circles of blooms wild with color. Langley kept walking, his stroll taking them around the first circle created mainly of purple blossoms. Olivia smelled the distinctive sweetness of lavender, but the other aromas that drifted up, brushed by her gown as she passed, just smelled like fresh flowers to her.

"If someone accused me of going into his office and looking through his things, I would deny it most vociferously." He looked down at her without breaking his slow stride. "It took you a very short while to admit to being there, but you gave your reasons. Reasons I believed."

Olivia met his gaze. "If you can accept he might have been in your office, why not accept that he might want you dead? I know you don't believe I heard that threat, but I assure you, I did. It was not a fever dream."

Langley rubbed a hand across his eyes. "I had forgotten it until now, but he did say that he had a plan to get out from under my father's thumb. I assumed, as I always assume, that he either planned to steal something, or that he was gambling, and expected a big win."

"Or to inherit all that is yours?" She hated to bring it up, but he had come a long way, admitting that his cousin could be the thief in the office.

She might be able to save his life after all.

He stopped and turned to face her, his eyes shadowed both by his hat and by some darkness within. "Perhaps. I do not like to think it."

"You might have to, like it or not." It might be totally forward in his time, but Olivia reached out and touched his arm, a brief brush. "If it was him—and I don't know that it was, but I'd bet real money on it—you must be careful. Set men to guard you; don't go out without someone with you."

She suddenly realized what a risk he had taken even coming to her today. "I mean it. No more riding about the countryside alone."

His brows came down in a truly ferocious frown. "I am quite capable of defending myself." The frown faded; his shoulders went back, and he folded his arms over his chest. "I do not know what kind of men you have in your country, but here, men do not need women to stand up for them. However, if it will make you feel better, I have a set of dueling pistols, and can carry both of them, primed and at half-cock. Would that be sufficient?"

Men! "You aren't going to take this seriously, are you?"

Those expressive brows went up. "I have just offered to ride with arms at hand. I do not know what more you wish from me."

I want you to be safe. She didn't let herself wonder if the burst of panic was from more than feeling responsible for him. "I wish you would stay in your house and not travel around the countryside. The voice I heard said he would waylay you along the way back to London, but if you show no signs of going back, he is here, I heard him twice, and he will take whatever chance he gets."

He gave what might pass for a laugh. "I am not going to remain in my house. I am not a coward to hide. I would rather whoever this is, whether Vic—Mr. Stewart or someone else, show himself like a man."

His plan suddenly became clear. "You are trying to draw him out, aren't you?"

The frown reappeared. "You need not worry about it. The less you know, the less danger to yourself."

Olivia waved her hands to encompass the garden around them and the house behind. "I am here in your father's house, surrounded by servants. I can't wander from room to room without what feels like an entire entourage following me, or watching from the corners. How can I possibly be in danger?"

Those crystal eyes darkened, and he leaned forward, towering over her. "If the man you fear is my cousin, he knows about you. If he hears that you are no longer in my house, he will suspect where I have taken you." He took a deep breath, as if bracing himself for something difficult. "On the other hand, if it is a stranger and he knows only about my family and wealth, then I grant you, you are likely safe here."

But he did not believe that, any more than she did. She was certain of it.

CHAPTER 39

THE GAZEBO WAS LOVELY, SMALLER THAN SHE EXPECTED, BUT with real glass. Which shouldn't have surprised her, but oddly did.

They went down the rock stairs beyond the gazebo, laid out to look like natural steps and easy to traverse, to look at the pond. The stream bent into the distance, but it got lost between the trees.

"Where does that go?" She pointed toward the curve of blue.

Langley gave her a sharp look. "It is much faster to take the road."

He had guessed what she and Clara planned. He was a hard man to deceive. Getting back to his house might be harder than they thought. If her suspicions were right, he would set out men to watch the stream the moment he learned either of them was missing.

He switched his gaze from the green and blue curve of the land and water to her face, and a little smile curved his

mouth. "If you want the iron, you do not need to cross difficult land or risk falling into the stream. You can simply ask."

She opened her mouth, but before any words came out,
he continued speaking. "But the answer will be no." The
smile disappeared, and he became serious. "I have grown to
trust you on some things, but it is strange and unsettling
how attached you are to it. Besides, I believe it to be a danger
to you. Whoever sent you here, and whatever they want
from you, they undoubtedly will want the iron as well. It
hides something. While I cannot find the secret, those who
sent you will know how to use it."

Know how to use it. If only she could tell him the truth! It
hurt to continue keeping her secret. Worse, he had grown to
trust her.

And he was right: the iron was a danger. Not just to her,
but to him.

What if Clara was wrong? What if the iron was not dead?
What if it whisked her away before she could find out the
threat? For a moment, she couldn't breathe.

If the iron still worked, if she suddenly found herself back
in her own time, would she ever know whether Langley
lived or died?

W hen they came back around the house, the sun had
lowered in the sky, not twilight, but no longer
midday. A small carriage sat before the front door, the single
horse nibbling on grass poking through the stony drive. The
dressmaker was there. Langley stopped, and turned to face
her. His expression was serious, his eyes capturing hers. "You
are not to consider cost. You are to order everything Lady

Stafford tells you. I assure you, whatever you purchase will not cause so much as a ripple in their finances."

Olivia glanced at the window beside her, catching glimpses of the frames in the parlor that held the awful paintings. She knew enough to realize the dressmaker would not be permitted to wait there. That was only for the upper class, and servants who were expected to clean in silence.

Besides, she didn't want to be measured where anyone might possibly walk in.

She met his gaze again. "I promise I won't make an issue of anything."

"You realize invitations will come to gatherings around the neighborhood." His gaze flickered away and came back, with a sternness she only saw when he was about to warn her not to spy. "You might be in danger. You were left for a reason, and I can only assume you were to meet contacts hiding about here. They will not know you cannot remember. If anything happens that seems untoward, if anyone gives you a message, you are to tell my father."

He stepped back, his body as rigid as the look in his eyes. "You say you are not a spy. This is your chance to prove it."

She flinched at the cold reminder that in his eyes—all of their eyes—she wasn't totally trusted. *I have grown to trust you in many ways.* That left a lot of room for lingering doubt.

The door opened beside them, and Langley's face went blank, hiding his thoughts from the footman who stood waiting for them to enter.

"Enjoy yourself. And do not worry if your trunk is found. No woman ever can have too many gowns." A faint twinkle gleamed in those pale eyes. "Or so my sister tells me. Who am I to argue with her?"

Olivia smiled despite the lingering sting. "I will take her word for it."

And then, much to her surprise after his stern warning, he held her gaze as he raised her hand . . . and kissed it. Which was real, the harsh caution, or the gentle kiss? Olivia thought he held her hand a moment longer than necessary before letting it go, but then, she didn't know the rules for hand-kissing. Under any circumstances.

"I will leave you to the care of my stepmother and the dressmaker, then." Langley bowed and turned, walking toward the corner of the house and around it, leaving her staring at the empty path, totally confused.

Behind her, Clara hissed, "Are you going in, or not?"

Olivia gave a start, and spun around. "Oh! You startled me."

Clara's brows came together, and she gave Olivia a thoughtful look. "You don't even see me when you are with him."

"Oh, Clara." Olivia couldn't deny it. "I'm sorry. It's not that I don't remember you are there. It's just that he's got a title, which makes him unique in my experience, and he's been so good to me, and I . . . I like talking to him."

"No, it's okay. Really." Clara looked down at the pebbles of the drive, and back up. "Just be careful, okay? We don't know what's going to happen." She shooed Olivia toward the door. "You need to get in. The dressmaker is waiting for you."

Olivia stepped across the threshold, to see Lady Stafford leaning over the staircase at the far end of the hall, her gown a splash of pink between the mahogany spindles and vivid against the cream wall. Did she have clothes in any other color? "Olivia, oh good! You are back. The dressmaker is here to measure you. She brought the most divine samples." She beckoned with a regal gesture.

Olivia turned to Clara. "Come with me? I don't want someone I don't know stripping me so I can be measured."

Clara nodded. "I'm probably expected to be there, anyway." A little smile touched her mouth, to Olivia's relief. "Besides, it might be fun."

They walked down the hallway toward Lady Stafford, but Clara turned toward the cross hall that led to the servants' staircase.

"There is no time to waste," Lady Stafford called. "Come along."

Olivia caught Clara's sleeve, tugged her back, and smiled. "Yes, come along with me." As they walked toward the large staircase, she whispered, "I don't think Lady Stafford minds. Her own maid follows her around, so why can't you?"

Clara hissed back, "I didn't want to step out of line."

But they were at the stairs now, and started up the first flight together. Lady Stafford waited until they were nearly at the landing before turning and heading up the next flight with surprising speed for a woman who had been worn down by the stress of pregnancy's first term.

"It was so good of the dressmaker to come here, but she wants to get back tomorrow, so we have to do everything we can today. She will sleep with the servants. There are plenty of beds."

At the strange noise one step below, Olivia glanced back at Clara, whose brows had gone up her forehead.

No doubt Lady Stafford had never gone up to the servants' quarters. She had a moment of gratitude that Clara got to sleep in the little room next door.

L ady Stafford scurried down the hall to Olivia's room. "We shall work in here. The light is coming in nicely, and we should take advantage of it while we have it." She beckoned to Olivia, a few feet behind. "Come, come, the dressmaker awaits." She opened the door, and stepped inside.

A large portfolio sat on the bed, and an equally large satchel sat on the floor.

"So, this is the woman who wants a wardrobe?" A voice came from the left, and Olivia turned to see a tall, thin, sharp-featured, well-dressed forty-ish woman.

"Yes, indeed." Lady Stafford gestured to Olivia.

Being measured by a stranger was an odd experience. The dressmaker, with the oddly appropriate name of Mrs. Berrycloth, was most thorough. The width of her shoulders, the measurement under her breasts, the length of her arms, the circumference of her upper arms, and her wrists, how long from shoulder to elbow, and elbow to wrist, how far from her shoulders to the floor, all were taken down in careful penmanship. She even measured Olivia's feet.

"I must have the shoes match," she had said when Olivia stared at her. "I will give this to the cobbler." Then she shook her head. "The ones you are wearing do not fit properly."

Of course they weren't a perfect fit. They had belonged to Langley's sister.

Then the sketches came out of a large portfolio, a whole sheaf of papers tied with a ribbon. Lady Stafford ordered Clara to pull the orange curtains wider, and sent her off to stand by the wall.

Lady Stafford and Mrs. Berrycloth hemmed and hawed over the stack of designs. Long gowns with high waists, some with long sleeves, some with short puffy sleeves, some with several layers of ruffles at the hem, some with slender strips of lace.

This was not as much fun as the day when they played dress-up with Cecelia's gowns.

The two women looked from the sketches to Olivia, standing in her chemise and growing colder by the minute despite the sunlight coming through the window, and back to the sketches, setting some aside while others went into a growing stack.

Olivia pointed at the stacks. "Can I see them?"

Lady Stafford looked up, startled. Olivia wondered if she had broken some rule. After all, she wasn't paying for all this luxury. The Staffords were.

But the lady smiled. "Forgive me. I know the latest styles have almost certainly not reached across the sea to your country. By all means, you may look." She pointed at the stack that Olivia liked the best. "These are the ones we shall commission." She looked over at Mrs. Berrycloth. "How many more, do you think? She must have a ballgown or two to start. And did you say you brought some fabric samples?"

The sun was low enough now that it shone directly in through the window, and the warmth of the day was fading into the coolness of early evening. Olivia shivered. "Can I get dressed?"

Lady Stafford looked up from the display in front of her, eyes wide. "Oh, forgive me." She looked over at Mrs. Berrycloth. "Have you taken all the measurements you need?"

Mrs. Berrycloth looked Olivia over with a thoughtful gaze. "I believe I have everything."

"You may get dressed. Have your maid get your gown."

The two women went back to shuffling sketches. "And I thought these should be in velvet." Mrs Berrycloth looked Olivia up and down again. "With that red hair, we must be careful which colors we choose." She shook her head and clucked her tongue. "If I had known about the hair, I should have brought other colors, but I think I can give a good enough account with what I have."

Mrs. Berrycloth then picked up the satchel and set it on the bed with a solid *thump*. She looked at Lady Stafford as she unfastened the straps. "I will match the fabrics with the patterns. We must discuss colors."

Tiny bits of fabric came out, pinks and yellows and whites, blues and greens and even purples, some of fabric so delicate and thin Olivia could see the orange bedspread through it. Then came heavier fabrics, velvet—she could tell from the shimmer—and what must have been wool.

Her skill at visualizing came in handy. The fabrics were pinned with straight pins to the papers, where holes showed from other matches. From where she stood, she agreed with the choices. Delicate fabrics with short sleeves, heavier fabrics with long sleeves, and the velvet matched with what Olivia could tell was a ballgown, with a note that said, "Green."

Olivia wondered if the Staffords missed having their daughter around. Maybe that was one of the reasons they had been so generous.

Or maybe Lord Stafford viewed her as a way to bridge the divide between him and his son.

CHAPTER 40

"MISS UNDERWOOD?" FARLEY APPEARED IN THE LIBRARY DOOR, where she was reading. "Lord Langley is here. Are you receiving?"

It had been three days. The dressmaker had gone back to Bristol to sew. After the flurry of activity, the days had become . . . boring. She had often longed for days to do nothing but read, but now she found she longed for work, for something to *do*.

Besides, some of the writing from this time was so convoluted and confusing that it took a lot of the fun out of it.

A visit from anyone was welcome, but a visit from Langley set her heart fluttering. Olivia closed *The Nun*—probably too quickly, she must look too eager—and rose. "Of course. Where is he?"

Langley appeared behind Farley. "I am here."

"Thank you, Farley," she said at the same moment as Langley. Stereo, she thought, but held back the smile as she turned to him. "I'm glad to see you alive and well. Did you take precautions? Did you bring a pistol?"

It was rather appalling, she thought, for someone as opposed to guns as she was to actually be checking to make sure someone was carrying.

He pulled a tiny pistol out of his coat pocket, so small his palm dwarfed it.

"Is that even real?"

Langley scowled at her, but a twinkle in his eyes told her he wasn't really angry. "Of course it is. I would recommend it be treated with care. I kept this on my person, within easy reach. You surely can have no complaints about that."

Modern guns killed at quite a distance, but she didn't know how far bullets traveled in this time. Olivia didn't want to spoil his visit, though, and he had listened to her and taken her seriously.

Which was more than she expected. "No, I have no complaints at all." Except that he was out riding on the road, where anyone could lie in wait, and a bullet traveled faster than a man could pull out his gun.

He was here, though, and for now he was safe.

Langley tucked the little pistol back in his pocket, and smiled down at her. "Would you like to go down to the pond today? I think this year's ducklings are about ready to leave the nest. This might be your last chance to see them together.."

"Ducklings! I would love to see them."

"Send for your maid, and we shall go out for a stroll again today."

The ducklings were hardly the babies she was expecting. The only indication that this was a family was that they all stayed close together, paddling near the reeds. The whole group was dull in color, just brown, although she caught a glimpse of yellow eyes.

Probably most American ducks were brown, but she was so used to seeing mallards with their shiny green heads that the brown was just the tiniest bit disappointing. The day was nice, though, warm and sunny, and the sky as blue as a robin's egg. Well, as a Minnesota robin's egg. She didn't know what color English robins' eggs were.

She had seen English robins occasionally from the windows, and been surprised by how little they were, as well as by the smaller patch of red, but just seeing the russet flash as they flew about the place brought back memories of home.

If she was stuck here, at least there was something vaguely familiar.

Another duck paddled out of the grass, a striking black and white, a lovely contrast to the brown ones. "Is that the male?" The duck turned its head, and something fluttered on the back of its neck. "It's got a feathered neck!" A silly thing to say, since the whole bird was feathers, but he understood, and chuckled.

"That is a tufted duck. We have a couple more families along the pond." He looked down at her. "I thought you might like them." His head tilted a little, and he studied her with a thoughtful gaze. "Are you the kind of woman who loves puppies and kittens, too?"

Olivia smiled. "Yes, who doesn't? But I'm more of an adult pet person. Kittens and puppies are lovely and great fun, but I prefer mature animals. You can tell their personalities better. Baby animals are just mischief on four legs, but adults have calmed down."

His gaze still held her face. "I have some stable cats. The mother just had a litter of kittens. When they are weaned, would you like a kitten?"

The tales of drowning unwanted kittens sent a chill over her. "What will you do with the rest of the kittens if I say yes?"

"There is always someone who wants to take kittens home to rid the house of vermin."

"Promise you won't drown any that don't get claimed?"

A flicker of what might have been guilt slipped across his eyes and was gone.

Spaying and neutering likely wouldn't be invented for decades, maybe longer. She thought about female cats going into heat, and male cats spraying, with the stench that went with it. Much as she wanted to save all of them, sight unseen, she knew it wasn't practical. "If you kill any of them, I don't want to know about it." In her own time, the decision would have been simple, and keeping an adult cat of either sex wouldn't be a problem. In this time . . .

She shoved down the longing, and sighed. "I would love a pet, but kittens grow into cats and cats, wonderful as they are, can make a mess of the house."

"I am sure we can find a way to keep the cat when it becomes a nuisance."

We? She felt her brows rise.

He must have seen it because he clarified his statement. "Just ask any of the servants. They will find someplace to use them. The barns always need cats, and the grooms might want one or two in their rooms by the stables."

So by *we,* he meant the household, not the two of them.

She didn't know if she was relieved or disappointed. "In that case, I would love a kitten."

He smiled. "I will tell the stable staff to set one aside for you." He held out his arm, and she took it.

This walk was as lovely as the other one. The sun shone, and he pointed out some of the things that had changed from when he was a child. A maze larger than the one at his house—"Mother's family did not have the wealth or the inclination to rip out what was there and start over,"— and trees that had been left in place despite the renovation. "I am pleased that Mr. Brown did not find it necessary to destroy everything. I am past the age of climbing trees myself, but if Lady Stafford has a son, it is nice to think another boy will have the same fun climbing them as I did."

"You don't mind having a half-brother so young?"

He almost stumbled. His eyes went wide. "No! Of course not! I rather think it would be fun."

Olivia smiled up at him. "What about a sister?"

Langley's face softened, and a faint smile played about his mouth, and lightened his eyes. "I find myself very protective over the sister I already have. I will probably be insufferable. Thank goodness she will have the earl to watch over her."

She heard a snicker from behind, and gave a laugh herself. "Unless he is worse than you? How was he with your sister? Cecelia, is it?"

"Yes, and I fear he was too lenient. I did tell you she married at barely seventeen?"

She nodded. "Yes, and it made me feel old."

A chuckle ran through her hand as it brushed against his

coat. If he tightened his arm even a little, held her hand more closely, she might feel the muscles of his chest as he laughed.

She would like that.

He kept talking, oblivious to the thoughts running through her mind. "I found a new letter from her when I went through my bills. She thinks she could be with child."

"So soon?" Olivia could have bitten her tongue. Of course a teenage girl would get pregnant quickly in this time.

He shifted, and she knew he was looking down at her. "Do women in America have a secret to keep from getting with child?"

This is 1811, not twenty-something. "No, I guess not. It's just . . . seventeen, or even eighteen when the baby comes, seems awfully young to be tied down to motherhood."

If she didn't go home soon, if she married . . . someone, she too could expect to have a baby nine months later.

How did a woman avoid her husband in the middle of her cycle, when conception was most possible?

C lara unfastened her gown in the light of the candle on the dressing table. "Are you really going to let Langley give you a kitten?" She started pulling up from the bottom and Olivia raised her arms. In short order the gown was off, and Clara hung it on one of the armoire's hooks, then turned back around. "If you want to go home, you shouldn't get too attached to anything in this time."

Get too attached. The feel of her hand in the crook of Langley's elbow, the sketches she had gone through when the dressmaker came here, and excitement of waiting for the gowns to be delivered.

Wearing gowns that had belonged to Langley's sister. Talking to Lady Stafford, who had told her that very morning to call her Abby—"We are becoming friends, are we not?"—and wondering what her sudden disappearance would do to a woman who was an older, possibly at-risk, mother in pregnancy terms . . . Was she already becoming attached?

Clara had made it no secret how badly she wanted, no, *needed*, to get back home to their own time. Olivia raised her arms for the nightgown, and with new skill, her friend bunched the fabric together and worked it over her arms, and tugged it into place.

The question had nagged her brain ever since she arrived, and she was positive it had tormented Clara, too. *How long was their stay? Were they here for good?*

Clara pulled down the covers for Olivia, the perfect lady's maid. Olivia wanted to yank the covers away, order Clara to go to bed and rest, but when she had tried it before, Clara had turned on her. "If I don't have something to keep me busy, I'll go crazy!"

So she stood there, nibbling at her bottom lip, and wondered if she dared ask, *what if we won't ever go back?*

Clara bolted upright, and turned stricken eyes on her, and Olivia realized she had spoken words aloud. "Don't say that! I have to go back! I have to!"

"I'm sorry, Clara. I didn't mean . . . but it's been on my mind ever since I got here. I don't know how we'll ever get back to Langley's house, and he's sure not going to bring the iron here." An odd smile tugged at her heart. "When they are ready to leave their mother, he'll bring a kitten, but not the iron." The smile faded inside.

Clara stood stiffly by the bed, and her hands clenched

into fists at her side. "What if we are linked somehow, and the more you like it here, the less possibility I will ever go back?" She leaned forward, and grabbed Olivia's hands. "I need you to want to leave. We are in this together."

CHAPTER 41

THE MESSAGE WAS BRIEF, BUT EVEN SO, CROFTS COULD FEEL the anger.

Come to my residence. I require an explanation.

Explanation of what? It had been days since he last heard from the man. He wished he could ignore the note, but Victor Stewart was not one to brush off. Crofts straightened his worn cravat, closed up his little house with the key that, for now at least, he had the right to use.

When he fled—and he would have to flee—he would leave it here in the house. Langley would have no trouble replacing him.

Thank goodness he had been frugal, because he doubted Stewart could get in and steal anything with staff roaming about the house, and Langley's valet standing guard over his master's possessions. If Langley had the veriest hint that Stewart had been in the office that night, he would set men to watch every window and door.

The sun was bright and cheerful, the sky blue and brilliant. The horse could go faster than the gentle trot he set it to, but he wanted to delay his arrival as long as possible.

Even with his dread of what Stewart would do if he arrived later than ordered, he refused to push the horse. He would get there when he got there.

It might be time to book passage to New South Wales. He wished he dared wait and see if Stewart managed to steal anything to sell, but even if the man did, what were the chances that he would share the proceeds?

Maybe he should go to the dock first. Or instead.

F ear crept along Crofts's spine as he stood before the house in Portishead that Stewart had rented. He hated being a coward, hated that he was more afraid of arriving in New South Wales poor than of the man he knew had no honor.

The slow ride had given him lots of time to think. Too much time, perhaps. Time to consider what it would be like traveling to New South Wales with the pitiful amount he had squirreled away in the cottage. He had another small sum in a bank in Bristol. He needed to get on a boat to the other side of the world before anyone knew he was gone, and dared not make the journey to get those funds unless he was certain it was necessary. His little house on the edge of Langley's land was close enough for a message to reach him from Portishead. Bristol was too large, too far away, and too obvious a place from which to flee.

Why had Stewart chosen this village to hide, anyway? Was there a fisherman willing to row him some place where no one would think to find him?

Stewart might promise him a share of what he inherited

when Langley was out of the way, but he knew the man now, knew he would get nothing unless he found the spine to demand it.

So here he was, building the courage to lift the knocker. It felt warm against his fingers as he made himself lift it, and when he let it go, the clang seemed to echo, not just into the house, but down the street.

Footsteps came toward the door, and it jerked open. Stewart glared down at him. "Inside." He turned toward the room where their other meeting had taken place, and snapped over his shoulder, "Shut the door behind you."

Crofts obeyed, leaving the lock undone. If he had to leave quickly, he did not want to waste time.

Stewart stood where he had the last time, only this time coals showed a faint glow and the room held lingering warmth of a fire. Portishead being on the water, the man must have decided the nights were too chill for the fireplace to stay unused. Unless the landlord provided the coals as part of the rent, Stewart must have dipped into his small funds or sold something to purchase them.

The curtain was slightly open; the sun painted a pale stripe on the floor, but the window had not been cleaned on the outside—not well on the inside either—so even if someone were to pass by, they would not see much. The knowledge gave him faint reassurance. And faint concern. No one could see what happened in this room.

Crofts did not have to wait. Victor spat out the same word as in his note. "Explain yourself."

"About what?"

"You said there was a woman in the house, and that we had been overheard. I took your suggestion and paid my cousin a visit. What good did it do me? Langley now knows I am around, and what is more, there is no woman there. He told me when I visited him. I have been back several times to watch the house, and never once have I seen a woman who was not a servant. How am I to believe that anyone knows our plan? I have only your word."

If the woman had heard them from the hallway and then again in the library—and he was convinced she had, wherever she had been hiding—she knew his voice as well as Stewart's. They were both in danger. "She was there, I tell you! He told me about her himself. He said that she was American! I learned of her presence and her room from *him*. I did not invent her. If she is no longer there, then I do not know where she went. The woman existed, and she *was* there."

"Yet you did not see her."

Crofts straightened. He did not realize he had been sinking back into himself until his anger was pricked. "Whoever she was, you know Langley. Do you doubt that he would have a woman in his house?"

Stewart's hands curled into fists at his side. "Then where is she now, and why did he deny her to me? American women can be mistresses as easily . . ." His hands relaxed, and a smile curved his mouth. "Ah. Now I think I understand. He still holds the one I stole from him against me. No doubt he is jealous of her now that he knows I am around, and sent her away."

"Langley said she was left there by someone unknown. He never used the word 'mistress.' Nor did any of the servants I overheard suggest such a thing." Crofts's mind made another leap. Something else Langley told him pricked his thoughts. "If she was a mistress, why did he need to provide her a maid?"

That stopped Stewart. "A maid? He gave her a maid?" A

brief pause, then, "I wonder that the woman did not bring her own. Servants love a trip to the country."

Those hands tightened again. "It seems you left out a great deal when you first came here. You tell me we were overheard, that the woman was in the room next to his. And now you tell me she needed a maid, did not bring her own, and he provided one? This woman becomes more and more unusual."

A pause. Crofts kept his mouth quiet.

Stewart looked at the dirty window, then back to Crofts. Every time the man's gaze met his, Crofts felt a chill run along his spine. "And my dear cousin now tells me she is not there. I can only come back to the conclusion that he is hiding her from me." His brows furrowed. "That still leaves me with having to find her. From what Miles told you, she heard too much. You must find out where she is."

A sly smile tipped one edge of his mouth. "An American here in England, with tensions rising and Napoleon rampaging around Europe—if she disappears, I might be doing England a favor." Stewart gave a snort of laughter. "Two favors! Eliminate an American, and replace my cousin."

Crofts fought down his shivers. "You wanted to steal something. Why not wait until you get the title? You will get it all then."

Stewart glared at him. "Do you see where I am living?" He swung his arms wide, encompassing the dingy room, the worn curtains, the faded cover of the settee, and the worn wood of the chairs. "Me, the grandson of an earl, living in this place? They will come for the rent soon."

He did not say it, but Crofts knew Stewart likely had no funds to cover it. His predicament was of his own making.

Stewart pointed his finger at Crofts. "You find out where the woman is, and let me handle my cousin."

"How do you propose I do that?" Crofts surprised himself by his own boldness.

"You are his man of affairs. Think of something!" Steward strode past him, back to the door.

There was nothing to do but follow him out into the hall, where the outer door stood open. The man now knew it had not been locked. Did he think it to be an oversight? Crofts eased past Stewart, but his expression said nothing new. When Crofts stepped into the street, the door slammed shut behind him.

Find out where the woman is. If Crofts could not do it properly, he would have to find her himself.

Victor stood at the door, and waited for Crofts to get on the borrowed horse and trot away. The man did not know it, but they were both going to the same place. However, he could tell Crofts was taking the main road, while he intended to take the secondary routes. Miles knew he was around—if he knew how things were going to fall apart, he would have told his cousin he was on his way back to London—so he would have to slip into the house quietly.

He would not leave until he had something worth selling. If he did not pay the landlord of this pathetic place, he would find himself sleeping in a haystack somewhere.

His horse waited in the stable behind the house. Poor beast. Its accommodations were no better than his own. Victor had paid some of his last coins to ensure the feed was fresh and the water clean.

If this did not work out, the horse and his clothes would be all he had until he found a way to return to London, and that could not happen until he had the funds to pay off his creditors.

The street was crowded when he rode out, but Crofts was nowhere to be seen, and the crowds had far too many other distractions to notice a man on a horse. Victor wove his way through the carts and people until he reached the outskirts. Instead of turning left to the main road, he turned right, onto the narrow path that wove into the woods.

It would take him half an hour to reach his cousin's house, plus time to watch, see when he could slip in and get back out. Thank goodness Miles did not have the number of servants his father did. Getting around should be possible.

V ictor tied his horse to a tree some distance from Miles's house, and crept toward it, keeping in the trees. The stable rang with voices and hammers, likely the blacksmith shoeing one of the magnificent beasts, the grooms holding them still.

He eased away from the tree's protection, crept past the laundry house all whitewashed and clean, then past the bushes that lined the path toward the servants' entrance at the back.

He did not want to take that route. The hallway would lead him directly past the kitchen, but with any luck they would be too busy to notice a figure strolling past.

Hurrying would attract attention, but a steady walk would be one of the normal sounds in the house.

The back entry, as he hoped, was unlocked, and Victor slipped inside. If only he could remove his boots! But if he was unlucky and ran into a stray servant, stocking feet would be remembered and remarked. So instead he made sure to land on the balls of his feet and kept his heels from clicking on the floor as he walked the plain hall to the door he knew led into the family's part of the house.

If God had been on the side of thieves, Victor would have given Him credit for the kitchen door's being shut. Even so, his heart pounded as he walked quietly past and through the entrance into the main hallway.

The kitchen was certainly loud. He wanted to pause, see if he could figure out what was going on, but he had to keep moving. He weighed the laughter as the noise followed him to the far doorway, and the main hallway. If he was not mistaken, there might be some kind of party going on, which meant that Miles was not in the house.

Better and better.

He cracked the door to that long gallery with the windows that lined the front of the house, where anyone could see him. No new sound met his ears, but the party's din could have drowned it out.

This house belonged to Miles's mother's side of the family and he knew he never would have claim to it, but he had been here enough to know the floor plan. The servants' stairs were at the far end on his left, right across the hall from his cousin's office. And Miles's bedroom was one floor up.

He took a breath and opened the door the rest of the way, looking in both directions. The long hall was empty, the narrow door to those stairs closed,

Victor threw caution aside and ran down the hall as though hounds were on his trail, grabbed the stairway door knob, and flung it open. He caught it just before it slammed against the wall, and forced himself to close it slowly, hearing the latch catch with the faintest click. When the door shut behind him, he took his first deep breath since the house came into view.

Now to find Langley's bedroom empty.

Up the curving stairs of the tower and into the hallway where he and Crofts had laid their plans. Had the woman been in Miles's room when she chanced to overhear? Where had she been when she realized they were in the office? That still troubled him.

He stopped outside Langley's room, and pressed his ear to the heavy wood. Not a sound came from inside, but the doors were thick and blocked any attempt at eavesdropping.

Would he find the valet there, mending one of Miles's shirts or polishing his boots?

With a sweaty hand, he turned the knob and eased the door open a fraction. No challenge came from inside, no sound, no breathing.

Victor slipped inside the quiet room, his heart pounding so hard his ears buzzed, and shut the door behind him as silently as he had opened it. No other sounds came. The place was still; no breathing soughed from the door where he assumed Thomas's sleeping area was.

The curtains were open, and the midday sun lit the room brighter than a candle ever could. Victor waited one more moment for someone to jump out behind that servant's door, but nothing happened.

The man must be down in the kitchen, celebrating Miles's absence.

He had to move fast. Victor scanned the room, the large burgundy bed, beautiful bedposts with carved vines winding up to blossoms, a wooden-framed screen with matching burgundy fabric that he knew hid the commode. An armoire where Miles hung all his fancy suits.

And finally, a dark chest of drawers against the near

wall, not tall, not wide, just the right size for a man to keep small items like handkerchiefs and cravats, gloves and stockings.

And cufflinks? Cravat pins?

He glanced back at the hallway door, still shut tight, went over, and pulled the top drawer open.

A small box sat among the neatly folded cravats. Aha. Victor flipped the box open. Gold glittered against the black velvet, rings and pins and cufflinks, rich ruby, golden amber, matching squares of emerald.

It was so unfair!

He had to think. Thomas would notice if something on the top was missing but how long before he took something from the bottom of the box? With a careful finger, Victor reached past the tempting ruby cufflinks, the ring with large amber set in heavy gold, an enameled cravat pin, not allowing himself a close look.

Down at the bottom, a gold watch chain, unattached to any watch, lay curled as if dropped there and forgotten. He pulled it out, to discover it had been broken and was actually two pieces, not one. With no watch, that meant it had been replaced with a new one at some time.

It would take that valet months to realize it was missing.

Victor slid it into the empty pocket in his vest, and something beneath the little box glinted in the sun, something that might have fallen out and been overlooked.

He picked it up, and as it came into view, he recognized it as a cravat pin he had occasionally seen Miles wear. An emerald surrounded by a swirl of diamonds on a straight stick of heavy gold.

A handsome piece, one he wished he did not have to sell, but both together would pay his rent for months to come, even get some of his creditors satisfied.

Or at least mollified. He shoved it in the pocket next to the broken chain.

Something creaked nearby. Victor snapped the small box shut, dropped it back in its place, shoved the drawer to with more speed than care, and scurried to the door. He pressed his ear to the door this time, too, listening, but the creak did not return. It was time to leave. He stepped out into the hallway.

But the long corridor was empty, thank goodness, the sound must have come from elsewhere. Victor closed the door, leapt for the round tower's protection, and ran down the stairs without worrying about being careful. He almost fell as he took the curves, but he grabbed the railing and stopped himself, his lungs clenching so tight he could barely breathe.

"Slow," he whispered into the air, not sure if he was telling himself or his heartbeat, but no one shouted behind him, the air was still, and his legs found their strength again.

Along the empty hallway, but with no one there to see, he slipped out the main door instead of risking the kitchen a second time, then eased along the front, pausing at every window. The corner of the house with round tower, and few windows.

Victor ran for his horse.

He had done it.

CHAPTER 42

THE WEEKS ROLLED ON. OLIVIA COULD FEEL THE PAIN hanging over Clara. Every now and then, her friend would look out the window toward the creek, the urge to run so palpable Olivia felt the muscles in her own body tense in sympathy.

Her new gowns had come, and her armoire bulged with the bounty. Day gowns of sprigged muslin and smooth cotton, silk, and velvet evening gowns with short, puffed sleeves, and gowns for the cold weather with longer sleeves and heavier fabrics.

Abby had even made sure she got a spencer and a longer pelisse for the coming winter, shawls so soft she was amazed at their delicacy, nightgowns and new chemises, plus stockings of both silk and cotton, and the ribbons to tie them.

Every fancy gown had matching embroidered slippers that actually fit, and she got half-boots for everyday wear.

Those boots—not at all as durable as she had supposed when they were mentioned, and nothing like the sturdy boots Clara wore—had seen plenty of use.

Abby had agreed to give Cecelia's old gown to Clara. "They are old, and they do not fit you properly," she said when Olivia asked. She turned to look at Clara as if she had never seen her before, and looked from the maid to Olivia and back. "Yes, I think she is more Cecelia's size. Especially on top." A faint smile tugged on her mouth.

So Clara finally had the gowns she had wanted.

The other change was that Langley had taken to visiting every day or so.

It would have been flattering if she had not known he was trying to draw out the potential killer. Or prove that she was wrong, that she had only imagined hearing any threats.

Her heart did not seem to get the message. Every visit it gave happy leaps, and her smile felt like a permanent fixture inside. She had to force herself not to let it show, but even as she controlled her expression, every minute with him made it harder not to believe there might be a happily-ever-after.

A sudden rap interrupted her thoughts and made her jump. Clara turned from the window. Olivia whirled around, hoping her friend didn't see her thoughts on her face. Maribelle stood at the bedroom door they left open to help the air circulate.

"Miss Underwood?"

"Yes?"

"Lady Stafford would like to see you in the parlor." Her face was serious. It was usually that way, but something in her eyes and the tone of her voice this time held a warning.

As kind as Abby had been, Olivia knew a command when she heard one. "I will be right there."

Maribelle turned and walked down the hallway, her shoes clicking on the floor.

Olivia turned to Clara. "Did that sound as ominous to you as it did to me?"

Clara nodded. "I have heard talk among the servants when they don't know I'm listening. Langley's parents are becoming alarmed. All his visits have them scared that he's getting serious."

Olivia wanted to pretend she didn't know what Clara was talking about, but she knew what they didn't. He was trying to draw out the man she had heard, whether he believed it to be real or not. He had as much as told her so.

It made the ongoing visits all the more painful. Every walk, every farewell kiss on her hand, every conversation over tea on the days it rained and walking was out of the question, buoyed her hopes and let her forget, if only for a few moments, how impossible this was.

He looked at her, on those visits. Long, silent looks when their eyes met and conversation failed. He would look away, and conversation would begin again. Stories about the ducks, family legends, explanations of the books she struggled to enjoy. Then there were the pauses, quiet, comfortable pauses, when they would sip tea in silence, always in front of the parlor windows, where he made a perfect target.

And she fought the urge to grab him, and pull him away.

Did he still believe her?

Who would have thought she would meet a man who made her heart both soar and ache two hundred years before her own time?

Clara motioned to the door. "You better go. You don't want to make her wait."

The walk down the stairs to the main hall felt longer than usual.

Abby was sitting by one of the small tables in the parlor when she arrived. A tea set waited, steam drifting from the spout, and cakes sat on a decorative plate.

Maybe this wasn't going to be as dreadful as she feared.

"Sit, sit, my dear." Abby gave nothing away and gestured to the chair opposite. "Tea should be drunk when warm."

Olivia sat, and reached for the cup Abby had just poured.

"You know that we have enjoyed your company these past weeks, do you not?" Abby made no move to pick up her own cup.

"You have been most generous, and I have enjoyed myself. I can't thank you enough." Olivia gestured to her pretty green gown. "I don't know how I can repay you."

"We can hardly have you wander about the house wearing Cecelia's old gowns. On the other hand, should anyone see your maid and recognize the gown as Cecelia's discard, no one will think anything about it. They all have done the same with their maids." Abby took a breath.

Olivia knew more was coming. She took another sip, and waited.

"We are planning a stag hunting party for some of the local gentry. It is essential that you be properly attired. We have to think of a reason for you to be here. You are not English, and that will be obvious to all who come. You also have no family, which presents another problem. We must come up with some explanation for why you are here. For now, you will be a cousin of mine."

"I could stay in my room." She wasn't at all certain she wanted to meet any more people. Things were complicated enough.

Abby did not acknowledge the offer. "But that is not all. I am most concerned about Miles's interest in you."

Olivia went still.

Abby continued, "I can hardly give him orders, but if his attentions continue, it will make his life difficult. You are American. You cannot see the complications this will have for him." She held out a hand, almost beseechingly, before drawing it back. "A man of his stature simply cannot marry a woman of unknown family, and an American at that."

"We're not getting married!" Olivia's voice was too loud, and she clapped a hand over her mouth as if to tamp down the volume, but too late.

She could not explain the real reason for his constant visits. Tell Abby he was testing to see if there really was a killer waiting the opportunity?

Abby sighed and settled against the straight back of the chair. "I am always amazed at the difference between our two countries. No man visits a woman as often as he has been unless he is quite serious in his intentions." Another sigh. "It is not just the visits. It is the look in his eyes, the way he listens to you, even the way he leans toward you when you are out walking. I know what a man looks like when he is falling in love. I see those signs in him. And that cannot be."

She straightened with a stifled groan. "I am but his stepmother. I have no authority to tell him what to do, but his father and I agree. Neither of us can endure him being so enamored with you."

Enamored. The word tugged at her with startling pain.

Abby, who had known Miles for almost twenty years, believed he was *enamored* with her. The word wasn't love, but it could lead there, couldn't it?

Olivia's whole being hurt; her lungs burned with air trapped by her stillness, her heart clenched with a longing that had been creeping in for weeks, and her mind tumbled with the knowledge that her time here may well be limited and she would leave only pain behind.

She couldn't think of a single thing to say. Abby waited, the quiet in the room palpated with the words the other woman wanted to hear.

If Miles really was enamored, if she had the choice to stay, would she leave the modern world behind to be with him?

Olivia knew her answer, but what if Clara was right and they were linked to the iron somehow, and what happened to one would happen to both?

She could not condemn Clara to a lifetime of working as a maid in this world.

But she didn't want to think of what it would cost herself to leave.

Something must have shown on her face, because Abby leaned over the small distance between them, and her fingers brushed Olivia's arm. "Do not cry. Forgive me for being so blunt, but it must be said. There are plenty of young men in the area who do not have as much to lose as Miles, and they would be happy to take you as a wife. That is why we provided you with a trousseau. I want you to meet an appropriate husband." Her voice softened. "You will find another man to marry. When you have children, your life will be full of purpose."

She leaned back and touched her growing belly with gentle fingers. "I cannot wait for your babies to arrive. You will be nearby, and our children will grow up together."

The few sips of tea she had managed to get down threatened to come back up. Olivia forced herself to swallow and took breaths as deep as her tight lungs would allow, hoping to calm the tension that threatened to burst through her skin. She couldn't open her mouth yet, or the pain that was growing and swelling would explode out in a wail that would shake the walls.

A tap on the door broke the spell. She jerked around, banging the table with her knee and jostling tea out onto the surface.

A footman opened the door, a smile on his face. "Miss Underwood, Lady Stafford. Are you receiving?"

Abby's face fell. Olivia watched the tiny sparkle that had begun when she spoke of Olivia's children—by some unknown man—fade, leaving disappointment behind.

"Of course we are. He hardly needs to be announced. Tell him to come in."

The door opened wider, and Langley didn't wait for the footman to move, just stepped around him. "Abby, Miss Underwood. What is this I hear about a hunting party?"

Abby struggled to her feet. "Stafford said he had sent a note. You must discuss that with him. It is his idea. The larder needs replenishing, and Stafford thinks a stag would go a long way to feeding us for the winter. We cannot shoot a doe for a few more months, but a stag would do nicely for now."

Langley strolled inside, ignoring Abby's hint, and stopped by Olivia's chair. "I smell tea. Is it warm enough for a cup for me?"

Abby actually glared at him, fleeting but unmistakable, before it faded into her usual gracious smile. "I am certain it is cold by now. You will want fresh. Go talk to your father, and have him order it, or give you something stronger."

His brows rose. "Have I interrupted a discussion for women only? Forgive my intrusion." He bowed, but Olivia didn't know which of them it was for.

Abby made a delicate sound in her throat, and Olivia blinked, suddenly realizing she and Langley had been staring at each other. Color crept up his cheeks.

He was blushing!

Olivia felt her own cheeks heat. His mouth tilted on one side, an embarrassed smile, he gave another elegant bow, and turned, walking with what seemed hurried steps to the door. It clicked behind him.

She felt Abby's gaze on her as the other woman took her seat again with a rustle of silk, but her own eyes were fixed on her hand, where the expected kiss had not happened.

He always kissed her hand.

"My dear, do you see now what I mean? He is becoming far too attached to you." Abby's voice was kind, but there was iron in it.

I am a modern woman, and we know how to stand up for ourselves. Olivia straightened her spine and turned her head, meeting Abby's gaze. Instead of the condescending look she was expecting, she only saw sympathy.

"I am sorry, Olivia. I should not have allowed things to go this far. I promise I will look for a kind man, one you can learn to love." Abby looked at the teapot. "I do not wish any tea, strange as that is to say."

She struggled back to her feet, and Olivia rose with her. These new formal manners were becoming second nature. She might have risen anyway in her own time, just in case a pregnant woman needed help, but now it was almost second nature.

"It is easier to breathe when I stand, and the hardest part is yet ahead." Abby smiled, but it looked strained. "I think I need to sleep." She stepped around the small table and stopped at Olivia's side. "My dear, I do not do this lightly, but Miles is like a son to me, and I must do what is right for him. You are still welcome here, you must not worry about that."

Then she walked to the door and out, leaving Olivia standing there, feeling emptier than she had since her mother's death.

How had it happened? All the rational thinking in the world hadn't kept her heart under control, and here she was, falling in love with a man from a different world, wanting him more than she ever had wanted a relationship before.

And knowing that she could not have him.

How long had she stood there? She could not stay in this room any longer.

Olivia whirled around, almost tripping over her own feet, and stumbled toward the door. Out into the hall, past the footman waiting for someone to let in or out, grabbing the knob of the heavy outside door and pulling before he knew what she intended. Olivia flew down the flagstone walk along the front of the house, past the path that led to the creek.

The windows looked over that path. Instead she turned to the left, to the more sheltered path that led through the small woods, where benches had been placed under sheltering boughs.

Where she could cry alone, unwatched.

CHAPTER 43

"I WILL HAVE CROFTS AND DENTON GO THROUGH THE LARDER and see what we need before the cold weather comes. I expect I will take a portion of the stag." Miles leaned back in the chair.

Father was sitting in the same position. "I thought the same. We also need a portion to get through the winter. Mutton does get terribly tiresome. I do not intend to go back to London until it is time for the Season. Abby will be well enough by then and the babe old enough for the trip." He smiled, a proud smile, even his head lifting. "I should rather like to gloat over my potency at my ripe age."

Miles had to chuckle. "No doubt men at the club will comment on the long years between Cecelia and this one."

Father straightened as if someone had poked a pistol in his back. "No one will say a single untoward word about my wife or our child, or I will call them out." He tapped a finger on the desk in a slow, ominous pattern. "And I do believe they know that."

"Everyone knows Abby would never be untrue. I did not mean that."

"I hope not." Father looked back down at the papers on his desk. "I believe we may have to schedule a second hunt later, when we can take a doe. I have found that a gift of venison, even scraps for stew, helps keep good relations with the tenants."

"It is better than having them feel forced to poach." Miles looked at his pocket watch, and rose. "I should take Miss Underwood for our walk before the day grows too late."

Father's head lifted, and a flash of guilt crossed his face. "I believe you will find her unavailable for your stroll."

There was something in those words, a flatness, that warned Miles he was not going to like the answer. "And why is that?"

Father folded his hands. Despite the guilt of a moment ago, he met Miles's gaze straight on. "You must stop walking with her. You cannot marry her, and I will not let you despoil her. Abby is inviting all the young men from good family for the hunt, and she will find a husband for Miss Underwood from among them. You are the son of an earl. You will marry a woman your equal."

The room was strangely silent. Miles looked at his father, the words still ringing in his ears. *"What have you done?"* He leaned on the desk, his hands in fists. It was a good thing the desk was wide.

"We have merely acquainted her with the situation. I am confident she will do the right thing." Father did not stand, just sat there, looking at Miles without flinching. "You may go downstairs and check for yourself, but I am confident she will refuse to see you."

Miles jerked the door open and strode quickly down the side hall, turning into the main foyer. The parlor door was open. He ran the last feet and skidded in, catching himself on the jamb.

Miss Underwood was not there. Neither was Abby. He turned around, looking for a servant, but there were none in sight. He stepped over to the bell pull, and gave it a solid yank.

It took but a moment for a footman to appear. "Yes, my lord?"

"Where is Miss Underwood? She was in the parlor with Lady Stafford."

"Yes, sir. I believe she went outside in a hurry."

"Thank you." Miles beat the footman to the door, and rushed outside, only to stop, not knowing which direction he should head first, just needing to find her.

"She went toward the woods," the footman called from behind, and the door shut.

The woods. Not the pond, not the garden. Miles ran along the front of the house and kept going, following the flagstone into the small copse.

He did not have to go far; he heard the sobbing before he saw her on a bench, uncovered red hair a beacon, her face in her hands, weeping as though her world had ended.

Miles had to stop before she could hear him. He had not the first idea of what to say. His father's words rang in his head, painfully true. *You cannot marry her. You are the son of an earl. You will marry a woman your equal.*

Had he been misleading Miss Underwood about his intentions? He enjoyed her company, missed her when she was not around and could not seem to stay away, but had not thought as far as marriage.

Abby and his father both had seen something that alarmed them, but what? And from whom? Himself? Or Miss Underwood?

He was not sure how deep his own feelings were, so he did not want to believe it was his actions that worried his stepmother. Which left Miss Underwood, alone in a strange country, in need of protection and support, even friendship.

Had she read more into his visits? Time with her had been easy and pleasant, but what had it meant to her?

And what did he do now? If she had been his mistress, he would know how to cut her off, but she was not that kind of woman.

He did not want to cut her off.

The mere thought of giving her a necklace, or a bracelet, and saying goodbye pricked him like nettles across his skin. She was a woman of honor and honesty. He could not treat her that way.

Could he salvage something from this debacle? Was there some way to keep her friendship?

He took a step toward her, and something crackled under his boot. Miss Underwood jerked, and turned her back to whoever she thought was coming from that direction, rubbing her cheeks to dry the tears. She gave a loud, unlady-like sniff, and he knew he had to move forward, if only to give her his handkerchief.

Only to give her a handkerchief? Was that all he could do?

He hoped the words would come and be the right words. He could not imagine never coming here to walk with her again, never laugh with her, or share his thoughts.

With a lash of pain that must be but a fraction of what she was feeling, Miles realized her pain was of his doing.

And he did not know if he could save what was becoming precious, and still keep his family name.

She had become his friend, and he could not bear to lose her.

He sat down next to her, and she scooted as far away as

she could without falling off the other side. He reached in his coat pocket and pulled out his handkerchief, then took her ungloved hand despite her resistance—her skin soft against his own, she had run off without gloves in addition to her bonnet—tucked the silk cloth in it, and folded her fingers around it.

"Thank you," she choked, and he could feel the aching there in the scratchiness of her voice.

"I am so sorry." He straightened his shoulders. He was a man; he had caused this pain, and it was up to him to salvage what he could of the wreckage.

"I believed we were becoming friends." He had to be as honest as possible if he was to heal her pain. "I valued your friendship." No, he could not leave it in the past. "I still value it. You are unlike any woman I have ever known, and I do not want to lose that."

In a voice he could not make louder than a whisper, he asked, "Can we still be friends, at least?"

Miss Underwood was so stiff he could have rested a poker flat to her back. She blew her nose, another raspy and wet sound, but all he heard was the pain. "I don't know," she said in that same scratchy voice. "I know it is silly, I should not have let my hopes . . . I don't belong . . . and I probably can't stay anyway . . . It was stupid of me."

"No!" He could not let her demean herself that way. "Friendship is never silly, and I will not hear you say so. Also, *stupid* is a cruel word and I will not have you using such a word about yourself."

She gave another sniff, and dabbed at her nose again, but did not turn to face him. He saw her shoulders go back even further and her chin raised; he could tell by the way her head shifted. "You will want to leave now. Your parents have seen enough of us together. Abby told me she will find me a"—her voice caught and she had to clear it—"husband from a suitable family around here, and then I will no longer be your responsibility."

At the word *husband*, his hand clenched, and his breath caught. This was worse than hearing it from his father. Olivia—*Miss Underwood*, he dared not let himself get too familiar, and why did her Christian name come to mind so suddenly—had accepted the decision and dismissed him.

He rose, his legs oddly stiff and uncoordinated. "First of all, I do not consider you my responsibility." That made her turn, and her look was blatant disbelief. "Perhaps I did at first, but things have changed, and I no longer consider you as such. I understand, perhaps more than you can, the difficulties in our continued association, but you are American, and much can be excused. I am sorry if my visits have complicated things for you."

She rose, and now that they were facing each other, he saw the marks of her weeping. Guilt and pain lashed him anew.

His handkerchief was clenched in her hand so tightly that her knuckles were white. Her face blotched with red, especially around her nose, and her eyes were swollen. Her hair, he could now see, had blown free in front, and the pins had fallen out somewhere along her run.

For she had run, that was obvious.

Despite her dishevelment and the strain of her expression, she met his gaze, and her chin lifted. "I am not sorry we met." Then her gaze drifted away, and he saw her green eyes fill again. A hand jerked, as if she wanted to reach out to him but stopped herself. She did not look up, but spoke to the nearest bush. "I don't believe in playing games."

"Games?" What would she know about gaming?

Those big eyes lifted, met his, determination and something like desperation in their depths. "I'm just going to say it straight out: I would hate to think you have simply been amusing yourself with me."

Her words jolted him like a slap in the face, and Miles actually took a step back. So *that* was what she had meant. Not cards, but hearts. *Amusing yourself with me.* Had he merely used her as a distraction, a momentary pleasure? He would have to think on that, but later. "I have found you amusing, but that is not the same thing." Was it?

"I wish things were different. I wish . . . " She heaved a great, shuddering sigh. "But as long as I am here, I have to live with things as they are."

"We both do." He did not realize what he was going to say until the words were out. Live with things as they are. The heaviness in his chest swelled, pressing pain from the inside out.

How could he miss her when she stood in front of him? He had dismissed mistresses who had shared his bed for months with less introspection than this woman from America with a strange past, who did not even remember how she came to his land, whose intimacies went no further than a kiss on the hand.

He needed to think.

Miles bowed to her, a deep, respectful bow. "I will bid you farewell, but you are on my father's land and in his house. We will see each other from time to time, and I hope will greet each other with some affection."

Before he changed his mind and gave in to the roiling inside that urged him to clasp her against himself and find out what her lips tasted like, kiss away the tears that slid down her cheeks once more, he turned and strode back up the flagstone path.

CHAPTER 44

OLIVIA STIFLED A YAWN UNDER HER HAND AND PRETENDED TO brush something off her cheek. If anything had been there, it would have been a tear.

She had not seen Langley for a week.

This was the third man Abby had invited for a dinner party, and once again, he was the lone man without a partner. Olivia had done her best with the other two, had tried to be gracious and seem interested, but her mind kept drifting, and her heart hurt.

She might well wind up married to one of these men. Every time the thought slid across her brain, her heart sank to her shoes, and her stomach roiled.

Women of this time actually lived this way! How many of the mothers and sisters of the men invited to dinner had been married to the most "logical" choice? A couple of the women invited to Abby's parties looked happy, or at least not miserable, but she couldn't help but wonder if they had learned to make the best of their situation.

She remembered Elizabeth Bennet's friend Charlotte, and how she settled for the idiot Mr. Collins.

Charlotte might not have been romantic and might have been happy to settle for a Collins just to have a home of her own, but the world Olivia left was not like that.

Or at least, not among her friends. They had married for love, and most of them were still married.

That hidden iron hung over both Clara and herself. They didn't even know if it was still in this time. It had gone back once before without Clara. They discussed it again last night. Maybe the cursed thing only allowed one-way trips.

"Like a cheap airplane ticket," Clara had said.

"Miss Underwood?" A male voice interrupted her thoughts.

She jerked her attention back to her dinner partner, a tall man with dark blonde hair and blue eyes that he seemed to think she found alluring because he kept raising his brows to open them wider. "Yes?"

"I asked you if you are upset by the idea of a hunt? Or will you ride out with the women to see us off?"

She took a sip of her tea while she tried to decide how to answer. "I understand the necessity of hunting game. People have to eat. That said, I am against hunting for sport. If you are going to kill an animal, you should at least not waste it."

He smiled. "I am against waste myself."

But what did he consider waste? She didn't want to ask, so instead borrowed the vague almost-agreeing non-answer she had seen Abby use so many times. "I am glad to hear that."

Unfortunately, that gave the man an opening. "Yes, foxes kill chickens, and can wipe out an entire flock. That is a terrible waste. They have even been known to kill lambs. They are a menace. Fox hunts are good for the local people, and the landowners." He leaned forward and said in what was supposed to be an alluring tone, "I hope you will come to the next fox hunt. I would be happy to have you there."

She shuddered. Not just at the thought of watching a fox hunt, but that he might view her attendance as some kind of acceptance of his suit.

This one would be hard to drive off. He had an inflated view of his own appeal.

The next course came, and Olivia was happy to end the conversation. Some kind of bird, about the size of a small chicken, but with a stronger flavor. She didn't want to know what it was, or wonder if it was one of the ducks she had enjoyed with Langley.

Olivia pushed his image from her mind, but the damage was done. Her appetite had fled.

Or maybe she was just full. They had already had three courses.

And then someone said Langley's name. Olivia froze, hardly breathing, and tried to pinpoint where the speaker sat. There were four couples here, not counting herself and the obnoxious man across from her, but Abby had seated her at the end of the table, no doubt hoping she and this latest choice would have some time to talk in relative privacy.

The speaker sat next to Abby. Olivia remained still, barely breathing, watched the little group out of the corner of her eye, and waited for Abby's answer. "No, he has not gone back to London yet. He says he will leave once the hunting and shooting seasons are over. It will be near winter by then, but young men love wintering in London." She shook her head. "I hope he will find a suitable woman and marry."

The woman she was talking to laughed. "Men will marry only when it is required, and not a moment before."

Olivia prodded her memory for the woman's name. She

wasn't the vicar's wife; they had come for the last dinner party. This one lived on the nearest estate, which must be at least a half hour carriage ride away in the opposite direction.

Abby was spreading a wide net, just to keep Olivia away from her stepson.

"How many stags will Stafford allow? We would gladly take a portion for our own larder."

They were done discussing Langley. Olivia poked at her bird again, but couldn't bring herself to take a bite.

"Is duck not to your liking?" Her dinner companion was not ready to be ignored.

And now he had completely ruined her meal. Olivia knew she wouldn't be able to go down to the pond and look at the ducks again, just in case one of her favorites was missing.

Miles threw his cravat onto the floor, wishing it would land with more force.

"M'lord, you should have waited for me." Thomas held out another crisp cravat, no doubt pressed by himself. "Sit down, and let me fasten it for you before you have none left, and I will have to send to the nearest tailor for more."

Miles pushed Thomas's hand away. "I do not even think I want to wear one today. I am going nowhere, and no one is coming to see me." But he flopped down in the chair by his bed, anyway.

Thomas did not bring the cravat over, though, merely stood there, the white cloth dangling from his hand. "Just go get her and marry the woman. The servants are beginning to complain about your foul temper, and the cook has threatened to serve nothing but soup."

"Henri's soup is worth as much as anyone else's finest

meal, and he knows it." But Miles could not wipe Thomas's first sentence from his mind.

Just go get her and marry the woman.

If anyone else had said that to him about any other woman, he would have cut them down to size with a few well-chosen words, but coming from Thomas, they had a different ring.

Ring. He immediately visualized his ring on Olivia's finger. He had inherited his mother's wedding ring. Father had saved it, and given it to him upon attaining his majority, with the instruction that it be given to the woman he married.

Miles had saved it, and it sat in a small carved box in his desk.

"Go ahead and put the cravat on. If the servants are complaining, there is no point in my giving them another reason."

Thomas hesitated, but must have decided he had pushed it as far as he dared because he came over, bent down, and with efficient movements, had a neat knot tied. He went over to the small chest of drawers, and began rummaging around.

He turned around with a frown on his face. "M'lord, what happened to your emerald cravat pin? It was here, and now it is missing."

"It has to be there. I saw you put it there the last time I wore it. Check again." He rose and strode over to look at the open drawer. Thomas stirred the box where all the jewelry Miles left here was kept. They both looked, both stirred, Thomas lifted the box and looked under it, but it was nowhere.

Then Miles noticed something else. "Where is the broken chain from my grandfather's watch?"

Thomas looked at him and back down at the box. "I

cannot imagine. It is gone, too." His eyes were alarmed, and afraid. "I did not take them, m'lord. I would not do that. I would not take anything of yours, I swear."

Miles clasped Thomas's shoulder. "I know that. I would never accuse you, but someone has been in here and taken them." He looked down at the box. "Let us see what else is missing."

Piece by piece, they went through, but only those pieces were gone. The broken watch chain would mean little to anyone else, but it meant something to him, and he had long intended to bring it in and have it mended so he could use it for his own watch.

"Call the servants and I will question them." Miles tucked the ends of his cravat into his vest, sat down, pulled on his boots. "I will meet the staff in the great hall. See that the stable staff is there, as well."

He strode out the door and down toward the main stairway, anger and betrayal churning inside.

Who dared to steal from him?

He paced back and forth across the hallway, each turn reminding him of walking the length with Olivia.

Would she take something? His chest hurt at the thought. She had gone into his office looking for her iron. Would she be bold enough, dishonest enough, to go into his room and search for something to give her money?

All she had to do was ask. He would give her whatever she needed, or find a way to ease her path.

The servants trickled into the hallway and took their places in front of him, some frightened, some defiant, some determined, their shoulders braced as though against some accusation.

A faint tinge of horse came with the grooms as they filed in behind the rest.

Miles stood, legs braced, arms folded across his chest, and looked at the group, going from one face to the next, but every servant met his gaze. A thief might do the same, he thought, to throw off the questioners. "I am missing some jewelry from my room."

No one blinked, no one looked guilty, but a few looked angry. "Who would do such a thing," came from one of the grooms in back. His grooms, he had learned, were confident men, convinced of their worth and not overly impressed by the fancies who came and went.

"That is what I am trying to find out." He shifted his attention to the maids. "Do any of you go through my chest of drawers?"

They all shook their heads, some with more vigor than others, and one on the end whispered to her neighbor, "We got enough ta do without dusting inside the drawers."

No doubt that was true.

"M'lord?" A voice came from the back where the grooms stood. It was Ian, Irish and a wizard with horses. "Ah saw summat the other week. A man were skulking about by the laundry house, an' 'e went in through the back door, 'e did. Ah were shoeing a 'orse and Ah couldn't 'ardly leave it ta challenge th' man, but Ah thought 'e looked familiar, so Ah just tucked it in the back o' me mind, an' then Ah fergot. Ah might niver given it another thought til ye asked."

"A man, you say? Did you see him come out?"

"Naw," Ian shook his head. "Ah were too busy."

Relief and anger mingled inside Miles as he dismissed everyone but Ian. Another suspect, and a man, not a woman. Olivia's hair was far too distinctive to be missed, but he grabbed at this new clue eagerly.

The servants left with more alacrity than they had entered, no doubt relieved to be cleared of accusation.

"Tell me what you remember about this man."

Ian scratched his chin. "Ah were far away an' Ah dint see much, ye know, but 'e were tall, and I recall 'is 'hair were light, but that be all Ah 'member."

Tall and blonde.

Victor.

And he was possibly still in the area.

Time to pay Father another visit, warn him of this latest bit of news.

If he happened to see Olivia at the same time . . .

Just go get her and marry the woman. The thought teased him.

It was not that simple, but she had insisted she heard a man threaten his life.

Perhaps she had.

CHAPTER 45

CROFTS LOOKED AT THE KNOCKER ON STEWART'S DOOR, AND wished he had the courage to turn and walk away.

A hunting party. With many people around. Was this better than lying in wait on the road, and shooting Langley where no one might pass for an hour? Crofts resented his employer's wealth, but he did not want the man's blood on his hands.

With so many eyes, he hoped someone in the group would see Stewart and capture him.

Today was the day to demand his share. He had booked passage to America, and his trunk was locked in his room by the Bristol docks, several hours' journey away. Hopefully, it would still be there when he got back.

He needed the reward Stewart had promised.

The knocker clanged in the house; he heard the echo. A minute passed, and footsteps vibrated on the air.

Victor Stewart opened the door, grabbed Crofts's arm, and jerked him inside. "Why are you here again? I told you to stay away until I sent for you."

"Stafford is planning a stag shoot soon. He has invited most of the gentry around the area." It was done, and Crofts wondered if he might be sick. But he plunged on, "I need my reward. You promised."

Stewart's mouth twisted in a parody of a smile. "Planning to leave the country?"

Crofts knew better than to tell the man where he intended to go. "I need to find another position."

Stewart's eyes went, if possible, even colder. "I do not have the full reward yet. What makes you think that I can pay you?"

"You stole some jewelry from Langley. Do not deny it. The gossip is all over the house. Langley called the staff together and reported a theft. I know not what was taken, he did not say, but one of the grooms saw a tall, blonde man slip in the back door by the kitchen." His heart was pounding so hard he could hardly take a breath. "I know it was you, so I know you have enough dosh to pay me. I gave you your solution, the way to find him and get away free. Now give me my reward."

Stewart looked away, a quick glance, then his eyes came back. "I suppose you have helped enough. Wait here." He turned and walked out of the room, leaving Crofts standing there. The fire had burned well recently, the coals still glowed, and it was a larger pile than before.

Crofts had wasted no time spending the money he got from selling Langley's pieces.

Something clunked in another room, something heavy, and he heard rustling, followed by one slither-thump, then another.

He had seen derringers being loaded, knew the sound of the ball, and the ramrod.

Crofts ran for the door, flung it open, took the porch steps two at a time.

He jerked the reins free, flung himself on the horse's back and kicked its flanks, knowing Stewart pointed a derringer at him but not daring to turn. He did not want to see the bullet.

The crowd of people, carts, and dogs scuttling between legs and wheels alarmed his horse and made it hard to keep the animal under control, slowing his progress.

But nothing slammed into his back, the horse kept moving, the crowds still milled around him, and finally he turned the corner, heading toward the road to Bristol.

He would have to go without funds. Crofts fought the sickness in his stomach. It would be a long ride to the docks.

At least he still had his life.

Victor lowered the derringer, cursing under his breath as he backed into the house and shut the door behind him. He wanted Crofts dead; that was the only way to remain free. The man knew too much, and he was too weak to stand up to Langley. Or worse, Stafford.

As long as Crofts was in the world, he would not be safe.

But he could hardly have shot Crofts from his stoop in front of everyone on the street. They had no love of the law when it came after them, but if a reward were dangled in front of their face, they would happily tell what they knew.

He looked at the primed and loaded pistol.

A stag hunt. A derringer was not accurate at a distance, but he did not have a rifle.

Whoever thought he might need one?

He would have to use the forest cover to his advantage and wear dark clothing.

With Crofts gone, finding out the date of the hunt would be more difficult, but he could hang around the local pubs where the servants gathered on their rare times off. Someone always talked.

———

M iles pulled the bell, leaned back in his big chair at his big desk beneath which Olivia said she had hidden, and waited for his butler to answer the summons. A moment later, Denton knocked and entered. "Yes, my lord?"

"Send for Crofts, will you? I need to find out how many of my tenants need meat. We are planning a second hunt in a month when the doe season starts."

Denton bowed and left. Miles waited, drumming his fingers on the desk.

He did not like to be at loose ends. Every time he found himself alone, his thoughts went back to Olivia. He could not think of her as Miss Underwood, despite her dismissal.

She had not sounded happy about Abby finding her a husband. Every time he heard her voice in his head, he remembered the pause, the choke before she got the word out. And her last words, *I wish things were different.*

He did not realize how much Olivia meant to him until she was so forcibly removed from his life.

The wretched thought of her finding a husband made him ill.

I wish things were different.

Denton appeared in the door, without even a tap on the jamb, but then, his arms were full of the rental books. "Crofts has disappeared. The house was unlocked, his clothing is gone, the key was left on the desk."

Miles stared at him. "Crofts's clothing is gone?"

Denton walked in and deposited the rental books on the desk in front of Miles. "I might recommend you check to see if any monies are missing. I cannot believe he would flee unless he had stolen some funds and did not wish to be caught."

Miles looked at the books, and back at Denton. "Was there any letter?"

"The footman did not say so. He just took the books off the desk. They were not safe being left where anyone could take them. He also locked the house and took the key." Denton fished in his vest pocket and pulled it out, setting it next to the books. "You should keep this."

Miles looked at the key, back to the books, and then to Denton. "Thank you. I will give the footman a bonus in his weekly wages." He nodded at Denton. "You may go. I will ring if I need you."

After the door shut behind his butler, Miles opened the most current book. He had been careful, had checked every month during the whole time the man had worked for him, and only once did he catch Crofts in a mistake. Crofts had quickly corrected it, and it had never recurred.

If Crofts had begun to embezzle funds, it would have happened recently. Miles's finger ran down the list, but every rent was right, and the totals matched. At least Crofts had not stolen the rents, which was reassuring.

So why did he run away?

The next question was: *had* he run off? Or was he kidnapped?

Miles quickly eliminated that possibility. A kidnapper

would not take clothing, nor would he leave the books and the key. So Crofts had fled.

But why?

Olivia—Miss Underwood, he must remember to keep it formal—had heard two men, and he was beginning to believe her. He suspected one of the conspirators was Victor, especially since he had been seen around the house, and some of his own treasured jewelry was now missing.

Was the other person in the plot his own trusted man of affairs?

It was time to pay a visit to Olivia, apologize for disbelieving her, and see what else she could remember.

See *her.*

Miles locked the rent books in a drawer and rang for Denton. The man must have been right outside the door, because it opened within a minute. "Have my horse brought around. I am going to see my father."

"Yes, my lord." Denton slipped back out, closing the door on his way.

M iles drew up at his father's house and dismounted. Someone inside had been watching, because it swung open before he reached it.

"Have someone take my horse to the stables for a rubdown. I need to see my father and Miss Underwood. Can you direct me to them? I wish to talk to them both." He started down the hall.

"Your father is in his office," the footman said from behind him. "I will find Miss Underwood. Shall I bring her there?"

Miles paused. After their last discussion of Ol—Miss

Underwood, his father would watch closely. But with his greater experience in government intrigues, Father might think of things to ask that he would not. "Yes, send her to Father's office."

When he got there, the door was shut. Miles rapped. He did not have much time to wait.

"Come," came from inside. Miles opened the door and stepped in. "Hello, son. What brings you here today?"

Miles shut the door behind himself—he wanted no one else to hear what he had to say—and turned to his father. No point hesitating. "I have been robbed, and my man of affairs . . . has disappeared."

Father closed his eyes, and sighed, then opened them. The familiar disappointment was there. "I told you to watch over anyone who handles your money."

Miles shoved down his irritation. "You did, and I have been, but my steward has always been responsible. We go over the rents and reports together. I do not permit him to run rampant with my incomes and tenants." He walked over to the chair and sat, but he was too tense to relax. Instead, he braced his arms on his knees, and leaned forward, pinning Father in his gaze. "I think this fiasco might be part of what O . . . Miss Underwood overheard. I believed it was a fever dream, I even told you the same, but I cannot think that any longer."

Father's brows went up, and his eyes lost their disappointment. "How bad is it?"

"Grandfather's broken watch chain is missing from the box in my chest of drawers, as well as my emerald and diamond cravat pin. But the worst of it is that one of my grooms saw a man slip into the house a few days ago, and the man he describes sounds like Victor." He could not sit any longer, but got back to his feet, and leaned against Father's desk. "I know you wish to defend my beloved cousin, but he is a thief and a scoundrel."

Father sighed and slumped back against his chair. "He perhaps was spoiled. He lost his father so young and was James's only child. My father did not wish him to feel lost and forgotten."

Miles scoffed. "That clearly did not work. He now feels the family owes him. He will not consider finding employment, but will take what he needs. Or what he wants." He remembered their conversation those weeks ago, when he challenged Father to give a reason why he persisted in believing Victor's version of the truth. "You remember I told you Olivia said she overheard a plot to kill me?"

As the words he was about to say bubbled to the surface, Miles found he needed to sit. "Victor would have everything he wants if I am dead. My title, my portion of wealth, and all that you have upon your death." The rest of the plot hit him like a fist to the jaw at Gentleman Jackson's. "This plot she heard to kill me—it must have been Victor. I think he might be desperate enough to actually mean it. And now that he has taken something of mine."

Father looked up at him. "Do you realize what you are saying? Men of our class do not do such things."

"Father, you know men of our class do anything they want if they believe they can get away with it. If someone from the docks or a highway man did what I am suggesting, he would either hang or be transported to Australia. But one of our class? No one has been hung for ages. Thrown out of clubs, cut off from parties, made a social outcast, yes, but Victor might feel he has nothing to lose."

A tap came on the door.

CHAPTER 46

"OUR GUEST, I BELIEVE. COME!" FATHER EXCHANGED A glance with Miles as they rose.

It was indeed Olivia, and Miles suddenly realized he had said her name aloud, and Father did not correct him.

Which was rather odd, but perhaps the idea of Victor stealing from him and plotting his death had distracted him.

Olivia walked in, wearing a lovely sprigged muslin day dress of soft green with white designs of some kind, probably flowers, scattered lightly across it. The color was perfect with her red hair.

She wore no mobcap of any type, and Miles had to bite his cheek to keep from smiling.

Farley shut the door behind her, but she made no move to walk in any further.

"Miss Underwood." Father gestured to Miles's chair, and Miles took the hint, stepping over to the second one. "We need to find out everything you remember from your first days. What you heard, what the men sounded like. Anything you can tell us will be appreciated."

She did not take the hint, just stood in place and looked from Father to him and back. They remained on their feet, waiting for her to sit. "Something has happened, hasn't it? You didn't believe me before, so if you believe me now, what made the change?"

"Sit, please."

She looked at Father, her eyes narrowed, but she walked to Miles's abandoned chair and seated herself. He and Miles sat at almost the same moment, but before Miles got fully down and without further invitation, Olivia asked, "What happened?"

Father looked from her to himself. "American, as always. Well, son, I will leave the explanations to you."

"Some items of mine have disappeared"—she stiffened at his words, and Miles remembered with a flash of shame his first thought was that she was the thief—"and one of my grooms saw a man who looked like my cousin Victor."

She relaxed, obviously realizing that she was no longer suspect. "I never saw the man. You already know what I heard."

"Just tell us again, whatever you can remember." Miles glanced at his father, then his vision caught as he realized what he was seeing. The man looked at Olivia with a sad, almost resigned, look on his face. The firmness and resolve, the set chin, the stiff shoulders, the hard eyes of the day when he told Miles there could be nothing more between them, were gone.

Father looked at him and gave a soft sigh. His shoulders drooped, and his eyes glistened. But then he straightened again, and turned back to Olivia, listening as she spoke.

Olivia leaned back in the chair, frustrated at herself. If only she remembered more! If only she had seen the men and could describe them.

If only Stafford wasn't watching the two of them, his eyes seeming to stare through her every time she spoke. He watched Langley with equal intensity, but she dared not turn her head that way unless answering a question for fear Stafford would see something in her face that she did not want to share.

It was hard enough sitting next to Langley.

The two villainous men's voices had faded into words without intonation in her mind. Perhaps if she heard them again she would recognize them, but it had been too long. While the exact words were gone, there were two men both times, and she knew the voices had been the same each time. Now his cousin—and thank God Miles had finally accepted that much—and some employee were both missing.

She wished she dared believe the villians had gotten what they wanted with the theft, but there was still the title and all that went with it. The very walls of this room screamed *money*.

Every instinct told her the danger had not subsided. If anything, it had grown with this blatant theft. If this was why she was here, she had to be ready. "This hunting party you are planning scares me. It's the perfect opportunity for someone to shoot Langley."

Langley shook his head. "Unlikely. We will have quite a large group in the woods, and the dogs will be out."

"Well, riding about the countryside all those weeks didn't work, and I don't believe they have given up."

Stafford shook his head, too, the gesture a copy of Langley's. "The hunt cannot be cancelled. This is part of our meat for the winter, and we share it with our tenants. We plan a second hunt for a doe."

She had nothing more to add. Olivia decided the men would talk more freely without her. She rose, and they rose with her. "If you don't have any more questions, may I leave?"

The men exchanged a glance, and Stafford bowed his head in dismissal. "Thank you for trying."

As she walked out, she heard Langley ask his father, "What should we do about Victor?"

She stopped out of sight, hoping they weren't listening to her steps.

Stafford grunted. "You are quick to blame your cousin. We can do nothing until we have some kind of proof, which we do not have. The word of a groom? Who was not close enough to identify anyone? I admit, it sounds bad, but we do not accuse someone of our own class, and more especially of our own family, unless we are absolutely certain."

"Then I need to find some proof. I know not how, but perhaps I can hire a Bow Street Runner to search pawnbrokers and jewelers, see if they can find my stolen goods and get a description."

"That is a place to start." Stafford cleared his throat. It generally presaged a change of subject. "That is for another time. We can do nothing at the moment. For now, we must plan the hunt."

"Very well. We will change the subject. Whose dogs should we use? Have you seen signs of deer around? They have not slipped off your grounds, have they? I have a stallion I would like to take through the woods."

They were going to chase the deer with dogs, and follow on horses?

How could she keep track of his movements if he was on a horse?

His cousin, or whoever it was that made the threats, could easily follow Langley—if he had a horse, and of course he must have one to get to and from the house so easily—and there was nothing she could do to prevent it.

T he day of the hunting party was here. Olivia sat in the parlor next to Abby, wearing her favorite day gown, pink with embroidered flowers, in hopes that it would give her courage. Things were tense between them after she rejected each of Abby's choices, but there was no place else to sit that wouldn't cause gossip.

The vicar's wife sat to her left. Also in the group were the mothers of two of the men Abby tried forcing on her, as well as a sister of a third.

One of the mothers came over and sat next to her. "My son was quite taken with you when he met you last. So you are from America?" She didn't wait for a reply. "It was most wise of your sister and her husband to send you and your maid here to find a husband. Our men are hardly the rough, uncivilized farmers and woodsmen of America."

Sent here to find a husband? Was that Abby's story? "Our men are far more varied than that." Olivia had no idea how much of this America was city and how much the rough country the woman thought, or what the men were like, but she had to defend them.

And she certainly didn't intend to marry the lady's son!

Horses and dogs caught the women's attention, milling about outside the parlor window, the men calling to each other, the dogs whining and yelping. The sun poured down, glinting off harnesses and stirrups, and brightening the grass behind the milling group. The first hints of fall gilded the leaves on the trees along the road.

Langley, tall and surprisingly elegant for the day's activities in tan breeches, a blue suit coat, a white cravat with his white shirt, stood next to a large brown horse equal to his size. He held the reins with a casual confidence that seemed to transmit through the leather to the beast, because it was among the calmest there.

"Do you see my son?" The woman interrupted her thoughts. "There?" She pointed to the group outside the window. Sure enough, there he was, mounting a large brown horse with skill.

Miller. The name popped back. The man was Alfred Miller, and this was his mother, so she was Mrs. Miller. If she had a title, Abby would have flaunted it.

Just because she didn't like Miller didn't mean that he was totally incompetent, Olivia told herself as she smiled back at the woman and said nothing.

Langley stood next to Miller, and she knew if she continued to watch, someone would guess which of the two she was looking at.

She still wasn't sure what to make of the look on Stafford's face during that last inquisition. Langley had not come to visit since, but perhaps he had written her off, and meant what he said about merely being friends. Her heart sank further.

A horse whinnied outside, and she automatically turned to look.

Langley didn't turn away fast enough and their gazes met. And held, for a moment too long.

He had been watching her.

And not as a friend, either.

Olivia's mouth curved in a smile as they looked at each other. The room behind her was quiet, or perhaps she simply did not hear them.

Langley touched his hat, turned back to the horse, and swung himself up with fluid ease.

The hunt was on.

And she was trapped here with the rest of the women.

CHAPTER 47

LANGLEY GUIDED HIS HORSE DOWN THE TRAIL INTO THE woods, following the sound of the dogs. They were fortunate to have deer on their land, established centuries ago, and even more fortunate that they stayed. Deer had little trouble going over the fences and hedges, but his father's land was rich with food sources, and the deer stayed close.

The other horses and riders were spread out, picking their way through the brush and branches. The baying became fainter, and he knew the dogs were on the trail of a stag. They would keep baying until the men caught up.

He recognized Alfred Miller, riding a little ahead on a big brown gelding, and knew he had been Abby's latest attempt to find Olivia a husband. His hand clenched on the rein, his horse hesitated, and Miles had to force himself to relax his fingers.

Thomas's advice sounded better all the time.

Had Father's resigned look said what he thought it was saying? Father had looked between the two of them, sitting in his office side by side, and Miles could swear that he was giving—

A doe burst from the underbrush, directly in front of them, and a *crack* cut through the air. His horse reared with such force, Miles lost his seat—*how silly, I never fall*—as something lashed across his side in a sudden, sharp pain. The ground rose to meet him, so swiftly he barely thought it before he hit, the impact jarring his head, rattling his bones, knocking the air from his lungs.

Miles fought the tightness around his chest; black dots danced in his vision. *He needed air.* Strange noises came from his throat as he struggled to breathe.

With a sudden rush, his lungs finally relaxed, sweet air rushed in, and he could see the landscape again. His horse had stopped a short distance away. He would get up in a minute, he told himself, as soon as the world settled a bit more. His hand went to rub the ache from the scrape as he fell, but the coat was sticky.

A flash of red on the edge of his vision caught his attention. He held up his hand.

Blood. He was bleeding. Miles angled his head and looked down. A rip ran along his coat, stained with red, but the tear was straight across and the gouge in his skin burned...

Then the reality hit him. He had been *shot.*

Olivia had been right.

He had to get up. Whoever had shot him must still be nearby, and he was a perfect target, lying on the ground like this. Miles lurched to his feet, ignoring the blood that still trickled down his shirt and into his breeches, and whistled for his horse while he searched for the rifle.

Something whizzed by his head and thumped into a nearby tree, and Miles ducked. The horse shied, but he caught the reins, swung himself up, and kept low on its neck. A kick against its side, and the big beast lurched forward.

He could not gallop. There were too many trees and the path was too narrow, but he pushed his stallion as fast as the animal could go.

If that doe had not startled his horse at the very moment she did and the stallion had not reared, lifting him above the bullet's path . . .

The white stone of the house glinted through the trees, and he knew it was just moments until he could kick the horse into a gallop. He would go to the front, where the shooter could not catch up, and where footmen would be waiting on the women.

He looked down at his wound, and the red stain that was slowly growing. Odd, that it did not hurt worse, or maybe he was concentrating too much on getting away to notice.

They passed the last trees, and he gave the horse a kick, wincing at the sudden throb from the wound. The big stallion stretched out, its legs thundering as it covered the ground in giant strides. The back corner of the house flashed past, and he was sheltered from one direction. Down the side, around the front corner, and he had the whole house between him and where the shooter had been.

Miles drew up the animal; it nearly sat on its haunches as it shuddered to a stop, and he flung himself off the back. The wound tore, he felt the wetness grow as he ran for the door, and wrenched it open, stumbling inside with a thudding of boots.

A footman appeared from the parlor, took one look, and gasped. "My lord, you are bleeding!"

Miles knew he should not frighten the women, but he did not think he could make it to his father's office. "Send someone for the doctor," he ordered, and stepped into the parlor.

A chorus of gasps and shrieks met him. He looked around the shocked female faces, but only one drew his gaze.

Olivia rose, and hurried to his side, a rush of pink silk. "You need to sit down."

Sitting down felt like a very good idea. She grabbed the nearest empty chair and thumped it down in front of him, then grabbed his arm and pointed.

He sat, grateful for her hand on his arm.

"I need some scissors." Olivia snapped out the order.

"What do you need scissors for?"

Miles was grateful to the owner of that voice. Someone else must have wondered the same thing and spared him the asking.

Olivia said in that same brisk voice, "We need to cut off his shirt so we can get to the wound."

"*Cut off his shirt?*" Another woman fairly shrieked the question.

Miles caught Olivia's hand. "I am perfectly capable of removing my own shirt. There is no need to cut it off."

She met his gaze, her eyes wide and alarmed, surprising when her voice was so firm. "We need to clean out that wound." She looked up, and must have found the footman. "Go get hot water and soap." Then she propped her hands on her hips and looked at him. "We might have to get you on the floor. I don't think we can clean out the wound with you sitting like that."

She turned to someone, and asked, "Is there a table or a bench we can lay him on?"

Abby stood, and hurried to his side. "There is a bench in the library. Can you make it that far?"

Miles rose. That brief respite had settled his brain and

body. He still felt shaky, but he would never admit it, and especially not in front of a room of women.

With Abby walking close by on one side and Olivia on the other, arms ready to grab him if he fell, he made it down the hallway to the intersection and turned left to the library. A maid came from the servant's doorway at the end of the hall, carrying a bowl of water so hot it steamed, no doubt ordered by the frightened footman.

Miles winced at the thought of that touching his raw flesh. The wound burned already, and with steaming water added, it might really begin to hurt.

"We're going to the library. Follow us." Abby opened the library door, and Miles followed her in, blinking at the sun pouring through the windows. Footsteps came down the hall, and he knew he had gained a larger audience.

And men thought women were the delicate sex!

Olivia turned to shut the door, but it was too late.

"You are not really going to be here with an unclothed man?" The scandalized voice sounded like the vicar's wife, but he was not going to turn and look. She was not done, though. "You should send for the doctor. This is not the place for women."

Olivia turned to her. "In America, women take care of injuries all the time. Would you rather he just bleed?"

The woman huffed, but she stayed. Someone muttered, "Men and rifles are a bad combination. They get careless."

Another voice said in a sharp tone, "My husband is a good shot. He would never do anything careless."

"Nor would my son," another woman snapped. "I sincerely hope no one is going to try to blame him!"

Abby must have had enough. "Women! Mrs. Kirkman does have a point. Since Miss Underwood is familiar with this type of injury, she must stay. Lord Langley is my stepson, so I will stay to help. The rest can either help, or go back to the parlor."

There was some muttering, but the women began to shuffle out.

"The water is getting cool," Olivia said, and took his arm. "Which bench is okay for us to use?"

The bench was only long enough for his midsection, but Olivia brought a chair for his head, and Miles decided his feet would be just fine braced on the floor. He sat in the middle and began to turn himself lengthwise when Olivia spoke.

"If you won't let me cut off your clothes, you have to remove everything from your waist up."

He was not anxious to begin whatever torture she had in mind for him, so raised one eyebrow in teasing. "Everything?"

Olivia propped her hands on her hips, and glared at him. "Yes. Everything."

Olivia ignored that eyebrow. She was not in the mood for teasing. He was *bleeding*. He had been *shot*. And whoever had done it was still out there.

What had been damaged inside? People could walk around after an accident and suddenly drop dead of massive internal damage. He could be hemorrhaging inside, the bullet might have ripped his intestines and their contents might be poisoning him even now.

She didn't know what she would do if that happened. How did one even begin to repair that kind of wound?

Someone had sent for the doctor, but there was no way of

knowing how long it would take, first for him to be found, and then to get here.

So it was up to her. And Abby. If—big if—they could manage it without getting sick or passing out. She hadn't seen it yet. He was talking and walking; several minutes had already passed. If he was bleeding internally, wouldn't he show some signs by now?

Maybe it wasn't as bad as she feared.

Langley stood again, with barely a wince, and began untying his cravat. Olivia didn't know anything about gun wounds, but he certainly wasn't acting like he was at death's door.

Still, a bullet wound was a bullet wound, and who knew how it was treated in this time? She knew Dr. Reed— presumably he was the only doctor around and he seemed a man of reasonable good sense—but would he attach leeches or put some disgusting poultice on the hole?

The only thing to do was to clean it out as best she could and hope Dr. Reed wouldn't undo whatever meager services she was able to provide.

While her thoughts had been on keeping him safe, Langley got his shirt off, folded it with the bloody side up, and looked around. "Where dare I put this?"

"Put it on the floor, if you please." Abby said over her shoulder. She had turned her back as soon as Langley began removing his cravat. "The maid can take it with her when she goes, and see that it is burned."

She did turn her head enough to meet Olivia's eyes. "I do not know what I am to do if word were to get around that you were in the same room as an undressed man, so both I and the maid will remain here."

"Thank you." Olivia knew how much it cost the woman to even allow this much. Were it anything less than a gunshot, she was certain Abby would order her out. Or never let her in.

"I presume you want me to lie down on the bench now?" Langley stood there, his chest bare, blood smeared around the ugly gouge on his side.

It was an impressive chest, a smattering of hair and sculptured muscles, and under other circumstances she would have enjoyed the view, but the blood stopped her cold. Red wetness dripped into the waistband of his breeches. How much had he lost?

"Turn around. Let me see the wound." She didn't care how she sounded; she had to find out just how bad it was. And hope it wasn't horrible, and she fainted.

She didn't normally faint, but then, she didn't normally have to look at a bullet wound.

Langley obediently turned. Olivia took a deep breath and stepped closer. "It didn't go in!" Her legs felt wobbly, either with relief or with reaction to his raw, open flesh. At least it wasn't a hole.

A hole would have been bad. A gouge was still scary, but she didn't know how she ever could dig into him and take out a bullet.

Thank goodness it didn't go in. *Thank you, God.* "You can lie down again."

He obliged. She knew he was a big man, but somehow, seeing him there, taking up the whole bench with no room for his legs, only holding him from shoulders to rear, his feet braced on the floor and his head resting on the chair, he looked bigger than ever.

The wound dripped a red splotch on the wood beneath. Her legs began to wobble, but Olivia refused to let it show. "I need a chair, and the water and soap. Also, something underneath him so we don't ruin the floor."

Something Olivia said must have worried Abby because she finally turned back. She gasped, her hands flew to cover her mouth, and the color drained from her face. "Oh, Miles!"

Olivia snapped out of her own dread and dashed over to grab her. The maid, and a footman Olivia recognized as the one who had been at the door when Langley came in, were already there with the chair meant for herself. Together, the two got Abby down before she fainted.

Telling a woman big with child to put her head on her knees wasn't going to work, so instead Olivia said, "Close your eyes and lean your head back." In as reassuring a voice as she could manage, she said, "It looks worse than it is. Really. We'll clean it out, and he'll be fine."

Eyes still closed, Abby said, "I am sorry. I think the sight of it . . . I was fine until I saw . . . How different your country must be, that you can handle this so calmly."

Olivia gave an unladylike snort of laughter. "I assure you, this is a new one for me, too." A strange noise came from the bench, Langley likely unnerved at putting himself in her inexperienced hands, so she hastened to add, "But I've heard of it, and the most important thing is to clean it well."

The maid, almost as pale as Abby, handed over the bowl and the soap. Rather than ask for a second chair, Olivia knelt at his side and, with careful dabs, started washing away the blood.

CHAPTER 48

LANGLEY WAS CLEAN, THE BLOOD WASHED OFF HIS CHEST, when Dr. Reed arrived.

Olivia was back on her feet, wiping the last spots of blood off her fingers. She looked up when he was announced, but other than a nod to her, he focused his gaze on Langley. He held his black bag with fingers so tight they were almost colorless, his hair was windblown, and his dark trousers coated in dirt.

"I was told you were shot, and are dying."

Langley twisted his head from where he was still prostrate on the bench. "Edward. You certainly came with dispatch." He sat up with only a single grunt and gestured to his side. "My guardian angel has been hard at work."

Dr. Reed looked at her with wide eyes. "*You* treated him?"

Treated was a bit of a strong word, Olivia thought. "I just washed it out. It will scar, and it's still bleeding, but it was only a graze. The bullet didn't go in, thank goodness."

Dr. Reed turned his attention back to Langley, and

walked over, setting his bag down. "I am pleased to see you still breathing. I was quite concerned."

Olivia had to speak up again. There was no antibiotic cream, no sterile bandages, no medicines to keep any potential infection at bay. "No one can touch him without washing thoroughly first. The wound has to remain clean."

Abby gasped.

Dr. Reed barely glanced at Olivia. "You have done well, but you should not be here. This is no place for a woman."

Olivia didn't move. A YouTube video on animal healing popped into her head. She should have remembered it earlier, probably would have if she hadn't been so rattled. "If there is any honey around, it should be put on the wound. Is there something we can wrap around him to keep germs from getting in? It has to remain sterile."

Dr. Reed's gaze was riveted on her. "What did you say?"

Olivia realized she had thrown out several terms that wouldn't appear for several decades. "It's what America uses on wounds. Honey will help heal and keep it from getting infected."

"I know *that*," he said with a snap. "I was going to use it without your advice. What were the *other* things you said?"

She had probably damaged time enough. "They are American words. The important thing is to keep the wound clean."

He gave her a narrow look, his brows tight, his lips compressed, but she set her jaw and met his gaze, and he must have decided patching up Langley was more important than prying definitions out of her. "Since you have already cleaned it, there is no reason for you to remain."

Her hands clenched. "*Wash your hands first.*"

Langley had been sitting there, shirt still off, side still moist with her bathing, watching them. He turned to his friend. "If it matters that much to her, wash your hands. She has worked hard to clean away the blood. Perhaps our American opposition knows something we do not."

Dr. Reed scowled, but the maid had already grabbed the bowl of stained water and was disappearing out the door.

Olivia didn't move, just stood there waiting for the maid to come back.

Langley caught her hand, raising it to his lips for a quick kiss on the back. "You have done well, and I am grateful, but Dr. Reed is right. When you were the only one to provide the healing, it could hardly be objectionable, but now that a proper doctor is here, it is time for you to go."

He glanced at his friend, and she could have sworn there was a twinkle in his eye. "Dr. Reed will wash his hands. I give you my word."

Abby pushed herself to her feet. She was still pale. "The men are right, Olivia. This is no place for us now. I stood up to Mrs. Kirkman when Miles was first bleeding, but now that the doctor is here, it is time for us to take our leave." She held out a hand. "I could use your support."

Olivia was sure Abby could have made it out of the room on her own, but this was a fight she knew she would not win, so she reluctantly stepped over and took her hostess's arm.

As they left the library, Abby whispered, "Thank you for saving Miles's life."

"He was in no danger of dying." It was rather nice to be admired after the tension of the last few weeks, but she couldn't take credit for something she didn't do.

Besides, while the wound itself wouldn't kill Miles—his first name popped so easily into her mind—it still could get infected, and in this era, that might well be fatal.

She wasn't going to tell them that, though. No doubt they knew more about infections than she ever would. Maybe she would stay long enough to keep an eye on him. Not that she knew what to do if an infection started, but she'd think of something.

Olivia didn't want to face the judgement of those women. "Do I have to go back in?"

Abby stopped and faced her. "Perhaps you are right. Give them a chance to forget." She touched Olivia's arm. "I am sorry things have been so . . . uneasy between us these last weeks. I judged you rather harshly, and I apologize."

"You had your reasons." Olivia wished she could promise not to hurt any of them, but she still didn't know how long she would be here. It had been too easy to think she might stay, it had been so many weeks now, but there were no guarantees, and the iron was still several miles away.

At best. Had it gone back by now?

Olivia looked at the main door as they neared the parlor. She needed air. She needed to get outside and sit alone. Maybe she had fulfilled her purpose. If Miles—*Langley*, she reminded herself firmly—had been meant to die by the shooter's bullet, he was still alive. Whether she had anything to do with that, whether her warnings had kept him more alert, he had survived.

She had taken care of his wound. Hopefully, Dr. Reed wouldn't do anything to contaminate it.

For now, she wanted, no, needed to be alone and catch her breath. She felt the shakes building, tingling down her arms, threatening to buckle her legs.

If she was going to fall apart, she didn't want an audience.

"You go to your guests. I need a moment alone." Abby nodded. Olivia turned around, heading for the doorway hiding behind the dining room. She hurried past the main stairway, ducked into the hallway that led to the outside door, lifted her skirt, and ran, pulling it open and bursting into the freshness outside.

Air that did not smell of blood.

The same sunlight that had brightened the library glared at her eyes. Olivia pulled the door shut behind her and leaned against it, closed her eyes, and let the brightness warm her.

The shaking started. Not from what had happened, but from what could have happened, what almost did. Did she need to be in the same house as the iron for it to work? Miles was alive. Perhaps that was why she had been sent here.

Her purpose was done.

So why hadn't she disappeared, gone back to Minnesota and her job and her house? The thought made her heart sink, and tears threaten.

Olivia's hands clenched, and she realized her feet were braced, pressing her against the wooden door behind her as if to resist some pull. There was no pull, only the fear that she might go back.

The door was warm against her back, the sun bright against her closed eyes.

And she was still here.

She was still here!

There was still time to find out what was behind Langley's gaze through the window, his kiss on her hand in the library.

Olivia couldn't stand there any longer. The shakes hadn't faded; if anything, they were stronger now.

She was still here, and Langley hadn't died.

And the shooter was still around. Was she supposed to figure out who he was? And then what?

The force that brought her here wasn't one she could reason with, beg for time, or make a bargain.

Because she would plea for time, give whatever was required, if she could only stay.

But what about Clara?

She needed to think, but not where anyone could see her. The garden was visible from every room on this side of the house, and the gazebo with its glass walls was too open.

That left the benches scattered throughout the copse.

Olivia walked along the back of the house, glad her legs were working. Past the dining room, the section that held the staircase, past the ballroom that had not been used since her arrival, and now to the library.

She slowed, and peeked into the window. Dr. Reed was busy wrapping a bandage around Langley's middle, neatly covering the wound. The long white strip showed no red stains yet. That had to be a good sign.

No one was looking at the window, they were absorbed in the task, so she clutched her skirt and hurried past the stripes of glass. No one had called her name when she reached the corner of the house.

Down the next wall, she refused to look into the parlor windows, just strolled along and decided to let anyone who saw her think what they would. Maybe, if she got lucky, Mrs. Miller would side with Mrs. Kirkman and decide her precious son could never marry any woman who looked at a shirtless man and tended his wound.

The path finally branched into the woods. She had gone only a few steps before she realized this was the very route Langley had taken the day he informed her that they could only be friends.

He had not acted that way today.

The bench, that same bench where he had broken her heart, loomed up ahead, and she stopped. He had met her gaze through the window, and that look had been only for her. She had not seen that warm in his eyes after that, but then, they had been surrounded by gossipy women, or his stepmother.

Which was the real Langley?

If she sat on that bench, would he come find her? Or would that bench forever be the place where she learned that she would never be good enough?

Olivia stood there, unable to move, and stared at it.

Footsteps came up behind her, and she turned around eagerly.

CHAPTER 49

SHE DID NOT RECOGNIZE THE MAN WHO STOOD THERE, TALL like Langley, but blonde. He held a rifle negligently at his side, pointing the barrel down at the ground, and smiled.

That smile sent chills down her spine. It was scarier than the gun.

Olivia took a step back. He took a step forward. "You have lovely hair, my lady."

That voice. She knew that voice, and every nerve went cold. It was *him*, the man who had haunted her, the man who threatened Langley. "Thank you." She would not let him know she had guessed, but could not stop herself from taking another step backward. "You are not with the hunters."

"Oh, but I was. In fact, I do believe I got my quarry."

Her heart beat faster, and her lungs squeezed. Not a deer, but *quarry*. "Did you?"

His smile widened. "One of them."

She looked at those eyes and knew what he was saying without the actual words. Langley had been his first target.

She was the second.

He was in trousers and could move fast; she was in a gown. He stood between her and any kind of safety. Did he know Langley had survived?

He must.

She glanced at the rifle again. She didn't know much about guns, but the hammer didn't look all the way back, more likely at half cock. How much time would it take to pull it that last click? No longer than a breath.

Olivia knew she should say something, humanize herself, but not a thing came to mind. Except for one warning from a safety instructor: *Never let them move you to a second location.*

She did have one weapon, she realized, whirling to run anyway, and opened her mouth to scream.

Something crashed into the back of her head; she felt a flash of searing pain, and the world went black.

***

She was waking! He must not have hit her hard enough. Victor reached into his pocket for the small vial of laudanum he had tucked there, just in case. Hopefully it was intact.

It was.

She raised a hand and rubbed her head. Victor crouched beside her, pulled the cork with his teeth, grabbed her hair, and tugged her head back. She opened her mouth to scream. He poured.

She coughed and flailed at him. Victor let go of her hair, plugged the laudanum, slid it back into the pocket, rose and stepped away.

"What? Who?" She tried to stagger to her feet but her legs

did not cooperate, she kept stepping on her pink skirt, and her eyes were already fighting to stay open.

She got her feet braced beneath her, but her hands never left the ground and she could not get herself upright. The woman swayed, her arms shaking as she tried to push herself upright but only got her bottom in the air. Her knees buckled, and she went down on all fours.

Victor watched, ready to clap his hand over her mouth if she screamed again, but she wobbled, then slumped over on her side.

The dose he got down her might not keep her quiet long enough to get her to Portishead, but he would manage. He had the laudanum bottle handy, and she was his bait. Miles would come for her; Victor was certain of that. Either he had not aimed right or the bullet had not flown true, if his cousin could get on a horse and ride to the house.

Victor looked down at the woman, waiting for the laudanum to take full effect. Red hair, Crofts—faithless man! —had said, and this woman certainly had that. There was no longer any question whether she knew too much, not after her reaction. She went white at his first words.

This might be easier than his original plan to portray her as a thief. Miles would not bring a woman for whom he had no concern to his father's house, and she really was quite lovely, even lying on the ground, hair a vivid flame against the flagstone.

All he had to do was get Miles into Portishead and do away with him. And her. Two threats at the same time.

Right now, he had to get her on the horse.

He did not relish the idea of balancing an unconscious woman while in the saddle, but he would not let her take up the whole horse while he walked beside it back to town, and her elegant gown would take a bit of explaining if he was stopped. It was an hour's journey on a horse. He might as well surrender now if he had to walk the whole way.

Victor grunted as he tugged her up and got his shoulder under her middle. He wobbled as badly as she had when the laudanum was taking effect, but found his feet and began staggering through the woods, heading away from the house and toward his horse.

He had not seen Crofts in days. He had taken a chance and ridden to Bristol, afraid he would run into someone who knew him—or worse, someone to whom he owed money—gone to the docks, and checked the manifests of the ships that had recently departed. That had cost money he did not want to spend, but he found out what he needed to know. Sure enough, the man had left the country.

But that left him with an unconscious woman and a horse, and the trip back to town. He did not intend to take on his cousin on Miles's own land.

Victor paused, adjusted the unconscious woman, and trudged on through the small woods. His horse was not far away. He had to stop and rest a couple of times, but at least he managed not to drop her into the forest detritus.

He did not know if he could have picked her back up.

She made sounds from time to time, odd, soft whimpers, and he thought the branches scratched her, but at last the horse came into view, a dark shape among the black woods.

Hoisting her onto the horse's back was harder than he expected, but with a bit of pushing, he got her balanced. He tucked a foot in the stirrup and got up behind her—although the fit was tight—pushed her forward on the small flat pommel, settled himself higher on the cantle, prepared himself for a miserable ride, and kicked the gelding into movement.

He would have to cross the road and keep to the trees on

the other side until he was past the windows, but once he was out of sight, he would catch the road again and head for Portishead. He would not take her to his rented residence. No, he had a place in mind where no one would ask questions, and she would find escape difficult, if not impossible.

Once he had her drugged again and securely locked in, he would send word to Miles. She had not been in Miles's house when he slipped in and found the jewels, but in his uncle's.

Victor guided the horse away from the house, looking for the path that crossed the road and kept him in the opposite woods and out of sight, his mind chewing over his predicament.

He had the woman now, and Miles would certainly come for her. He knew what to say in a letter that would bring the man to Portishead and his trap.

The path appeared, and Victor looked and listened. No carriage, no horse, no one nearby who might see him. He urged the horse across the road, one hand firmly on the woman's back to keep her from slipping, and back into the woods.

His cousin already suspected him. That conversation of weeks ago had told him as much.

If only his aim had been true! Miles would be dead, and he would be the heir. Even a presumptive heir had access to funds that were out of reach now.

Miles had to die.

And this woman would bring him close enough to do it right the next time.

Victor carefully wended his way through the back alleys of Portishead. The woman lolled in his arms—Victor had stopped far enough outside the city to eliminate anyone seeing him, and pulled her into his arms before entering—and his muscles strained at their burden. He had stopped once to give her another dose after she had begun to stir, and it was holding nicely.

He had had one close scrape along the road. One of the neighbors, a man a generation older who often picked the berries along the road despite them being on Stewart land, and then sold the jams—"the man has to eat," his uncle had often said, and let the minor theft go—had been walking his horse when Victor came around a curve.

His heart had nearly stopped, but it was too late to turn around; the man knew him.

He could not possibly miss the woman dangling over the withers.

"Mr. Stewart! What have you there?"

He pulled up, his heart racing enough to make him breathless. It had taken a moment for the name to come. "Mr. Martin? Why are you not on your horse?"

"He threw a shoe." Mr. Martin had removed his hat and scratched his head, then pointed at the woman. "What have you there? She ain't dead, is she?"

Victor managed a laugh. "A drunken whore. She served her purpose, but I am bringing her back." He had waved a hand that thankfully did not shake. "You can see she is hardly in any position to walk all the way."

Mr. Martin only nodded. "Pity such a pretty one got led down the path of sin, but good o' you to take her back."

And that had been the end of it. Victor had lifted a hand and kicked the horse into movement again, but it had taken a while for his panic to subside.

The chance of anyone questioning Martin, whose status was far beneath them and who might well reach his little holding before the search began, was slim.

Now all he had to do was get her inside before any more people saw her. That hair was memorable.

The place he chose had a back entrance, and he had the room closest to it, but one floor up. She would be a bit of a load to carry up the stairs, but he had lifted heavier.

He drew close to the back door, tied his horse to the pole, and tugged her down easier than he had gotten her up. Sounds came from the kitchen, and laughter drifted from the open dining room at the front, but no one appeared. Victor worked her over his shoulder—hopefully no one saw him because her position would cause comment—pushed the door open, and began to climb, listening with every step to any sounds that indicated someone moving upstairs.

But it was quiet all the way, the only sounds his own puffing and the thumping of his heart. He bumped her head twice as he climbed higher, but at last he reached the landing. A quick peek around the corner, but the hall was empty, and he hurried to his room.

The key was still in his waistcoat pocket, a minor miracle considering the last hours. He got the door unlocked without dropping the woman, turned, and kicked it shut, carried her to the bed and dropped her down in a puff of pink silk. At last, he could relax.

And get some food. She would not wake for a while. Victor rolled his shoulders to get the strain out, stretched his back to ease the tightness there, slipped out of the room, and locked it behind him.

He would have to eat with relative dispatch. It was hard to dose her while riding a horse, and he feared he spilled as much as she swallowed. There had to be an apothecary close by where he could get more. He also had a letter to write and get delivered, and he dared not let her wake.

For now, he would get some food in his stomach and keep his ear to the ground. Someone would drop a name of a man willing to take a message as far as Miles's house.

Heir presumptive. He turned the words over in his head as he went down the stairs to the main room. In a short time, he would have access to all the money he could ever want, and no collector would ever come after him again.

A s he waited for his food to come, Victor sipped his ale, watched, and listened. He had found a ragged, smelly boy in the street who was happy to get a ride out into the country, but now Victor needed someone to drive him.

He certainly could not do it himself, not and watch over his flame-haired captive at the same time. Getting the child back here was not his responsibility, and besides, Miles would almost certainly see to the boy's return. After all, once he had read the letter, he would come here himself.

Men in rough clothes sat in clusters at the circular tables. The smell of fish, perhaps from the men but more likely from the kitchen, lent its own scent, and ale joined it, making the air a veritable advertisement of the edibles on hand.

He knew he looked to have money. As he was about done with his own fish and vegetables, a man with the strong odor of farm gave his order to the maid. "An ale and some bread, if you please, and make it quick. I have to get back before the wife worries about me."

A few ribald calls came from those well in their cups, but the farmer ignored them.

Victor put down his fork, took one more swallow of ale,

rose, and walked to the man. He pulled out a chair opposite and sat down. "Which direction are you headed, my man?"

CHAPTER 50

EDWARD HAD ORDERED HIM TO HIS ROOM TO REST. MILES struggled to get comfortable in the strange bed, but finally closed his eyes. When he opened them again, the sun was streaming in.

Based on the angle of the golden rays, perhaps two hours must have passed. He was surprised that he had managed to sleep. A tap came at the door, and Thomas peeked inside. "Oh! You are awake. Your father wishes to see you." He smiled a weak smile. "I believe he needs to reassure himself that you have not died of your wound."

It took some effort to get out of bed without causing more pain, but once he got onto his feet, he was pleased that the room remained still.

"Do you wish me to accompany you?" A frown puckered between his valet's brows.

"I will make it. I think it will be more reassuring to Father if I arrive without assistance. The wound is sore, but not so bad that I cannot move on my own."

Despite his reassurances, Thomas followed him down the

stairs and along the hallway to Father's office. He stayed out of view when Miles tapped on the door and walked in. He closed the door behind himself, strolled to the chair in which he always sat, and took care to sit without wincing.

Father looked at him, a frown creasing between his brows and real concern in his eyes. "Tell me honestly, son, now that we are away from the women, how badly do you hurt?"

Miles shifted in his chair, grateful for the bandage and the lack of a waistcoat. Edward had forbidden him from wearing one for a week, so as not to disturb his wrapping. "I am sore, but the bleeding is almost done. I suspect I will feel it tomorrow."

Father leaned back in his chair, relief obvious in the sag of his shoulders and the sigh that puffed out of him. "Your guest was right all along. She did hear what she said. It was not a fever dream."

Miles wished he could slump, too. The wound was better when he kept his back straight. "I can no longer deny what she heard. And if she was right about the threat, then I am certain the shooter was Victor. She insisted he had mentioned a family head who was an earl. I let myself think it was a coincidence, but that no longer holds."

"We do not know if your cousin is still in the area." Father tapped his two index fingers together in a quiet rhythm.

"Not that long ago, he stopped at my house for what he called 'a pleasant chat.' It did not end well, but it was not so acrimonious that he would have gone back to London." Miles leaned back, only to have his wound twinge, and straightened again. "There is no reason any longer to defend him."

Father stood and adjusted his waistcoat. "I should like to thank Miss Underwood. If she did well enough that Dr. Reed praised her efforts, it is only right that I thank her as well."

"I caught a glimpse of her walking past the library window toward the front when Edward was wrapping me. I suspect she is still sitting in the copse." Miles doubted she would be at the bench where they last spoke, but there were others scattered through the small woods, and he knew the location of each.

"It is the middle of the afternoon." Father strode toward the door. "She may have come in for a cold collation. Meats and bread are in the dining room, and cakes were served the women in the parlor."

A smile tugged at Miles's mouth. "I do not think she will eat with the women. They were . . . less than approving."

"Let us go find her, and thank her appropriately." Father opened the door, and Miles followed him out.

He had a question to ask Olivia, and the fear that she would reject him in favor of returning to her own land was a pain deeper than the gouge in his side.

Olivia was not in the dining room, and none of the servants busy there had seen her.

The women in the parlor had not seen her, either. Despite their judgmental words of earlier, Mrs. Kirkman said, "She was so calm. No doubt she did as well as Dr. Reed could have. I was most impressed."

"But where did she go?" Miles looked around the faces staring back at him, all of them most obviously surprised to see him walking unaided.

"She wanted fresh air," Abby said. "I believe she went out by the garden door. I would not be surprised if she is still there."

Cakes and scones sat on delicate plates about the room,

and the tea smelled fresh. "She did not come in to enjoy your repast?"

Abby shook her head. "No. I have not seen her since we parted."

He bowed to the women. "I think I know where she might be, then." He turned around, nearly bumping into Father.

"When you find her, tell her I wish to thank her myself." He bowed to the women as well.

The two men exited the room together. Miles could not resist a smile. "You are not going to stay with your wife?"

Father actually shuddered. "Along with those other women? No. I will have the servants bring me a little something, and then I will join the men when they arrive. We will eat in the dining room. The women will no doubt join us, but there will be enough men to go around."

Miles chuckled as he turned to the front door. "Enjoy your food. I will bring Miss Olivia in when I find her."

The footman opened the door for him, and Miles headed for the path. He would try the bench first, but he did not expect to find her there.

Less than a minute later, he found himself staring at that bench. Something did not feel right. He could not figure out what troubled him, but the hairs rose on his neck.

And then he saw what caused it. Her jade and gold bracelet lay open on the flagstone walk. He reached it in three strides and picked it up. Olivia was never without it. He had never even seen her take it off.

The clasp was bent, badly enough that it had come apart. A spot of red stained one of the pieces of jade.

He spun around in a circle, hoping to see her red hair, or a flash of her pink gown. But all that caught his eye was a section of broken twigs. His hand clenched on the bracelet, and he hurried over to the wounded bushes.

Where the flagstone ended, footprints began. Men's footprints, long and heeled, the ground broken where the shoes had pressed in. Whoever made those prints was carrying something heavy enough to leave clear impressions in the dirt.

Panic rose in his throat, tight and strangling, and his heart began pounding hard enough to thunder in his ears, but Miles forced himself to breathe, forced himself to walk slowly and keep his eyes on the ground. His fingers held Olivia's bracelet so tightly the prongs holding the stones dug into his palms, but he could not release it.

It was all he had of her.

Where is she, where is she? The words thundered as loudly in his brain as his heart did in his ears. He caught himself running, but forced himself to slow down for fear he might miss the footprints and lose the trail.

This had to be Victor. He knew about her presence in the house; at least, he had known about her having been in Miles's own house. The traitor who carried the tale about her presence had to be Crofts. It was a good thing the man had disappeared, because if he was behind this kidnapping, Miles might take justice into his own hands.

At last he came to the end of the trail, where horse's hooves marred the ground, and the footprints became muddled.

A bellow of rage burst from his throat, echoing off the hills. There was no point in going slow now. She was not here, and if they were to catch a horse, they had to move fast. Miles whirled and ran back toward the house, cutting through the copse, not bothering with the path.

He burst through the door before the footman could

reach it, shoving it open so hard it hit the wall, and shouted into the house, his voice rebounding off the walls and echoing from the far corners. "Olivia has been taken! She is gone! Get the horses saddled!"

The women burst from the parlor, and a moment later Father appeared at the end of the hallway. "What is this?" His voice cut through the chatter of the women.

Miles fought for breath and held up Olivia's bracelet. "I found this on the path. It has blood on it. There is a trail through the woods, and it ended at a horse. The hoof prints are matted and jumbled. Someone struggled with the horse, probably getting her on it."

Abby hurried over and grabbed at the bracelet, but Miles could not let go. He held it out, though, firm in his hand. "See?"

She gasped and clapped her hand over her mouth. For the second time that day, she went pale, but the footman reached her just as Father arrived. Together, the two men got her—as well as the rest of the women—back into the parlor.

Once Abby was lying on a settee, one of the ladies fanning her while another patted her hand, Father turned to him. "Not here."

He stomped out the door, and Miles followed so closely he nearly stepped on Father's heels. They stopped halfway up the hallway.

"We must saddle the horses!" Miles wanted to shake his father, wanted to roust all the servants, to jump on his stallion and ride.

But where would he go? What direction? Toward Portishead and the sea, the perfect place to toss a body? Miles went cold. He would not let himself think that, but the chill went all the way to his bones.

"Take me to the place where you saw the signs of horse."

Father turned to the footman. "Go get some grooms. I need men who understand horses. And have them meet us by the copse. Quickly, man, quickly!"

The footman took off running in one direction; Miles turned toward the door again, running himself, hoping his father could keep up.

He forced himself to stop at the path's turning, and Father came up behind, moving quickly, but his running days were past.

They had no sooner met up than a ruckus came from the area of the stables, grooms running toward them, several with pitchforks.

Father waited until the men had caught up and stood around, restless and curious, the pitchforks bobbing over their heads. "Miss Olivia has been kidnapped. Lord Langley will show you where he found signs of the horse, and we will spread out and see if we can find out which direction they went."

Miles beckoned the men to follow. Once the men got to the trampled ground, he stood back and let them search. These men knew horses better than he would do in a lifetime; if there was something those marks could tell them, they would find it.

L ess than ten minutes later—Miles knew the time, he had checked his pocket watch repeatedly—a groom shouted, "This way!"

"Don't disturb the tracks!" Miles ran after the voice, afraid he was doing the very thing he warned the others against.

The men stood around a faint line of prints, heading

directly toward the road, and Miles began to shake inside. He patted the pocket where Olivia's bracelet now rested, neatly buttoned so it would not fall out.

One of the grooms went into the road. "I think he crossed it here. Look!" He pointed at his feet. "It is going across." He drew an imaginary line in the air with his finger. "He went into the woods there." And he suited the gesture with action, walking in a straight line into the woods.

The grooms followed, but before they reached the outer trees, the first groom shouted, "Here! He headed west! He went toward Posset!"

"To the horses," Miles shouted as he turned back and ran.

The men followed him.

Father was no longer in the small clearing where he found the hoofprints.

Thomas, however, was.

"Thomas! What brings you here?"

"A boy arrived at your house." Thomas took a quick breath. "He had a note, and he will not give it to anyone but you. He says it is urgent, so I thought it best to come for you."

The ransom letter! It had to be.

CHAPTER 51

D ENTON WAS OUTSIDE BY THE FRONT DOOR WHEN M ILES
pulled up his stallion and tossed the reins to the groom. He
heard Thomas's horse thundering up the road. "Take care of
him," he said as the groom caught the leather, and ran toward
his butler. "What is this about an urgent letter?"

"A rather smelly little boy has arrived with what he says is
a matter of life and death. He will not be dismissed, and says
he must be paid by the lord of the house before he hands
over the message he carries."

Miles pushed past Denton, jerked the door to the
servants' hallway open, and saw at the far end of the hallway
a little boy, no more than seven or eight, his clothes dirty
rags, the pants hanging below his knees, his feet bare. A cap
that had originally belonged to someone much larger than he
covered most of his hair, but it might be blonde under all the
dirt. An unrecognizable odor rose from him, reaching Miles
before he was halfway down the hall.

As he passed the kitchen door, standing open, he noticed

his staff clustered there, eyes wide. Mrs. Flaherty held her apron over her nose, but she looked as anxious as the others.

"I gots a note for the lord." The little boy stood there as confident as a prince. "Ye got any of the ready? I hain't turnin' it over fer nuthin'." The little chin stuck out pugnaciously.

The child had brass, Miles thought. If it was not so urgent, it would be humorous.

"Who brought you here?"

"I ain't s'posed to tell. I gots me rules, and I ain't gonna get paid lessen I follow em."

"I will pay extra."

He saw the boy calculating, and finally he said, "'Ow much extra?"

If this child could help them find Olivia and catch whoever had stolen her, it would be worth paying a grand sum. "How does a quid sound?" He was tempted to offer a sovereign, but feared the gold would cause more problems where the child came from than it would solve.

The boy's eyes went wide. "A quid? A whole quid?"

Under other circumstances, Miles would have smiled at a single pound being so valuable, but the whole situation was not funny, and might well turn tragic. "Yes. A whole quid."

"I don't know 'is name, but 'e promised me e'd make it worth me while. 'E were all dressed fancy-like, not like ye are, and were all tall an' blond."

Miles exchanged a look with Denton. He could see the other man reach the same conclusion as himself. Victor. He turned around to the child again and folded his arms to make himself look more authoritative. "Would you be able to take me to where the man found you?"

The boy ran his gaze over Miles again. "Ye don't look like ye could walk to town."

Miles chuckled. "Walk? No. You will ride in my carriage."

The boy's eyes were more excited than even at the offer of a quid. "A real carriage?"

Miles had been around a number of the ton who had not caught the new craze for bathing, but not even they could match the awesome odor coming from this little body. "Yes, but only after you have bathed."

"I ain't takin' no bath, and you cain't make me!" Color rose up the child's cheeks, visible even beneath all the dirt. "Bathin' ain't nacheral. Hit'll kill ye!"

"It has not killed me," Miles said, keeping his voice low and unthreatening. His hands were clenched in impatient fists behind his back at this odd delay, but if he was going to ride in the carriage with this boy, he would not get in with that smell. Neither he nor the carriage would ever be the same.

"Denton? Go get some coins for this enterprising young man." Miles smiled, but still kept his distance. The odor was getting stronger the longer the boy spent in the hall. The doors would have to be left open for an hour to clear the air.

Miles held the boy's gaze while he heard Denton's feet go down the hall.

When they were alone, Miles scowled down at the boy. "Very well, I am getting you your reward, but before I give it to you, how do I know you even have a letter? Let me see it or you will not receive a ha'penny."

The boy reached down into his shirt and pulled out a crumpled paper.

"Let me see what it says. That could be anything."

"The ready, first."

This child did not trust anyone, did he? Miles had seen enough of the note to think he recognized the writing. "No, open the page. Let me see that it is what you say it is."

Denton showed up then with the jingle of coins in his hand. Miles did not know where he found them, but the timing was perfect. The boy saw the coins and held out the letter one second too long. Miles snatched it. "You have seen your reward. You will get it after you are bathed."

He turned to Denton, the letter clutched tight. "Have some of the footmen take him outside and pour some water over him. If they can find some soap in the process, all the better. Do it quickly because as soon as I am dressed in something that will fit in there, we are leaving."

He walked back down the narrow hall and across the main one to his office, shutting the door behind him. The letter was closed with wax, but no seal. What kidnapper would have his own seal, anyway? Even worse, be stupid enough to use it?

He broke the wax and opened the letter. The words were jagged and sprawling on the page, but still readable.

"I have your woman. If you want her, come to Portishead, and wait in The Eel's Tail. Someone will meet you there."

There was no signature, but he did not need one. Victor might think he had disguised his handwriting, but as children they had practiced writing with both hands. The lines might have matured, but he could still see the childish ploy they had invented.

He knew this was a ploy to get him close enough for Victor to do away with him and claim the inheritance for himself.

Olivia had told him, and *told* him, over and over, that someone wanted him dead.

Would she die, too?

He had to set the letter down; the paper was shaking so hard the words blurred. How much danger was she in?

I have your woman. Yes, she was his woman. Could he find her in time?

How far from her hiding place had Victor walked to find the little boy being bathed right now? If they were to put the child down where he requested, would it bring them anywhere close to where Olivia was hidden?

Miles sagged into his chair and stared at the letter.

The Eel's Tail indeed! He would find any footmen who could ride, send someone over to his father's house and ask for more, all that Father could spare, all in common clothes to blend in.

A quill and paper. He scribbled a note to his father and sealed it, then rang the bell.

His butler appeared after a minute, a long time for him. Miles blinked when he saw the man. He had never seen Denton so rumpled. "What happened?"

Color rushed up Denton's normally impassive face. "The young man did not take kindly to a bath."

"How does he smell now?"

Denton's lips actually twitched. Was that a smile? "Much better, my lord. I do believe he will no longer offend."

"Good. We have an issue." He did not wait for Denton to ask, just hurried on. "I believe this is a trap. We have been given a place to meet the kidnapper, but I do not intend to get there alone."

He held out the letter. "Will you send this word to my father, and quickly? And, Denton? Find any of my own men who are good on horses and do the same. They will need to fit in on the rough streets of Portishead. Tell them to get there quickly, but quietly."

"Consider it done, my lord."

Olivia squinted and blinked, trying to bring the room into focus, then wrinkled her nose at the reek of spoiled food and unwashed bodies that crept through the very walls. The powerful yeasty smell of beer clung to everything, along with something else, more primitive, like someone had missed the chamber pot more than once.

Where was she? How did she get here?

The memories crept back, the man with the evil smile and the rifle, of trying to run, having him pour something nasty down her throat. She thought she remembered jostling on a horse, and tenderness along her abdomen verified that.

What time was it?

Her brain throbbed in her skull, and her legs felt like overcooked noodles. She struggled to sit, fighting the spinning of the room and the pounding in her head. From what she could see, the room was small and dirty, the grey curtains were stained and torn, the hems beyond washing. In fact, Olivia decided the whole room was beyond saving.

She did not know the time, but anemic light crept through the tears in the curtains, so it was either growing late, or nearing sunrise.

Scrabbling sounded in the wall close to her ear, and Olivia lurched off the bed, falling onto her hands and knees with a thud that surely could be heard out in the hall. She held her breath, trying to listen, and sure enough, footsteps pounded up the stairs.

Olivia clambered to her feet, feeling the traces of whatever he'd drugged her with ease. She scanned the room frantically, but whoever was responsible for this hadn't been stupid enough to leave her with anything resembling a weapon.

Except the chamber pot, a solid piece of porcelain that

had seen better days. It had been cleaned before it was left in here, but she hated to touch it.

It was either fight with what she had or stay in the bed feigning sleep, so Olivia swallowed her gorge, grabbed the pot, slipped behind the door, and held it over her head. The small slit of the hinges would only give her a flash of time to recognize whoever opened the door.

The man—his face abruptly familiar—threw the door open. She jumped out of the way before it hit her and swung the pot with all her might.

He dropped to the floor like a felled tree. She vaulted over him . . .

Only to have him grab her ankle and bring her down so hard her ears rang. Her forehead burned against the floor, and splinters tore through her hands.

Olivia flipped onto her back, wrenching that foot free, kicking, hitting any part of him that got close with everything she could flail. The air was singed with his curses. His nose was bleeding, she saw in a quick flash, and aimed for it again with a lashing foot.

He caught that foot before it landed, twisting it so sharply she cried out. She rolled with the turn, and the chamber pot was there, right within reach. She grabbed it and kept rolling onto her back, her free foot going like a piston, back and forth, trying to avoid his grabbing hand. She felt the chamber pot slam against his shoulder and the force ripped it from her hand.

"Hellion!" the man yelped, dropping her foot.

Olivia ignored the pain in her wrenched ankle, and flung herself toward him, the heel of one hand going for his nose, the other a claw, going for his face, scraping against his skin.

Blood spurted; he made a sound she never hoped to hear again, but it got her on her feet and to the door. He lurched upright, but Olivia didn't wait, it was now or never, and she had to *move*. Out the door, stumbling down the hallway toward the opening in the wall that hinted at a way down.

Yes! A stairway! She hurtled down; the stairs were narrow and slippery, the railing loose, and her ankle didn't want to hold her up, but she didn't dare slow for the startled faces sitting at stained tables, dirty faces and greasy unwashed hair, the ragged clothes of the patrons of the inn, mugs in their hands suspended on the way to their mouths. She went past before any of them could rouse themselves to get involved.

She burst outside, dust swirling around her, static electricity sparking along her arm when she shoved at the metal handle. The discharge startled her, but Olivia didn't pause, just ignored the pain in her ankle and kept running. The street was covered with straw; the houses leaned against each other as if they all worked in collusion to stay upright. The sun was low in the sky, the shadows growing long, warning of evening to come, yet the street was filled with people.

Faces flew past, eyes blank with hopelessness, staring past her, none of them able to excite themselves enough to help. She didn't hear any shouts from the man coming from behind her, didn't hear anything over the pulsing of blood coursing through her veins, throbbing in her ears, and her heart pounding in her chest, lungs burning until finally her body gave up and she fell flat on the dirty street.

The ground barely hurt, it seemed soft beneath her, or perhaps she was already so bruised and shocked that she couldn't feel it. Sparks flashed before her eyes, static arced around her, blurring her vision, her hands tingled and shivers ran up her arms.

Olivia lay there just long enough for the buzzing to stop,

then pushed herself back to her feet when the dizziness eased. People around—there seemed to be people every-where—shrieked and pointed as if they only now saw her, and beneath the dirty faces Olivia thought she saw them pale.

"Please, what city is this?" she asked a small group of dirty women leaning over a tub of washing when she reached the nearest building and could hold herself up against the crumbling brick.

No one answered. The children huddling near the women scuttled into doorways, staring with big eyes, showing the first sign of interest she had seen since she careened out of the room. A couple of the smaller ones burst into tears and ran back down the street to disappear around the corner. The reaction was out of all proportion to her innocuous presence.

"Please? Where am I?" Her ankle twinged, but it wasn't as bad as she feared. She might be able to run on it if she had to.

One of the women, braver than the rest, propped a wet hand on her hip. "Don't ye know? This is Posset. How ye get 'ere iffen ye don't even know where ye be?"

She didn't dare explain. "Thank you." Then she pushed herself away from the wall. Behind her, she heard a muffled shriek, but she didn't turn around. Her vision was fading, everything growing dim. The true danger of her position struck her, limping, vulnerable, and alone, dressed in a gown the like of which the women of this place could only dream of.

Would they kill for it?

As she turned the first corner, her vision cleared, and she paid attention to the expressions around her. She garnered only faint curiosity, and she realized her lovely pink gown was torn, her exquisite hairstyle was nonexistent, curls dangling in her eyes and hanging loose down her back. Olivia picked a clump of mud off one drooping curl, and threw it away, afraid to wonder where it had originated.

Her old Minneapolis street sense came back sharp, watching without seeming to watch as she limped along, eyes straight ahead, aware of everyone nearby, keeping track of their steps, watching the long shadows for movement, listening behind her for whoever might be coming too close. Few people even turned her way, most passing her without a single glance. Olivia was grateful for their inattention because her vision kept going vague, people turning hazy and distant.

A man to her side turned without warning, moving too quickly for Olivia to get out of the way, and walked directly into her, then jumped back to glare with a mixture of anger and fear. "Where you come from?" he snarled, his bravado paper-thin.

Olivia didn't answer, just stepped around him and kept shuffling along, trying to match the hopelessness weighing the whole area, blending into her surroundings.

Behind her she heard the man shout angrily at someone, "She weren't there, I tell ye!"

CHAPTER 52

THE OLD CARRIAGE RATTLED ALONG, CREAKING THROUGH THE narrow streets of the little fishing village. He had taken an old vehicle. It might not look like much, but his staff kept it in good repair, and it would not attract attention.

Miles had not seen any of the footmen who had gone ahead, but he knew they were here. Several of his own men and a couple more of his father's were from this place. They had been most helpful in giving suggestions on which streets would handle a carriage this size, and which would not.

He dropped the boy just inside the city. The feisty child flatly refused to give his name, and had told them where to set him down.

As they drove off, Miles saw the boy scuff some dirt on his legs, and rub his hands on his face. Through the entirety of the trip here the child had squirmed and fussed, and looked at his hands and legs with a scowl. "Nobody'll recognize me, and I'll be pummeled into jam, I will."

Not quite an hour had passed since Miles had read the

ransom note and set his plan in motion. No doubt his stolen jewelry had already been sold. Several of the pieces had come from Grandfather. He would miss them.

If he was very lucky, he would find them still in the possession of Victor, although the chance of that was small.

Best of all would be to find Olivia safe and sound, and have her be able to give enough information to convict his cousin.

And his man of affairs, who had to be mixed up in this mess. Somehow Victor had known about her, but more, had recognized which woman to grab.

Miles would like nothing better than to see his cousin on a convict ship to New South Wales.

His hands clenched on his knees as the forced inactivity gnawed at him. The carriage horses plodded along, the wheels barely turning, but there were other vehicles around, hacks and wagons with the day's supplies, a mail wagon taking a shortcut through the town, handcarts with flowers or fruit, likely heading home for the night, and horses.

Lots of horses. In fact, as he peered through the long shadows, Miles recognized a number of familiar horses. He felt his hands relax, his shoulders ease.

His men were here. They would scour the alleys; he would go to The Eel's Tail and watch from a distance.

He patted his coat pockets, feeling the pistols on either side. They were double-barreled, which gave him four bullets if needed. He was long familiar with these guns and knew they shot straight.

The thought of putting a bullet into his cousin made him sick, but Miles consoled himself that the chance of anything that violent happening was small.

Unless any harm had come to Olivia.

For Victor's sake, she had better be unharmed.

Olivia clung to the corner of the dusty building and pressed her forehead against the cool wood. No one bothered to look, just as no one had in the past several blocks. She might as well have been invisible.

She was grateful she had been ignored during those blocks. It was probably the torn gown and the tumbled hair, but apparently she looked no different from the other women in the street and the coming twilight helped her disguise.

She hadn't seen despair and squalor like that—ever. Even in her own time, driving through areas with boarded-up houses, and businesses closed, iron gates locked across the abandoned storefronts, windows smashed, groups of men on street corners likely selling drugs—knowing they had weapons hidden—not even then had she seen the equal of what she'd just walked through.

A knife could kill as finally as a gun and with less noise, and she'd caught flashes of a few of those.

She looked down at her hands as she brushed the dust away.

And saw the street through her palms. Olivia held out her hands, staring at them—through them—in disbelief.

She really was invisible.

For a moment, she couldn't move, just stood there staring at the filthy street, knowing that her hands were extended, hovering in space. Even where her gown should be was clear, empty.

No wonder no one had reacted. She looked around her.

The building was solid; she had felt it against her head, but the people who acted as if they did not see her actually had not.

Olivia felt a hum of electricity inside her. On a hunch, she lifted a hand. It was solid again. She was solid again. Her dress was back, her shoes were visible when she lifted her skirts.

A woman screeched. Olivia jerked around at the piercing cry, to see an elderly woman in elegant blue gown and hat, being carried in a chair on the shoulders of some burly men in matching uniforms.

The woman pointed at her, and the scream went up a notch. Olivia picked up her skirts and darted around behind a large covered wagon piled with cabbages.

When she arrived in 1811, it had been quickly, a shocking flash and she had been whisked across time, complete with clothing. This was different. She was slipping in and out of solidity, and there could only be one reason.

The iron was waking.

She didn't even know where it was. Olivia could only assume she was too far away for the iron to find her. It was calling her, sending out pulses, seeking her, but she was just out of reach.

What about Clara? Was the same thing happening to her?

What if they were right, and the iron was misfiring? How long would it do this? What if it found her, and whisked her away before she had a chance to tell Miles the truth?

She wanted him to know everything. She wanted a ride in the country, wanted another dance, even the sound of his voice.

She wanted to tell him she loved him.

The old woman stopped screaming. Olivia heard servants' voices crooning to her, and hoped the poor lady's blood pressure would settle. Taking a chance, she peeked around the edge of the wagon. The only sounds were the bickering of buyers and sellers, and scolding of people who were taking too many liberties with the produce for sale.

Someone came over and plucked a basket of cabbages off the wagon, and jumped at seeing Olivia. It was a fat man not much taller than Olivia herself, wearing an apron that must have been white at the beginning of the morning's work, but now had green cabbage colored streaks down his front. "'Eere, ye, wot ye be doin' there? Ye wanna cabbage, ye jest get in line with the rest of 'em." He set the basket down and grabbed Olivia's arm. "I mean it, jest get away from back there." He dragged her out from behind the wagon.

The old woman saw her, took a deep gasping breath, opened her mouth, and truly impressive shrieks cut the air once again.

With her bad luck, between the woman's caterwauling and the cabbage seller's grip on her arm, Olivia knew she would be accused of stealing, and the woman would accuse her of witchcraft on top.

Olivia knew about the choices for thieves, death or transport to Australia. Being accused of witchcraft would be the nail in her coffin.

Panic gave her strength. She jerked her arm out of his big hand with a quick twist, and ran, clutching her skirts, moving as fast as her sore ankle would take her, down the street toward a building, even a gap or a doorway, any place where she could hide.

Where was invisibility when she needed it?

M iles heard a woman scream suddenly, and even without hearing the words in that frightened cry, he knew it had something to do with Olivia. "Follow that," he shouted to the driver.

An elderly woman in shimmering silks, her gown's every seam trimmed with lace, and riding a sedan chair, was pointing down the lane. "A witch, a witch!" she shrilled over and over.

Miles looked the direction of her finger. A familiar sprigged pink gown, tattered, with lace dragging behind it, disappeared around a building. He jerked the carriage door open and leapt outside, running toward where the gown had disappeared.

A small opening separated two buildings. He ducked into it, hoping against hope that it was her, that he had found the right turning—and there was Olivia, limping hurriedly further into the crack between the building and flashing an anxious glance over her shoulder, her dress tattered and dirty, her hair tumbled, her skin pale. Miles's heart clenched in fear. He had heard of women being abused, hurt in the worst ways, and Olivia looked like one of them.

"Olivia! Stop! It's me!"

She did not seem to hear him over her fear.

As he ran for her, she began fading, like a wisp of smoke.

O livia heard her name shouted, in a voice so familiar she couldn't believe her ears, stumbled to a stop, and jerked her head toward Miles, desperate with relief.

Miles stopped; she saw his steps check in mid-flow. A look of horror swept across his face. "Olivia? Olivia?" His voice sounded strange, thinner, as if from a throat suddenly grown tight.

She knew the feeling of displacement she saw on his face, as if everything had suddenly been uprooted, as he searched for her, turning around, peering behind him to see—Olivia could only imagine what thoughts ran through his nineteenth-century mind.

She cursed the iron's timing. It couldn't wait until she was in his arms once more, could it? No, it had to make her disappear right before his eyes. She didn't know if he could hear if she spoke; silence had been important before as she'd run away from her prison, and silence had been vital during her mad journey through this city's slums.

"Miles?" Her voice was creaky and tight. Olivia cleared her throat and tried again. "Miles?"

He closed his eyes, rubbed them, and opened them again. Blinked. "No, I am not blind. I see everything else." He whirled around, looking behind him, and called as if he expected her to be hiding, "Olivia, where are you? Where did you go?"

Olivia took a deep breath, trying for power in her voice, and called, "I'm here." She watched his face, hoping to see him hear her. A funny idea, seeing sound.

"I can hardly hear you. How did you get away?" He was shouting, but he had heard *something*.

Olivia wanted to laugh in relief, and cry in fear. "I'm still here. I'm fading," she yelled. "It's the iron."

Still turning around, peering in the dimness of the shaded alley, he kept up his muted yell. "Come back here, where I can see you. You are safe now."

She needed to be near him, needed to touch him. She had felt the building. Surely she could feel him. Olivia picked up her dragging skirts and ran, stopping at his side.

Miles had heard something, the patter of her feet, the rustle of her skirt, *something*, because he turned, and looked at her . . . but his eyes did not focus. He was looking at where she stood, but he did not see her.

"Who was that?" His voice sharpened. "Show yourself!"

"It's me," Olivia shouted the words, hoping their nearness would make them more audible. "I'm standing next to you." *Please hear me*, her heart pleaded, but even as she thought it, she saw his gaze sharpen. His mouth dropped open and his face paled, but his eyes met hers straight on.

She looked down at her hands, and they were solid. She was visible again.

None of her other appearances had happened that fast. They had to get back to his house, back to Clara, and the iron.

Or run away, far, far away, out of its reach.

She longed to throw herself into his arms, hold on against the pull of the iron, but the look on his face was so shocked that she did not dare. Olivia just stood there, shaking and wishing. "I'm still here, I haven't gone anywhere. Didn't you hear me say it was the iron?"

He snapped out of his surprise, and in a rush of movement, pulled her close, holding her in a fierce embrace. Olivia clenched her fingers in his coat, and felt his heart thundering against her face.

"Stop that! I am so happy to see you safe,"—his voice roughened—"you must know that, but you are talking nonsense. I do not know what you are doing to hide and return, but this is not the work of something as silly as an iron."

His voice was gruff and strained, a vibration of emotion sending shivers through her skin. "Just to feel you safe is enough for now, but I have not lost all sense. I do not want to hear about the iron again. You have tried every trick imaginable to get it away from me. I am tempted to toss it into the Atlantic."

She clutched at his coat, felt her finger slip through a tear in the fabric, and blinked. "Where did you get this thing? It looks like it was rescued from the garbage."

He stared at her as if she was speaking gibberish, and she hurried on, "Never mind. There isn't much time." She grabbed his arms and tried to shake him. "You have to listen! Any minute I might disappear altogether. The iron is calling me. I may not last until we get to your house. I've been drifting in and out of sight; you saw that yourself."

"We won't discuss it now." Miles cut her off, becoming once again the lord of the manor, wrapped his arm around her waist, and turned her to the alcove's opening, hurrying her along. "My men are looking for Victor. I need to get you away from here before he sees us. He has a gun; we know that. I would not put it past him to use it."

She looked up in surprise, almost tripping over her torn skirt. "You finally believe me?"

At the alcove's entrance, Miles held her out of the way as he peeked around the corner, and scanned both directions. "Come!" He hurried her through the carts in the road, and across to where a ragged carriage waited, the driver sitting with a pistol resting on his knee, in full sight of everybody.

Miles pulled open the carriage door and bundled her inside. Her skirt tore again, another rip to add to the many. He slid into the seat beside her, close enough that his thigh pressed against hers. He barely got settled before blurting, "What do you mean, disappear altogether? You deny it, but is this some kind of trick? Were you making a mirage? It can hardly be tricks with mirrors; you do not have one on you.

Whatever it is, I will protect you, you need not fear that, but I must know what you are doing."

Olivia fixed her gaze on Miles, trying to memorize every detail. The carriage rumbled beneath them, taking her further and further from Victor—hopefully—out of the city and closer and closer to his house and wherever Miles had hidden the iron, closer to its power. "I am from the future. The iron is a time tunnel—or a time key."

CHAPTER 53

MILES'S MOUTH FELL OPEN. "THE FUTURE? HAS YOUR FEVER returned?" He touched the back of his hand to her forehead. "You do feel warm, but I am not a physician. I do not know how to tell a fever."

Olivia caught his hand and pressed it between both of hers, twisting to face him. Carriages were not as wide as cars; the fit was tight, but she did not mind. She wanted, no, *needed* him close.

He was tense; she felt it in his hand between hers, and in the hard thigh. "I'm fine, and you have to listen. I don't know how much time I have. If I disappear, listen for me. I will keep talking because you heard me before." She squeezed his hand tighter. "Think back. Why did I not know where I was? Or how much time had passed? Why did I tell you not to look for my trunks on the ship, that they wouldn't be found? *Because I didn't come by ship.* I came by that iron."

His brows came down, and she felt his impatience through his hand. "I know it sounds silly, but I promise it is the truth. That iron has to be the key."

The last few houses of the city passed by slowly enough that Olivia could see through the windows, but she was not interested in anything outside this carriage.

Miles turned his head away, staring out the window at those same houses, but she did not think he was any more interested in what was happening there than she was. Whether he was remembering things that made sense now or angry at what he thought was a ridiculous lie, Olivia needed him to see her, to see the truth on her face as well as in her words, so she let go with one hand, and turned his face back to hers.

And he let her. His brows were still furrowed, but not in anger. More in . . . sadness?

He suspected she had gone insane. Somehow, she knew what he was thinking. She did not move her hand, just held his face and his gaze. "I am not crazy. Let me prove it to you." Although she didn't know how to do so in a moving carriage, without a pen and paper to draw the miracles of her time.

The lowering sun flashed into the carriage, and the answer came. Benjamin Franklin and his experiment with lightning!

"You know about lightning, don't you? How it conducts electricity? Have you heard about Benjamin Franklin and his experiments with the kite?"

His brows went up rather than down. "You Americans want to take credit for everything, don't you? Of course I know about lightning and electricity. You are talking about the Leyden jar, but Franklin did not invent it. A Dutchman did."

He was paying attention, so Olivia let go of his face, and clutched his free hand again, holding on as if she could keep both of them anchored. "Well, I don't know if he ever found a decent use for that, but in my day, everything runs on electricity. We use it to light our homes, and cook our food, even heat our houses."

How much of the future had she changed? But she had to convince him, so Olivia hurried on. "I had never used an iron like the one that brought me here. I warmed it up just for fun. We still have irons, but not like that one. Ours run on electricity. We don't light candles anymore except for atmosphere. We use electric lights. We even have a box that shows pictures that move."

Was she convincing him yet? She continued, her words tumbling out, not knowing what she was going to say until it was said. "We have carriages that run without horses, and a way to talk across long distances. We can go to the top of tall buildings without using stairs. Our chairs are soft, filled with something called foam."

His brows came down again. "Every word that comes out of your mouth is more strange, but you do not look like you are babbling from fever. Perhaps the kidnapping was harder on you than you realize."

Time was so short, and here she was, wasting precious seconds on an explanation! "You are stubborn as a mule! You know we're not dealing in normality right now!" She took another breath. "I'm sorry, that wasn't polite, but how else could I land in your house except by something out of this world? No one saw me enter; I know you checked that out. So how did I get there, then? You never even heard me, and you were in the adjoining room."

He turned his hands around, holding hers this time. "You cannot expect a rational person to believe this. You came across on a ship. Everyone knows that's the only way to get from America to England."

Olivia leaned forward, holding back her own frustration. "I realize this is startling. Remember when you found me today? One minute I was there, and the next minute, what had happened? I saw you looking around for me. What did you think as I disappeared?" She decided to indulge herself. "And just for my own curiosity, what did it look like? Did I fade, or what?"

"Something like that." A faint frown pulled his brows closer, then eased. In a voice that lacked his usual confidence, he said, "Surely it was magic."

She nodded. "That's probably not a bad description. I'd call it science, though, because there has to be a logical explanation, something we haven't discovered yet. There's speculation about wormholes in space that will let people zip across the universe, but no one's discovered one yet. That doesn't keep them from trying. Who knows, maybe one of these days someone will find one."

"Worms in space?" Miles's voice was strangled, his lips twitched as if trying to keep from laughing.

"Not worms, but holes like the tunnels they make in the ground, only in space. It's an expression, based on what people presume they look like, I guess," Olivia said, smiling back at him despite herself.

"So if you think you are from another time,"—his voice was kindly, pampering her delusions—"what time do you think you came from?"

"Brace yourself." She took a breath to brace herself. "I'm from over two hundred years in the future. It was 2023, in fact, when I left."

"Two hundred years?" He stopped smiling and shook his head. "First traveling using an iron as a ship, then worms in space, and now you want me to believe you are from the future? There is a limit to how far I can stretch my powers of belief."

"I don't blame you." She could explain all she wanted, but

he had to get used to the idea, or accept her on faith. "Truly, I know what it sounds like. But remember, you saw me disappear and come back."

"Yet you claim you are not a sorcerer, and this is not magic. I have been to performances, and seen men pull coins from behind ears." He smiled again.

His face abruptly changed, disbelief and stunned shock and a horrified dismay filling it. "No! Not again!"

The tingling started, prickles running along her skin. She didn't even have to look down at herself to know she had vanished again.

Olivia tightened her grip on his hands, but it felt like she was holding mist. She raised her voice. If his hands felt far away, no doubt her voice came from an equal distance. He had heard her earlier, when she disappeared. She had to try. "Miles? Can you hear me?"

His face was a study of anger, bafflement, and confusion mingled with shock. "Olivia? What are you doing? Are you still here? What spell is this?"

She tried a different tack, shouting at the top of her voice, "If you can hear me, say 'yes!'"

Miles drew back, then leaned forward, just a bit, as if afraid whatever happened was contagious. "Is that you?"

She yelled again, *"Say 'yes' if you hear me!"*

"I think so, yes." His face was still that odd study of emotions, his brows flicking from up to down, his mouth opening and closing before he spoke. He had pulled his hands away, and why not? He could not feel her, did not know her hands had still been in his after she vanished. "How can you be here, yet I cannot see you?"

If she had to shout the whole way, she would be hoarse by the time they got to the iron. The carriage continued down the road, moving swiftly, but O! for a car!

The thought stopped her. A car would get them there more quickly, but would that also make her disappear all the sooner?

And what was happening to Clara? Was she disappearing and reappearing in front of the servants, and frightening them to bits?

Another thought hit Olivia like a blow. If Clara was fading in and out as well, she might have run to his house and found the iron. It was what she had been hoping for all along, a chance to go back. Was the iron holding off, idling like an engine, just waiting until they were both in the same room to whisk them away?

Olivia took a deep breath. One question at a time. Miles first; her own questions would not be answered until they got to his house. *"I don't know, but I am still here!"*

"What kind of magic is this?" He must be talking to himself.

"It is not magic, it is science!"

"Why do you think the iron is to blame?" A blush rose on his face. He was too dignified to be comfortable talking to an empty carriage, even if a faint voice answered.

"It is the only thing I was doing when this happened, and it came with me." Not just her voice was hurting. Her heart hurt now, too. These might be the last minutes she had with him. Olivia could not tear her gaze from his face, memorizing every feature. If she was gone in a few minutes, at least she had met him, walked with him, met his family, treated his wound. Pain clamped around her heart.

Would she ever find a man to compare? Or would she spend the rest of her life wishing she had stayed?

"We are close, only a few minutes away. What will happen when we arrive?" *Now* he believed her? *Now*, when they might only have a few minutes together?

"I don't know!"

"Will you vanish as quickly as you came?" The question was so soft, she almost didn't hear it over the creaking of the carriage and the thumping of hooves.

"I don't"—the flashing came again, and her voice echoed in the carriage. *"KNOW!"*

His mouth dropped open, and a strangled sound came from his throat. "You are back!"

Olivia looked down at her hands, and they were solid, but she only had a glimpse before she was crushed against his chest. His mouth came down on hers, fierce, wild, molding her lips to his, tasting her with an urgency that matched the tumbling thoughts in her head. And her heart.

She slid her hands from between them, and wrapped them around him as tightly as she could, feeding on his taste, his breath, his questing tongue. *I must remember this, I must, I must*; the thought ran through her mind again and again, the only concept she could hold as he pulled away, gasped for air, and came back.

The carriage jerked, and settled; she clutched him tighter and gasped out, "Are you still here?"

"We are home." He drew back, but did not let go. "Let me remember you. I should have hired a painter. How will I remember your face if you are gone?"

"And I yours?" She tried to smile, but it wobbled, and her voice shook. "In my day, I would take a picture."

"Do we have to go in?" Miles looked out the door that the coachman must have opened. The man stood there, his face a mask. Olivia wondered how much he had seen. "What will happen?"

"I don't know." How many times had she given that answer? She had to tell him the rest, and leaned over to pull the door shut again. In an urgent whisper, it spilled out.

"Clara is also a time traveler. Neither of us knew who the other was until I said something that made her guess. I think we will find her ready to disappear as well."

His brows came down. "How many people from your time have come into my house?"

"Just us two. And we think it was an accident. We think the iron might be shorting—breaking down. We weren't even sure it still worked. She must be as surprised as I am."

He leaned forward, caught her head in gentle hands, and pressed another fierce kiss to her lips, longer this time. "Remember me." Then he eased around her, turned the latch, opened the door, and lowered the steps. Once out, he turned back, held out his arms, and swung her down. He just stood there, his hands still on her waist, looking at her. "I want to believe what you have told me is not true, that I am not looking at you for the last time, but I have seen too much to allow myself much hope."

In front of any onlookers, he gave her another kiss. "Know this, take this with you wherever you go: I am glad you found my house." Then he stepped back and bowed, a deep and elegant bow. "It has been my pleasure, Miss Olivia."

He held out his elbow, that painfully familiar gesture, and Olivia slipped her hand into the crook. In a soft whisper, he added, "Try not to disappear while we are walking. I will look rather foolish leading no one into my house. If you are still with me when we get inside, we will discuss whatever spell you have cast. I want it to stop."

Olivia felt no tingle; her hand remained visible on his arm, and the door opened right on time as they neared it. Denton stood there, his hair askew as if he had run his hands through it, a broad smile creasing his face, almost shivering with excitement. "My lord! You found her!" Then he remembered himself. "Have you found the blackguards as well?"

"My men are searching the city. I am sure they will find them soon." Miles hardly slowed. "I have more details to settle. We will talk later." His voice sounded strained.

They walked in silence to his office, but just before they reached it, a series of thumps, like books hitting the floor, came from inside.

CHAPTER 54

CLARA SAT ON THE FLOOR, BOOKS AROUND HER, AND PART OF the bookshelf open. Olivia blinked. So that was where it had been all this time!

From the dark box that the books had hidden, sparks spat, and the edges of the box, even the shelves above, seemed to dissolve into a wavy blur stripped of color.

The iron was awake.

"Clara, have you been fading in and out?"

Clara's eyes were wide and excited, happy. "Yes! You, too? It's starting! We're going back!"

Olivia stayed where she was. Not that it would matter, but Clara was closer. What if it could only take one? Would it grab the nearest person? If it could take both, *wanted* to take both, she needed one more minute here, one more touch of her hand in Miles's. One more kiss . . .

Miles spoke first. "How did you find the iron? No one who did not know the secret has ever found the safe."

Clara did not move from where she sat. Her voice was strong, modern, all traces of the servant gone now that rescue was at hand. "I kept appearing and disappearing so I knew the iron was waking up. I ran along the river because someone said once that it connected both properties, and I hoped it was a shortcut."

She rose and looked in the dark hole at the iron. "I felt it as soon as I got into the house. The power was so strong, I knew it had to be in here. I was standing on his chair,"—sure enough, it had been moved next to the shelves; Olivia had not noticed before—"and I lost my balance and caught the shelf, and the books fell off, and the cubby opened, and there it was."

Her words had tumbled out, running together with her excitement. Clara reached in and pulled the iron out before Olivia could shout a warning. Despite the strange sparks, it didn't burn her hands. "I am ready to go back, believe me." She looked over at Olivia. "You should probably come over here. I think it will be easier, and reach you better."

Olivia felt the tingle start, but something was off, Clara was fading, too, and Miles yelled, "No!" His arms came around her, holding her tight against him. "No!"

The tingling eased, and Clara was suddenly clear and sharp. She looked at Olivia, heartbreak on her face. "What did you do? Why did it stop?"

Miles turned Olivia to face him, and stared down into her eyes, his own gaze filled with heartache. "I want you to stay. I want you as my wife. I was going to ask you today; my father knew that, but then you were kidnapped."

His eyes were wet, his arms fierce and tight around her. "I need you. I care not when you were born. I think that thing brought you here for me. I will not let you leave me!" His mouth came down on hers again, tender this time in contrast with the tightness of his embrace.

Someone was talking, a constant buzz, but Olivia could not be bothered to listen.

Miles broke off the kiss, and lifted his head, looking over her, and Olivia turned to look at what had interrupted them.

Clara held the iron tight against herself, both arms holding it as if someone would wrest it away. "I think he is right. I think taking me was a mistake."

Her face went sad. "You have a life here. I do not. It must be correcting its mistake, and that is me. I have a boyfriend. I need to get back to him before he finds someone else. He must think I'm dead. I want to marry him. I thought he was going to propose soon."

The tingling started and Clara grew dim again. "Make up your mind,"—her voice sounded oddly distant—"but I'm going, no matter what!"

Miles bent down; Olivia felt his breath on the side of her face. "I think it is waiting for you to decide." He turned her around a second time, his hands firm on her shoulders, his gaze warm with love.

She had seen that look before, when he was staring at her through the parlor window with the men and horses eager for the hunt, but now Olivia saw it for what it was.

He loved her as much as she loved him.

"Marry me, Olivia? Please stay. Please put that thing out of its indecision and let it take Clara."

His mouth came down again, his lips soft and appealing, the kiss over too soon. "You must be the one to choose. I cannot, *I will not*, force you into a life you do not want, but I cannot see what life will be like without you in it."

He caught her hands and pressed them together. "Stay with me, Olivia. Be my wife."

She looked up at him, his anxious, hopeful, handsome face, his crystal-grey eyes, that mouth that kissed with such skill, confusion tumbling through her. Memories of her other life raced through her mind, like a reel of film on fast forward, as if the iron was reminding her of everything she had to lose. Leave her sister forever? Leave her career, her customers, *her friends?* Her company?

Stay with Miles forever?

Her heart must have decided before her head did, because suddenly a gust of wind buffeted her hair, strands slapping her face, a voice no louder than a whisper called from a far distance *I'm sorry*, and when she remembered Clara and she and Miles both turned as one, the office was empty. The box that had hidden the iron so safely was bare, and the books still sat on the floor in tumbled disarray.

The iron was gone. There was no way home. She was here to stay.

Oh, thank goodness.

His arms went around her, his chest tight against her breasts, his lips came down.

It was a long time before they came up for air.

———

Miles adjusted Olivia on his lap and looked around his office. The books still sat on the floor. He pressed a kiss to her cheek. "We need to put these back and hide the safe again. It has held many a secret, and doubtless will hold many more in the future."

He chuckled. "Future. That word has a different meaning now." Then he lifted her off his lap and stood to join her.

It took but a short time to put the room back to rights. As he shoved the last book into place, Miles suddenly realized . . . "You will need a new maid."

Olivia gave a start. "I will, won't I?"

He pulled her back into his arms. "I shall have to get a marriage license. It will be easy enough. The nearest bishop is in Bristol. I can be there and back in a day." He leaned back and smiled down at her. "We can be married within a week. I am certain Abby will wish to arrange for your wedding dress. That should be the only delay."

CHAPTER 55

It was not the only delay.

"You are not going to give her a rushed wedding." Abby stood next to Stafford in the dim light of the setting sun when they walked into the mansion hand in hand half an hour later, and glared at Miles. "I will not have people thinking that we did not protect her. You will wait a respectable time. I will send word to Mrs. Berrycloth, and we will order the gown. Olivia is not going to wear something she already has, as they are mostly day dresses."

Olivia clearly remembered getting some ballgowns, but she suspected that with their low-cut bodices and their short puffy sleeves, they would be inappropriate for a wedding. They had been hanging in her armoire, unworn, all this time.

If Abby wanted to order a gown for the wedding, she, Olivia, would keep her mouth shut. It wouldn't be the sleek, white gown she often envisioned, but just the thought of a wedding gown—and the wedding, O the wedding!—made her heart soar.

Miles stood there, looking between his father and his stepmother, listening without protest. "Very well. She has lived here long enough. I will ask for the banns to be read. That gives us three weeks."

Abby and Stafford exchanged looks. A whole conversation seemed to pass between them; the air was thick with tension.

Olivia looked up at Miles, to see him looking down at her. Someday, would they be able to communicate like that?

His eyes were warm, and she was certain she had her answer. They already did. They shared a secret Stafford and Abby would never understand.

Someone cleared a throat; they jumped apart and turned to the parents.

Abby's face was as set as her eyes, determination in the gaze and the chin. "Three weeks is not long enough to guarantee that she is not with child."

Miles stiffened. "You saw how quickly I brought her here. There is no question of her being compromised."

Abby shook her head, her face gone sad, and Olivia knew exactly what she was going to say. "Not by you, Miles."

He gasped, a strange sound coming from someone as dignified as he was. "No!" He turned to Olivia, his eyes wide. "Did my cousin touch you?"

She smiled, and some of the tension left his eyes; even the air felt lighter. "No. I hit him over the head with a chamber pot when he came into the room, and then I ran."

Miles relaxed, his whole body losing the rigidity of a moment ago, and he smiled back. "A chamber pot? I would have liked to see that."

He looked at her, then, his eyes thoughtful. The room went quiet.

Olivia felt her heart sink.

"I will have no one count on their fingers for the first babe and come up short." Oddly, that pronouncement came from Miles, not Abby, much to Olivia's surprise. He took her hands, right in front of Abby and his father. "Abby is right. I told you I would not force you into a life you did not want. Now I must defend you and your reputation before I can bring you into a life you *do* want." He hesitated, then rephrased. "A life we both want. I will not have anyone accuse you of anything, and so we will wait." Miles turned his head and looked at his parents. "Two months. Not a day more."

Abby nodded. "Two months will be sufficient." She looked up at her husband. "I will go to Bristol and discuss fabrics with Mrs. Berrycloth." She gave Olivia a long, measuring look. "I wish it to be a surprise. You will have to trust me once again."

Before Olivia could respond, Stafford tilted his head, a single nod of agreement. "An excellent idea, my dear. You will take your maid, and several footmen."

Olivia jerked at the word *maid*. She was short a maid now.

Miles glanced down at her; one eyebrow rose, and he patted her hand. "Olivia needs a new lady's maid."

She interrupted him, because she knew more about Clara's other life than he did. "Clara eloped to marry a man she had met. I have never seen him, she had done such a good job of concealing her feelings,"—although only to everyone else—"and I cannot forbid her the happiness I have."

Miles gave her hand a quick squeeze, but addressed his father. "Do you have a maid that might serve the purpose? Otherwise, I will have to advertise for one."

Stafford snorted. "Not yet. That will be your responsibility soon enough. For now, you must leave that to Abby."

"I will talk to my housekeeper." Abby smiled at Olivia. "I am certain we can find one among the household staff." Then she stepped away from her husband and walked over to Olivia, arms outstretched. "Welcome to the family."

The hug felt genuine, and Olivia hugged her back. "Thank you."

"Now," Abby turned to her stepson, "you may stay for supper, but then you will go back to your own house. You may visit Olivia as often as you wish, but you will never be alone together. If we are going to protect Olivia's good name, we will do it right."

T wo days later, Abby and her small entourage climbed into the big carriage, travel trunks strapped on top. She leaned out the door to give Stafford last instructions. "If Mrs. Berrycloth needs to order the fabric, I will stay and make sure it is right. There will be no mistakes." Her voice was firm. "This wedding will be of necessity quiet, but no one will be able to fault our family on anything."

Stafford kissed her hand, and murmured, "Come home safely." Then he stepped back and spoke to the rest of the group. "Men, do you have your guns?"

The footmen and the driver all patted their jackets.

"Take care of my wife," he ordered, and the driver nodded.

When the carriage vanished behind the trees, leaving only the clop of the horses' hooves and the creak of the springs behind, Stafford turned to his son. "I am concerned about sending you back to your house. You have come and gone without incident so far, but you are not fully healed yet, and I fear that he will come after you again. I am here to chaperone, but I fear talk will spread, anyway."

Olivia bit her tongue. She didn't want Miles to go back, either, but there was a possible alternative. "What about following the stream?"

Miles shook his head. "Victor knows that route. He grew up running along it. I am convinced Victor is hiding. He knows he has been identified. He might well be on a ship to America, but he would not dare set foot on the family land." He turned to his father. "I am in no danger now, I am certain. You will not have to air a room for me."

Stafford nodded. "I will pray for your safety."

And so Miles came every day, taking Olivia for walks, obediently within sight of the house—although that did not prevent him from stealing kisses regardless of those who might be watching—or riding along the road with his father playing chaperone and watching eagle-eyed for any indiscretions.

Two weeks later, Abby came back, all smiles and with another trunk strapped on the back of the carriage. "Wait until you see it," she crowed.

After the trunks were offloaded and the footmen carted them upstairs, Abby turned to Olivia. "Stay here. Not a peek until I send for you," she ordered.

Olivia braced herself for a pink wedding dress, obediently paced the parlor, and wished Miles was there.

At last, Maribelle came down. "My lady is ready for you now."

She didn't know if she wanted to run up the stairs with excitement or drag her feet, but Olivia followed the maid, not to Abby's room, but to her own. Maribelle stopped in the doorway, smiled, and waved her in.

The bed was covered with the shimmer of ivory satin. Olivia stopped dead, tears filling her eyes, and stared at the lovely thing.

"Try it on," Abby said with a smile both proud and hesitant, "and we shall see if it fits. We have time for adjustments, should they be necessary."

A few minutes later, Olivia stared at herself in the small dressing table mirror. "It's perfect, absolutely perfect," she told Abby, and it was true. The embroidered bodice had a low, square neckline, puffy sleeves that went to her elbows with the same faint embroidery on the band, a lace ribbon ran under her breasts, and a single flounce of lace trimmed the bottom. A ribbon identical to the one under her breasts edged the gathers of the flounce above and below.

It was simple, elegant, and so close to her old dreams that she suspected the iron's magic had reached from the future to grant her this last wish.

The weeks flew by, and at last the banns were read. Three Sundays, the announcement came: "I publish the banns of marriage between Miles Cedric Stewart and Olivia Anne Underwood of this Parish. If any of you know cause or just impediment why these persons should not be joined together in Holy Matrimony, ye are to declare it."

Of course, no one objected. And Victor had not shown up.

The discussions of a wedding at home or in the church had finally been resolved.

Church it would be.

A bby helped her dress, bubbling with joy. "You look lovely. I cannot wait for you to have your first child. Our children,"—she patted her belly—"will be close in age." She paused in buttoning the back of the gown. "I owe you an apology. It should have been said weeks ago. I told you to have children from one of the men of the area, and that it would not be Miles's child, and I was wrong. How foolish I was to think I could stop him once he made up his mind. And his mind had been made up. It was wrong of both Stafford and myself to try to prevent it."

Olivia looked at Abby's reflection in the mirror. "If you need forgiveness, I give it gladly, but it really isn't necessary. He pushed me away himself."

"Because we pressured him to do so."

"Well, everything is working out." It certainly was, she thought as she stared at herself, a Regency woman with her hair pinned up and a bonnet waiting to be tied on the curls.

She had been given an unexpected gift: a man to love and a whole new life.

But it was time to climb into the carriage, Abby so big there was no hiding the coming babe, was helped up the steps, with Stafford climbing in afterward to sit beside his wife.

The church was ready and full with nearby families, including those of every man Abby tried to pair her off with, all delighted to finally see Lord Langley leg-shackled, even if it was to an American.

Miles stood outside the church door. "At last," he said as he helped Olivia down. "You look beautiful. I am a lucky man."

And he kissed her right there, in front of all the watchers, before he walked her in and they took their places.

The bishop began the ancient words, and Olivia's throat tightened with tears of happiness. "Dearly beloved, we are gathered together here in the sight of God, and in the face of this congregation, to join together this Man and this Woman in holy Matrimony; which is an honorable estate…"

CHAPTER 56

TWO WEEKS LATER, AS MILES SAT AT DINNER WITH HIS WIFE, the candles glowing on her face, the rich scent of roasted venison filling the air, a ruckus came from the front door, shouting and cursing and thuds against the walls.

Denton appeared in the dining room door. "My lord, Victor has been found."

Miles looked at Olivia, their eyes met, and she let go a soft sigh. He had done his best to reassure her that she was safe, but now she finally was.

Then a smile tilted her mouth. She turned to Denton, still waiting in the door, through which the noises still came. "I assume that awful racket is him, and he's not happy."

"Yes, my lady. They had to resort to binding both hands and feet, and he made their journey difficult."

"But the footmen were only on horses." Miles felt his own mouth curve. "Did they throw him over the back like a sack of flour?"

"No, the footmen hired a hackney from Posset, which you will have to pay for, I fear, but they got him here safely."

"Take him to my office and watch him. I will be there momentarily." Miles turned back to his wife. "Do you want to see him in custody?"

She nodded. "I do. It might erase the nightmares."

He caught her hand, and kissed it in a gesture that never grew old. "Very well. Let us finish our meat, and then we shall go together."

Victor slouched in the guest chair, his face red with both embarrassment and scrapes. One eye promised to turn black in another day, his lower lip was split in one corner, one sleeve of his shirt had torn from the shoulder, and his boots were dusty. Despite his hands tied behind his back and his feet still tightly lashed as well, plus the two burly footmen standing on either side, still in their rough disguise, he managed to look scornful and haughty.

When Miles walked in, Victor lurched forward. One footman clamped a hand on his shoulder and shoved him back, but he still spat out, "You will never get me hanged!"

"Hanged? What made you think I would have you hanged?" Miles led Olivia around the desk, keeping between her and Victor. "I believe you already know my wife." He turned to her, then, ignoring Victor's sputtering.

"Take my chair. I will stand." He leaned down and whispered in her ear, "I rather like the idea of looking down at him."

She took the chair. He gripped the back with both hands. It was safer than grabbing Victor's neck.

His cousin stared at Olivia. "She is not your mistress? You truly wed her?"

"I truly did." The details did not need to be aired. "Now, I think I have decided what to do with you." He turned to the footmen. "Did you find any of my gold? And what about Crofts? Did you find him?"

Both footmen shook their heads. "No, m'lord. No gold. I believe he sold it all. We found nothing in his room." The footman held out a pouch. "We also found this on him." The contents were poured out on the desktop: four sovereigns, several guineas, and a pile of shillings.

Miles looked from the coins to his cousin. "I suppose if I ask you where you fenced my jewels, you would refuse to answer. So I will not try. I will merely sketch out what I am missing and send my men back to Portishead. I'm sure we will reclaim most, if not all."

The footman cleared his throat, and Miles was only too happy to turn away from his cousin again. "As far as your man of affairs," the footman said, "according to Stewart here, he is already on a boat to America."

A soft gasp came from his wife. Miles touched her shoulder. "I believe the country will survive his presence."

He was done with Victor. Miles stepped from behind the chair and leaned against the desk next to Olivia, his back to the prisoner. "I'm of a mind to throw him on a ship to New South Wales. What do you think? You were the one to suffer most under his hand. I leave his punishment to you."

From behind him, a mocking scoff. "You are going to leave my fate in the hands of a woman? You must not think much of her. She will never bear the guilt."

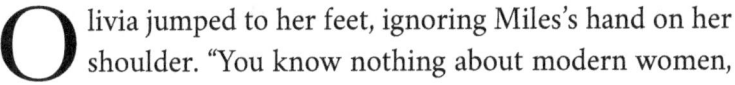

Olivia jumped to her feet, ignoring Miles's hand on her shoulder. "You know nothing about modern women,

Victor! Or ancient women, for that matter. We are stronger than you think."

She turned to Miles. "I think New South Wales is a wonderful solution for him, but there are things you must know first. I need to speak with you in private." She turned to the footmen. "Keep your eyes on him. We will be right back."

As she headed for the door, she realized that she had basically ordered her husband to listen to her, just as she might have done a modern, twenty-first century man. And he was following her, ignoring the laughter from Victor.

As soon as the office door shut behind her, he pulled her into his arms, and placed a kiss on her lips. She had not embarrassed him, she decided, and leaned into the kiss. He did that a lot, kissing her at every opportunity, and it made her smile every time.

It did now, too, even though he did not know what she was going to say, and might not like it when he heard.

He looked down at her, his arms still around her waist, his eyes gleaming. She knew where they would go as soon as they got rid of their inconvenient guest, and she couldn't wait to get there. "What modern secret are you going to reveal now?"

"New South Wales is a rough country in this time, but it is going to become very wealthy. At some point, and I don't know when, they discovered opals, and men got fabulously rich. He might go there and struggle and starve, or he might become richer than you someday." She touched his face, marveling that she could do that now. "You have to decide how badly you want revenge. I only want him far enough away that I don't have to worry."

He pursed his lips in thought, and then nodded. "Perhaps making his own wealth will heal his bruised spirit. Very well, we will ship him off. And what do we do about the money he got for fencing my jewelry?"

Olivia looked down at her bracelet. What would she pay to get it back? When Miles had returned it to her, clasped it back on her wrist, it had been as powerful as a vow. "That I will leave to you. I say, let him have some of it to buy food and maybe a place to live when he gets there, but keep what you think fair."

Miles smiled down at her. "I think I can be more generous than that. I will give him all the coins, put him on a ship to New South Wales, and let him fend for himself."

"But what will your father say?"

Miles's eyes went hard. "When Victor kidnapped you, Father was done with the man. From now on, he is on his own."

Olivia felt her shoulders slump. "I'm sorry to cause problems in your family, but this might be the making of him."

O livia rolled over, away from the morning sun that prodded insistently at her eyes. A deep voice chuckled nearby. "Good morning, my dear."

"Uh, huh." Then she remembered, and opened her eyes, to see her husband dwarfing the small dressing table chair and smiling at her.

"He is gone. I watched the ship sail away at dawn. And I do not recommend pacing the docks of Bristol overnight."

She sat up and ran her gaze over him, but no bruises, no scrapes. "You didn't get into any fights, I see."

"No. I must have looked the very husband eager to return to his wife." He rose and tugged off his coat, then unfastened his cuffs, setting the links on the table. A pull, and his shirt came over his head, revealing a truly impressive six-pack of abs. Olivia smiled, wondering what he would think if she told him that, then wondered how long she would remember the future.

Would it stay with her? Or would it fade as she settled into this new life?

Miles moved to his boots, and winked. "I could use some sleep. Will you help me?"

She slid out of bed and went over to the door, sliding her hand across his rippled middle as she passed. A twist of the key, and they were locked in. She turned back to him, dangling the key from one finger. "I think I can do that." She tossed the key onto the small table, and started back to the bed.

With a laugh, he tossed his breeches to the side, caught her, whisked off the nightgown, swung her up into his arms as he turned to settle her into the crinkly mattress, then followed her down.

DO YOU WANT TO READ CLARA'S STORY?

Of course Clara has her own story! This tale wouldn't be complete without it.

To read Clara's Story, how she got there, what her life was like beyond Olivia's presence, and what happened when the iron took her away. click here.

ABOUT THE AUTHOR

Mary Ellen Boyd is a romance author of Regency and Biblical fiction, although if the muse strikes, she will happily branch into other genres.

She has been happily married since 1982, in May, the prettiest month of the year. She and her husband have one adult son.

ALSO BY MARY ELLEN BOYD

Days of the Judges Series

Temper the Wind

A captive bride, a new land, and the chance of an everlasting love.

His Brother's Wife

By law she must face her worst nightmare, and wed a total stranger.

A Man to Marry

In a world of brideprice and arranged marriages, she finds her own love.

Warrior of the Heart

A bitter war, a stolen bride, forgiveness, acceptance, and love in unexpected places.

Love Among the Lilies

A captured enemy bride. An unwilling widow bound by law to another, and a feisty young woman breaking the rules. Three tales of unexpected marriage in an ancient land.

Regency

To Heal a Wounded Rogue

She might not agree, but she needs him, and he will risk everything to win her heart.

The Thief's Daughter

An audacious plea for help, and a forbidden love.

This Time Love

An antique mirror and a trip through time. A mesmerizing man, a sudden love, but for how long?